MATTHEW'S REDEMPTION

MADELYN S. PALMER

ISBN: 978-1-4907-9453-2 (sc)
ISBN: 978-1-4907-9455-6 (hc)
ISBN: 978-1-4907-9454-9 (e)

Library of Congress Control Number: 2019903675

Trafford rev. 04/16/2019

 www.trafford.com
North America & international
toll-free: 1 888 232 4444 (USA & Canada)
fax: 812 355 4082

Contents

CONTENTS

CHAPTER 1

STERLING CASTLE

Matthew gritted his teeth, bit back a couple of swear words, then turned and stomped off the jousting field, pulling off his helmet and chest-plate and dumping them on the ground. He was done. Absolutely finished with the knight training. If Sir Lamborgini didn't see enough potential in him, then it wasn't worth battling the other squires for promotion. They always teamed up against him anyway. Just because his birth station was different didn't mean he got special privileges. Well, sometimes it did, just not here in knight training. Here he got special expectations and insults.

He sighed. He understood now what his older sister, Amber, went through as a teenager, trying but not quite able to fit in with the other girls at the castle. Always being held to a stricter standard and higher expectations, few real friends, the future planned out for you...

Matthew smiled slightly to himself. At least he had a little more freedom than Amber had in deciding his own future. He wasn't expected to rule a kingdom like she was. He could choose knighthood, tradesman, farmer... The problem was he wasn't sure what he wanted to do. Other eighteen year old boys were already well established in their trades.

Matthew missed Sir Bentley. Sir Bentley had taught him the modern fighting skills of a knight, but also many of the old moves and tricks. Maybe that was what Lamborgini and the other squires resented. Lamborgini had been brought to Sterling Castle when Bentley died. Then when Matthew's older sister Amber got married to Harry, Sir Royce and his wife Shelley moved to Adonia with them. Sir Lamborgini was then put in charge of training the squires into knighthood, while Sir Rover stayed training the younger pages. The arrangement worked, except for some reason Lamborgini had made it his special purpose to single out, stress and correct Matthew in front of the other squires every chance he got. If there was a tie in contest, Lamborgini voted the other squire the winner. One time Matthew got so angry, he actually attacked Sir Lamborgini with his mace. Lamborgini parried the strike with his shield so deftly that Matthew found himself on the ground in moments.

"Never let anger guide your actions or cloud your judgement," was all Lamborgini growled before sending him off the field in shame. The other squires whispered behind his back a lot after that, and Matthew felt even more excluded from their circles.

Matthew became aware that during his reverie he had already walked halfway back to the castle. Suddenly he felt more free and light of heart than he had in the past three years. To him it felt like the right decision to leave the knight's training.

At the foot of the hill where Sterling Castle perched, he took a detour to the south, exploring niches and climbing slopes he hadn't explored in years. He came to a big stone slab that covered a human waste cistern that he and Tom the Smith had designed when Matthew was twelve. It was one of the inventions of which he was most proud. It minimized the need for the castle's inhabitants to depend on emptying chamber pots, a chore he and his sister had been given the year prior as a punishment for disobeying their parents. He determined at that moment to design a waste system that brought people to a toilet place that would drain the waste down and out of the castle through a drainage system. They had to revise the receptacle area after a couple of years, when they discovered an open sewage hole attracted more flies and varmints to the castle hill. After enclosing the waste into a large cistern, Hortense the Cook advised them that the smell coming up the drainage system could be decreased by throwing a yeast and ash pottage down the system once a month. The women of the castle were particularly delighted by the addition of polished wood seats of different sizes over the toilet holes designed by Roger, the new castle carpenter and artisan.

Finally tired and dusty, Matthew returned to the castle, washed up and changed into clean clothes. Then he lay low, staying in his chamber suites until dinner time. He wasn't sure how he was going to tell his parents that he wasn't going to pursue knighthood after all. He felt restless, cooped up and stifled in this castle. Not that it was particularly small, but life here was too predictable, the people all knew each other, and thought they knew how everyone's lives would turn out. Matthew wasn't sure what he wanted with his own life, but he did know he wasn't going to find it here.

When it was dinner time, Matthew walked quietly down to the royal dining room in freshly changed clothes. His mother, Queen Elinore, sat at one end of the table dabbing a damp napkin to her seven year old daughter, Stephanie's face. His older sister, Amber, was trying to quiet her hungry two and a half year old daughter, Sabrina, who was sitting on some books stacked on a chair. Amber's husband, Prince Harry from Adonia, was carrying on a frequently interrupted conversation with King Robert at the other end of the table. Matthew sat down next to Stephanie.

Stephanie crossed her arms and looked grumpy. "I already washed my face, Mother."

"You missed a spot, dear."

Stephanie turned to Matthew. "My face looks clean enough, doesn't it, Mattie?"

Matthew grinned. "Except for the spot of dust on your nose!" He wiped his finger underneath the table, and then wiped the dust onto her nose.

"Ooh, Mother! Look what Mattie did!"

Elinore glared at Matthew momentarily, but then turned back to washing Stephanie's face, which she was now allowing willingly.

"Robert," Harry asked, furrowing his brow. "I have an economic question for you. In Adonia we are finding that foreign traders seem to be paying lower prices for our country's goods, and charging higher prices for theirs. Our local farmers and tradesmen can't get good prices for their goods either. Have you experienced anything similar in Sterling?"

Robert frowned slightly. "I don't know that I am the right person to ask. Elinore? Have you noticed any economic changes in the trade business lately?"

She looked thoughtful for a minute. "Hm. The merchants have been complaining about the increased danger of piracy near the main continent, but I haven't heard much about change in prices locally. I can certainly look into it."

Just then Cook's assistant chef, Monica, brought in the soups. There was sudden silence as hungry little Sabrina slurped her soup. King Robert's face relaxed at the sudden quiet. Harry gazed lovingly at Amber, who smiled glowingly back at him. Matthew averted his eyes and bent over his soup, slightly embarrassed.

Robert was the first to finish his soup. "How is the packing coming, Harry?"

Harry looked up from his soup. "Almost finished, Sir. We'll be heading back to Adonia right after breakfast in the morning."

"It surely has been exciting having your little family staying with us this past month, Harry and Amber," Elinore commented.

Matthew nearly choked on his soup. Exciting was not the work he would have used. Unpredictable, distracting and loud would be more descriptive.

"Can I go back to Adonia with Sabrina?" Princess Stephanie asked her parents.

"'May I go' is the correct way to say it, Stephanie dear. No you may not, but thank you for asking," Elinore told her. "Your schooling starts back up after they go."

"Aw…phooey." Stephanie put on her pouting face and crossed her arms again.

Matthew leaned over to her. "Maybe you could become Sabrina's assistant nanny, live with her in Adonia all year round and play with her every day."

Stephanie sat up in her chair hopefully. "Mother, can… I mean may I?"

Queen Elinore paused and looked at King Robert. "No, that would not be possible…"

"Maybe that would not be such a bad idea, Elinore. We could send her tutor, Lady Charlotte, to Adonia with Little Steph for half the year, say Fall and Winter, and have the girls here for Spring and Summer. How does that sound?"

"Her name is Stephanie," Elinore corrected, then looked thoughtful. "Maybe that would work."

Amber piped up. "That would be wonderful, Mother and Father! The girls get along splendidly, and Sabrina is always so much easier to tend when she has a playmate she adores. We could teach the girls to ski in the mountains of Adonia, and to swim on the beaches of Sterling."

Elinore nodded. "You have convinced me. I do love spending time with my girls when you are here. But it will be at least a day before we could get her things and her tutor ready to go."

Harry looked at Amber and nodded. "We could postpone our journey an extra day."

Stephanie jumped out of her chair. "Hurray!" she shouted. Elinore gazed at her sternly, and she sat down demurely. "Sorry. That is wonderful!"

Robert's glance flickered in Matthew's direction. Matthew looked up at the ceiling innocently, recalling how he used to jump out of his chair the same way when excited.

Monica took away the soup bowls and brought in roast beef, carrots and potatoes. Matthew took a big chunk of bread, dunked it in the gravy, and took a big bite.

"How was your day today, Matthew?" Robert asked him.

Matthew gulped his bite of bread, caught off guard by the question, and he felt it going down his esophagus uncomfortably. "Um...I quit the training for knighthood today."

There was silence around the table. Queen Elinore was the first to speak. "Why ever would you do that? I thought that is what you wanted to do. You are so close to finishing the training."

Matthew took a drink of water. "It's not that I don't appreciate the training, skill and experience. I have learned quite a lot. But I feel that my future lies in a different direction."

"You aren't thinking about wanting to rule Sterling after us, are you?" King Robert asked quietly.

Matthew looked at his father. "I think you already promised Amber that she and Harry could rule Sterling jointly with Adonia someday." He shook his head. "No, I don't want to rule a kingdom." He gazed out the tall window behind Robert that looked out over the rolling farmlands of Sterling. "I would like to see more of the world outside of Sterling."

Robert and Elinore gazed at each other wordlessly. "Shall I see if my brother, John, wants to use him on the family farm in Danforth?" Robert finally asked.

Elinore nodded. "That would be an option. He could go there after escorting Stephanie to Adonia."

Matthew remembered the summer he turned eleven visiting his cousins in Danforth and helping Uncle John bring in their wheat crop. "That would be different. But that wasn't exactly what I meant by 'seeing more of the world.'" He saw the expression on his parents' faces. "I am still willing to take Stephanie to Adonia."

Stephanie looked up at her big brother adoringly. "I would like that. I will have my own knight to escort me to my new kingdom."

Sabrina giggled at her Aunt Stephanie.

"I am not a knight, nor am I likely to ever be one," Matthew told her softly. Part of him was relieved, but part of him also felt empty at the declaration. If not a knight, who or what was he supposed to be?

The next day was a whirlwind of getting Stephanie packed up. Of course she wanted her favorite dolls and dresses brought with her. When Queen Elinore told her she could not take everything with her, she melted into tears. Elinore left Stephanie's chambers with her hands lifted in the air in frustration. Matthew counted to ten, and then sauntered past the door to Stephanie's rooms.

"Mattie, Mattie!" Stephanie appeared in the doorway with tearstained face. "Mother won't let me take all my dresses. You need to talk to her for me."

Matthew knelt in front of her. "Steph, if you take all your dresses from here, then you won't have room to bring back your new ones from Adonia."

Her eyes widened. "I'll be able to get new dresses in Adonia?"

Matthew nodded. "Yup. You'll probably get the latest styles of dresses too. You should probably leave a whole trunk empty for the new dresses."

She smiled brightly. "Do you think I ought to leave an empty trunk for new toys too?"

Matthew smiled. "Sure! Do you need help packing?"

She nodded and grabbed his hand, dragging him into her room. She set about commanding him on what things to pack into which trunk. He obeyed her calmly and formally like a butler. "Yes, Your Highness. As you wish, my Lady."

Finally she sat back on her bed. "Thanks, Mattie, I think we are all finished here. You are dismissed."

He bowed solemnly. "Yes, Princess."

Matthew discovered there was not much he wanted to take with him: a couple of changes of shirts, pants and stockings, a travel cloak, and the long dagger Amber's husband Harry had made for him seven years before. Matthew packed them all in a travel bag he could sling over his shoulder, and then sat on his bed looking at it, wondering where he was going to take it in the near future.

That night dinner time was filled with parental advice.

"Stephanie, dear," Queen Elinore told her for the fifth time. "You need to listen to Amber as if to me. You need to help take care of Sabrina, and be on your best behavior at all times and places. You are a princess, and no one should doubt that you are of good upbringing when they watch you."

"Yes, Mother," Stephanie murmured between bites of food.

King Robert was talking at the same time to his son. "Always stay alert, Matthew. There are people out there who would take advantage of the innocent and unsuspecting. You will be responsible to get Stephanie, Lady Charlotte and George safely to Harry's castle in Adonia. After that you can stay the winter in the mountains of Adonia, or return to Uncle John's farm in Danforth, or strike out in another direction as you desire. Just make sure you send us letters occasionally so we know where you are and what you are doing."

"Yes, Father," Matthew replied.

"And Matthew, your mother and I would like you to come by our chambers tonight about eight o'clock before you go to bed."

At eight o'clock Matthew knocked on the door to his parent's personal chambers. Queen Elinore opened the door to let him in. She was dressed in a simple yet elegant white dress. King Robert had on a green tunic over a white dress shirt and nice dark pants. He welcomed Matthew into the parlor and indicated that he sit on a chair in the center of the room.

Robert laid a hand on Matthew's shoulder. "This is our blessing chair. The night before your sister Amber was married, we brought her in here to receive a father's blessing. This is a family tradition: my father gave each of my brothers, John and Edward, a father's blessing before they started on their life journeys as adults. He gave me a blessing before I came to Sterling to work. I would like to give one to you tonight before you head out on your own into the world. It is a way I can provide you with my direction and protection."

"Wonderful," Matthew whispered. "I would like that." He sat down on the chair, and Robert placed his hands on Matthew's head. He was silent a moment, and then began speaking.

"Matthew Robert of Sterling, I Robert of Danforth give you a father's blessing at this time. As you go forth into the world, I bless you with the gift of discernment, that you will know good from evil. I bless you with wisdom to be able to make decisions properly, that you will be able to keep yourself and others from harm. I bless you with good health and endurance, to be able to perform all the tasks set before you. Know that your parents and your sisters love you. Remember who you are; represent the royalty that you are at all times and in all places. May God keep you safe from harm. In the name of the Father, and the Son, and the Holy Ghost, amen."

When Robert was done, Matthew kept his head bowed for a minute. When he looked up at his father, his eyes were moist. "Thank you, Father. This is something I will always remember."

Robert embraced his son. "Now go get some rest. You leave early in the morning with Stephanie."

The next morning Matthew was a little late to breakfast. He could barely pass through the second floor hall, as servants carried trunks and luggage down the stairs to the front door. Amber rushed by, strands of hair coming out of their tresses at her neck.

"Mattie," she panted, holding up her hands carrying Sabrina's jacket and shoes. "Have you seen Sabrina? I was packing our luggage, Stephanie was playing with her, and now they are both gone! I need to get Sabrina dressed for the journey home."

Matthew shook his head, and Amber rushed on down the halls away from the family suites. On a sudden hunch, Matthew went down the back servant stairs toward the kitchen, and opened a door leading into an enclosed courtyard, in which an old shed had been fixed up as a little playhouse. The two girls were in the house's little kitchen having Tea. Sabrina was chatting away like a little mother, telling Stephanie what to do with the tea cups, and about the news of their kingdom. Stephanie wore an apron and lacy bonnet, and was pouring water from a dented teapot into a mix-matched set of chipped teacups.

"Lady Sabrina's presence is required at the carriage!" Matthew announced, standing like a doorman outside the little house. "Lady Stephanie is requested to escort her to the carriage."

"Ooh!" giggled Sabrina. "Come, Aunt Teffanie!"

"Do we have to go now, Mattie?" Stephanie sighed. "We haven't finished Tea yet."

Matthew knelt down and scooped Sabrina up in his strong arms. "Yep," he replied firmly. "Amber is beside herself worrying about where you two went. She is very anxious to get going so we can get through the Black Forest before dark."

"Okay." Stephanie followed them past the kitchens, where Cook handed each of them a fruit tart as they passed. At the front door of the castle they met Amber and Harry, who was directing the last of their traveling cases to the top of the carriage. Sabrina stretched her arms to her mother.

"You found her! Oh, thank you, Mattie!" Amber put her down to dress her in shoes and jacket. "Come, Sabrina, Daddy almost has the carriage ready to go home."

Sabrina reached her little arms out to her grandparents. "Bye bye, Gamma, Gampa!" She hugged them both, but her biggest kiss was for Elinore. "See you soon!"

After Harry helped Amber and Sabrina into the coach, he turned and shook King Robert's hand before climbing in himself.

Matthew helped Stephanie climb into the carriage next to her tutor Lady Charlotte. Charlotte was in her mid-fifties, white strands of hair mixed in with her strawberry blonde, giving a cinnamon effect to her bun. Her children were grown, leaving her free to travel with Princess Stephanie for whatever length of time she was needed. After helping George toss up Stephanie and Charlotte's trunks on top of the carriage, Matthew turned to meet Malcolm, the castle butler, who came hurrying out with a triangular wrapped package.

"Your father wanted to loan you this from the armory for the journey," Malcolm explained.

Matthew nodded, wedged it in amongst the trunks on top of the carriage, and then climbed up on the front seat next to George.

Robert and Elinore stood on the bottom of the outside castle steps to wave everyone goodbye. The children waved back until the carriage drove out of sight.

Elinore dabbed her eyes with a handkerchief. "I don't know if I am doing the right thing, letting Stephanie go for so long," she sniffed. "Although I know it is the tradition of other royal families to send their children off for years at a time at the same or earlier ages."

Robert put his arm around her. "I know what you mean. Who knows what kind of challenges and dangers Matthew will face, out there in the big wide world?"

"Maybe she will get homesick before the mountain passes close, and she'll want to come home again right away."

"Depending on where he goes and what he does it may be months or years before we see him again."

Elinore turned to Robert and leaned her forehead into his shoulder. "The castle is going to feel so empty!"

Robert got a wicked grin on his face. "Then we can run naked through the castle together!"

She slapped his shoulder in mock dismay. "What will the castle help say?"

He shrugged and patted his well-fed belly. "Nothing; they are too polite. They will avert their eyes in modesty (or horror), and keep their vow of silence and secrecy."

Elinore laughed and rolled her eyes. "I will keep that to our bedchamber. I would rather spend a week together in the farm cottage."

Robert's eyes lit up. "A second honeymoon! I love that idea, Elinore. Let's leave right away."

She looked around the castle hall as they walked inside. "I would have to cancel my meeting with the town magistrate, Robert. I was going to guide Joseph trimming the Queen's Garden hedges this week, and what about all the people that are expecting me to hold court this week?"

Robert laid a finger on her lips. "Let Malcolm perform his butler duties and organize all that. He is not too old to know how to rearrange your courtly schedule. And your Lady-in-waiting Celia can run the inner castle just fine in your place. Leave a note on your dressing table, and let's sneak off on our horses now. It will be fun to see how long it takes for anyone to find out we are gone."

Elinore giggled. "Okay. I'll slip on my riding clothes and be right down."

Hardly anyone paid attention to Robert saddling their two horses, Flint and Paré, in the stables. Elinore joined him as he was finishing up. As they rode out through the courtyard only a little boy, sous-chef Monica's youngest son, saw them leave as he stood in the kitchen doorway eating an apple. Robert waved briefly and the little boy waved back.

Robert and Elinore trotted their horses down the winding road below the castle. Once they reached the flat straight road that ran east and west parallel to the seashore, Elinore glanced at Robert and smiled teasingly. "Catch me if you can!" she kicked her horse into a full gallop.

Robert tried his best but could not catch her. As they neared a barn half filled with hay among ripening wheat fields, she finally slowed her horse. Both animals came to a walk, sides heaving.

"I think Flint is finally feeling his age," Robert remarked, sliding off his horse and reaching out to help her off hers. "The last time we raced I nearly beat you."

"Nearly is the operative word," Elinore smirked. "Paré is a year older than Flint. He can't use age as an excuse."

"Ah, but I am one-and-a half times your weight."

"Flint is a bigger horse and weight shouldn't matter."

Robert kissed Elinore, holding her mouth hostage. She finally broke away.

"That's not fair! You know I can never remember what I am saying when you kiss me like that!"

Robert grinned. "That's exactly why I do it. I can't win a debate with you any other way." He grabbed two handfuls of hay from the barn to feed the horses. After munching it gone, the horses went back to tearing meadow grass with their teeth.

Elinore plopped down in the shade of the barn. "I hope we have enough food at the cottage. I didn't think to bring any."

Robert pulled two biscuits and two apples from his tunic. "I slipped these past Monica and Cook while they were putting something in the ovens. We at least have lunch."

Elinore munched thoughtfully on her apple. "I haven't checked the cottage garden since we planted it. It's probably full of weeds by now."

"Probably," Robert swallowed his biscuit. "Or else everything has dried up and died."

Elinore jumped up. "We need to go check the garden right now!"

Robert finished his apple slowly, savoring each bite. "Almost ready," he drawled.

Elinore drummed her fingers on the side of her saddle. "I could leave you, you know."

"You know you won't find anyone out there better than me." Robert pulled a string from under his tunic, from which dangled an old brass key. "And I have the cottage key," he stated matter-of-factly.

She sighed exasperatedly. "Of course. But I could start the gardening while waiting for you."

Robert got up from the ground and sauntered toward his horse. "You could. But I know you prefer when we ride together."

She tossed her head. "Fine, I'll wait for you, but not forever."

He grinned. "Yes you will. You promised on our wedding day we would be together forever." He straightened his tunic, tugged on his stirrup, then swung into the saddle. "I'm ready," he announced.

"Finally!" Elinore rolled her eyes but she was smiling, watching his still handsome figure as he rode comfortably in sway with his horse's stride. She wasn't sure how he managed to stay looking as muscular as when she first met him, working as a stable hand at the castle and then for the old farmer who left Robert his cottage and farm. Castle life tended to make royal people go flabby. She rubbed her own thighs thoughtfully. Or maybe having three babies had done that to her.

As they neared the cottage, Elinore was almost afraid to look at the yard. But the front path was lined cheerfully with daisies, tulips and sunflowers, the family's favorites. Inside the hedge surrounding the house, the vegetable garden's plants looked green and well-tended. Elinore gave a cry and leaped from her horse.

"Robert! Someone has been tending the garden!" She rounded on him. "We agreed that only our family would take care of this house. Please don't tell me you hired someone to weed and water the garden!"

He shook his head. "No, unless bribing our own children counts as hire. Once a week while you were working I have snuck out with one or both of the children to help me in the garden. Matthew swore us to secrecy. He wanted you to be surprised."

"I am!" Elinore walked around touching the plants here and there. "The blackberries are producing this year!" She tasted one that was almost ripe. "Tomatoes, lettuce, beans,…no turnips?"

Robert shook his head. "Stephanie wouldn't let me plant those. We put in potatoes instead."

Elinore squeezed Robert's biceps. "Now I know how you have stayed in shape."

He patted his belly. "Yes, Cook and Monica's great cooking have given me shape all right."

"Oh! We need to harvest some food for supper!" Elinore started picking vegetables. "Go put the horses away in the stable, dear."

He finished unsaddling and brushing the horses about the same time she filled a basket with produce, and they walked into the cottage together. It was not as dusty as she expected.

"Stephanie helped me clean in here also," Robert explained. "And Matthew was very good at fixing the broken shutters off the back bedroom."

"Amazing! Our children are growing up." Elinore wiped down the table with a cloth dipped in rainwater from the barrel by the front door. She stopped and looked up at Robert who was gazing at her adoringly. "I suppose our children will be all right after all, won't they?"

He wrapped his arms around her waist and kissed her. "Yes, they will."

They cut and washed the vegetables together, then set the table with mix-matched plates and mugs while the vegetables sautéed over the fire. After eating, Robert leaned back with a sigh. Elinore folded her hands and gazed at him.

"I am not going to know what to do with myself here for a week, you know, with the garden and house all taken care of."

Robert held up a finger, walked over to a cabinet near the fireplace, extricated an armful of books, and plopped them down on the table beside Elinore. "Your homework assignment is to read one book a day. One fun book. No homework."

Elinore signed dramatically, placing the back of her hand against her forehead. "If I must. You are such a hard taskmaster. But I love you anyway!"

CHAPTER 2

DANFORTH

The royal carriage rumbled down the hill on which Sterling Castle stood and turned north. The road passed between farm fields, where the harvest was already gathered and the fields were browning in the autumn days and chilly nights. They passed the hay barn where the castle and town of Sterling held the May Day Festivals and some of the Autumn Harvest celebrations, and which belonged to King Robert, formerly Robert of Danforth. He had inherited the farm property from an old farmer he had worked for prior to passing the suitor's Test of Rimrock Island and marrying Princess Elinore. A couple of miles later they passed the track that led to a cozy little cottage that once belonged to the old farmer, which Robert had renovated, and now was the Royal Family's summer cottage.

From the driver's seat, Matthew saw Stephanie leaning out of the carriage window to gaze toward the cottage longingly.

"Shall we stop and visit the cottage, Steph?" he called down to her.

She shook her head. "No. I was just wondering what Mother will think of it when she next visits the cottage."

"Hm. There won't be much work left for her to do when she gets there, will there?"

Stephanie giggled. "Mother won't know what to do with herself, will she?"

Matthew grinned and shook his head. "We'll leave Father to solve that dilemma."

Just then Sabrina started wailing within the carriage. "No want that! Want out!"

Stephanie pulled her head inside to try and distract her young cousin. Sabrina was quiet for only three minutes. "No! Don't want to. Want out!"

Matthew gestured to George to stop, and then jumped down from his seat. He opened the coach door.

"Rest stop, my Ladies," he bowed. "Time to stretch our legs."

Sabrina scrambled out of the carriage and began running down the road back toward Sterling Castle. Before Amber could even get up from her seat, Stephanie had jumped out after her young cousin and caught up with her.

"Sabrina! Where are you going?" she panted, scooping her up into her arms.

"Wanna go home!" Sabrina tucked her face into Stephanie's shoulder and cried.

"You are going the wrong way," Stephanie explained. "Your home is that way." She pointed toward the Black Forest.

Sabrina looked at the Black Forest, then back toward the castle. "Want to go to Teffanie's home."

Stephanie hugged her. "I am glad you want to go to my house. But I want to come visit your house in the mountains."

Sabrina looked interested. "You come for Christmas?"

Stephanie nodded. "Yes, for the whole winter."

Sabrina wiggled out of Stephanie's arms, dropped to the ground, and grabbed her cousin's hand. "Come!" she commanded, walking back toward the carriage.

Amber finally had managed to get out of the carriage after Charlotte. "Sabrina, my love! Come to mama!"

Sabrina towed Stephanie toward her mother. "Teffanie go home wif me."

"Yes, dear. Stephanie is going home with us."

"Good." Sabrina continued walking up the road past the carriage, pulling Stephanie along with her.

Amber moved as if to stop her, but Harry grasped her hand. "Let the girls walk a bit, Amber. It will help her get the wiggles out. In fact, let's join them."

Amber didn't move. She looked down the road, then off to the side toward a field and irrigation ditch. "I have to go," she whispered.

Harry grinned. "Matthew, George! Follow the girls with the carriage!"

They nodded and prodded the horses to follow the little girls while Charlotte followed Amber. Harry stood guard at the roadside while the women did their business, and then they hurried after the carriage to catch up.

"Whew! That was refreshing," Amber sighed as Harry helped her back into the carriage. "Come girls! Time to get back in."

Sabrina did not want to climb back inside.

"Tell you what, Sabrina," Matthew suggested. "Why don't you climb up on the driver's seat with George and me for a while, and help me drive the horses?"

"Yay!" Sabrina stood by the high step at the front of the carriage and held up her arms. Matthew lifted her up onto the high seat next to George, and then climbed up beside her. He showed her how she could hold onto the ends of the reins behind George's hands.

Inside the carriage Amber opened her mouth in horror, and then covered it with her hand.

"Matthew will watch over her," Harry reassured her.

"But she is just a little girl and a princess," Amber protested.

"She will have plenty of time to be a proper princess a few years from now. Meanwhile, she needs to survive this trip." Harry rolled his eyes. "Or we need to," he muttered under his breath.

Amber turned to him sternly. "You are going to turn her into a Tomboy at this rate. She is not going to become your horse-around boy. You will have to wait until you have a son."

Harry leaned back against the seat cushions and closed his eyes. "Any time now would be fine with me."

Amber turned on him. "What is that supposed to mean? You know I am trying." She folded her arms across her chest. "Even my father has been asking me for a grandson. It is getting embarrassing."

Harry stared out the window at the fallow fields they passed. Stephanie twisted the handkerchief in her lap, pretending she wasn't listening. Lady Charlotte pretended to be sleeping. When she couldn't stand the tension any longer, Stephanie began to hum a tune. At first it vaguely resembled a tragic folk song she sort of knew, then it led to a more familiar ballad melody, and then a dance tune. Soon Harry started humming with her, tapping his foot. Amber finally unfolded her arms, then reached out her hand and laid it on Harry's.

"I am sorry," she whispered.

He nodded and grasped her hand in his. "I am too." She laid her head on his shoulder and closed her eyes. Stephanie smiled and laid her head back and also slept.

Mid-afternoon the carriage stopped briefly. The road had entered the Black Forest heading northeast, and the shadows were cool compared to the autumn sun over the farmlands. Matthew carried Sabrina into the carriage interior where Amber tucked her in beside her. George unloaded some blankets from the top of the carriage to wrap around the riders. They rode on until the light was nearly faded, then stopped to set up camp underneath the canopy of trees.

Harry fetched cloaks for all the ladies, while George tied up the horses in a grassy area. Matthew started a fire, using sticks the little girls brought him. Amber and Lady Charlotte cooked some dinner over the fire while George set up tents. After supper Amber and Matthew taught the little girls camp-fire songs their parents had taught them when they were younger. Then they told stories about their cousins living in Danforth, and some of the adventures of the summers they spent there.

"When will we be at our cousin's house?" Stephanie asked.

"Not until tomorrow night," Amber replied. "We have to get through the Black Forest, cross a small mountain, and go through the valley of Danforth."

Sabrina yawned. "Night-night," she declared.

"That's our signal," Harry stated. "I'm tucking my ladies into bed."

Lady Charlotte stood up. "It is time for you also to retire, Princess Stephanie."

Stephanie gave her brother a hug. "Good night, Mattie." She hesitated, and then stretched herself up tall to whisper into his ear. "Are you sure it is safe here in the Black Forest? I heard that there are bandits or bears."

Matthew leaned down near her. "I promise I will let nothing and no one harm you, Steph."

Stephanie hugged him one more time, hard. "I don't care whether you are knighted or not. You are still my favorite brave brother."

He watched her run to the tent she shared with Lady Charlotte. "I am your only brother," he murmured.

George stood by the fire warming his hands. He yawned and then shook his head hard. "I am tired."

"Go to bed, George. I'll take the first watch," Matthew commanded. "I am not that tired yet. And Harry offered to take the midnight watch.

Sabrina gets him up at least once in the night anyway. You can take the last watch."

George nodded gratefully, and rolled up in his bedroll by the fire. He was soon snoring. Matthew chuckled to himself. He wondered if all old men snored. He had heard his father's snores through his parent's suite doors the last few times he happened to be walking through the castle halls at night. He wondered if he would snore one day. He felt sorry for the poor lass who ended up marrying him if he did.

He let the coals go low, adding just enough small twigs to keep the fire from going out. He wrapped his blanket tighter around himself against the chill night air. He might be colder with the small fire, but he felt a little safer being able to adjust his eyes to the dark. Looking up he could see an occasional star twinkle through the trees. His thoughts drifted again to the problem of what he was going to do with his life, but no solutions came. Maybe he would wander the world forever never knowing.

Two and a half hours later Sabrina cried in her tent, waking her parents. Harry took her behind a tree to pee, tucked her back into bed, and then came back out to join Matthew.

Harry held his hand out over the coals to warm them. "Small fire," he commented.

"I like to see what's out in the dark," Matthew told him.

Harry nodded and wrapped his cloak closer about him. "Go to bed, Matthew. I've got this from here."

Matthew nodded. "Thanks, Harry. Don't forget to wake George when it's his turn." He stretched out next to Stephanie's tent and was soon asleep.

Harry and George changed shifts three hours later without mishap. Then sometime just before dawn, something woke Matthew. His ears identified the crackling of the fire, and then a different sound tickled his senses. Breathing? Twigs cracking? A low whine?

Matthew opened his eyes, trying to avoid looking toward the bright fire. His hand gripped the hilt of his long dagger. Out of the corner of his eye he made out George's shape hunched toward the fire, poking it with a stick. Matthew couldn't see it yet, but he could sense a presence out there beyond the light. His muscles tensed, and he quietly loosened the blanket from his arms and legs.

There was a sudden snarl, then howls and barks erupted, and four wolf shapes leaped toward George. He had just enough time to raise his left arm to block one of the animals hurtling toward him. He poked it in the eye with the stick in his right hand. It immediately dropped to the ground yelping, while one of its companions plowed George toward the side of the fire. Matthew was on his feet in seconds, slashed the wolf on top of George across the flank, and stabbed the first one as it tried to get up again. George was struggling to keep the other two from finding purchase on his throat. Matthew hefted one up by the leg and stabbed it in the heart. The fourth wolf snarled and bit at George's arms held up over his face. With one final slice, Matthew disposed of him also. George let his arms fall to his chest and groaned.

Harry leaped out of his tent, clumsily unsheathing his sword. "Who goes there?" he shouted.

Matthew leaned over, panting. "Wolves, Harry. They are gone."

Harry stumbled over the body of one of them. "Oh. So they are, bro."

Amber crawled out of the tent after him. "What is all this commotion, boys?" She rubbed her eyes and tried to focus.

"Some wild dogs wanted supper, I think, Sis." Matthew pointed toward George, and then gazed into the trees. "Check on George and make sure he is all right."

"Oh, my!" Amber immediately went into mothering mode. "Harry, fetch my pack. I should have some cloths for bandages in there."

While Harry fetched the pack, Amber examined George. He was fading in and out of consciousness. The commotion had awakened Stephanie and Lady Charlotte. They watched Amber dress the wounds on George's arms in the gradually approaching dawn.

Matthew calmed the two horses who were prancing where they were tied up near the tents. He checked the perimeter of camp for any more wolves, and then dragged the four carcasses into the trees. He stared at the largest one, obviously the leader of the pack, then on an impulse he turned the beast over, pulled out his dagger and sliced the beast's skin open down the stomach. It took several minutes of careful work, but when he was done he had skinned off a handsome pelt. When he was finished he tied it to the upper back of the carriage where it could dry. Then he went back to check on George.

"Mama!" came a shrill cry from Harry and Amber's tent.

Stephanie ducked inside the tent and came out carrying Sabrina. "Your mama's helping George right now, Sabrina."

"Daddy!" Sabrina squirmed in Stephanie's arms, looking for her father.

"He is fetching more wood for the fire."

"Teffanie, I hungry," she announced.

Lady Charlotte smiled. "I will make us some breakfast."

George slept while the others ate. As they were finishing up, Matthew took Harry aside.

"Harry, how common is it for forest wolves to attack someone near a fire?"

Harry was thoughtful. "It is not very common, but it has been known to happen. Usually it occurs more often in times of greater hunger or drought. This year's harvest was a little more lean than usual, but not noticeably so." He gazed out into the trees. "It is still early in autumn, so we haven't reached the late winter hunger yet. Maybe they sense a harsher winter is coming. I don't know why these wolves attacked George. I would have expected the horses to be more of a target."

Matthew studied the place where he had been sleeping. Any one of them could have been a target. He walked around the fire looking for clues. Near where George had been sitting he saw a ham bone from last night's supper. Perhaps George had been snacking during his watch. Matthew turned back to Harry.

"Let's take down the tents and get moving again."

Harry and Matthew carried George into the carriage to ride with the ladies. Then the two of them climbed up onto the driver's seat.

"You drive," Matthew directed. "I want to watch the road." Harry noticed that Matthew held a crossbow in his lap. He wasn't sure whether to feel more worried or less.

But their journey through the Black Forest was without further mishap. Soon they were traveling through farm fields, then a town, and then past more farms before heading into the foothills where Robert of Danforth's older brother, John's homestead lay.

The little girls were very ready to get out of the carriage when they arrived. Aunt Beth greeted them at the door of the farm house.

"Stephanie! Sabrina!" Aunt Beth knelt and hugged them both at the same time. "Come in for some hot tea!"

Matthew and Harry helped George walk groggily into the farmhouse, while Uncle John put away their horses. Amber and Lady Charlotte brought in some of the little girl's luggage. Aunt Beth assigned George into the front guest room, and then showed the others into rooms upstairs.

"All of my children have their own homes now; you take their rooms," she told them. "I will see to George."

Amber and Matthew followed Aunt Beth into George's room to help her with the dressing changes. Aunt Beth carried a bowl of warm soapy water while Amber brought in clean cloths.

"Tell me what happened to him?" Aunt Beth asked quietly.

"Wolves attacked just before dawn," Matthew replied guiltily.

"Wolves!" Aunt Beth gasped. "That is unusual."

"His arms look fairly shredded," Amber told her. "He probably needs stitches."

Beth laid her hand on George's clammy brow. "He will also need something for fever and an analgesic. Matthew, help him sit up while I pour a bit of this herbal concoction down his throat."

After George drank some of the tonic, the women unwrapped his bloody dressings and washed his lacerated arms. Then Amber and Beth set to work stitching up the wounds. Matthew held George's head while he gritted his teeth enduring the procedure with an occasional groan. Finally Beth proclaimed it sufficient. She applied some drawing salve and then wrapped up his arms in clean dressings.

"Now we let him sleep for twenty-four hours. I will check the wounds again tomorrow," Beth declared.

Amber looked disconcerted. "Aunt Beth, we were hoping to be back on the road tomorrow."

"Amber, dear, unless you plan to go on without George, I advise you to let him rest for at least two days. He is no good to you otherwise. And you run a greater risk of infection. I would not advise that."

Amber sighed. "If we must, we must." She and Matthew left Beth to watch over George through the night. "I was hoping to get back to Adonia more quickly, before the weather gets colder," she murmured.

Matthew shrugged. "We are still early enough. We should be fine."

The next morning Sabrina and Stephanie accompanied Aunt Beth in feeding the chickens, gathering eggs and milking the cow. Matthew and Harry helped Uncle John feed the horses, cow and goats, and repair a section of broken fence surrounding Aunt Beth's garden.

"What are your plans this year?" Uncle John asked Matthew as they worked.

Matthew sighed. "I'll probably stay through the winter in Adonia. After that, I don't know."

"Ever thought of farming or sailing?" Uncle John queried.

Matthew smiled. "I'm not so fond of farming. Sorry, Uncle John. But sailing might be interesting."

John nodded. "I'll write you a letter to take to your Uncle Edward. If you ever think of sailing you should look him up in Portsmouth."

When done with chores everyone trooped inside for a breakfast of ham and cheese omelets prepared by Amber and Charlotte. While they ate, Beth took some breakfast to George, and gave him another draught of analgesic. When she returned to the kitchen, the visitors were laughing merrily with Uncle John.

"With all these helping hands, John, we should take a trip up Elephant Mountain to finish harvesting the apple orchard," Beth suggested.

"I remember that being a fun trip when I turned eleven," Matthew recalled. "Bidden was very quick at picking strawberries. And good at eating them too."

"And Bard and Brian could chuck apples quite a ways," Amber commented.

Aunt Beth leaned back in her kitchen chair and let out a bubbling contagious laugh. "I always suspected they were having apple fights. But I never could quite catch them at it. It was nice having them around to climb the trees for us though."

Uncle John rubbed his shoulder. "I miss that too. Now that they are off with their own farms, I can usually only get their help once or twice a year. I had to build a ladder to reach the higher tree branches, and even then the rheumatism in my shoulders limits me."

"We would love to help you, Uncle John," Matthew offered.

"Someone will need to stay with George," Amber reminded him.

"I'll stay," Charlotte offered. "My hips don't like much walking any more, especially up and down mountains."

Amber looked at Aunt Beth with concern. "I'd rather not stay overnight up on the mountain. It will be all I can do to carry Sabrina up the trail, let alone overnight packs."

Matthew looked over at his sister. "I seem to remember you were trying to carry a wet wool blanket in your pack last time. I don't know why you wanted to do things the hard way."

Amber punched him in the arm. "I fell in the creek, silly. It was not on purpose."

Harry smiled at her. "I will carry Sabrina, Amber."

"I walk!" Sabrina protested, pausing in her chasing cats around the kitchen just long enough to pat her mother's arm.

Beth laughed. "John built a little cabin by the lake a couple of years ago. Then if he has to stay overnight there is a cook-stove and straw mattress right there. But I anticipate we could get most of the apples picked in half a day."

"Any chance Bidden can join us?" Matthew asked hopefully.

"Or Breanna?" added Amber.

Uncle John grinned. "Well now, seeing as how we have a bit of a family reunion, I might be able to convince them to join us tomorrow. While I am off alerting the clan, I could use some firewood chopped."

"And I would love some help in the garden today," Aunt Beth added. "I have some harvesting and canning to do."

"Yes, Aunt Beth. Charlotte and I can help," Amber smiled.

Harry and Matthew chopped and split logs behind the barn while Amber, Charlotte and the girls helped Beth pick the last of her garden's corn, beans, cucumbers, tomatoes and squash. Then they dug up potatoes, beets, carrots and turnips, loaded much of the food into baskets and bags for the men to carry into the cool cellar below the farm house. John was back in time for a quick lunch, and then everyone gathered for the canning and pickling. Beth watched the fires in the kitchen, while John tended the outdoor fire-pit. As jars were filled with beans, corn and tomatoes for canning, Beth set them to boiling over the cook-fires. John lugged out a big vat of vinegar to pickle the beets and cucumbers. As dusk fell, the canning was finally done, and everyone carried jars of pickled and canned foods to arrange on board shelves in the cellar.

As John closed the cellar door, Beth sighed in contentment. "Thank you all. You just saved us a week of work. This will help us get through the winter nicely."

After supper everyone fell into bed exhausted. Even Sabrina didn't resist going to sleep.

At dawn the next morning, all the cousins arrived with their families in wagons or on foot. John hitched his horse up to his wagon while Beth passed warm muffins around for breakfast. Then everyone climbed into wagons for the one mile ride to the foot of Elephant Mountain.

At the foot of the mountain trail they led their horses into a little corral built among the trees, with plenty of grass and a trough of rainwater for the horses to drink. The men unloaded wheelbarrow wagons, armfuls of burlap sacks and some baskets to bring the produce in from the mountain. Then they all headed up the trail.

Stephanie and Sabrina were very excited, running up the trail ahead of the adults and back again. In short order cousin Breanna and her older sister Betsy assigned a few of the older children to stay with the younger ones and they ran ahead, whooping and calling through the trees.

"I won't see the girls again for a long time, will I?" Amber moaned.

Breanna laughed. "We'll catch up to them at the stream. The children know not to cross the stepping stones without an adult present."

Sure enough, the adults found the children at the stream, throwing rocks and dipping their toes in the water. Once the children were helped across, the men paired up to carry the wheelbarrow carts across. Then they were off again up the trail.

The trail grew steeper as they neared the lake's plateau. Just before the trail's last ascent they abandoned the carts, loaded the adults with armfuls of burlap sacks and baskets, and climbed the last bit of steep trail. As they broke through the trees, the clear mountain lake greeted them, reflecting the bright blue sky, surrounded by trees adorned in autumn colors of red, gold and orange.

Stephanie and Sabrina squealed in delight and ran toward the lake. Amber dropped her baskets and dashed after the girls. Betsy laughed and sent her older children after them. Soon many of the children and even cousins Bidden and Brian had stripped off their outer clothes and were swimming in the water near the edge of the lake. Other adults took off their shoes and socks and waded in.

"Amber, do you remember when Father threw you into the lake the last time we were here with him?" Matthew asked, grinning.

"Don't you dare, Mattie!" Amber raised her hands defensively. "It may be warm here for September, but the water is still cold!"

"Besides, teasing her is my job now," Harry commented, splashing up beside them. He dipped his hand in the water and flicked a few drops of water at her face.

Amber jumped up on the shore and scooped up Sabrina. "If you splash me you also splash Sabrina, and she will NOT appreciate that."

"I think Amber is serious about not getting wet," Matthew commented drily.

"I think you are right," Harry looked after her as she walked toward the little cabin.

"Lunch!" called Beth. She had laid out bread, cheese and sausage on a wooden table John and Bard had carried out of the cabin and placed out in the sun. Children ran up to collect their food, followed by the adults. They sat around on the ground, chatting and eating together contentedly.

After eating and getting shoes back on, everyone grabbed a basket or burlap sack and headed further up the mountain toward the apple orchard.

The apple orchard grew out of a hillside meadow where the western sun kissed the mountainside. The orchard trees were a little wild and overgrown, but the dozen trees were loaded with reddish green apples. With whoops of excitement, the older boys began climbing the trees with burlap bags in their hands. Men stood below the branches picking apples and filling bags.

Meanwhile, the women ushered the younger children with them a little further up the trail. They crossed a little stream, and then they came upon a multitude of blackberry bushes and wild grapes. Some of the children were old enough to pick fruit, while the younger ones played around their mother's skirts. A couple of hours later the baskets were full of berries and grapes, and the burlap bags were full of apples.

Everyone headed back to the lake, where the youngest children were laid out on blankets to nap, while the men and boys went to the water to catch some fish. Cooking fires were readied, and as the fish were caught and cleaned, the women cooked them over the coals. Added to the bounty were fresh berries, grapes and baked apple.

After supper, Uncle John stood to address the group. "Thank you, family, for coming up this day to harvest the orchard. You know how hard it has been the last few seasons to make ends meet. The bounty this year should allow us to get through the winter..." His voice cracked and he bowed his head, unable to continue. His son, Bard, came up and hugged him.

Aunt Beth stood up, all business. "Now enough of this sentimentalism. Let's get packed up and take this harvest back down the mountain."

Adults and children alike hefted bags of apples and baskets of fruit, and then headed down the steep part of the trail. When they reached the wagons, the bags of apples were loaded inside. The men and older boys guided the wheelbarrow wagons carefully down the trail, one holding the handles and one in front of each wagon to keep it from careening down the trail. The women and children followed behind carrying the baskets of berries and grapes. At the stream's cross-stones the wagons were unloaded, the wagons and bags of apples carried across separately, and then reloaded.

Matthew took a turn on a wagon with Bard, while Brian and one of his sons guided a wagon behind them. The men were talking about their grain crops and the challenges of keeping growing families fed.

"I have a question," Matthew suddenly asked during a lull in the conversation. "Why was Uncle John so emotional about us helping him with the apple harvest today?"

Bard and Brian glanced at each other. Bard finally spoke. "Well, cousin, times have been hard the last few years in Danforth. It seems that the cost of trade with other countries has increased to the point that we are better off trading amongst ourselves than with neighboring cities. That puts financial pressure on a lot of people, and limits the goods we can get that we aren't able to produce locally."

"What would cause the prices to go up?" Matthew asked. "I haven't heard of any changes in trade agreements between our countries."

Brian shrugged. "I don't think there has been anything official. But when the merchants do come through town, which is happening less often, they demand much higher prices for food and goods than we can pay. And they pay us less for our goods. They cite the high cost of international business. They won't barter for lower prices any more either, nor trade for equivalent goods. If we can't pay in coin, they take their goods on to the next country that is willing to pay more. Maybe the supply is limited."

As they trudged down the trail, Matthew remembered what he had overheard his father and Harry talking about before leaving Sterling. "What would limit supply?" he asked his cousins. "I know of no drought or war that would affect production. It doesn't make sense."

Bard shook his head. "No it doesn't. But it is hurting the poorer common man. Maybe you can find the answer at the castle level, Mattie."

Matthew wasn't so sure. If his parents and brother-in-law didn't know the reason, how would he figure it out?

They reached the foot of the mountain as the sun set. The produce was divided amongst the families, good-bye hugs were shared all around, and the families departed to their own homes.

CHAPTER 3

ADONIA

George felt well enough to resume travel the next morning. His fever had broken, and though he was sore, he didn't need the herbs for pain anymore. Matthew and Harry told him they would drive the coach, and made him sit inside with the women and girls. The morning sun was shining as they drove away from Uncle John's farmhouse, their stomachs full from Aunt Beth's bounteous breakfast.

"Barring no more unforeseen adventures, we'll arrive in Adonia tomorrow," Harry told Matthew. "We'll stay overnight in a little cabin at the top of East Adonia Pass that my father had built thirty years ago for travelers going between Adonia and Danforth or Renling."

The day traveling had pleasant weather. They passed more agricultural fields and several farms. Then the road wound its way up a mountain the size of which made Uncle John's Elephant Mountain seem like a little hill. The carriage entered a pine forest as the horses pulled it steadily uphill, and the air grew colder. Harry and Matthew put on their cloaks while the travelers inside the carriage pulled blankets around themselves. George told stories to entertain the little girls and keep his mind off the pain returning to his arms.

Then just before sunset the road crested the mountain pass and Harry pointed to a little house by the side of the road. While Harry let George and the ladies inside, Matthew led the horses into a little stable, fed them hay and water, and brushed them down. By the time he entered the house, Harry had a nice fire roaring in the fireplace, and Charlotte had hot tea prepared for everyone. Amber brought out muffins and salted pork sent by Beth and John.

"Hmm," Matthew sighed, settling into a chair by the fire. "I could sleep right here and now."

"You may have to," Amber responded. "There are only two bedrooms in this house. Charlotte and Stephanie get one, and—"

"And Amber and Sabrina get the other one with me," finished Harry. "Sorry, Mattie. You have to rough it again tonight."

Matthew grinned. "Roughing it near a warm fire, inside where I'm protected from wolf attacks, hot tea and food filling my belly... I think I can handle that."

George looked around the room. "As long as I have a bedroll, I think I can sleep anywhere. The floor is fine with me."

Sabrina yawned and relaxed into her mother's lap. "Night night," she said, closing her eyes. Harry picked her up and Amber followed him to their bedroom.

Lady Charlotte motioned to Stephanie. "It is time for you to go to bed too, young lady."

Stephanie sighed. "All right." She turned and gave Matthew a hug. "Good night, big brother. I am glad you are traveling with us."

He hugged her back. "Me too."

While George stretched out in his bedroll, Matthew placed two more logs on the fire to keep the house warm. Then he rolled up in his blanket by the fire, and watched the dancing flames until his eyelids became heavy and he slept.

Matthew came suddenly awake sometime before dawn. He listened to the night sounds outside the little house, his instincts telling him that something had been different. Then he heard it, a distant howling that reminded him of the wolves in the Black Forrest. He lay quietly, trying to guess where the wolves were traveling in relation to the little house. Some of the howls sounded closer and then faded off again. Matthew wasn't worried; he had carefully shut tight the door to the stable, and the house's door and windows were also barred shut.

George groaned in his sleep; he rolled over to his side, grunted and rolled to his back again. Matthew watched him a few minutes to see if he would need some analgesic herbs, but George began softly snoring. Matthew drifted off to sleep again.

Matthew awoke to Stephanie sitting down on his chest. He rubbed his blurry eyes and looked up to see her grinning down at him.

"Wake up, sleepy head," she poked him in the cheek. "Charlotte has some hot porridge for us this morning."

"And I have a sister asking for it this morning," Matthew told her. He grasped her around the waist and heaved her off to the side. She giggled as he tickled her.

"I was so glad when you were born, Stephanie," Amber told her while helping ladle porridge into bowls. "Mattie was always trying to tickle me, and didn't leave me alone until you were about thirteen months old. Then suddenly you were more fun to tickle than I was. I almost felt abandoned."

Matthew stood up and wiggled his fingers toward Amber. "I could correct that slight if you wish, dear sister." He advanced toward her threateningly.

"Oh no, you don't," Amber glared sternly at him and backed up a step. When he stepped toward her again, she flung the porridge ladle toward him, and a clump of porridge went splat on his cheek.

"Hey, Amber," Matthew spluttered, wiping off the oatmeal and advancing toward her again. "You don't have to hit me with it!"

She giggled and stepped back again. "You touch me and I'll throw more at you!"

"Hey, you children," Harry wagged a finger at them. "No food fights in someone else's house."

"Oh, so we can food fight in our own home?" Amber asked innocently.

"Uh, no…" Harry mumbled.

Matthew stuck his hand in a bowl of porridge and raised it as if to throw it at Amber. "This is sort of your house."

"Oh no you don't, Mattie!" Amber shrieked and reached for his hand.

He dodged her hand and smeared the oatmeal on her face. She wiped it off and rubbed it in his hair. Harry and Charlotte stood helplessly by as porridge began flying across the table. Stephanie quickly snuck two bowls off the table for her and Sabrina. Pretty soon Amber and Matthew collapsed into chairs, giggling. Charlotte handed a towel to Harry to wipe porridge off his shirt where he had gotten in the firing line of one of Matthew's barrages.

"That was awesome," Matthew sighed. "I've missed having you around, Sis."

"Well, I haven't missed this," she replied tartly, but her lips betrayed a smile. "I guess we will have to make another batch of porridge and clean this place up before we go."

Frowning disapprovingly, Charlotte handed Amber and Matthew each a damp towel. She didn't have to say a word for the two mess-makers to get the message.

Amber sighed. "We are in trouble again, Mattie. Remember when we had to clean the whole castle for a week as punishment?"

Matthew nodded. "I seem to remember you were particularly fond of emptying the chamber pots."

"Eww!" Amber wrinkled up her nose. "At least it inspired you to invent an indoor outhouse."

"Yes. Malcolm disapproved of any changes to the castle's internal structure, but Mother and Father overruled him. That was a great victory!"

"And all the court ladies thank you very much," she replied, finishing wiping up the table.

Harry was grinning. "She loved the invention so much she made us make similar changes to Adonia Palace before she would marry me."

Amber swatted him with her wipe rag. "I would have married you anyway. I just wouldn't have moved to Adonia."

After everyone had their fill from the second batch of porridge, Matthew hitched the horses up while Harry loaded the carriage. George put out the fire and Harry closed the door to the little cabin. There was thick frost on the ground, so everyone kept their cloaks and blankets in the carriage with them. Charlotte had heated up some stones by the fireplace so they could keep their feet warm while traveling. The wind was blowing snowflakes around them, though not much was sticking to the ground yet.

Harry shivered in his cloak, blowing on his cold hands while Matthew drove the horse team. "Good thing we didn't stay in Sterling any longer," Harry commented.

Matthew nodded and wrapped the edges of his cloak around his hands. He wished he had brought a pair of work gloves on this journey.

The snow stopped and the air grew a little warmer as they descended the mountain. They passed a couple of pristine lakes surrounded by pine trees. Stephanie spotted a couple of deer in the trees. They stopped and ate some cold lunch near one of the lakes. Then they rounded a bend in the foot of the mountain and saw the capital city of Adonia filling the valley before them. Adonia Palace perched on a hill in the middle of the city, and a lake glittered behind it in the mid afternoon sun.

"Oh, it is beautiful!" Stephanie gasped, leaning out of the carriage window. "I can hardly wait!"

Sabrina pounded on her mother's shoulder with a little fist. "Want out! Want dinner!"

Amber tried to soothe her with one of the last of Aunt Beth's muffins. "Just half an hour more, dear. Why don't you take a nap?"

"Not sleepy!" insisted Sabrina.

In a rescue attempt, Stephanie engaged her in a game of "I spy" that became more interesting as they came into the city. Then the game lost momentum as Stephanie became distracted by the fine carriages and beautiful dresses the city ladies wore. They also sported large hats or fancy hair-do's, hair piled up on their heads with ribbons woven in.

"The hair styles are amazing, Amber! Can I get my hair done up like that?" she asked.

"That can be arranged, Stephanie. Keep in mind that it takes up to two hours to have your hair done that way, and it feels a little top-heavy. Most women only do it for special occasions."

"I don't care!" Stephanie replied. "The hair style is magnificent!"

Finally they were driving up the road to the palace on the hill. Sabrina was bouncing excitedly on her seat.

"Teffanie come to my house!" she chanted.

"That's right," Stephanie soothed. "You get to show me your toys now."

As soon as the carriage reached the front palace entrance, the little girls jumped out of the carriage and ran up the steps and inside. Adonia Palace staff surrounded the carriage, taking over the care of the horses and unloading their luggage. Harry helped Amber out of the carriage, while Matthew helped Charlotte out and then George. George grimaced when Matthew accidentally grasped on of his bandaged arms.

Harry turned to his head butler. "Steven, would you please take George to see Physician Coates? His arm wounds will need new dressings, and I think he will need more analgesic."

"Yes, Your Highness." Steven bowed and escorted George into the palace.

One of the court ladies stood on the top step near the door watching the royal family unload. Matthew gazed at her thinking she looked familiar, but could not imagine how he might know her. As Amber started up the steps carrying a blanket, the young woman dashed down the steps to carry it for her. Amber smiled at the young woman as she approached and gave her a hug.

"Thank you, Roberta," Amber told her.

Matthew smacked himself mentally. Of course! Roberta had been Amber's bane when she was fourteen years old. Roberta teased Amber and dared her to do something 'brave'. Amber talked Matthew and Harry into going with her to Rimrock Island to re-enact the Test that their father, Robert of Danforth, had taken to win Elinore's hand in marriage. The task was to find seven treasure objects hidden around the island. The children hid them for each other, but all of them were injured while finding them again. And then they discovered that Rimrock Island was also the home to a pair of Komodo dragons guarding a nest of eggs. To date no one knew how the dragons ended up on the island.

Matthew however, had been fascinated by the dragons, and spent many summer days on the island studying them, unbeknownst to his parents. He also found some books in the castle library about dragons, but doubted much of what was common belief about them. He was always extra wary of the male dragon that had attacked Harry, and never approached the female dragon when she was around her eggs. But as he observed them interact with their young, Matthew developed a working theory of how he might tame one of the young dragons. He brought meat to feed them, and learned to mimic some of the sounds the mother made. Soon he had three of the young dragons following him around the island, begging for food scraps. One of the dragons would actually crouch and watch Matthew for hours wherever Matthew sat in the sun. Matthew would whistle and talk to him and the dragon would croon back. Matthew named him Creedo because the dragon perked up when Matthew made those sounds.

Amber and Roberta eventually made up and became friends. When Amber married Harry, Roberta followed her to Adonia to be her main lady-in-waiting. There she met Jack, a handsome Adonian courtier and married him a year later.

Roberta looked up and recognized Matthew. She waved at him and smiled. Matthew waved back. Roberta continued to walk up the stairs with Amber and Harry.

Everyone seemed to know where to go, taking luggage upstairs to rooms, taking the horses to the stables, and getting food ready for supper. Someone whisked Lady Charlotte and Stephanie away to their guest suite in the west wing, leaving Matthew standing uncertainly in the front hall, his knapsack tucked under one arm. Matthew studied the entryway, with its rich cherry wood walls, oak pillars, and marble staircase curving elegantly upward. Four stained glass windows on either side of the front door let in the light through mountain scenes of trees reaching up to the sky from a forest floor.

"Beautiful windows, aren't they?" a female voice commented behind him. "King Gilbert's grandfather had the work commissioned from a famous glass maker a hundred years ago."

Matthew turned to look into the face of a pretty, dark eyed, black haired girl about his age. She smiled at him. "You must be Princess Amber's brother."

He nodded. "My name is Matthew." He bowed.

"Oh no! Don't bow to me! I'm just one of the palace workers." She curtseyed deeply to him. "My name is Sarah, Prince Matthew. I am here to show you to your room."

He nodded and followed Sarah up the grand staircase and down a long hall on the west wing. She stopped in front of a door and opened it.

"This is one of the smaller suites, but should be comfortable," she told him. "You have half an hour to wash up before dinner is served." She curtseyed again and left him.

Matthew went over to the window that looked out onto the central palace garden below. Beyond the opposite wing of the palace he could see snow covered mountain peaks. He turned around and looked around the room. There was a couch and two chairs circling a fireplace, and a table by the wall with goblets and a water pitcher on it. Next to the fireplace a door led to a bedroom, which shared the same fireplace, and also had a window looking out onto the palace garden. Next to the bed stood a table with a wash basin and a little mirror, and a chamber pot underneath. There was also a wardrobe where he could put his clothes. Despite being called little, the suite felt more than roomy enough for him.

Matthew washed his face and hands and pulled on fresh clothes. Then he went back down the hall and downstairs to find the dining room. A pair of arms suddenly hugged his legs from behind.

"Uncle Mattie!" Sabrina smiled up at him.

He squatted down and gave her a hug. "You live in a beautiful palace, Princess Sabrina. Now where do we dine?"

She giggled and grasped his hand. "This way."

She led him into the dining room, a long hall with beautiful wood floors, more stained glass windows depicting hunting scenes, mirrors on the opposite wall, and three large glittering chandeliers overhead. The table itself was made of highly polished dark cherry wood, set with matching gold china and crystal goblets. The center of the table was laden with a feast rivaling a Christmas celebration.

Sabrina led Matthew to sit at the table next to her. "Eat," she commanded.

He leaned over to whisper loudly in her ear. "Shouldn't we wait for your parents?"

She rolled her eyes upward. "Yes," she sighed dramatically. "But I so hungry!"

Matthew picked a bread roll from a plate near them. "Maybe you can nibble on this while we are waiting."

"Thank you," she replied daintily, and took a big bite.

Princess Stephanie, Lady Charlotte and George came in next, and sat at the table opposite them. A few minutes later Harry and Amber arrived. Harry sat on one end of the table, and Amber sat between him and Sabrina. Harry nodded at everyone, and they filled their plates and began eating.

About ten minutes later King Gilbert came into the dining room.

"My Lord," Harry greeted him, beginning to stand up.

King Gilbert waved him back down. "We are amongst family, Harry. Save the formalities."

Lady Charlotte started to pass a plate of food toward King Gilbert, but he shook his head. "I have already eaten. Carry on."

Sabrina finished eating her mashed potatoes, then slipped out of her chair, went to King Gilbert, and climbed into his lap.

"Pappi, I brought Teffanie to our house," she told him.

"I see," he smiled down at her. "And what did you do at Stephanie's house this summer?"

"We played house. Teffanie is my lady-waiting. I am Queen Sabrina."

"Very fine." Gilbert laid a hand on her head and caressed her hair. "What else did you do?"

"I went to the beach and got seashells!"

"Marvelous. Anything else?"

She wrinkled her forehead. "No."

Stephanie piped up. "Yes there is! We rode ponies, went on picnics, and played dolls!"

Sabrina smiled. "I love Teffanie!"

King Gilbert gave her a hug. "And I love you Sabrina. I missed you this summer."

After dinner Harry and his father left together to discuss business, and everyone else retired to their apartments for a well-deserved rest.

Matthew woke early the next morning, and left his suite to go exploring. He wandered down halls, up some back stairs, and found a roof access door. He walked around a roof walk that circled the west wing of the palace. He could look across the inner courtyard gardens toward the east palace wing and its rooftop walk. One end of the palace contained the entry hall at the front. The opposite end was connected to the palace stables and carriage house. Matthew could see the kitchens on the ground floor of the opposite wing, workers already bustling around getting ready for the day.

In the center of the courtyard garden was a magnificent fountain, with stone ladies dancing around the spraying water. Walking paths meandered around exotic flower plots, fruit trees, and a fish pond, with scattered benches in strategic places. Shrubbery surrounded the garden, separating it from a covered walkway circling the inner walls of the palace.

Matthew went back down the stairs and went out the front door. He followed the carriage road around the outside of the palace to the back stable area. He went inside and found the two horses, Dawn and Dusty, who had brought them from Sterling. Grabbing a brush from the wall, he started brushing them down.

As he finished the second horse, he leaned his forehead against the horse's warm neck. "What am I doing here?" he asked the horse. "What am I going to do all winter long? What am I going to do with my life?" He sniffed and ran the back of his hand across his nose.

"Hallo! Who is in here?" called a voice from the front of the stable. "Who left the main door open?"

Matthew poked his head out of the stall door. "It is I, Matthew, visiting from Sterling. I am taking care of our horses."

"Matthew!" A familiar figure appeared around the corner, a handsome man in his late twenties, dressed in green tunic and boots. He approached and grasped Matthew's hand in greeting.

"Sir Royce!" Matthew pumped Royce's hand energetically. "Am I glad to see you! What have you been up to lately?"

Sir Royce leaned back against the stable wall. "Well, it is pretty much a full time job running the page and squire training here. Unfortunately we have fewer young men who stay on for the full knight training any more. I think more of them want to join Adonia's military force. That training is less intense and allows the men to pursue other careers around their weekend service. Have you made knighthood yet?"

Matthew frowned. "No. Sir Lamborgini was making it extra hard for me. I am not sure I will continue."

Sir Royce shook his head. "That's too bad. You were showing some natural talent." He pulled an apple out of his pocket and rolled it in his hands. "Sir Lamborgini is really good. His teaching techniques are a little different, but he produces some of the best knights I have ever seen. He demands the highest quality from his men. Those who have the greatest potential he pushes the hardest."

Matthew didn't know what to say. He fiddled with the brush in his hands. "I didn't mind the hard work so much. But the idea of pledging my fealty to one Lord concerned me. It felt restrictive." He looked up at Sir Royce suddenly. "Speaking of fealty, how were you able to move to Adonia and leave Sterling?"

Royce laughed. "I pledged to protect the royal family of Sterling. Since Sterling still had two other knights, and Adonia had only one aging fellow, Queen Elinore directed me to be Princess Amber's protector." He lowered his voice. "Between you and me, I would have worried more about that assignment seven years ago. I think Princess Amber had a crush on me. It would have been very awkward being her special protector."

Matthew laughed. "She did have a crush on you. So did just about every other young court lady in Sterling."

Sir Royce cleared his throat uncomfortably, and then suddenly tossed the apple in his hands to Matthew, who barely caught it. "Here, feed your horse." Royce pulled out another apple for the other horse.

Matthew rubbed Dusty's nose while he crunched the apple. "So how is your wife, Sir Royce?"

Royce grinned. "Shelley is doing very well. My son turns four this winter, and our daughter recently turned two. I just found out that we are expecting again. Shelley has her hands full caring for them. She had to give up her palace job after our daughter was born."

Matthew nodded. "Shelley's brother Roger was so lost after you moved to Adonia. "I almost think he married Mary Stone just to have some woman to care for him."

Sir Royce smiled. "It was a good thing he married her. She has been pining for him ever since he bought her May Day basket when she was sixteen."

"And they are both very happy now. I think it was her pushing that got him to accept the head gardening job when Joseph died. She actually does more of the gardening now while Roger builds and fixes things around the castle. Mother declared the Queen's Gardens never looked so good under a man's care. She is trying to make it official that a woman can supervise the royal gardens." Matthew cocked his head and gazed at

Sir Royce curiously. "Why did you marry Shelley? I thought you had your eye on Lady Alyssa?"

Royce looked uncomfortable. "I think Alyssa had her eye more on me than the other way around. Then she fell head over heels for that foreign Ambassador. She is now living with him on the continent, traveling all around the world and living the elegant life. I wanted to marry someone who loved me and not the color of my armor."

A female laugh peeled out from the front of the stable, and Shelley appeared, carrying two buckets of water. "Who is to say I didn't marry you for the color of your armor?"

"Well, it won't do you any good now, Shelley. I had to change color from red to green when I moved to Adonia." He took the buckets from her and put them down in front of the horses. "And you are not supposed to be carrying heavy things, missy."

She stretched up on her toes and kissed him on the cheek, then turned to Matthew. "You should have seen the kind of man I married, Matthew. Talk about a man who needs a woman around to pick up after him. You should have seen the state of his quarters before I moved in."

Royce playfully swatted her bottom. "Don't go talking like I am the only one. You could barely ride a horse when we married."

She gazed at him lovingly. "So we are even. I think you loved me for me first, you big lout."

Matthew left the two of them kissing in the horses' stall, smiling at their antics, but also feeling acutely lonely.

After breakfast Amber and Harry left to take care of duties in the city, leaving Sabrina in the care of her nanny. Lady Charlotte took Princess Stephanie to the school rooms to start her tutoring, and George went off to see Physician Coates again. Matthew was left at the dining table with King Gilbert, who was still finishing up his breakfast.

King Gilbert finally wiped his mouth on his napkin and pushed his chair back. He patted his ample stomach. "My wife Geraldine always chided me for eating too much, but I believe a good day starts with a good breakfast." He leaned toward Matthew conspiratorially. "Actually I did sometimes overeat just to irritate her. But now that she is gone I am trying to lose weight. I am not eating as much in the evening, and I engage in a daily calisthenics program. I do it in a private room so I don't embarrass anybody." He laughed a deep rich laugh.

Matthew smiled. "Yes, Your Highness."

King Gilbert peered at him. "I think you need to visit our palace library today. Read up a bit on the history of Adonia. How much do you know about our country?"

"I learned a little bit in my studies," Matthew confessed. "But I was not a particularly avid reader."

"Noted. Neither was I. I preferred to be out on my horse hunting." King Gilbert pushed his girth up out of his chair. "Off we go to the library. Our librarian will show you around while I go off to my duties."

Aberforth, the old librarian, welcomed Matthew without a smile. He led Matthew over to the shelves containing the history of Adonia and other neighboring countries, and then left him to read to his heart's content. Matthew found a couple of smaller volumes that seemed more like cursory summaries of Adonia's history, then sat down in a comfortable cushioned chair to read. A couple of hours later he woke with a start, and realized he had only read two pages into the first chapter.

"This won't do," he muttered to himself and placed the books back on the shelf. Aberforth was poring over a frail old volume at his desk, and looked up briefly as Matthew passed him. Matthew nodded at him, and Aberforth bent over his studying again.

Matthew wandered into the palace garden. He threw some grass into the pond and watched the fish dart toward the blades and then meander slowly back around the bottom of the pond. He sat down in front of the fountain and gazed at the stone dancers. He imagined himself dancing at a court ball, and wondered what kind of dance steps they did in Adonia. He tried to remember the steps to the Pavane he had danced years ago when Amber turned fifteen.

He heard a noise behind him and turned, his hands still raised as though leading a dance partner. Sabrina was running toward the fountain, a little boat in her hands. She placed it in the water, the fountain spray making it bob in the rain. Then she turned back to point it out to someone behind her. Matthew looked to where she gestured and saw Sarah coming down the walk. He dropped his hands quickly and tried to look natural.

"Hello, Sarah," he greeted her.

"Hello, Prince Matthew," she curtseyed. "Dancing with the stone ladies, were you?"

He blushed. "Just trying to remember how… Never mind. What are you doing here with Sabrina?"

"I am her nanny. I attend the princess and cater to her every whim." Sarah smiled. "What are you doing today?"

Matthew shrugged. "Not much. I tried to read up on some of the history of Adonia, but I fell asleep."

Sarah's peals of laughter were warm and genuine. Matthew liked it. "Did Aberforth help you find the books? He picks the ones that are the most dry and boring. I am not surprised that you fell asleep."

Matthew sighed. "I am not a very good reader. But I don't wish to be ignorant of your country's history either."

Sarah nodded. "If you like, I can tell you some of Adonia's history. It is rich in lore and legend, as old as the mountains that surround our land. I could tell you a different tale every day."

Matthew was intrigued. "You make it sound more interesting than any old book. I accept your offer."

Sarah sat down on a bench to watch Sabrina play in the water. She patted the seat next to her and Matthew joined her.

"Before I start the stories, you will need an outline of our country's history first. How much do you know about how our countries first came to be?"

Matthew tried to remember. "There were four brothers who divided the land. But I don't remember how there came to be five countries."

"There was also a sister," Sarah explained. "The land of Adonia was named after her. The four brothers were Sterling, Renling, Borden and Mordred. Their father was an explorer from the mainland, who about three hundred years ago came seeking a place where he and his people could settle, free from servitude, war and poverty. He founded our island continent, Browning Isle, and eventually divided the land amongst his five children: Sterling in the South, Renling in the East, Borden in the West, and Mordred in the north. The sister took the land in the center of the island continent, surrounded on all sides by her brothers, who vowed to protect her from any invaders from the mainland. The countries also promised to always cooperate with each other, and never go to war."

"As I recall, that didn't always work out as planned," Matthew commented. "There were some kings who wanted to rule the whole island continent for themselves."

"Correct. But the other countries would band together to put down the warring king and keep their countries intact. It was a beautiful balance of powers."

"But then the area of Danforth became an independent city-state a hundred years ago," Matthew pointed out.

Sarah's expression clouded over. "That was an unfortunate hiccup in our land's history. It almost caused the break-up of the five country system. Other cities tried to become independent after that, and it took thirty years to stop all the little factions from seceding. There is still hope that Danforth will agree to rejoin their mother nation."

Matthew shook his head. "I don't think that will ever happen. Danforth seems to be happy as an independent entity. And they were given that right by the king of Sterling for valor during a particularly nasty war."

Sarah sniffed. "An unfortunate turn of events then."

There was an uncomfortable silence between them. Sabrina came up to Matthew then and tugged on his sleeve, a pleading look on her face. "Fetch my boat, Uncle Mattie."

Sarah giggled. "Mattie? Did Sabrina make that up?"

Matthew shook his head. "My sister, Amber, started calling me that when I was little. I am trying to change it to something that sounds more masculine, but I am not having much luck."

He looked over to the fountain and saw that Sabrina's boat had floated to the relatively protected center of the fountain, within the circle of cascading spray. He looked around for a stick he could use, but the garden was kept immaculately clean. There was nothing for it but to go in himself to fetch it. He pulled off his boots and stockings, rolled up his pant legs, and stepped into the fountain. He ducked under the spray, seized the boat, and jumped out again, but not before getting soaked from head to toe. He handed the boat to Sabrina who ran off down the path with it. Sarah was holding her side and laughing uncontrollably.

"What?" Matthew asked, standing drenched before her.

"You looked like a drowned cat," she told him, and ran off down the path after Sabrina.

Matthew sighed and turned back toward the palace to get changed into some dry things. So much for impressing the first girl his age that he had met here.

Matthew slogged upstairs to his suite to change into dry clothes. He draped his wet ones on the chair in front of the fireplace, and started a little fire to get them drying. Then he went downstairs to get some lunch. Charlotte, Stephanie and George were in the dining room, already eating.

Stephanie was pouting. "I don't want to go back for more studies," she told Charlotte, folding her arms. "I want to play with Sabrina."

"Sabrina is taking a nap right now," Charlotte told her. "How about we have a sewing lesson until she wakes up?"

Stephanie heaved a sigh. "Okay. I suppose."

Matthew sat down and dished up some food.

"How was your morning?" George asked Matthew.

Matthew shrugged. "I found the library, got a nap, and took a shower in the garden fountain."

Stephanie looked up at Matthew and giggled. "You took a shower where? Don't you know where the palace baths are?"

Matthew stared at her accusingly. "I was fetching Sabrina's boat. Her nanny laughed at me through the whole thing."

Stephanie rolled her eyes. "You are such a geek, Mattie. I can't believe you jumped into the fountain! How embarrassing."

Matthew sighed. It *was* embarrassing, but he wasn't going to let Stephanie know it bothered him. "Do you have any better suggestions how I should spend my time here in Adonia?"

George cleared his throat. "You might want to stop by the training field at the foot of the palace hill," he suggested. "Sir Royce was working with several young squires who looked pretty green to me. He might be able to use your help this afternoon."

Matthew brightened up. That sounded more interesting than reading in the library. He quickly finished eating and headed outside. One of the palace workers pointed out a trail down to the training ground. When Matthew arrived he saw several young men practicing various sword techniques. Matthew watched a few minutes while Sir Royce demonstrated a technique and had the young men try it again. Matthew almost laughed. It was obvious they were not catching on very quickly.

Sir Royce pulled at his hair in frustration. "No, no, no!" he cried, stopping them. Then he caught sight of Matthew. "Matthew!" he called, delighted. "Help me demonstrate the Lamborgini Disarming Technique!"

One of the squires handed Matthew his sword. Matthew hefted it in his hand, swung it several times, and then faced Sir Royce in a ready stance.

"You attack, I'll defend," Sir Royce instructed.

Matthew came at Royce with a variety of strikes, which Royce parried, waiting for the right moment. Then when Matthew came at him with a diagonal slice, Royce twisted his sword around Matthew's blade, yanking it out of his hand. The sword went flying up, spinning end over end and landing point down in the dirt.

The squires clapped and Sir Royce bowed.

Matthew grinned. "Do you want to see the defense to the Lamborgini Disarming Technique?" he asked them.

The young men nodded.

"Sir Royce, start again defending, and do the same maneuver on me you did before," Matthew instructed.

The two began again. Matthew sliced diagonally, but this time when Royce twisted his sword, Matthew twisted his wrist right along with him and then kept twisting. This time instead of Royce disarming Matthew, Matthew disarmed Royce. As Royce's sword arced up and then down, Matthew watched carefully, then shot his hand out and caught it by the hilt.

Royce rubbed his wrist. "Well done. I have not seen that one before."

"Yeah, Sir Lamborgini caught me with his disarming technique so many times I had to invent a maneuver to defend myself," Matthew grinned.

Sir Royce waved everyone over. "Young men, I'd like you to meet Prince Matthew of Sterling, one of my previous squires."

Technically Matthew was only a squire to Sir Royce for about six months. Before that he was a page under Sir Bentley until he died, then Sir Rover took over training the younger boys. Shortly after Matthew started with Sir Royce, Amber and Harry married, Royce moved with them to Adonia, and Sterling hired Sir Lamborgini to take his place. But Matthew wasn't about to correct Sir Royce.

Sir Royce introduced Matthew to the ten squires he was training. Then they began practicing the Lamborgini Disarming Technique. Sir Royce did not let them practice the defense against it; that would be for another day.

Mid-afternoon the young men were tired and ready for a different skill. "Archery!" they clamored.

Sir Royce threw up his hands, smiling. "Fine! Archery it is."

The boys ran to their equipment shed and exchanged their swords for bows and arrows. "Come, Matthew!" they shouted.

Beyond their tournament field lay their archery range. It was unlike anything Matthew had seen before. They had the standard straw bale targets spaced near, medium and far, but they also had targets in all shapes, sizes and heights. Half the field was arrayed like a forest: trees, logs and bushes partially masking stuffed large and small animal hides as targets.

"This is awesome!" Matthew breathed, turning to the young man next to him.

"Just wait until you see the actual contests we do here. Archery is our national sport, hunting our favorite pastime. Show us what you can do, Matthew."

Matthew was one of the better archers in Sterling, but compared to the Adonian archers they were pros and he was barely an amateur. After an hour of shooting he decided to sit back and just watch. Some of the boys were very steady and precise, hitting small targets from great distances. These would be the winners of archery tournaments, Matthew judged. Other boys loved to creep among the bushes and trees, sneaking up on unsuspecting animals and shooting them consistently in the kill zones marked on their bodies. These would be the hunters.

But the archer who impressed Matthew the most was a sandy haired young man who had his own style of shooting altogether. It was almost like watching a bird in free flight. He would run past the targets loosing arrows as he ran, barely aiming, but hitting targets every time. In the forest range he climbed trees, jumped from rocks and leaped over animals as he shot. One time he even hung one handed from a tree branch, braced his foot against the bow and pulled the string with his free hand. The arrow found its mark in the animal below, and he leaped to the ground, catching his bow mid jump.

"That was amazing shooting," Matthew told him. "Where did you learn to shoot like that, um…"

"My name is Karl," the young man smiled. "I am not a native of Adonia. We are actually from the mainland. My father is an ambassador here. He taught me some techniques and I made up the rest. My mother and I have what you might call acrobatic ability."

"I would love to learn some of your techniques, Karl. Will you teach me?"

Karl bowed. "I would be honored to, Prince Matthew."

"Please just call me Matthew."

Over the next several days Matthew and Karl became fast friends. Karl showed Matthew places in the palace that none of the workers would have shown him or even known about. One of the most interesting was a wooden trapdoor in one of the kitchen storage rooms that opened up into a tunnel that sloped down and curved out of sight. Karl thought it might be a secret escape exit off the palace hill, but he had never explored it for fear someone would close the trapdoor and seal him inside.

Each afternoon of the week the squires practiced a different skill: sword fighting, lance and javelin, wrestling, archery, and horse riding. Of course, the boys all wanted to shoot with their bows for an hour after each day of training, which Sir Royce would allow if they worked hard on their other skills. Matthew discovered that he was better at the free-style archery shooting that Karl exhibited than the steady strength and precision shooting of the Adonian men. He never figured out how to hold the bow with his feet and hit the target accurately, but he became fairly adept at quickly shooting while running past targets.

In the mornings while Sir Royce worked with the younger boys training as pages, the squires went into the city of Adonia three days a week to learn from various trades: smithing/ metalworking, carpentry/ woodworking, and livery/ horses. The other two days they learned from the court matron etiquette and home care skills (cooking, washing, mending). The squires had complained about the homey skills until Sir Royce pointed out that first, armies had to take care of all their own care needs while out on campaigns away from home, and second, the best way to impress a lady was while displaying fine manners. Matthew was no stranger to any of these skills and had seen first-hand how it served a knight well at castle life to exhibit these skills.

Matthew tried as much as possible to eat breakfast and dinner with his sisters. Lunch was usually bread, sausage, cheese and fruit on the go between training sessions with the squires. He found he excelled at the carpentry, livery, and sword fighting, and was only passingly adept at the other skills. However, he much preferred training with Sir Royce over reading books in the library or wandering bored through the palace.

CHAPTER 4

FIRST SNOW

A week after Matthew and his sisters arrived in Adonia, a snowstorm in the mountains closed East Adonia Pass. The air grew colder, and everyone took to wearing cloaks outside. The high hills filled with red and gold colors as the trees turned in the autumn air.

Three weeks later, Matthew awoke in the night to howling wind and blowing snow beating against his bedroom window. He saw a curtain of white particles blowing horizontally past the window blinding any view of the palace wing on the other side of the courtyard gardens. No lights could be seen beyond the driving white. He shivered and put two more logs on the coals in his bedroom fireplace, and blew on them until they burst into hot flame. Then he dived back into his bed and piled more blankets on top of himself until his shivering stopped. He dozed until dawn, listening to the ice particles hitting the window glass.

Matthew finally got out of bed when the fire in his room died, and pulled on his socks, long pants, long sleeved shirt, tunic and boots. He went downstairs to the kitchens to get warm. The palace staff were already up and cooking for the day. He saw Charlotte by the fire, where she was heating a pot of tea for Stephanie and herself.

"Good morning, Charlotte," he said, coming up behind her.

She nearly dropped the teacup she was holding. "Prince Matthew! I did not expect you here this early in the morning."

He sat down in a chair near the fire. "My room got cold. How about you?"

"Yes, the same. Stephanie would not leave her blankets and bed, but the poor dear is shivering herself to pieces. Do you want to help me take up something warm for her?"

Matthew nodded. "Yes, if I can have some hot tea also!"

"Of course. The water is almost ready."

Matthew carried the tray with the hot water pot and teacups, while Charlotte carried a basket of scones. When they entered Stephanie's bedroom suite, they found a fire already burning in the fireplace and the room was warming up.

Stephanie poked her head out of her blankets. "Lady Roberta sent someone in to restart the fire," she explained. "Is that the tea?"

"Yes," Charlotte nodded and poured her a cup. Stephanie held her hands around the warmth and sipped in utter contentment.

Matthew looked around the suite. The sitting area was on one side of the fireplace, and the bedroom on the other, but it was a more open arrangement and much larger than Matthew's. A door led off of the bedroom side. Charlotte noticed Matthew gazing at it.

"That leads into my bedroom," she commented. "It has its own fireplace, but most of the time I am in here with Princess Stephanie."

After eating scones and drinking her tea, Stephanie was ready to get out of bed. She pulled on a long sleeved dress and stockings and padded over to her window.

"I can't see anything out there," she complained. "It just looks white." She shivered and ran back to the fireplace to warm her hands. "And it is colder by the window."

There was a knock at the door and Roberta came in, carrying an armful of winter clothing. "Princess Amber instructed I bring you some wool stockings and undergarments to keep you warm now that winter is trying to arrive." She sized up Lady Charlotte's tall height. "You are a little taller than many of our ladies, Lady Charlotte. I will try to find you some longer leggings."

Charlotte bowed her head. "Thank you. That will be appreciated."

Stephanie was already rummaging through the pile of clothes her size. "These look so much warmer!" she squealed, then looked at Matthew. "Turn around, Mattie, while I change."

He smiled at her sudden modesty, but acceded to her wishes and walked over to the window to look out at the blizzard. There was a definite draft around the window. He ran his fingers around the edges where the window's wooden frames met stone walls. He could feel little gaps where the wind blew in cold air. He wondered if there was a substance he could use to seal in the spaces.

"Ta-da!" Stephanie announced. "You can look now, Mattie."

He turned around and she showed off her thick wool stockings pulled over long legged underwear, and an extra petticoat under her skirt. Over the top of the dress she wore a little wool cape that covered her shoulders down to the waist. It also had a hood that she could pull over her head to keep her ears warm. On her feet were a pair of boots with fur lining inside.

"Isn't this cute? Oh, I feel warmer already!" Stephanie twirled around. "Mattie, let's go exploring the palace!"

While Charlotte put on her own warm underclothes, Matthew and Stephanie wandered around the palace. Other than everyone now staying warm indoors, all the palace workers went about doing their normal work. Matthew led Stephanie through some back halls and nondescript doors to get to the palace stables. There they found Sir Royce pitching hay to the horses.

Matthew looked around, but saw no one else. "Where are the pages and squires this morning?"

Sir Royce leaned on the handle of his pitchfork. "Most of them are staying in their homes in the city. Traveling is not safe in this kind of weather."

"Oh." Matthew grabbed another pitchfork and tossed some hay to Dusty and Dawn.

"Karl should be along soon. He lives with his father in the east wing of the palace." Royce gazed at Matthew. "What are your plans today?"

Matthew leaned his head toward his sister. "Entertaining her Royal Highness and trying to keep warm during this blizzard. Any ideas?"

Royce pointed to some buckets by the stalls. "As for keeping busy, the horses still need to be watered. You can fill them at the courtyard well just outside the stable door."

Stephanie shook her head. "I am not going out there. I just got warm." She sat down on an upturned bucket in one of the stalls and began petting Dawn's nose.

Matthew opened the door leading to the courtyard, and was hit with a biting gust of wind blowing snow into his face. He stumbled toward the well and pulled up the well bucket to fill the bucket for the horses. By the time it was full, his hands were frozen stiff. He stumbled back into the horse stables and set down the bucket of water for Stephanie's horse.

"I am not going out there again!" Matthew stuttered. "There has got to be a better way to water these horses."

Stephanie was giggling. "You look like a snow beast, Mattie!"

"I feel like an ice-man, that is for sure." He shook snow out of his hair and Dusty next to him snorted. Matthew placed his hands against the horse's warm hide and sighed pleasurably. "Sir Royce, this stable is warmer than other rooms in the palace, and it doesn't even have a fireplace. How is that managed?"

Royce scratched his ear. "We are next to the kitchens, and the horse bodies also help heat the stables. Other than that I am not sure. But it is one of the more pleasant places in the palace in the winter time."

There was a clattering near the courtyard door of the stable and a figure came in, covered in furs from his head to fingertips to his toes. He was carrying two buckets of water for the horses. He set them down in front of two other horses, and they began to drink. Then he pulled off his gloves and removed his fur cap, complete with ear flaps.

"Karl!" Matthew exclaimed, surprised. "What are you wearing? I have never seen anything like it!"

"We call it a fur coat in my country. Look, it has sleeves to fit around the arms. No open flaps to let in drafty cold air."

"I wish I had one of those," Matthew remarked enviously. "It looks warm!"

"Very. Do you want to try it on?"

Matthew nodded and pulled on the coat. Karl showed him how to fasten the front. Then he put his hat on Matthew's head, tying down the ear flaps. Karl then offered him his gloves.

"Oh yes! This is warm! I think I could go out into the snowstorm again!" Matthew picked up two empty buckets and ran out to the well again.

When he came back, Stephanie looked at him critically. "Now you look like a snow bear."

"Much better than an ice-man! Karl, I have a wolf pelt I picked up on the way here. Where I can I get one of these coats made?"

Karl sized him up. "I know a fellow in town that can make it up for you. Meanwhile my father may have an extra one he can loan you."

"Excellent! I am interested. I am going to fetch more water."

After they finished watering the horses, Sir Royce led the boys up to a little loft above the stable where extra hay bales were kept. They tossed two more into the hay stall below to be prepared for the horses' next meals. Near the hay the loft was warm, but near the ceiling Matthew could feel the cool air of the palace again.

After finishing with chores, Karl beckoned Matthew and Stephanie to follow him. He dropped his furs off in his family's living quarters, and then led them back downstairs to one of the kitchen storage rooms.

"What are we doing here?" Stephanie asked curiously.

Karl put his finger to his lips and led them over to a trapdoor in the floor underneath some barrels. He moved the barrels, lifted the trapdoor, and indicated the tunnel inside.

"Two of us to explore, and one to guard the entrance," he whispered.

"Where does the tunnel go?" Stephanie asked quietly.

"We don't know. That's what we are here to find out," Karl answered.

"Do you want to go with Karl?" Matthew asked Stephanie.

She looked in the hole and shook her head. "No. You go, Mattie."

Matthew jumped down into the hole. "Don't let anyone close and cover the trapdoor with a barrel or anything," he told her.

She nodded and watched them descend. The tunnel went pretty straight toward the outer walls of the palace, then turned and started sloping down. Karl and Matthew were feeling their way along at first, then Matthew bumped into Karl, who was fumbling in his pocket in the darkness.

"I know I put it in here somewhere."

"What?" Matthew asked.

"My flint and a candle," Karl responded.

Matthew could have kicked himself. He was usually the one prepared with his flint stone.

"Found the candle," Karl remarked.

They noticed a faint bobbing light coming down the tunnel toward them. Matthew and Karl held their breaths. Then Stephanie rounded the bend. "There you are," she commented. "I decided I didn't want to be left behind. I brought you a candle."

Matthew grinned. "Thanks Steph. Excellent timing."

"What about the trapdoor?" Karl asked.

"Don't worry. I pulled a table over it to shield the opening from view."

Stephanie lit Karl's candle, and they followed the tunnel down as it wound in a large circle inside the hill. After what seemed like a mile, the tunnel ended at a heavy wooden door. The wood felt cold to the touch. Karl tried to turn the handle and pull on the door, but it was locked or stuck.

"Let me look at that." Matthew studied the lock in Stephanie's candlelight. Then he drew a wire out of his pocket, stuck it in the lock and wiggled it for a couple of minutes. He felt a subtle click, and then the doorknob turned. The door still would not open by push or pull. Matthew ran his hands along the door frame.

"It feels like it should open outward," Matthew told the others. "Karl, put your shoulder to the door with me and let's see if we can force it open."

Together on the count of three they rammed against the door. On the third attempt the door popped open a foot. There seemed to be some dirt or plants on the other side. A cold wet wind blew in at them. Matthew couldn't quite reach or see around.

"Let me look," Stephanie pushed forward and squeezed through the space. She pulled some plants away and the door opened another foot. They found themselves in a little alcove filled with growing plants, beyond which daylight was visible and the snowstorm swirled. Karl's candle blew out.

Karl poked his head out of the alcove for a minute. "I think this is the base of the hill near the squire's training ground, but I can't tell for sure. I say we check it out another time." He shivered and came back into the warmer tunnel.

They closed the door again, but left it unlocked. Stephanie relit Karl's candle and they hiked back up the tunnel to the storeroom. Luckily the trapdoor was still open. They closed the trapdoor but left the table over the area.

"No word of this to anyone," Matthew advised Stephanie. "After we find out where it exits we can talk to Harry and Amber."

"Okay," Stephanie smiled, obviously proud to be part of a big secret.

The next morning dawned bright and clear, the sun glinting off the newly fallen snow. Matthew could hear the squeals of Sabrina and Stephanie down the hall as they saw the snow and begged to go outside.

There was a sudden pounding on Matthew's door. "Come on, Mattie! Come play in the snow!" Stephanie called through the door.

"Coming!" Matthew threw on his borrowed winter clothes over his shirt and breeches, pulled on his boots, and grabbed the winter hat, coat and gloves. He ran down the hall and jumped down the steps two at a time. Stephanie and Sabrina were already in the palace courtyard wading through snowdrifts between the garden hedges. Matthew met Charlotte standing by the courtyard door in her cloak, shivering. He paused and raised his eyebrows questioningly at her.

"I will stay here, if you please," she told him.

He nodded and stepped outside. He trumped through the snowdrifts, working his way toward the fountain in the center of the garden. A few minutes later Sabrina came running around the hedge toward him. She took one look at Matthew in his furs, screamed, and turned around to run. She bumped straight into Stephanie who was right behind her.

"Bear!" Sabrina cried.

"Sabrina! It's just me." Matthew pulled off his hat, and stooped down to her level.

Stephanie hugged Sabrina and turned her around to look at Matthew. "Look, Sabrina. It is just Uncle Mattie."

Sabrina studied Matthew a minute, then walked over to him and fingered his fur coat. "Uncle Mattie play bear with us?" she asked, looking up at him.

He nodded and put his fur hat back on. "The snow bear is fishing by the frozen stream. He sees two beautiful princesses. What are they going to do?"

"Oh no!" Stephanie took hold of Sabrina's hand. "Princess Sabrina, there is a giant snow bear. What shall we do?"

"Run!" Sabrina squealed. She led Stephanie around the trails while Matthew stomped after them, swinging his arms and growling like a bear.

"Make snowballs!" Sabrina commanded Stephanie.

"I don't know how," Stephanie confessed.

"I show you." Sabrina cupped her gloved hands around a handful of snow and packed it into a ball. Stephanie followed her example. Then Matthew staggered around the hedge. The girls squealed again, threw their snowballs against his chest and ran to the next section of garden.

After a few rounds of snowballs Matthew changed the game up. "I am now a giant, coming to get you!" He made some snowballs of his own to throw at the girls. Again they ran from him screaming gleefully, hiding behind hedges to make more snowballs to throw at him.

Several volleys later, armed with four snowballs, Matthew rounded a hedge and instinctively threw a snowball at the cloaked figure standing there. She turned at the noise he made, and almost in slow motion, he watched as the snowball he threw smacked her squarely in the face. She gasped and Matthew stood mortified realizing this was not Stephanie, but Sarah, Sabrina's nanny.

She sputtered and wiped snow from her face. "I beg your pardon!"

"I am so sorry!" Matthew pulled off his hat and reached out as though to help her wipe off the snow. "I was intending to hit my sister Stephanie."

"Well, you got the wrong target, Prince Matthew." She looked around. "I am here to fetch Princess Sabrina for lunch."

"I'll help you find her." They went different directions to locate the girls. Matthew heard Sarah's voice one hedge over addressing Sabrina's protestations, then their voices fading in the distance. Matthew found Stephanie sitting on the edge of the frozen fountain.

"Sabrina had to go in," Stephanie commented.

"I know."

Stephanie looked up to see Matthew's glum expression. "You look sour."

"Yeah, well you should have seen Sarah's expression when I hit her in the face with a snowball."

"That was not very smart. No wonder she looked unhappy." Stephanie giggled.

"I didn't intend to hit her. I meant to hit you."

"We look so much alike. She is at least a full head taller than I am."

"It is hard to tell from the back side in your matching winter cloaks," Matthew defended himself. "I suspect she won't want to talk with me for a week."

"Probably not." Stephanie slid off the fountain wall and grabbed his hand. "Come on, big brother. Let's go eat lunch."

With the training fields covered in snow, Sir Royce cancelled the afternoon outdoor training sessions all week. However, the squires were still expected to go into Adonia City for their morning indoor apprenticeships. Matthew bundled up in his borrowed furs for his journey down the palace hill the second day after the snowstorm. Karl came up behind him on horseback.

"Do you want to ride with me, or do you prefer to walk?" Karl asked.

"I'll ride with you. Do you have livery today?"

Karl nodded. "I find in the wintertime it is much nicer to ride than walk through slush and snow. Do you want to go skiing with me this afternoon?"

"Skiing? What is that?"

"Only the most glorious sport in the mountains in winter time! You strap a wooden ski board to each foot and you can glide across snow faster than you can run. Downhill you can go faster than a horse can run."

Matthew looked confused. "Wooden boards on your feet?"

Karl laughed. "After lunch today I'll take you. You can use my father's skis. Meet me at the horse stalls in your winter furs."

Karl dropped Matthew off at the woodworking shop. They had a fire going at the back of the shop where the workers would go periodically to warm their hands. Matthew was glad he had worn an extra tunic over his long sleeved shirt. He was working on building a wardrobe, and was currently carving a basic edging design in the front panel doors. He found he had to warm his hands about every half hour over the fire.

At lunch time Karl was waiting for him with the horse to take him up the hill.

"I don't know if I am ever going to get warm in this cold," Matthew complained. "I don't remembering it ever getting much below freezing near the ocean."

"Oh, you'll get used to it," Karl grinned. "Of course it is warmer at the smithy and livery stables."

"I was wondering about that. Why are some places so cold and others keep the heat in better?"

Karl shrugged. "Never thought about it. In the past some families slept with their farm animals inside their thatched huts to stay warm. I hear they were cozy."

"And I imagine a bit stinky." The boys laughed.

The boys grabbed a quick lunch and then met back at the horse stables. Karl was holding two pairs of long flat wooden polished boards with curved ends and leather straps fastened at the middle.

"Those are the skis?" Matthew asked.

Karl nodded and handed a set to Matthew. "We'll ride our own horses into the hills. There is a great meadow where you can get used to the skis before we go on the big mountain."

"Okay." Matthew saddled his horse and Karl tied the skis onto the back of the saddle.

"Follow me!" Karl led them down Adonia Palace Hill, through some back streets and then into the hills. An hour after leaving the palace, Matthew and Karl were in a meadow with rolling hills and a lovely view of Adonia City below. Karl went to the trees and broke off four straight shoulder-height sticks.

"You'll want these to help push you forward on the flat terrain," he explained. "Now let's strap on these skis."

While Matthew stood on the two boards that were his skis, Karl showed him how to wrap the leather straps around his boots and fasten them. Then he handed Matthew the two poles to hold, and put on his own skis.

"Ready?" Karl asked him.

Matthew nodded, uncertain what was next.

"Now we walk, sliding the skis forward in a gliding motion. Like this." Karl glided smoothly forward, arms and legs moving opposite each other, using the poles in the snow to push himself forward.

Matthew tried it. He couldn't get the arms and legs in rhythm. Then he went over a little rise, and as he came down it his skis caught in the loose snow, and he fell over face first. He rolled onto his side, spitting snow out of his mouth.

Karl nearly fell over laughing. "Oh, my. That wasn't any kind of hill at all. You are worse than the three year olds."

Matthew stuck out his tongue at Karl. "Thank you. I am sure I would have been a lot better if I had started as a three year old. But we don't have snow where I am from."

Karl looked contrite. "I am sorry. I forgot you have never done any of this before. Let me help you up." He stuck out his hand to pull Matthew up.

Matthew pulled Karl off balance and into the snow beside him. Then he took a handful of snow and rubbed it into Karl's face. "That's for laughing at me," he grinned.

Karl threw snow back at him. "Now I can demonstrate the real way to get back up." He showed Matthew how to position both his skis to one side, push himself into a squatting position over the skis, and then stand up. Matthew followed suit and soon they were ready to go again.

Karl led Matthew around the meadow a few times until he had the striding gait down. Then he led him to a little hill and they side-stepped up it.

"The real fun, Matthew, lies in going fast down the mountain." Karl pushed himself down the hill, first heading straight and then zigzagging side to side, sometimes with feet together, sometimes with one foot in front of the other in a running crouch.

Matthew watched nervously as Karl made his way back up the hill. "That looks complicated," he commented when Karl finally arrived.

Karl laughed. "I am a show-off. You do not have to do all that today." He winked. "We'll do that next week. First step today is to learn the controlled fall down the mountain, or how to slow down and turn. Start with your toes in and heels out."

Matthew imitated Karl. "Are you sure? This feels awkward. It is not how you skied."

Karl nodded. "I know. This is how all the little kids start out. Trust me. Just do what I do and follow in my tracks down the hill."

Karl started down the hill at an angle so the slope was milder and his speed slower. Matthew took a deep breath and followed him. Karl looked over his shoulder at him.

"Bend your knees a little more and squat slightly. It will help your balance!" he called.

Matthew lowered his stance and indeed felt more balanced. Then Karl turned directions to cross the hill the other way. Matthew tried to turn and fell over. This time he kept his face out of the snow, but his legs went out in opposite directions and he couldn't pull them back together. Karl came back to help untangle him.

"Try to fall to one side if you are going down," Karl told him. "You are less likely to hurt yourself if you don't get twisted up." Karl pointed out the hill to Matthew. "When you turn, you need to put more weight on the outer-turning, downhill leg." Karl went more straight down the hill, weaving slightly from side to side by shifting his weight from one foot to the other.

Matthew tried it, and found he could do the slight direction shifts better than the long turns. Soon they were at the bottom of the hill. Karl began unstrapping his skis.

"Let's walk up normally this time. Use some different muscles." He slung the skis over one shoulder and Matthew followed him back up the hill. They went down a few more times, and by the end of the afternoon Matthew felt fairly comfortable with smaller turns, some larger turns, and was even able to stop himself without falling down most of the time.

Karl eyed the sun dipping behind the mountains. "It is time to go. It will be dark by the time we get back, and you don't want to miss supper."

Matthew suddenly felt starved. "Let's go then!" They strapped their skis onto the horses and trotted down the mountain. As they wound up the hill to Adonia Palace, Karl turned in his saddle to look at Matthew.

"You will want to soak your muscles in the hot baths tonight and tomorrow. You should also do some leg stretches. You will feel your muscles tomorrow." He grinned. "Next week we go to the real mountain to ski!"

"All right! I am ready!"

The next day he wasn't so sure. His thighs and calves ached, and he could barely go up and down the stairs. Fortunately in the morning the smithy was warm, and they kept him walking from coal bin to fire to water and oil barrels and back again so he didn't stiffen up too badly. By the next week he felt pretty good.

Karl told Matthew to meet him at dawn Wednesday morning in the horse stables with his warm coat and skis. "We are skipping sewing class that day; sorry to disappoint you. And eat a good breakfast. We will be gone all day."

When Matthew arrived at the stables dressed in his new fur wolf coat, Stephanie and Sabrina were there also, dressed in warm wool pants, hats and gloves. They also had pairs of skis, albeit shorter ones for the little girls than Matthew had.

Stephanie looked at him curiously. "Mattie, you look like a wolf man."

He turned around for her. "It's not as bulky as the bear coat. I can move better in it."

She deigned to give Matthew a hug. "We are going skiing too! Isn't this exciting?"

Matthew nodded, thinking of the newly found skills he could teach his sister.

Sabrina tugged on his coat. "Sarah and I teach Teffanie to ski!"

"That's good, Sabrina! Do you ski too?" He picked her up in his arms.

Sabrina nodded. "Sarah teach me."

Just then Sarah rounded the corner into the stall area, wearing wool pants, pink wool cape and white fur hat. "There you are, girls. Sabrina, you forgot your tether."

Sabrina drew her lips into a pout. "I ski by myself. No tether," she declared.

"We'll see." Sarah turned to Matthew and gave a little curtsey. "Good morning, Prince Matthew, Karl."

Karl nodded. "Good morning, Sarah."

There were more voices at the door of the stable, and a four year old boy ran around the corner, bumping into Karl.

"Nathan!" a woman's voice called. The little boy ran into one of the horse's stalls and hid behind the wall.

Shelley came around the corner, carrying two children's cloaks and a bundle of food. She spied Matthew and Stephanie.

"Good morning!" she greeted them.

"Shelley! What are you doing here this early in the morning?" He asked her.

"Apparently we are going skiing with your family. Princess Amber insisted Royce go with the girls for protection, so of course he is bringing me and the children. You really have grown tall!" She looked up at his height. "What are they feeding you these days?"

Matthew laughed. "Pulse and water, or whatever healthy stuff the knights in training eat. Mother never did like it when I lived off of desserts."

Sir Royce approached. "Okay, crew, saddle up. It's a long way up the mountain."

Stephanie ran toward Dawn. "Mattie, help me with my saddle."

After Matthew got Stephanie settled with her skis on her horse, he saddled and mounted Dusty. Sabrina rode with Sarah, Sir Royce took Nathan, and Shelley rode with her daughter, Nellie. Karl brought up the rear. They rode through town, roads made muddy by the snow from three days prior. As they rode higher into the hills, the snow built up to a new six inches. They followed a woodcutter's trail up the mountain, which opened up into a view of the entire valley and city of Adonia. The sun was rising, giving welcome warmth to the crisp mountain air.

Sir Royce reigned up his horse. "This will be a good place to set up the warming camp," he announced.

He dismounted and helped his family off the horses, while Matthew helped Stephanie, and Karl helped Sarah and Sabrina dismount. Shelley ordered Karl and Matthew to fetch some dry wood for a fire, while the children gathered twigs for her. She welcomed both wet and dry with a smile of thanks, but separated out the ones that wouldn't burn. After good piles were created, Shelley stayed by the fire with little Nellie to heat up food, while the others went to ski.

Royce and Sarah led everyone with their skis further up the hill. Here there were fewer trees. Royce led them up the edge of a wide snowy hill that seemed to extend halfway down the mountain. Matthew felt his palms get sweaty at the thought of skiing down that slope.

When they reached the top, a cold wind was blowing. Matthew and Stephanie lagged behind the others, panting in the thin air. Finally Sir Royce stopped and let them strap on their skis.

Matthew glanced at Stephanie, expertly strapping her skis to her boots. "Have you done this before?" he asked.

"Yup. Been practicing all last week with Sarah and Sabrina." She sounded unafraid.

Sarah was helping Sabrina attach her skis. Royce already had Nathan standing on his skis. Karl was impatiently sliding back and forth across the top of the slope. Matthew watched from the top while Stephanie confidently started down across the slope, toes pointed in, heels out, skis angling in the V shape Karl had briefly shown Matthew. Royce followed his son, who zipped almost straight down the hill. Sarah led Sabrina back and forth across the hill, glancing back frequently to watch the little girl following in her tracks. Sarah's moves were graceful, feet together, hips turning with the skis…

Matthew nearly fell over. He righted himself and peered at the steepness of the hill, trying to discern the most gradual slope down.

"Come on, Mattie!" Stephanie yelled up to him. "Don't take all day!"

Matthew took a deep breath and plunged over the lip of the hill. He started across diagonally, and then tried to turn. He found himself going straight down the slope, going faster and faster. Horrors! He was headed straight for Sarah and Sabrina! He tried to remember what Karl had told him about falling up the mountain slope, and he threw himself to one side, landing in a spray of white powder.

He heard Sabrina's giggles and she threw herself on him. "Uncle Mattie! You went fast!"

He raised his head and saw Sarah staring down at him. She tried to suppress a smile.

"You and snow don't seem to be getting along very well," she remarked.

Matthew felt his face get hot. "I am so sorry, Sarah. I don't seem to have the knack of controlling my skis yet."

She reached out a hand to help him up. "Let me guess, Karl taught you the basics?"

Matthew nodded dumbly, brushing the snow off his coat.

"I thought so. He's reckless when it comes to skiing. Stick with Sabrina and me for a while and I'll teach you some of Adonia's finer beginner techniques."

Matthew watched, listened and tried Sarah's additional hints. He found it wasn't so much what Karl hadn't shown him as what he hadn't figured out how to apply well. Sarah's explanations helped him see what he needed to do, and pretty soon he was following in her tracks and turning as easily as Sabrina and Stephanie.

As they neared the bottom more gradual slope, Sarah suddenly called over her shoulder. "Race you all down!" She pointed her skis straight down the slope and shot away. Sabrina and Stephanie both followed. Matthew took a deep breath and followed them.

The speed was glorious! This time he felt more in control of his turning and felt more confident with his speed. At the bottom of the hill he slid to a stop sideways without falling down. Sarah applauded him.

"That was very good, Matthew! You have a good sense of balance."

Matthew shook his head. "You should have seen me the first day. I fell down over a bump."

Sarah laughed. "I am serious. It usually takes adults a little longer to get the knack."

Matthew shrugged. "Well, I have spent time balancing on boats and fences and horses."

She nodded. "It shows."

They started the long hike back up the mountain. Before long Sabrina claimed she was too tired to walk. Matthew picked her up and put her on his shoulders while Sarah carried her skis. He tucked his skis under one arm and held onto her feet with his other.

Halfway up, they stopped at the warming fire to drink some hot tea with biscuits. Little Nellie had been patting together a tower of snow. "Snowman!" she explained before going back to her work.

Matthew had been grateful for the rest at the warming fire. Carrying Sabrina had added to his huffing and puffing. When they started again, she raised her arms to him to be carried again. He managed for a while, but finally had to stop and rest. "I am sorry, I don't seem to be in good shape anymore."

Sarah stopped hiking. "It's the altitude. You are not used to it yet. Sabrina, you need to walk by yourself again."

The second time skiing down the hill went more smoothly for Matthew. He and Stephanie stayed together, while Sarah and Sabrina went ahead. By the time they reached the bottom of the hill they were hungry for lunch. When they reached the warming fire, Shelley had some hot stew for them to eat. Royce, Nathan and Karl had already eaten and were heading up the mountain for their fourth run.

As they started up the hill again after lunch, Stephanie walked slower and slower. Finally she stopped. "I can't hike up this big mountain any further. My legs are too tired."

Matthew had been feeling his thigh muscles for some time also, but wasn't about to tell anyone about it. "Shall we just ski down from here?" he asked her.

She nodded. "And then I'll stop at the level of the warming fire so I don't have to hike up again."

"Sarah!" Matthew called out. "I'm going down from here with Stephanie!"

"Me too!" Sabrina stated. She sat down in the snow with her feet out for Sarah to strap on her skis.

Sarah sighed. "All right. We'll all come."

They strapped on their skis and started down the middle of the mountain slope. When they reached the trail to the warming fire, Stephanie left them. Matthew continued down to the bottom with Sabrina and Sarah.

At the bottom Sabrina stayed sitting after her skis were unstrapped. "I tired," she announced.

Matthew picked Sabrina up and put her on his shoulders again, and tucked up his skis under his arm. "All right, let's go back."

Sarah followed him with hers and Sabrina's skis. After trudging up the hill a few minutes, she spoke. "You surprise me, Prince Matthew. For being a bumbling coastal newcomer, you have taken to mountain sports pretty well."

He cocked an eye at her. "Am I to take that as an insult or a compliment?"

She laughed and lowered her head. "A compliment now. I wasn't so sure initially."

"I figured." He shifted Sabrina on his shoulder and switched his skis to his other arm. "I really do apologize for hitting you with the snowball in the palace courtyard."

Sarah shook her head. "Yes, you did get me good that day."

"I thought I was getting my sister," he explained. They walked in silence a while. "Sarah," Matthew ventured. "How did you become a governess for Princess Sabrina?"

Sarah didn't answer right away. "I was working at Adonia's main orphanage when Princess Amber came to visit, soon after Princess Sabrina was born. She liked how the little ones took to me, I suppose. She offered me a position as Sabrina's nanny, which I refused the first time. Then Princess Amber spoke to the orphanage's head mistress, who strongly advised me to take the position as a "way up in the world". So I accepted it." She looked up at Sabrina. "I have not regretted that decision one bit!" Sabrina reached out her hand toward Sarah and waved at her. Sarah waved back.

Matthew considered what Sarah had told him. "How did you come to work at the orphanage, Sarah?"

She didn't look at him. "I grew up there. From time to time children would be adopted by families in Adonia, but I was not one of them. It is customary for the older children there to look after the younger ones. We all go to school together at the orphanage, and the older ones also teach the younger ones. Then at age eighteen we are expected to leave and apprentice to a trade. I left the orphanage at age fifteen."

"Oh, I did not know." Matthew had a hundred questions that he did not ask. His thigh and calf muscles were burning. He lifted Sabrina from his shoulders and put her gently on the ground. "Can you walk for a little bit now?" he asked her.

Sabrina skipped around in the snow, making and throwing snowballs. Matthew reached over to Sarah and took her set of skis to carry for her. He tried not to think about his tired legs, just putting one foot in front of the other methodically up the hill.

"Sarah, what kinds of things do you like to do in your spare time?" he asked her.

She smiled. "Not that I get too much spare time with chasing energy child here. But I do love to read." She glanced over at him shyly. "You will think this is silly, but I especially love to read fairy tale stories. I like the parts where the princess finds her true love and lives happily ever after." She paused. "I used to imagine myself being a princess and having my true love rescue me from the orphanage and take me to my new home." She sighed. "But that is not the real world. The real world is full of work and often disappointments, sometimes interspersed with joyful gifts, like working for Princess Amber and little Sabrina." She smiled brightly but Matthew detected a tear on her cheek. "Perhaps that is what every little girl wishes, to be a princess and to be special. I think now I will be content just to find a good person to share my life with."

"I don't think that is silly," Matthew told her. He thought of his parent's love story, which almost ended in disaster for Princess Elinore, until Robert showed up and rescued her from a mismatched suitor. He thought how nice life could be with a person like Sarah.

They walked in silence several minutes. "So what are your life plans?" Sarah asked.

"Ouch!" Matthew exclaimed. "That is exactly what I am trying to figure out. I planned to be a knight and trained for it, but...I don't know. It is hard for sure, but that is not the main reason; I've done hard things before. Maybe I don't want to pledge my loyalty to a specific Lord. I almost envy now my sister Amber's position to rule a kingdom, where one pledges one's loyalty to a kingdom, a people, a cause. Maybe I am looking for a cause to fight for; I don't know. I haven't found the right fit yet."

"What are you good at? Is there any trade you like?" Sarah inquired.

"Well, I am fair at building things, but I've seen others do better. I am really rather average at many things."

"'Jack of all trades, master of none'?" she smiled.

"Something like that. I don't really like book learning. I would rather be outside exploring new places."

"An explorer?" she asked. "Discover new worlds?"

He shrugged. "Maybe. But I prefer exploring closer to home."

She got a gleam in her eye. "I have a place to explore, come spring."

"Where is it?" he asked.

She merely shook her head. "You'll see."

They reached the warming camp. Shelley served them some more hot tea, while Matthew sat down on a stump. Stephanie, Sabrina and Nellie started building a snow fort. Soon Karl, Sir Royce and Nathan joined them. After quick drinks, Karl, Royce and Sarah left to ski some more, while Nathan joined the little girls at the snow fort. After resting a bit, Matthew walked through the trees toward the ski slope to watch for the skiers to come down.

It didn't take long for them to whiz by. Karl and Sarah were racing each other down the hill, with Royce close behind. Matthew couldn't take his eyes off Sarah. She almost seemed to be flying, graceful as an angel. Karl skied with energy and intensity, but Sarah slipped down the hill almost effortlessly.

Soon after Matthew got back to the warming fire, the three skiers arrived. Shelley started packing up camp, while everyone packed up their skis. Matthew helped Sarah load her skis onto her horse.

"When did you learn to ski?" he asked her. "You look like you have been doing it for years."

"I have," she confessed. "Even before hunting, skiing is Adonia's national sport. Even at the orphanage we had skis. Once a week through the winter after chores were done we went into the mountains to ski. It was one of the things I was good at."

"Good! You are incredible!"

Sarah's eyes met his and she seemed to glow. "Thanks," she said simply.

The little children fell asleep riding back down the mountain. Even Matthew dosed over his horse's reins. Back at the castle after a quick dinner everyone retired early to bed. Matthew especially slept hard, with intermittent dreams of skiing down a mountain, trying to keep up with Sarah as she twisted and turned ahead of him. She kept looking back at him, daring him to keep up. But his limbs were awkward, or his skis kept twisting up wrong and she drifted further away from him. Finally in a last heroic effort to catch up to her, he put on a burst of speed going straight down the mountain. He found himself flying off the edge of a cliff, and he saw her disappear out of sight into the trees before he landed in deep snow in a blinding spray of white.

CHAPTER 5

SARAH

M atthew couldn't stop thinking about her. He thought about the way she smiled, not just with her soft rosy lips, but the way her eyes crinkled up into the smile. He thought about the way her hips swayed gracefully when she walked. He admired the way she twisted up her silky dark locks, soft yet stunningly complimentary to her face. He pictured her in her small variety of dresses, modest yet always complimentary to her slightly plump figure. And her personality was warm and friendly, always with a funny, positive or insightful thing to say.

Sarah was beautiful.

And he had to admit, he was fast falling in love with her. He found out that every afternoon before dinner she took a walk in the palace garden with Princesses Sabrina and Stephanie. He left the squire training as quickly as possible so he could pass through the garden and visit with them. At Sunday Chapel service he sat next to his sister as she sat with Sarah and Sabrina. He could pick out Sarah's silvery soprano voice, sweetly singing the hymns.

Sarah usually ate dinner with the palace staff so the royal family could eat dinner together, and usually the little girls had already eaten lunch by the time Matthew returned from his apprenticeships in town. But most of the time if he timed it right he made it into the dining room in time to eat breakfast with the little girls and their governesses. He would listen to the girls chatter, and loved to hear Sarah's repartee, sometimes telling silly stories that would make the girls laugh.

Harry joined them often for breakfast; Amber had stopped coming for morning meals.

"So, Harry, where is Amber these days?" Matthew finally asked him one morning when they were the first ones at the table.

Harry glanced at Matthew darkly. "She won't say. She tells me she is not hungry and stays in bed sleeping until late morning. It's like she is angry with me but she won't tell me what I did wrong."

Matthew just started at him. "Have you asked her?" He finally queried.

"Yes I've asked her! She just rolls over in bed and ignores me. Then she chats normally with everyone else the rest of the day like nothing is bothering her. It is very confusing, and annoying." Harry gazed at Matthew helplessly.

"I don't know how to help you, brother," Matthew responded. "I've had my own confusing time with the opposite gender." They looked at each other until Harry finally cracked a smile.

"Women!" he said, sighing.

"Women," Matthew responded with a shrug.

"What is this about women?" Sarah asked, sweeping into the room with Sabrina and Stephanie beside her. The little girls were dressed in pink lacy gowns, which Matthew could tell were too big for them.

Harry stood up to greet Sabrina with a hug. "I was just saying how we can't live without the lovely women in our lives. How is my little princess this morning?"

Sabrina sniffed. "I a big princess, Daddy."

"Of course you are," he answered, putting her down gently so she could smooth her skirts.

"Is that really what you two were talking about?" Sarah asked Matthew as she settled herself at the table. "You sounded more exasperated."

"Uh, yes!" Matthew scratched the back of his head with one hand. "Okay, I confess. We are having some trouble understanding your gender."

"For example?" she asked, her eyes teasing.

"For example…Princess Amber has stopped talking to Prince Harry and won't come down to eat breakfast anymore with us."

"It's the morning sickness, sillies," Sarah replied. Then she noticed both of them looking confused. "Her pregnancy! She feels terribly sick in the mornings."

Harry nearly fell out of his chair. "She's pregnant?"

Sarah's eyes widened. "You didn't know, Your Highness? I shouldn't have said…" She covered her mouth with her hand.

"No, no, I'm glad you did," Harry said hurriedly. He shook his head. "First she's mad at me for not giving her a second baby, now she won't talk to me because I did. I should go talk to her." He began to stand up from the table.

"No!" Sarah commanded sharply, and then softened. "Don't bother her while she is sleeping."

"Okay." Harry sat down and ate breakfast with a silly grin on his face, ignoring everyone else, and periodically muttering, "We're pregnant!"

At dinner that night Harry looked happier than Matthew had seen in a while. He and Amber kept exchanging knowing looks. Even Amber was less irritable than usual. With her parents happier, Sabrina was less whiny and easier for Sarah to handle.

The days were getting shorter and the evenings colder. The girls' walks in the palace garden were short. Matthew joined them in the music room after dinner where Stephanie was teaching Sarah what she knew about how to play the harpsicord. Matthew either entertained Sabrina with a puzzle, or read to her from a book and listened to the music.

"Uncle Mattie?" Sabrina leaned in close to his face while he was reading.

"What, Sabrina?"

"What present does Teffanie want for Christmas?"

Matthew was taken aback. He had not thought about Christmas yet this year. He remembered as a child dreaming about what gift his parents might get for him. The past few years he had been in on gifts planning for his younger sister, but he was more interested in the food and youth games for himself.

"I am not for sure, Sabrina, but lately she really likes dresses and hair ribbons."

"Ooh! Hair ribbons. Yes!" She returned to her coloring.

Matthew started thinking about Christmas gifts. He figured he could carve a wooden jewelry box for Amber, and forge a leatherworking tool for Harry. He thought he might be able to carve wooden dolls for Sabrina and Stephanie. He realized he wanted to make something special for Sarah. But what would be appropriate? He wanted to make something nice and pretty, but not overly personal. It should be different from what he was giving everyone else. Carve a little wooden animal? A deer or swan came to mind, but he was not very good at making wood look like animals. Make a necklace or bracelet? He had not worked with anything finer than chain mail links, and he didn't think chain mail jewelry was nice enough for Sarah.

For the next two weeks he spent extra time at the wood shop and forge making Amber and Harry's gifts. He then started work on the little wooden dolls for the little girls, complete with hip and shoulder joints that one of the carpentry journeymen showed him how to make with hinges and rivets. When they were carved and polished he wrapped them carefully in cloth and laid them in an old box the carpenter was not using. He carried them up to the palace and placed them carefully in his room. After Sarah had put Princess Sabrina to bed, he tucked the box under his arm and went down the halls to her suite and knocked on the door.

"Who is it?" Sarah's muffled voice asked.

"Matthew. Do you have a minute, Sarah?"

After a moment the door opened, revealing Sarah wrapped in a robe over her dressing gown.

"I am so sorry to disturb you, Sarah," he bowed his head. "But I need your assistance with my Christmas gifts for Sabrina and Stephanie. May I show you?"

A smile dimpled her cheek. "Of course. You may come in." She stepped back and Matthew entered the parlor room she shared with Sabrina. The door to Sabrina's bedroom was closed, and a fire burned merrily in the fireplace next to it.

Matthew laid the box on a table and opened the lid. He carefully unwrapped the two dolls and laid them out for Sarah to see. She picked them up and examined their moving joints carefully.

"Very clever," she commented. "You carved these?"

He nodded. "With a fair amount of help from the carpenters. They still need hair and faces painted on, but I am most in need of someone who can sew dresses for them."

"I think we should ask Arlin, who does the portraits of the royal family, to paint the faces on these dolls. I am sure he would give you a discount since it is a gift for Princess Sabrina. What if he made the dolls look like Stephanie and Sabrina?"

Matthew grinned. "That would be amazing!"

"Do you mind leaving them with me then? I will hide them in my room until I can get them to Arlin without the girls seeing them. Meanwhile I will work on the dresses after the girls are asleep at night. Would that be all right?"

"Yes, thank you! I think the dolls should be from both of us then," he told her.

"I would like that! I didn't have a gift for them yet." She smiled.

"Then that's settled." Matthew glanced around the room and saw a portrait of a young woman in an exotic dress, standing in a sunlit garden, holding a spray of colorful flowers in her hands. He walked over to take a closer look and Sarah followed. "Who is this?" he asked.

"I don't know," she answered wistfully. "I think she is from the Eastern countries. I think she may have visited on an ambassadorial mission in the past. She is beautiful, is she not?"

Matthew nodded, and then looked over at Sarah. "I still think you are prettier."

Sarah blushed, but just shook her head. "Oh no, I am just plain Jane."

"I like 'Jane'." Matthew examined the portrait again. "What kind of flowers is she holding?"

"They are orchids. Aren't they beautiful? I hear there are many varieties and colors."

"I am not familiar with orchids," Matthew replied. "I only know my mother likes Daisies, Stephanie likes tulips, and Amber has an affinity to sunflowers." He turned to the door. "I should leave you now to get some sleep. Good night, Sarah. And thank you."

In the middle of the night Matthew suddenly awoke and sat up in bed. He knew what he was going to make for Sarah: an orchid. He just wasn't sure how he was going to do it. On that thought he fell back to sleep and dreamed of carving flowers.

Over the next week he tried carving flowers out of scrap wood pieces. He couldn't even get a surface design to look right. He needed a three dimensional shape. He went to the palace library to find pictures of orchids, and found a few ideas. He decided he needed a different medium to work with. He studied different sculptures around the palace. Clay? He didn't have easy access to any. Paper? Too amateurish. What about metal? Hm, that would give him the three dimensional look he was after, if he could make the petals delicate enough.

The next day after his morning apprenticeship work was finished he approached John, the master smith, with his idea.

John stroked his beard thoughtfully. "I suppose you could get it to work," he told Matthew. "Fashion each petal separately, and then weld them together around a central stem. I suggest you get Lance to work with you. He is more adept at the finer work than I am."

Lance was excited at the idea when Matthew asked him. They looked at different types of metals and scraps, Lance explaining the properties, pros and cons of each. They finally decided brass would be the best to work with.

Matthew spent every afternoon the next two weeks working in the forge with occasional help from Lance. Even when Sarah invited him to go skiing with her and the little girls, he begged her to excuse him.

"I am working on a project," was all he told her.

She narrowed her eyes suspiciously. "All right, if you would rather be somewhere else than with us."

He looked crestfallen. "No, that is not it."

She nudged him with her elbow. "Don't look so glum. I'm just teasing. I can tell a man with a mission."

It was getting closer to Christmas. Matthew stayed later and later at the forge working into the evenings. Lance sometimes stayed to keep him company, working on his own projects. At those times Lance's wife, Lark, would bring him a basket supper which Lance shared with Matthew.

Finally the petal pieces were cut, flattened, curved and polished. The stem piece was rolled and elongated, with a button end for the center of the flower. Lance explained how to heat the rod and edges of each petal so Matthew could weld the pieces together. They had to work quickly; Lance heated the petals while Matthew attached them, pressing and twisting them around the stem. When all the petals were attached, Lance inspected the flower, worked his fine tool in a couple of places, and then nodded.

"Dunk it into the cold water now," Lance instructed.

Matthew plunged it into the cold water barrel, and then drew it out. Other than a couple of petals twisting slightly different ways, the welding held and the piece was finished. Matthew sighed in relief.

Lance checked the welds. "Looks like it will hold," he approved.

Matthew stretched. "What time is it?" he asked.

"Late enough that Lark is waiting dinner for us. Come to our home tonight, Prince Matthew and join us."

Matthew's stomach rumbled. "I would like that."

Lark greeted Matthew warmly. Their home was small, but neat and cozy. There was a little fire going in the fireplace, but even the far corners of the room were warm.

"Dinner is ready." Lark led them to the table, indicating a chair at one side for Matthew to seat himself. Across the table from him sat an eight year old boy and his two younger sisters, sharing a bench. The girls looked at Matthew and giggled. Matthew waved at them.

"Quiet now, girls," Lark frowned at them briefly. "Papa needs to say Grace."

The children all bowed their heads and folded their hands while Lance said a prayer over the food. Then the children dove into the bread and turnip stew while chattering away merrily. Matthew found the stew delicious.

"I don't think I have tasted such good turnip stew before," Matthew commented between spoonsful. "I believe my mother detests the vegetable."

"It's all in the spices and how you cook it," Lark beamed.

Lance leaned over to Matthew. "I married her for her cooking, you know."

Lark elbowed him in the side. "That is not the only reason."

"No, but I don't want other men to get jealous of your beauty."

The little girls giggled. The son rolled his eyes. "Yuck."

Matthew grinned at him. "One day you will think girls are pretty." He leaned back and patted his stomach. "That was very good, Lark. Thank you."

"My pleasure." She stood to clear the dishes. "Come, children. Bring your dishes to the wash bucket."

The children filed past the bucket on a stool filled with clean soapy water. They dipped the dishes in the water, wiped them with a clean cloth, and then placed them on a cupboard shelf. Matthew brought his dishes behind them.

"Oh no, you are a guest," Lark protested, trying to take his dishes from him.

He held onto them. "I will wash them. This is my way of saying thank you."

After clearing the table, the little girls changed into nightgowns. Then they stood by Matthew, looking up at him. The littlest one tugged on his sleeve.

"Tell us a story," she begged.

Matthew glanced up at Lark. "Is that all right?"

Lark waved her hand toward the children's bedroom. "By all means, please. They know all my stories anyway."

Matthew followed the children into their bedroom. The girls shared one bed, the boy had his against the other wall of the room. They climbed into their beds and waited expectantly. Matthew tried to think of a story, and then decided to tell the one of his parents' courtship.

"Once there was a princess who needed a husband," he began. "Suitors came from far and near to take the Test of Rimrock Island. Finally, one named Prince Abram arrived to take the test."

The boy looked bored with the story until another suitor, Robert of Danforth, came on the scene to vie for Princess Elinore's hand. He seemed to like best the contest between the suitors, the kidnapping of the princess by an invading lord, and the battle for her freedom. The little girls sighed in contentment when Elinore finally decided to marry Robert.

"That was a beautiful fairy tale," the older girl sighed as she closed her eyes.

"It's a true story," Matthew replied. "It happened to my parents."

Lark was standing in the doorway. "You tell it well, Matthew." She came in and kissed each of her children. "Good night, little ones." She left and took the candle with her.

Sitting in front of the warm fire Matthew remembered the question he had had during the first snowstorm that fall. "Lance, I noticed your house has managed to stay warm in the winter, even in the children's bedroom. How have you managed this?"

Lance grinned. "It is a common village secret. Come, I'll show you."

He led Matthew over to a ladder in the corner of the room which led to a trap door in the ceiling. Lance climbed the ladder and pushed open the trap door.

"You will need a candle to see this, Matthew. But be very careful to hold the candle only in the trap door area."

Matthew grasped the candleholder and carefully climbed the ladder. Lifting the candle up through the trapdoor he looked around through the attic space. The floor of the attic appeared to be covered in 3-4 inches of straw or grass. He reached out his free hand to confirm his suspicions.

After climbing down the ladder Matthew gazed at Lance. "You line your attic with straw?"

Lance nodded. "It acts as insulation to keep the heat in. In the summer it helps keep the heat out. At harvest time we replace it with new grass or straw. Many of us use it also to feed our goats and sheep through the year." He shrugged. "It seems a practical way to store it. We just have to be careful about fire."

Matthew looked about the room. "I imagine."

Lance turned to his wife. "Lark, you should see what Matthew made."

"Oh, yes!" she exclaimed. "I have heard a lot about this project. I want to see it!"

Matthew pulled the package from his tunic, carefully unwrapped the brass flower, and laid it on the cloth on his palm. Lark touched it gently.

"It is beautiful. What kind of flower is it?" she asked.

"An orchid. It's not quite the shape I wanted though. But the color turned out nicely."

"Yes. The different shades of color on the petals gives it a nice touch. Your lady will like it, I think."

Matthew blushed. "She is not really my lady."

"Yet," Lark smiled. "Give it some time."

Matthew wrapped up the metal orchid and tucked it carefully back into his tunic. "It is late; I better get back up the hill. Thank you, Lance and Lark for a delicious meal. You have a wonderful family."

"It was our pleasure." Lance escorted Matthew to the door.

As Matthew walked back through the cold star-filled night toward Adonia Palace, his mind pondered the problem of the cold palace. He was formulating a plan but needed to run it by someone.

Early the next morning Matthew entered the palace stables and found Rolf, the palace stableman watering the horses.

"Have you seen Sir Royce this morning?" Matthew asked.

Rolf nodded his head sideways. "He's feeding his horse," he grunted.

Matthew hurried to the neighboring stall, where Royce was forking hay to his horse.

"Sir Royce," Matthew interrupted him. "May I ask your opinion about something?"

Royce leaned on his pitchfork. "Sure. What is it?"

Matthew took a deep breath. "I have an idea on how to make the palace warmer during the winter. But I want to make sure someone reviews my idea." He described his plan, and then waited for Sir Royce's response.

Sir Royce scratched his chin. "Sounds crazy, but it might work. You say you want it to be a surprise? We should probably at least get Rolf's permission, since it involves his hay supply."

They approached Rolf and reviewed the idea with him. Rolf stared at Matthew. "You can have some of the hay, but you have to keep it in good condition so the horses can eat it in the spring, and I will not be moving it for you."

"You have a deal," Matthew grinned. "I'll get Karl to help me."

After his morning session at the woodshop, Matthew approached the barrel maker to buy a bucket of tar. It was heavier than he imagined. As he lugged it up the street, Karl caught up to him on his horse.

"Would you like a ride with that load?" Karl asked.

"Would I ever!" Matthew replied. He handed Karl the bucket to hold while he mounted behind him, then took it back.

"What are you planning to do with the tar?" Karl asked, curious.

"I'll show you when we get back to the palace," Matthew replied mysteriously. "I need your help with a project. I hope you don't have much planned for this week."

"Apparently my plans are to help you," Karl answered, mystified.

After grabbing some apples, bread and cheese for lunch, Matthew led Karl to the stables, then up into the stable loft where the hay was kept. Matthew went over to one of the bales and lifted it up.

"You grab one too, Karl. We are taking it to the palace attic."

"Is Rolf okay with our taking these?" Karl asked, picking up a bale.

"He knows." Matthew led Karl up the back stairway to the second floor and down a hall to the narrow stairs leading to the attic of the East Wing. They found it was easier to get the hay bales up when the two of them lifted up one bale together.

The attic roof was sloped but high enough for Matthew to stand up in the middle. There were several small dormer windows set in the roof line to let in light. The attic was partitioned into three large sections, with a door between each. They carried their bales to the far front section, over the royal bedroom suites. Whereas the first two sections had a few pieces of old furniture scattered in the space, the third section was empty. Thick dust lay on the floor, and it looked like a family of mice had set up a nest in one corner.

"We need to sweep this out," Matthew mused. "We have to keep the hay in good shape."

"Some mouse traps too would be a good idea," Karl advised.

They went back downstairs and found two brooms and a trash bag. After sweeping up the dust and mouse nest, Matthew pushed the bales toward the outer walls and cut the ropes holding the bales together. The hay spilled out and he spread it out with his foot. It didn't cover as big an area as he hoped, especially when he tried to keep the layer two to three inches thick.

"So, what is the hay for?" Karl asked. "This is going to be a big mess to clean up, you know."

Matthew grinned at him. "Maybe we'll just bring the horses up here to eat it."

"Ha! Like they can get up the stairs." Karl grew serious. "No, really. What is the hay supposed to do?"

"I am trying to keep the heat in the palace bedroom suites. The townspeople are doing it and it seems to work."

Karl looked around the large attic space and blew a little cloud of breath in the frosty air. "Lots of luck. This palace is a lot bigger than a town house."

Matthew nodded. "I am seeing that. It might be a multi-year task to get enough grass or hay to keep this place warm. However, I am also planning to seal the windows in with tar to keep the wind out. I'll need your help with that too."

Karl nodded. "If all of this works, I want my family's suites fixed up also."

"No problem! Let's go get more hay."

By the end of the afternoon, they had managed to cover the whole floor of the far attic section, which covered the royal suites of the palace. Then they took up two more bales of hay to cover an area in the middle section where they estimated Karl and his father's suite lay.

Matthew stretched his arms and rotated his shoulders. "Tomorrow afternoon we tar the windows."

Karl nodded. "Meet you at the stables?"

"Yes. Then we can sneak into the chambers the back way and hopefully not be seen."

The next afternoon Karl waited in the stables before Matthew finally showed up, lugging the bucket of tar.

"What kept you?" Karl complained jokingly. "Rolf almost put me to work."

"It took longer than I thought to heat and soften the tar," Matthew explained. "I'm afraid it smelled up the kitchen a bit. They finally kicked me out. Next time I'll have to heat it in the fireplace in my suite."

"Or take it to my suite. My father almost always has a fire going. Where do we go first?" Karl asked.

"My rooms. I need to practice on a window first to make sure it works."

It took a while to find the right tool for the job. They tried spoons, trowels, knives, sticks, and finally settled on a painter's spatula. Matthew stepped back from the windows to take a look, and then shook his head.

"It looks terrible, like some child played with mud pies here."

Karl held his hand up by the window cracks. "But I don't feel any more drafts. Come, let's practice on my windows."

This time they finished with a much cleaner look. While the tar was thinning over the fire in Karl's suite, the boys sat down for a few minutes.

"Now the biggest trick will be getting into the royal suites when no one is there," Matthew told him.

"King Gilbert and Prince Harry usually hold court until dinner time," Karl observed.

"And Sarah usually takes Sabrina and Stephanie out for a late-afternoon romp in the Palace Gardens," returned Matthew. "That means Lady Charlotte is in her suite most of the afternoon and evening. She is only out in the morning to tutor Stephanie in the library, which is when we are working in town."

"We might have to let Lady Charlotte in on the surprise then," Karl commented.

Matthew sighed. "All right. Let's go do Charlotte and Stephanie's chambers."

When they arrived, Matthew knocked on the door.

"Come in!" Charlotte's voice answered.

They opened the door and went in. Charlotte was sitting in a chair close to the fire, doing embroidery. She laid it down in her lap.

"Good afternoon, Matthew and Karl. What can I do for you this day?"

"Lady Charlotte," Matthew began. "We are working on a project to diminish the drafts in Adonia Palace. We beg permission to seal the windows in your chamber suites."

She smiled. "You may proceed."

When they were finished she inspected the windows. "Yes, I see. This is more airtight. Thank you!"

The boys went next to Sarah and Sabrina's suite. There was no answer to their knock on the door, so Matthew tried the door handle. It was unlocked so he let himself in.

They finished the windows in the sitting room and Sabrina's room first. Matthew looked to the closed door that led to Sarah's chamber. Suddenly he felt awkward about going into her private chamber. He turned to go.

"Hey!" Karl stopped him. "Aren't we going to tar the window in that room too?" He pointed to the closed door.

Matthew squirmed. "I am not sure it is appropriate for me to go into Sarah's room."

Just then the main door from the hall opened, and Sarah and Sabrina swished in. Sarah stopped in surprise when she saw the boys.

"What are you doing in our suites?" she frowned. "These are our private rooms."

"Yes, I know," Matthew stammered. "We were just…"

"Ooh, that stinks!" Sabrina wrinkled her nose and peeked into the bucket Matthew was holding. "What is that?"

"Tar," he responded. "For sealing out the drafts of the windows." Karl nodded and pointed to the window.

Sarah walked over to the window to examine it. She ran her hand along the edge and came away with a black finger.

"You may not want to touch that until it is dry," Matthew began.

"Too late!" Karl moaned.

Sarah looked at her finger and then at the window. "Have you done my room yet?"

"I have not," Matthew confessed. "It didn't seem right…"

"Please seal the window in my room too," Sarah interrupted. "I would love to sleep in a room without drafts."

She opened her bedroom door and led the boys in. It was a small and simple chamber, but neat and clean. On a little table by the bed were some dried meadow flowers standing in a glass vase. Matthew noted that it looked just the right size for the brass orchid he had made for her.

Matthew and Karl went to work. Sarah and Sabrina sat on the little bed to watch them scoop tar into the cracks with the paint spatulas. Soon it was finished. Matthew stuck his spatula in the tar bucket with a final flourish, and Karl bowed to the ladies. Sabrina clapped.

"Thank you, kind sirs, for the service this day," Sarah curtseyed to them.

"I knight is always happy to serve," Karl bowed again.

Matthew shoved him playfully on the shoulder. "You are not a knight yet," he told him.

"Fine. A squire is always willing to serve," he started to bow again, but Sarah was giggling and pushing them out of her room.

"Whatever you are now or are going to be, I thank you for this service. But you really should not be in a lady's chamber."

"Right." Matthew looked at Karl. "Let's go do Amber's rooms."

"Oh, no!" Sarah stopped them. "The smell of the tar will make her sick again. You need to wait."

Matthew inclined his head. "Thank you for the advice. Good afternoon, Sarah and Sabrina." He and Karl left the suite with their tar bucket.

"Where to next?" Karl asked.

Matthew grinned. "To King Gilbert's suites."

Karl shook his head. "Oh, no. I am not going with you there. I don't have authorization."

Matthew nodded. "Okay. See you tomorrow then."

Karl left and Matthew went down the hall to the door of the King's suite. He knocked, and when there was no answer, opened the door and went in.

This was the largest suite in the whole palace, and the most elegant. It had large windows and large mirrors on the walls, between elegant tapestries. Gold lined the décor on the ceilings, and crystal vases sat on tables around the sitting room. The sitting room and main bedroom had their own fireplaces. There was an unused nursery, and a bath room adjacent to the bedroom.

Matthew merely glanced at the finery that surpassed even his own parents' suite, and went to work, starting in the back rooms. As he was finishing up the last window in the sitting room, the door burst open and King Gilbert strode in. He saw Matthew and stopped mid stride.

"What are you doing in here?" he demanded.

"Tarring the leaks in your windows, Your Majesty," Matthew stammered. "It was to be a surprise for Christmas—"

"Out, young man!" King Gilbert pointed his finger toward the door. "You are not allowed in my suites without permission. Go, now!"

Matthew quickly gathered his bucket and spatulas, and hurried out of the room. The door slammed shut behind him. He felt hollow inside. He had meant no harm or discourtesy, and was only trying to help. Now he had angered his sister's father-in-law, his mother's cousin, his host.

He dropped off the tar bucket in his room, grabbed a coat and hurried down to the stables. He quickly saddled Dusty and rode him out and down the palace hill toward the tournament training fields. A few Adonian squires were out shooting in the archery fields beyond, but Matthew had no desire to join them.

He rode the horse up and down the field, sometimes in a run, sometimes trotting. He felt a little better, but he couldn't shake the feeling of not belonging, more acutely now than he had ever felt before.

As he finally slowed Dusty to a walk, his eyes raised up to the palace hill. It was mostly bare, but surrounded by brush and weeds at the base.

Near the supply shed Matthew tied up Dusty and began walking around the base of the hill.

He remembered the tunnel exited somewhere near here, and wondered if he would be able to find it. He began looking behind every clump of brush tall and wide enough to hide a door. There was still some snow on the leaves, and soon his hands grew quite cold. But he was determined. About a quarter of the way around the hill he moved aside some bushes and noticed that they went deeper into the hill than they should have. He pushed aside more branches and crawled through. A short way in he found an old wooden door.

"This is it!" he thought excitedly.

He looked for a door knob or handle, but there was none. He felt around the edges of the door to see if he could grasp an edge for pulling, but the door was seated tightly into the frame. Maybe in the area of the inside doorknob there might be a keyhole. He ran his fingers gently over the area and felt a little hole. He pulled his metal lock pick out of his pocket pouch and stuck it inside. After moving it around a little, he found a way to push on the lock mechanism until it turned the tongue of metal holding the door in place. The door opened slightly in the door frame, and Matthew's fingers were able to get a little purchase on the edge of the door. Carefully lest he push the door back into place, he pulled it open a little more until he had it open a foot wide as before. He could see now the overhanging branch that blocked it from opening further, and pulled it out of the way. When he got the door open all the way, he could see into the tunnel leading into the palace hill. It may have been meant as an escape tunnel, but now he knew he could enter from outside too. He grinned to himself as he shut the door closed again.

Feeling better, he rode Dusty back to the stables, unsaddled and brushed him, then went to wash up for dinner. As he slipped into his chair next to Stephanie, he overheard her conversation with Amber.

"And when I got back from our afternoon walk, there was this stink in my bedroom." Stephanie wrinkled her nose. "It smelled like tar or something. And Lady Charlotte says she can't smell anything different!"

Sabrina bounced in her chair. "I know, Teffanie! I know what it is!"

Stephanie turned to look at her. "What, Sabrina?"

Sabrina leaned conspiratorially across the table toward Stephanie. "Uncle Mattie fix the windows." She nodded vigorously. "Keep out the cold."

Stephanie narrowed her eyes at Matthew. "Mattie, what have you done?"

He looked at her innocently and spread his empty hands out before her. "Nothing!"

She examined the black tar coloring under his fingernails. "Yeah? Then what is this black stuff under your nails?"

"Tar," he answered nonchalantly.

"And what were you doing with the tar?" she grilled him.

He hesitated, and then finally answered. "Sealing out the drafts from your windows."

Stephanie sat back and stared at him. "I thought so!"

"Happy Christmas!" he told her.

"That's still three days away," she responded.

"Yep. I still have more rooms to do. Do you want to help me?"

She looked at the black of his fingernails and shook her head. "No thank you."

Amber looked at Matthew. "You can make my bedroom warmer, Mattie?"

"Yes, but it will smell like tar for a day."

She considered it. "I think I could handle that for a day."

"All right. I will do your room too. But I recommend waiting until tomorrow morning after breakfast, when you are up and able to spend most of the day somewhere else." He realized this would make him late to his morning apprenticeship, but didn't see another option.

She nodded and looked at Harry happily. "Imagine being warmer in the winter," she told him. "I can hardly wait!"

King Gilbert put down his soup spoon. "So, Prince Matthew. You have been altering my palace in more than one place?"

Matthew felt his stomach sink again, but he raised his head and bravely met the king's gaze. "Yes, Your Majesty. If you find you do not like it, I will be happy to remove the tar from around the windows." He didn't think now was the right time to tell the king that he also had filled his attic with straw.

"Hmm, well, I will just have to wait and see, won't I?" King Gilbert looked at him mildly. "You may complete Harry and Amber's suites, but I request you wait until after Christmas before changing more windows."

Matthew inclined his head gratefully. "Yes, Your Highness. Thank you."

Later that morning Karl tracked Matthew down. "Tomorrow is the annual Boar Hunt. Are you going?" Karl asked.

"I've never been on one. Are we invited?"

"Sure! Anyone who wants to go is welcome. Most of the squires go, because for any pigs they kill they will receive an extra portion of the meat for their families. The rest goes to the townsfolk for the annual Christmas giving."

"Have you killed a pig before?" Matthew asked, feeling a little excited.

"Last year I got one." Karl lowered his voice. "It was an old sow who wandered close to where I was hiding when she couldn't keep up with the herd. Anyway, the biggest male boar is usually reserved for someone in the royal family to kill. That one is served at the palace Christmas feast."

Before dawn the next morning Matthew bundled into his furs at Karl's suggestion and brought along his father's crossbow and his own dagger blade. The hunting party met in front of the palace, where men brought their dogs and horses. Matthew was riding Dusty.

King Gilbert sounded his bugle horn and everyone rode off behind him into the North Mountains. At times the snow was up to the horse's knees, but under the trees it merely blanketed the ground. Soon Gilbert called a halt.

"My scouts say they have seen the wild pig herd recently between this valley and the ravine area. I will lead one group to the west, Harry will lead the other to the east. Good hunting!"

He turned his horse and trotted off. Karl motioned Matthew to follow Harry's group. After leading them past a ravine and up a hill, Harry stopped his horse and turned to his hunting party.

"The dogs are getting excited," he told them. "I don't know if we will find the sow herd or the males. Be careful; I don't want anyone gored this year." He peered into the trees. "Release the hounds!"

There was a sudden excited barking and baying as a dozen hounds were released. They raced into the trees and the hunters followed.

"Wait!" Matthew shouted to Karl, who was plunging through the brush and trees ahead of him. "What is this about being gored?"

"Just stay away from the front tusked end of a maddened boar and you'll be fine!" Karl called back to him.

Soon they heard the dogs baying even more intensely, and it was just ahead of them. Karl and Matthew slowed their horses. Karl held his long sword at the ready, and Matthew nocked an arrow to his crossbow. They pulled up at the edge of a clearing, surrounded by men holding spears and bows at the ready.

There was a very large boar, five feet long and weight over two hundred pounds, backed up against a massive tree, grunting "Unk, unk." Dogs darted in and out trying to avoid his thrusting tusks, yet keep him cornered at the tree. Prince Harry dismounted from his horse and cautiously approached the boar, tightly gripping his spear. While the boar was distracted by another dog, Harry's hunting dog leaped onto the boar's back and latched onto its neck with its teeth. Harry followed him in, driving his spear into the boar's side. It let out a high pitched scream and turned toward Harry, who stabbed the boar deep into its shoulder. It shuddered, and several dogs dove in to grab the boar with their teeth and hold him down. One final thrust with Harry's spear and the boar was dead.

A cheer rose up from all the hunters. "Hurrah, Prince Harry!"

Harry bent down to tie up the boar to carry back on his horse. In the midst of the dogs milling around, two of them started barking again and ran off in another direction.

"It must be another boar!" Karl cried. "Come on, Matthew!"

Other hunters followed the dogs, a full dozen now again. In another clearing the dogs danced around two boars, smaller in size and younger, sporting shorter but still deadly looking tusks. Several men shot their arrows at one boar who screamed, and charged at one fellow who had dismounted to approach with his sword. He quickly climbed a tree while two other hunters stabbed and killed the boar with their spears.

The second boar backed up against a tree, dogs dancing around him.

"Shoot him with your crossbow!" Karl shouted to Matthew.

Matthew raised his crossbow, waiting for a moment when no dogs would be in the line of fire. He released the trigger and the arrow stuck into the boar's rump. Screaming and maddened, he charged through the line of dogs toward Matthew, who was trying to load another arrow onto his crossbow. His horse suddenly turned and ran from the boar, unseating Matthew, who fell directly into the path of the charging boar. Instinctually he rolled off to the side into some bushes, and the boar charged past, then stopped and turned to face him. Dogs harried him on every side, but the boar only had eyes for Matthew. Matthew released another arrow, which stuck into the boar's shoulder, and the boar charged.

Karl was suddenly in front of Matthew, plunging his sword downward into the boar's flank. Two other men stabbed the boar with their spears. Still the boar's momentum carried him toward Matthew, who stood now holding his dagger blade in his hand. As the boar neared, Matthew sidestepped the tusks and thrust his blade into the underside of the boar's chest. The knife handle pulled from Matthew's hand, but after six more strides the boar slid to the ground dead.

"Prince Matthew!" voices cheered, and Matthew looked up into Karl's beaming face.

"Wunderbar!" Karl pounded him on the back. "We made quite a team, no?"

"Thanks, Karl!" Matthew could finally breathe. "That was… exhilarating!" He tried to hide his shaking hands as he retrieved his blade.

"Yeah. The best part was that I wasn't the one who had to climb a tree this time." Karl grinned sheepishly.

"I could see how that would be the safest course of action," Matthew consoled him.

"But not the bravest. Come on, we need to load the boar onto your horse."

Matthew shook his head. "You stopped it from killing me. Your horse should carry it."

"It is tradition that the man who delivers the killing strike is the one to carry the boar home," Karl explained.

As it turned out, Dusty was still skittish from being chased by the boar, so the boar was loaded onto Karl's horse. As the hunting party returned to town, the townspeople cheered Karl as his horse bearing the boar walked by. Karl waved proudly. Matthew grinned to himself to see his friend so happy.

King Gilbert's party had found the herd of sows, and they brought back six pigs to share with the townspeople. Prince Harry was the main center of attraction for killing the largest boar of the year.

On the last day of Advent, the palace halls were decked with holly and ivy garland boughs, which gave off a wonderful smell of the holidays. Ribbons and cranberries decorated the garlands, and the little girls ran through the palace squealing their delight at the decorations. Extra candles burned everywhere.

The day was spent in fasting, and then the family and courtiers gathered in the chapel for afternoon mass. The liturgy focused on repenting of one's sins of the previous year. Matthew couldn't think of any big sins, but there sure were a lot of little mistakes he made that he regretted and wished he had done better. He hoped tarring the palace windows and spreading hay in the attic wouldn't turn out to be next year's regrets.

After mass everyone trooped into the great hall for the Christmas feast. Extra tables were set up to accommodate all the guests. The tables were laden with food: mashed potatoes, platters of venison, pig and beef, roasted vegetables, pastries and breads of every kind, a roast goose at each table, and the boar's head on a silver platter in front of Prince Harry. Everyone took their places at the tables and waited for King Gilbert to offer the prayer over the Christmas feast. Then they dug in to demolish the plenty.

After dinner the tables were pushed back against the walls, and musicians filed in. While they set up at one end of the hall, Karl and his father carried in a big Yule log to lay on the fire. It was wrapped in garlands of herbs and flowers, and as it burned it gave off wonderful scents of spices.

Groups of people gathered for singing, while others met in the middle of the room for dancing. Candles flickered brightly from the chandeliers, and Matthew settled comfortably in a chair at the side of the room to soak in the sights and sounds of the festivities, his stomach comfortably full.

As one particularly lively song started, Matthew looked up to see Sarah standing in front of him, hand on her hip.

"Aren't you going to ask me to dance?" she asked, her mouth drawn into a little pout.

He stood up quickly and gave a little bow to her. "Lady Sarah, may I have the honor of this dance?" He extended an open hand toward her.

She curtseyed and laid her hand in his. "I would be honored, Prince Matthew."

Matthew felt an intense desire to make a good impression in front of Sarah. He walked gracefully with her to the dance floor, and then turned to grasp her waist. Instead his knuckles hit her in the ribs. "So sorry," he murmured. Then he tried to adjust his stance, took a step forward and stepped on her foot.

"Don't you know how to dance?" she asked.

"I used to," he laughed nervously.

"Then just relax," she told him. "It will come back to you."

He took a deep breath and tried to move with the music. Step after step it became easier, and soon they were waltzing around the room.

Dancing with Sarah was delicious and intoxicating. He drank in the smell of her perfume. He nearly melted at the touch of her hand on his shoulder and the closeness of her breath near his cheek. When the song came to an end he forgot to stop dancing.

But she stepped back to look at him. "There, that wasn't so bad, was it?" A smile dimpled her cheek.

He bowed slightly. "May have the pleasure of this next dance?"

She nodded as the music started again. Then her face fell. "Oh, no! It's a pavane! I don't know this one so well."

He took her hand. "That's all right. I'm actually very good at this one. I'll lead you through it."

This time it was Sarah's turn to stumble occasionally. Matthew had known the Pavane since he was ten, and had even taught his sister, Amber. He liked this particular dance at the time because there were a series of tricky steps without having to constantly hold hands with a partner. Now it reminded him of a bull elk showing off in front of the does in the mating ritual. He blushed slightly at the thought, and then focused on leading Sarah through the dance steps. The musicians gradually sped up the music until by the end all the dancers were laughing and breathless.

The song ended and Sarah leaned into Matthew slightly as she looked up at him. "I am ready for something to drink!" she requested.

There was a barrel of ale that many palace folk were drinking from freely, but Sarah led Matthew to the bowl of freshly pressed apple cider. Matthew poured goblets for both of them. Sarah drank hers down in one draught, and then held out her goblet for more.

"I love the flavor of fresh apple cider," she commented. "We didn't get it very often in the orphanage. Sometimes at Christmas we got fresh apples, but mostly we just waited for the palace to bring us the annual gift of a goose and fresh bread."

Matthew finished his goblet of cider and set it down on the table. "Come with me, Sarah. I want to show you something."

She set her goblet down too and followed him up the stairs to the second floor on the East Wing. He took her to the narrow stairs leading to the attic.

"What I want to show you is up there," he told her, pointing up.

She eyed the stairs. "That is pretty steep to negotiate in this dress."

"I can help you," Matthew offered. "Do you want me in front of you or behind?"

She thought a moment. "Stay behind me in case I fall." She hitched up the front of her full skirts and started the climb carefully.

Matthew kept his eyes on her feet as they negotiated the steps. She had very shapely ankles and calves.

They made it up the stairs without mishap. Matthew led her to the far section of attic and he opened the door. The smell of hay fields met their nostrils. Sarah stopped and stared.

"Why in the world is hay in the attic?" she asked.

"It is an experiment of mine, to see if it keeps the heat in and helps the palace chambers stay warmer. Apparently the Adonia townsfolk do it." He held out his hand in front of him. "But I don't think the temperature feels much different here."

"Probably not. The heat would stay below this hay." She smiled. "I do think my chamber has been warmer lately; I just thought it was all due to the tar you put around the windows. Does King Gilbert know you did the hay?"

Matthew shook his head and grimaced. "No. And I'm afraid to tell him after how he reacted to the window tarring. But Rolf the stable master gave me permission to borrow and rotate the hay."

"Borrow? How are you going to get the loose hay back out again?" she asked.

Matthew stared at her. "I hadn't thought of that. I guess we'll have to bundle it up again."

"Either that or you use meadow grasses next time so you don't have to give it back to Rolf as quickly." She started walking around the attic area across the straw. "It will get dusty and stale over time."

Matthew walked with her. As they neared the corner where the mice previously had a nest, he noticed they had set up another one in the straw. "Oh, no!" He knelt down to examine the nest.

"What is it? Oh!" Sarah covered a smile with her hand. "It looks like you have a mouse problem. You need some traps."

"I meant to do that last week," he moaned. "Do you know where I can find some?"

She nodded. "I'll get them first thing tomorrow morning." She paused. "I better wait until people recuperate from the festivities. I'll get them sometime this week anyway." She headed back toward the stairs. "Now, how to get down again? I think down will be even harder than up. I think you better be below me again, Prince Matthew."

He stepped down a couple of steps, and then turned to see how she was faring. She gathered her full skirts in one arm and put one hand against the wall. She tried to feel for the first step with her foot since the skirts blocked her view, but she missed the step and nearly fell. Matthew shot out his hands toward her, but she caught herself before he touched her.

"This won't do," she sighed. "I think it will be better to go down backwards." She turned around and managed to take a step down backwards. She stopped and looked over her shoulder. "Um, Prince Matthew? I still can't see the steps. Do you mind steadying me? You may hold onto my waist."

"Yes, Lady Sarah." Matthew's mouth went dry, but he reached his hands around her waist to steady her.

They went down a step at a time, and finally reached the bottom. Sarah dropped her skirts and turned around to face him. "Thank you," she spoke primly. "I think I shan't be attempting those stairs again any time soon. At least not in a ball gown." She smiled.

Matthew bowed. "I shall be happy to take the mouse traps up for you, Milady."

The next morning most of the palace residents slept late. Matthew, Sarah and the little girls were among the first up. After helping themselves to fruit and bread in the kitchen, Sarah led them to the palace wood shop to look for mousetraps. The type Sarah recommended that intrigued Matthew was one that flipped inside when the mouse ran through it, trapping them inside a chamber.

"It's more humane," Sarah explained. "You can check the traps every few days and set the mice free outside."

They chose four of them, and Matthew and Stephanie took them up to the attic, placing one in each corner of the straw-filled room. They decided to take turns checking the traps.

After lunch the palace staff and royal family gathered in the Great Hall to prepare for the Great Christmas giving to the people of Adonia City. There were mountains of bread loaves, bags of apples and nuts, wrapped packages of smoked partridges and goose and salted pig. Wagons pulled up to the door of the palace, and everyone loaded the bounty into them.

King Gilbert gathered everyone around. "We will have four distribution stations again this year. I will lead one, Sir Royce will lead one, Amber and Harry will lead one. That leaves one more." Gilbert looked down at his granddaughter. "Princess Sabrina, would you like to lead one this year?"

Sabrina jumped up and down. "Yes, yes! Me and Teffanie and Mattie!"

Matthew bowed. "I would be honored, Your Majesty."

"Whew!" Matthew overheard Amber saying to her lady Roberta. "I was afraid I would have to lead one of the stations by myself again this year. I don't think I would have felt up to it."

"I think the king knew," Roberta responded. "Either way I will be your arms and legs distributing the gifts. You may just sit and look regal."

"Just make sure we have extra food to eat in case I get hungry," Amber whispered.

"Already done, Milady." Roberta told her.

Once the wagons were loaded they were driven down Palace Hill into Adonia City. Matthew and Stephanie rode in one wagon, Sabrina and Sarah in another. Even Charlotte and George came in their group. Once they reached the eastside marketplace they pulled their six wagons into the center of the square. The townspeople were already gathering excitedly, some already singing Christmas carols. The mood was festive, everyone greeting one another happily. They lined up alongside the wagons to receive their gifts from the palace.

Although the air was chilly the sun shone brightly, and everyone kept warm handing out packages. An hour later an innkeeper and his wife brought the palace group mugs of steaming hot tea. Sabrina and Stephanie were particularly grateful for the hot drinks.

Soon the townspeople had received their gifts and the wagons were empty. They bundled back into the wagons and returned to the palace.

After dinner that night, the royal family and close friends gathered in King Gilbert's personal parlor chamber for gift sharing. Roberta accompanied Princess Amber, Charlotte and George attended, and Sarah was there with Princess Sabrina. Matthew carried his gifts for the family members in hand, but Sarah's gift was tucked carefully inside his tunic.

King Gilbert addressed the family briefly and then handed out his gifts: a gold coin to each person, carved with their likeness on one side, the symbol of Adonia on the other. Then everyone mingled, giving their gifts to each other. Matthew felt bad that he hadn't thought of gifts for Charlotte and George, but Stephanie had gifts for them, a soft fur hand muff for Charlotte and fur hat with ear flaps for George. Finally, Matthew had only Sarah's gift yet to give. He approached her shyly, where she watched Stephanie and Sabrina playing with their new dolls.

"Sarah," he spoke quietly behind her. She didn't move. He cleared his throat. "Sarah," he said more loudly.

She turned and gave him a smile. "Hello, Prince Matthew. Happy Christmas!"

"I, ah, have a gift for you." He retrieved the package from his tunic and thrust it out to her.

She took it and carefully unwrapped the cloth. The brass orchid lay on her palm glinting in the candlelight. She turned it, examining it carefully.

"It is beautiful!" she breathed.

"You liked the orchid in that painting so much," he explained.

"Yes. Thank you, Matthew!" She threw her arms around his neck and hugged him. Then she quickly stepped back. "Oh dear, I am so sorry. I shouldn't have done that."

"That's okay." Matthew felt warm inside, and his neck tingled where she had touched him.

"I have a gift for you too," she told him. "I didn't know what to give to someone who has everything."

"I don't have everything," he began.

She pulled from her skirts a long slender object wrapped in a soft white cloth. He unwrapped it and found a plain wooden flute.

"I don't know how to play this," he confessed.

"I do," Sarah smiled, showing her dimples. "I will teach you."

Matthew smiled back at her. "I would like that very much."

The next day it snowed, but that did not slow down the palace workers in the kitchen packaging up venison and salted pork from the country's pig farm. In the great hall others were pouring grain from large bags into smaller ones, and then setting them in piles against the walls. Cheeses were brought from the cellar and also placed against the wall.

Matthew worked with them carrying cheeses up, and then helped fill grain bags. Prince Harry directed placement of items. Matthew soon joined him.

"Where is all this food going?" Matthew asked him.

"For the next ten days of Christmas we will be delivering these gifts to the outlying towns and villages of Adonia, as a token of thanks from the king to the people." Harry sighed. "The past couple of years it has not been much, and we mainly are only able to give the same kinds of foods the people already have. We used to disperse imported and exotic foods, like rice, spices and citrus fruits. But they have been difficult and expensive to obtain recently."

Matthew felt again a sense of foreboding that had begun creeping inside him whenever this topic was discussed. He looked up at Harry. "May I come with the caravan to deliver the gifts?"

Harry grinned. "We would love to have you come along. We can use all the wagon drivers we can get, and I can show you more of my country."

At dawn the next morning everyone gathered to load the twenty wagons full of goods, and covered them with tarps, tied down against the winter weather. Among the drivers were Karl, Sir Royce, George, Harry and Matthew, all bundled in warm coats, hats and mittens. Amber gave Harry one final kiss, and they were off, lumbering down Adonia Palace hill. They took the north route out of town, following the road through a series of valleys, avoiding the snowed-in mountain pass roads.

Midday they came to the first big town, and stopped in the town square to distribute the goods from the first wagon. The townsfolk received the gifts cheerfully, some of them bringing gifts from their own trades and gardens to give back to the king. These gifts were loaded back into the emptied wagon, and the driver returned back to Adonia City. After eating a hot meal provided by the town inn, the wagons headed onward.

It was the same in each town and village the next several days. At night the inns provided bed and breakfast, which Harry paid for. Matthew and Sir Royce stayed with Harry to the last village, leaving their empty wagons at the previous towns and riding with Harry. After the drop off and wishing the villagers well, they returned for their wagons.

"This is a really nice tradition Adonia does for its people," Matthew commented.

"Sometimes I wish we could do more," Harry responded. "Life in the hill country is hard. The growing seasons are short and winter is long. But the people help each other out as best they can. And we are fortunate to have peaceful neighbors. We have managed better since establishing stable trade with them: we export pork and venison; Danforth supplies grain; Mordred in the north provides cement and building stone; Renling from the east most of our fine wood; Sterling from the south our seafood; Borden from the west our textiles and wool. At least they have held steady even when the foreign trade has petered down."

The journey back was faster, stopping once for the night. They made it back in time for the last feast of Christmas and the welcoming in of the New Year.

King Gilbert himself stood to offer the toast. "To a more prosperous year, good crops and good health!" he proposed, raising his glass of wine.

Everyone raised their goblets. "To a prosperous New Year!"

CHAPTER 6

DISAPPOINTMENT

The next two months returned to normal winter routine for Matthew, mornings spent at the trades, and afternoon squire training in the fields when it wasn't blizzarding. On Saturdays and etiquette days he joined groups going skiing in the mountains. Matthew found himself getting used to the colder weather. He also became more proficient at skiing, almost able to keep up with Sarah. He figured he would never get as fast or reckless as Karl.

Finally hints of spring came to the mountain valleys. There was not as much snow in the hills around Adonia City, the snow pack finally melted from the streets, and crocuses and tulips erupted from gardens in front of city homes.

Sarah proposed a Saturday excursion with the girls into the mountains. "I promised to show you my special place," she hinted.

Matthew felt as though something momentous was about to happen. As he pulled on his boots in his room that morning, he thought about the last five months in Adonia and about his life plans. It was pleasant here in the mountains, and he could picture himself taking on a trade, or continuing to train under Sir Royce, settling down with a wife and starting a family. Suddenly he realized he was thinking of Sarah being with him in that picture.

He dropped his foot to the floor and inhaled deeply. In a couple more weeks East Adonia Pass would open, and he and Stephanie would return to Sterling. Perhaps he could talk Sarah into coming with them? It would work especially if Sabrina would be spending another summer with them.

Sarah would get to know Sterling…and Matthew better. And when the time was right (Matthew's heart leapt in his chest at the thought), he would propose marriage to her…

He shook his head to clear it. Today was a hike into the mountains with a girl he liked very much. And hoped she would become a part of his life. Forever.

The little girls were excited to get out of the palace for an outing in the hills. They met in the stables right after breakfast to saddle their horses. Sarah brought a lunch basket, which she gave to Stephanie to carry, while she kept Sabrina with her on her horse. When they were ready, Sarah led them out of town a different way from the ski slope hill.

Once they were in the hills, Sarah led them up one side of a ravine toward a towering peak. The hill was steep, but the horses were sure-footed. So far the ravine was mostly free of snow, but a stream careened down the base of the ravine, pregnant from the snow melt. Under the trees it was cool, but occasional rays of sun warmed them. The trees grew taller, evergreen mixed with deciduous trees sprouting bright green leaf buds.

Another side ravine joined the first one, and Sarah turned their horses in that direction. The stream in this ravine was smaller, but still swift. They climbed higher and the ravine narrowed. At a small level clearing Sarah stopped her horse and dismounted.

"We leave the horses here and go on foot the rest of the way," she announced, lifting Sabrina down.

Matthew got off and helped Stephanie down with the basket. They followed Sarah along a narrow trail beside the stream up the ravine. After a twenty minute walk the ravine opened up to reveal a little pond. On the far side a waterfall cascaded down a cliff to fall into the pond. In the spray over the pond a rainbow formed.

"Wow," Matthew breathed.

"It's called Bridal Veil Falls," Sarah told him. "During Spring runoff it's at its best. It is just a trickle during the late summer and fall."

"I like that name," Stephanie announced, and then scampered off with Sabrina to the water's edge. Sarah and Matthew followed.

"How did you find this place?" Matthew asked her.

"One of the Sisters running the orphanage loved to take us exploring in the hills," Sarah explained. "Sister Agnes actually discovered it. She passed away a few years later, and I don't think anyone else has come back to visit. At least not that I have seen."

"Someone else should know about this place. It is beautiful!" Matthew gazed at Sarah where she stood framed by the falls.

"Yes." Sarah watched the girls playing at the edge of the pond. "Perhaps I will tell others about it someday."

Stephanie looked up at Sarah. "Maybe you could get married here!" She suggested.

Sarah blushed and avoided looking at Matthew. "Perhaps."

Matthew pulled off his boots and socks and stuck his feet in the water. "You should come in, Sarah! It is refreshing!"

She knelt and plunged her hand into the water, then pulled it out quickly again. "Oh no! This water is still icy from the snow melt. I think I'll wait until the end of summer." She glanced at him suspiciously. "Or are you just trying to get me to take off my stockings so you can see my ankles again?"

Matthew grinned. "I hadn't thought of that, but now that you mention it…"

Sarah slugged him playfully on the arm, and then stepped back from the pond. "I am not chancing it with you near the water. Amber told me how you liked to get her wet."

"Yes, she was fun to tease." He stepped out of the pond and sat down to put on his socks and shoes again. "You are right. The water is cold."

Sabrina ran up to Sarah and threw her arms around her. "I hungry!"

Sarah bent down to hug her back. "Good suggestion. It is time to eat."

Sarah opened the picnic basket and pulled out biscuits, salted pork, apples and fruit tarts. The girls ate quickly, and then ran off to float stick boats down the stream.

Matthew turned the apple in his hand half eaten. "So Sarah," he began. "What do you see yourself doing in the next ten years?"

She paused thoughtfully. "I suppose I will still be nanny for Amber's children. I do hope to have found a man to marry by then and start my own family. If neither of those work out, I will likely return to work at the orphanage. What about you? What are your life plans?"

Matthew laughed. "I used to want to be a knight, until Sir Lamborgini squashed my enthusiasm. I figured my sister, Amber, would co-rule Sterling and Adonia with Harry, so I don't have to worry about being tied down to a kingdom. I was actually feeling sort of lost until I came to Adonia."

He picked his words carefully. "I also see myself settling down to have a family, and perhaps working at a trade like smithing or carpentry, although I am not as skilled at those professions as others are." He gazed into her eyes. "I could see myself staying on in Adonia working my profession and courting the girl of my dreams." He took a deep breath. "Sarah, I like you a lot. I am falling in love with you. I would like to ask you to marry me."

She leaned back surprised. "Me? Why me? There are many other girls you could choose. I am honored." She suddenly stood up. "No, Matthew. That can't be. You are a Prince. I like you and everything, but I—I don't even know where I come from. How could your parents accept me? I could not measure up to what is expected. No, it could not work." She whirled around and walked toward the pond, one hand on the top of her head and the other over her heart.

Matthew watched her, his half eaten apple lying forgotten on the ground, a gaping hole torn in his heart. He could only watch dumbly as Sarah called to the girls that it was time to go. Forgetting the picnic basket, she hurried the girls down the trail away from Bridal Veil Falls. His sister, Stephanie, looked back reproachfully over her shoulder at him, as if to accuse him of ruining the perfect day. When they were out of sight, Matthew sank heavily onto a log and stared at the remains of their picnic lunch.

After a long time reviewing everything he had said and done, he decided he *had* ruined everything. He should have left things as they were, where he and Sarah were casual friends, to be parted as summer approached. Now that he had declared his heart, he had closed that casual door forever. There was nothing left for him in Adonia now. As soon as East Adonia Pass opened he would leave and let Sarah live her own life with someone else.

He sighed and knelt to pick up the forgotten lunch remnants. He had been looking forward to tasting the tarts, but they did not appeal to him anymore. He walked back along the trail until he reached Dusty, who whinnied joyfully to see him. Matthew leaned his face against Dusty's nose and noticed there were tears absorbing into his soft fur. Then he swung into the saddle and trotted back down the mountain, his face set and hiding the pain he felt inside.

Matthew didn't tell a soul about what happened, and apparently neither did Sarah. She continued watching Stephanie after her lessons with Charlotte, but Matthew no longer joined them in the afternoons or evenings. He spent more and more time in the stables with Dusty. In fact, he made it a point to stay away from places where he might bump into

Sarah. Once he saw her down the hall near the kitchens, but she saw him first and turned back the way she had come. He continued going through the motions of training with the other squires, but his heart wasn't in it anymore.

Karl noticed the change. "What's wrong, Matthew? You have been a bit moody lately."

Matthew shrugged. "I guess I am just anxious to return home. How soon will East Adonia Pass open?"

Karl gazed at the snow covered mountain peaks. "Soon. Maybe another week."

Matthew pressed Amber for an estimated date for when the girls would leave Adonia and go to Sterling.

"I can't go, Mattie, until after the baby is born. Probably mid-summer," she told him.

Matthew knew he could not wait that long and consulted George. "You must go when you are ready," George told him. "Harry and I can get the ladies safely to Sterling."

Matthew approached King Gilbert in his chambers to announce his intention to leave.

"We have enjoyed having you with us this winter," King Gilbert told him. "Thank you for your contributions to our comfort in the palace. You are always welcome back."

"Thank you, Your Majesty." Matthew noticed him eyeing him reproachfully. "Cousin Gilbert," he amended.

King Gilbert grinned. "That is better, Matthew. In private we are family." He grew more serious. "Which road will you be taking back to Sterling?"

"Which road? I only know the one through East Adonia Pass."

King Gilbert pulled a scroll from a book shelf and unrolled it over a table. It showed the land of Adonia, and various roads leading through the mountains to its neighboring countries. King Gilbert traced a road with his finger that led over East Adonia Pass, curved back through the city state of Danforth, then west again through the Black Forest of Sterling.

"The wider more commonly used route through Danforth takes about 4 days." He traced a different route with his finger. "But if you go through the southwest mountains here through South Wolf Pass, you can reach Sterling in a day and a half."

Matthew looked at his cousin in surprise. "Why don't more people use this road?"

King Gilbert shrugged. "Many people like to trade in Danforth along the way, and they have inns where travelers can stay. South Wolf Pass is a lonely road, plus in places it is too narrow to take wagons through. It is better for foot and horse travel."

Matthew thought of his trip to Adonia. "So I suppose there are wolves near South Wolf Pass?"

Gilbert nodded thoughtfully. "There have been stories of them, yes. They are more likely to attack the lone traveler on foot. I would be happy to find a traveling companion for you."

Matthew recalled George being attacked by wolves in the Black Forest. "Yes, I would like that."

Three days later King Gilbert pulled Matthew aside after dinner. "Good news. Word is that the passes should be open the day after tomorrow. A man named Thomas is traveling through South Wolf Pass heading toward the country of Borden. You share the same trail for the first day, before the roads divide. Is that satisfactory?"

Matthew felt excitement rising inside him. "Yes, thank you, Cousin Gilbert!"

He hurried back to his room and began sorting his belongings. The cross bow, heavy fur coat, hat and skis he would leave here. He would keep his good boots, traveling cloak, cap and work gloves, and an extra pair of pants, tunic and socks. He would bring his dagger blade from Harry, the sword he had made in the smithy, and the bow and arrows that Sir Royce had let him keep. He picked up the flute Sarah had given him for Christmas, and almost set it aside on the table. In the end he could not part from it. Though Sarah might never care what he did with it, he had grown to enjoy playing a couple of simple melodies on it, and he thought it would bring him solace on a lonely night.

The next morning he went to town to say goodbye to those who had taught him the trades, including Lance and Lark. At lunchtime he spent half an hour with Dusty, combing his fur and feeding him apples. He spent one last afternoon with the squires, but only on the way back from training did he tell Karl he would be leaving on the morrow.

Karl pulled him into a bear hug. "I will miss you. Don't forget me," Karl told him.

"Never," Matthew promised. "I will come back, if only to see you again."

"What are you planning to do?" Karl asked.

Matthew shrugged. "I have a letter from my uncle John, asking his brother Edward if I can sail on one of his merchant ships."

Karl rocked back on his heels. "Prima! I wish I could do that someday."

"Maybe if I get any good at sailing I can take you with me," Matthew grinned.

Karl pounded him on the back. "You do that. Then I can show you my home country."

"It's a promise then. Thanks, Karl, for everything." He pumped Karl's hand one more time and left before his voice got quivery.

After dinner Matthew went to Stephanie's bedroom suite to say goodbye. She started crying.

"There, there, Stephanie," Matthew hugged her. "I'm not going away forever, you know."

She wiped her nose. "I know. But it is more lonely here without you. I miss Mother and Father more when you are gone."

"You'll be back with them soon, after Amber's baby is born. And you have Charlotte."

"I know, but I've always had you." She hugged him one more time and then stood back with her best bossy expression. "You must eat your vegetables, stay warm, and don't do anything stupid. Promise me."

"Yes, Your Highness," he grinned. "I promise."

Before dawn the next morning Matthew gathered his travel pack, girded on his sword, donned his cloak and hat and slung his bow over his shoulder. In the kitchen he picked up some food for his journey: salted pork and venison, cheese and a loaf of bread. Harry met him at the front door.

"Amber sends her farewell," Harry told him. "Take care of yourself. Don't do anything I wouldn't do."

Matthew chuckled. "That leaves the door wide open. I seem to remember all sorts of adventures you and Amber dragged me into."

Harry shook his head. "Rimrock Island was Amber's idea, not mine."

Suddenly Amber's lady-in-waiting, Roberta, came running down the stairs toward them. She looked disheveled, like she had just jumped out of bed.

"Prince Matthew!" she puffed. "Will you be going to Portsmouth?"

"Yes. Why?" Matthew was curious.

"Have you found a place to stay yet?" she asked.

"No. I thought I would just find an inn for a decent price." He shrugged.

"My older brother, Dale, still lives there, in a little house on Fisherman's Lane. Would you please look him up and show him this?" She handed him a little package wrapped in brown paper.

"What is it?" he asked, tucking it into his tunic pocket.

"A fish talisman on a chain. My brothers Allen and Dale gave it to me when I left home to train at court at Sterling Castle. It was to help me remember them and where I had come from. At the time I wanted to get as far away from the life of fishermen families as I could." She laughed. "Of course I didn't picture myself deep in the mountains either. Anyway, if you are in need of housing or assistance, show it to my brother and he will know you are a friend of mine. You are welcome to keep it."

"Thank you, Roberta. You are most kind." Matthew inclined his head to her.

Thomas was waiting on the palace steps, a large bundle slung over his back. He was a large bearded man, who looked like he preferred living in the mountains. He didn't say much, but waited while Matthew gave Harry one last farewell hug.

Then Matthew walked down the palace hill road after Thomas, who was keeping a brisk pace. He looked back once, to the upper windows where he imagined Sarah still sleeping. He felt a pang of regret that he hadn't handled things better with her. Perhaps it was for the better…No, that old saying was not comforting him. He felt like he was leaving a piece of himself behind in Adonia, and Sarah held it captive.

Matthew followed Thomas across Adonia City toward the southwest mountains. They reached the canyon entrance to the pass just as the sun was coming up. Even going uphill Thomas kept up his fast pace, and Matthew sometimes had to jog to keep up with him. Matthew asked the occasional question, which Thomas answered with grunts, nods or one word responses. Finally late morning Matthew sank down on a rock near a stream.

"Thomas, I've got to rest a minute," he panted.

Thomas stopped and nodded, putting down his pack. They both gazed through the trees to the valley far below. From this distance they could see farmlands stretching beyond the city, brown dirt interspersed with trees showing their early spring green.

They both drank from the stream and Matthew broke out some of his bread and cheese. He offered some to Thomas, who merely shook his head.

"So what's the hurry up this mountain?" Matthew asked between bites.

"Get beyond the pass before nightfall," Thomas answered.

"Why?" Matthew queried. "Wolves?"

Thomas nodded.

"Oh." Matthew's stomach flip-flopped. He did not want to repeat George's misadventure. He stood up and packed away his food. "Guess we better get going then."

It was mid-afternoon when they reached the pass. It was narrow in places, where it appeared the passage had been chopped out with pick axes to make it wide enough for a horse and rider. At the high point Matthew stopped to look out over the land. To the north Matthew could see the mountains and valleys of Adonia. To the south east he looked over the forest portion of Sterling, and to the west the high plains of Borden.

Thomas glanced once over the vistas, and then marched on through the narrow rocky pass. Matthew walked quickly to catch up to him. They walked downward until it was almost too dark to see the trail. Thomas finally called a halt. He pointed to a rocky alcove that offered shelter overhead, but also a rock wall that protected their backs. Thomas pointed to a spot in front of the alcove.

"Build the fire here," he directed.

Matthew could see black charcoal of old fires on the ground in that spot. "Okay," he answered. He collected dry twigs, moss, and some larger sticks, and then started the fire with his flint. Thomas returned with an armful of logs.

"I assume the fire is supposed to keep the wolves away?" Matthew commented.

"Yeah," Thomas grunted his assent.

"I don't think that always works." Matthew proceeded to tell him about George being attacked by wolves near the fire on their journey to Adonia.

Thomas chewed on his jerky meat thoughtfully. "You say he may have been eating while on lookout?"

Matthew nodded. "Yes."

"Perhaps the wolves were hungrier than they were afraid." Thomas gazed into the branches of a tree nearby. "Tonight we tie our food up high in the tree. We take turns keeping watch, but with the fire low to preserve night vision. Agreed?"

"Agreed." Matthew felt a little better. A very little.

Thomas looked at him. "You look tired. I take first watch while you sleep."

Matthew nodded willingly, curled up in his cloak with his back against the rock wall, and fell quickly to sleep.

Thomas shook him awake a few hours later. "Your turn," he murmured. Thomas rolled up in his cloak and fell right to sleep.

Matthew sat up next to the fire and gazed out into the trees. He could hear the quiet sounds of the night creatures chirping at each other. He unexpectedly thought of Sarah with a stab of pain, and wondered if he would ever see her again.

The night sounds quieted suddenly, and he gazed into the trees more alertly. He could make out a dark form sitting by a tree at the edge of the clearing. He squinted his eyes, and then opened them wide. Yes, he thought he could see a pair of eyes reflecting the firelight. Matthew didn't move and neither did the animal. It seemed like the right shape to be a wolf, but slightly smaller.

He turned his head slightly to search the other trees around the clearing. He did not see any other animals, but that didn't mean no others were there. Matthew thought about how he had befriended the Komodo dragon, Creedo. It started with just being comfortable in each other's presence.

Matthew slowly moved his hands out in front of him, palms up, and started talking in low tones. The animal blinked periodically but otherwise didn't move. After about twenty minutes, Matthew slowly stood up. The animal stood up on its feet, but continued to face him. Matthew stepped slowly toward it, arms by his side, keeping his palms facing forward. As he got closer, he could tell it was indeed a wolf.

Matthew squatted down in front of it holding out his hands for the wolf to sniff. The animal sniffed, then sat back on his haunches and continued to watch him. Matthew continued to talk to it for a while, and then stood up again to back up toward the fire. The wolf took a couple of steps toward him. When Matthew stopped so did the wolf. A few more steps back and the wolf cautiously followed the same distance. It seemed to be limping, favoring its right front paw. Matthew stopped, uncertain. Dawn was beginning to light the sky, but it was still too dark to see much.

Matthew took a step closer to the wolf, talking quietly. The wolf sat on its haunches and let him approach. A few more steps and Matthew was close enough to touch the wolf. He held out a hand toward the wolf's head, and the wolf briefly touched its nose to his palm. Matthew sat down beside the wolf, still talking quietly to it. After a few minutes he slowly raised a hand and touched the wolf's shoulder. The wolf lay down on his stomach next to him. The sky grew lighter.

"Something seems to be wrong with your leg," Matthew murmured. "Do you want me to check it out?"

Matthew laid his hand on the wolf's shoulder and slowly slid it down the right front leg. The wolf looked up at him, but didn't otherwise move. When Matthew touched the wolf's paw, it emitted a low growl but held still. Matthew gently raised the foot and the wolf rolled slightly to its side and let him.

In the growing light Matthew could see the pads of the wolf's paw. The center seemed red and swollen. Matthew gently ran a finger over the swollen pad and thought he felt a thorn. The wolf drew back his lips. Matthew grasped the top of the thorn with his fingernails and swiftly drew it out. The wolf yelped and leapt to his feet. Matthew jumped up and faced the wolf warily.

"I pulled the thorn out," Matthew told the wolf soothingly, holding the thorn up to show him. "Your paw should be able to heal now."

Thomas had awakened at the wolf's yelp and now stood facing them. "Wolf!" he cried. He stepped toward the wolf, waving his arms wildly. "Shoo! Go! We don't have anything for you here!"

The wolf jumped back, looked at Matthew briefly, and then ran off into the trees.

"I just pulled a thorn out of his paw," Matthew told him.

Thomas shrugged. "I don't trust wolves, never will."

They retrieved their food from the tree, ate a little, packed their things quickly and headed down the trail. An hour later the path split, one branch headed west, the other southeast.

"You go south," Thomas told him. "Black Forest, then Sterling. Good traveling."

"You too." Matthew grasped Thomas' hand and they parted.

Matthew sighed and turned town his path. Thomas hadn't been the most talkative but he had been company. Now Matthew felt acutely lonely.

About twenty minutes later he thought he heard something in the trees behind him. He stopped to look but saw nothing. Yet he couldn't help but feel something was watching him. He walked a little farther and then looked over his shoulder. He saw a shadow moving in the trees behind him. It was the wolf he had helped! Matthew continued walking warily, trying to sense if there were any other wolves around. This wolf seemed alone. Matthew eased his pack around to the front and dug out some salted pork. He dropped a few pieces onto the trail behind him, and then glanced back as he walked.

The wolf left the trees hesitantly and sniffed at the first piece of meat. He lapped it up greedily and went to the next piece. Matthew dropped a few more pieces, walking slowly to let the animal close the distance between them. Soon the wolf was right behind him, tongue out lolling, waiting for the next piece. Matthew turned to face him and squatted down, holding out the next piece. The wolf sniffed at it, and then delicately drew it from Matthew's hand with his teeth. Now Matthew could see his gaunt appearance, ribs showing through his fur.

"Hungry are you? Where is the rest of your pack?" Matthew looked around. "Are you the runt of your litter? What did you do to become a loner?" He slowly reached out to touch the wolf's nose with his fingers, and then fed him another piece of meat. "I don't have much more, but you are welcome to come with me." Matthew stood up and began walking again. The wolf followed him.

A couple of hours later Matthew recognized that he was in the part of the Black Forest near the fields of Sterling Castle. He started looking for a certain smaller trail that led along a stream. Soon he found it.

"Keep coming," he said and the wolf followed him.

Soon Matthew found what he was looking for, a cave he had discovered as a boy, that used to shelter bandits before Matthew and his sisters turned it into a play cave. His mother once had been held prisoner here, when a certain suitor had her kidnapped to falsely win a test of Wit and Worthiness. Matthew lit a torch with his flint and entered the cave.

Things were as he had left it, a little table, chair and bed. He went into a corner and opened a chest containing some dried food. He offered it to the wolf, who only sniffed at the dried fruit but did eat some of the dehydrated meat. Matthew popped a few dried fruit into his mouth and sat down on the bed. The wolf climbed up beside him and lay down, looking up at him.

"This is my forest house, Wolf. You are welcome to stay here. There is not a lot of food, but you should find what you need nearby."

Matthew lay down on the bed and the wolf curled up against him. Matthew laid a hand on the animal's neck and scratched it. The wolf let him. Matthew closed his eyes and dozed.

Matthew awoke an hour later. The wolf sat near the front of the cave looking out as if to guard the entrance. Wolf turned to look at him when Matthew got off the bed.

"I must continue my journey, Wolf. Unfortunately, I can't take you with me to the ocean." Matthew emptied the rest of the meat scraps from his pack into the chest, leaving it open. "You stay here, Wolf. I will likely be back in a few months."

The wolf followed him from the cave and accompanied him downstream to the edge of the forest. There Matthew stopped and squatted in front of the wolf.

"You need to stay here now, Wolf. The forest is your home."

Matthew stood and held his hands palms forward in front of him to tell the wolf to stay. The wolf sat on his haunches and watched as Matthew walked away. He let out a single lone howl. Matthew turned his head once to see the wolf still sitting at the edge of the trees, as if to say he would wait. Matthew was once again alone.

CHAPTER 7

PORTSMOUTH

As Matthew walked passed the newly planted fields along the edge of the Black Forest, he realized how late in the day it was. He was not inclined to spend the night in Sterling Castle, having to answer his parents' questions about how the winter went in Adonia, what friends he made, or what his life plans were. Instead he turned down a familiar path toward a little cottage among the fields, surrounded by low hedges and a garden patch. The shutters were closed for the winter, but he knew where the key was for the door. He opened up the house, washed up and drank deeply from the rain barrel by the door, then found a jar of bottled vegetables for his supper. He went to bed and slept soundly despite his recent nap in the cave.

At dawn the next morning he left a note on the table explaining his plans. Then he was off traveling the road that ran along the beach, past Sterling Castle and through the village of Sterling. There one of the villagers recognized him and offered him a ride to Portsmouth, where he was headed anyway. Matthew accepted.

They reached Portsmouth late in the afternoon. Matthew paid a coin to the villager for the ride. Then he threw his pack over one shoulder and started walking through town. On the main street he thought about the time his family attended the Fall Harvest Festival in Portsmouth, when extra stalls had been set up for people to sell their wares. Now the street was crowded with wagon and donkey traffic, people milling past each other on the sides of the streets, hurrying to their various destinations. No one paid him much attention.

He made his way to the southwest end of town, and followed the road along the coast line about half a mile. He turned off on a dirt road labelled Fisherman's Lane. It led to a cluster of small fishing houses. He stopped at the third one and knocked on the door.

"Just a minute!" a deep voice called from behind the door. Matthew waited. Then the door was opened by a large bearded man in his early thirties, wearing a work apron and smelling strongly of fish. He was wiping his hands on a dirty towel. "What is it?" he asked gruffly.

"My name is Matthew," he introduced himself. "My sister's friend Roberta sent me to find her brother, Dale. She thought he might be able to put me up for several nights until my uncle's ship comes in."

"I'm Dale." The big man sized Matthew up and down. He folded his arms across his chest. "I don't have much room, and I don't babysit landlubbers."

"I can sleep on the floor, Matthew interjected quickly. "I can pay for my way, and I'm willing to work any chores you need help with. Roberta asked me to show you this." He unwrapped the fish talisman.

Dale examined the talisman, and then looked at Matthew's soft hands. "Humph. Well, all right, since Roberta asked. Come on in."

Matthew followed him inside. The main room had a cooking fire, two benches to sit on alongside a wooden table, and a cupboard loaded with a variety of pots and dishes. Another cupboard stored boxes of food and bottles of spices. Two doorways led off the main room to what Matthew presumed were bedrooms.

Dale pointed to one door. "You can have that bedroom. No one has used it for years, but you can clear off the bed and sleep on it. The outhouse is out back."

Dale went back to gutting and chopping fish on the wood table. The guts were scraped into a bucket, the fish heads tossed into a cauldron for soup, and the fish bodies laid into a crate.

Matthew entered the bedroom. There was all sorts of junk thrown onto the bed. He moved two old chairs, four boxes, and a pile of musty clothes off to make enough room. He left his knapsack beside the bed and returned to the main room.

"Wash your hands, grab a knife, and help me." Dale pointed to a bucket of water by the door.

Matthew washed and joined Dale at the table. He observed how Dale slit a fish along the underbelly, scooped out the innards and chopped off the head. It looked easy, but Matthew struggled to hold on to the slippery fish, and discovered it was harder than it looked to get the insides clean. Dale finished three fish before Matthew finished one.

"First time cleaning fish?" Dale asked.

"Second," Matthew confessed. "It's been a while." He thought about camping out on Rimrock Island when he was fifteen, fishing to feed himself, and using a spoon to scoop out the innards. He had wanted to spend more time on the island to try and train one of the Komodo dragons that lived there, but his mother had nixed the idea after she found out he had spent the night there. He had managed to sneak off several times since then, but never to stay overnight again. He sighed and concentrated on mimicking Dale's moves with the knife.

Soon the bin of fish was done. "Come," Dale commanded.

Dale lifted the crate of fish bodies and carried it outside the house door. In the back yard Matthew saw the outhouse in the corner. Closer to the house stood a brick smoker. Dale showed Matthew how to lay the fish out onto three trays, and then push them back into the smoker. Dale checked the hickory wood burning in the bottom, and then fastened the door shut.

"Tomorrow night the fish will be smoked and we can sell it in the market," he told Matthew. "Go to bed. At dawn we go fishing."

Though he was tired, the straw mattress was hard and lumpy, and it took Matthew a while to fall asleep. It felt like he had barely slept a few hours when Dale thumped on the door to wake him. Matthew stumbled through the door. Bread, cheese and sardines were on the table for breakfast. Matthew nearly choked on the strong fish taste of the sardines, but swallowed them down manfully.

"It is cold, bring a coat," Dale told him.

When Matthew brought out his cloak, Dale shook his head. "It is drizzling. You need a rubber coat." Dale went into his room and came back with a large ugly tan coat. It was large on Matthew's shoulders, but did look like it would keep him dry.

Matthew followed Dale outside and down to the beach. They climbed into a fishing boat tied to a little dock, and Dale set the sails on a course along the coast. Periodically they stopped near a rock or buoy and pulled up a net from the water. Dale swiftly emptied fish into large tubs in the boat, occasionally pulling out a starfish or other creature not good for eating. After a couple of hours Matthew felt chilled to the bone, but Dale kept working. Finally he turned the boat back toward home.

Back at the house Matthew put more wood on the fire while Dale prepared them a hot barley drink and soup. After eating they set to work sorting the fish into baskets by size and variety. Then Dale placed the baskets in a cold stream that ran by the house to stay cool. After that he checked the fish in the smoker, removing some of the smaller pieces and putting them into a basket.

"We'll leave the large pieces to smoke overnight. Tomorrow we take all the fish to market."

Matthew nodded and collapsed in bed again. This time he fell asleep right away. Dale knocked on his door before dawn. He had already collected all the fish out of the smoker. Together they pulled the baskets of fish from the stream and piled them into Dale's cart. Then Dale pulled the cart into town. Just as dawn broke through the sky, they finished setting out the baskets in a market stall. Then they sat back to wait for customers.

As Matthew observed, Dale sold individual fish to various men and women who put their purchases in their own baskets or bags. Occasionally purchasers from inns came strolling through, requesting larger batches of fish. Instead of naming a direct price, Matthew noticed that Dale started with a larger price, and then bartered with the purchaser until a mutually acceptable price was reached. Then the buyer carried off a burlap sack of fish. Matthew marveled at the process.

"The trick is to start the bid high enough that you can get a profit but not so high that the buyer loses interest," Dale explained. "As a buyer you shouldn't look too eager to purchase at the higher prices. Either way it helps to be familiar with the usual cost of things."

Mid-afternoon Dale sat back and had Matthew sell some of the fish. Matthew was very nervous and felt very awkward stating prices. Then a buyer from an inn stopped in front of the stall.

"How much for two dozen of these fish?" the buyer asked.

Matthew glanced at Dale nervously, trying to remember how much Dale had asked per fish. He calculated for a quantity of twenty-four, and then named a slightly higher price. The prospective buyer flipped over a fish.

"How fresh is it?"

"We just caught them yesterday. They have been stream chilled until today."

The prospective buyer named a much lower price. Matthew shook his head and named a different price. The buyer named a middle price which Matthew thought would be sufficient. Dale nodded almost imperceptibly.

"Sold," Matthew agreed. He took the money and helped the buyer bag the fish.

After the man left Dale nodded. "You did okay. Maybe another day I let you run the stall yourself while I get more fish. Agreed?"

Matthew hesitated. "Agreed. But tomorrow I need to check in at my uncle's shipping business office. They need to know that I am here so they can notify me when his next ship comes in."

Dale nodded slowly. "Okay. We still have some fish to sell tomorrow if you have time."

When they returned home they placed the few remaining fresh fish back in the stream to chill, and hung the covered basket of smoked fish from a tree to stay cool in the night air. Matthew washed his hands from the water beside the door, but even the Fuller's soap did not remove the fish scent from his skin. He found he was rather hungry by the time Dale put a bowl of fish soup again in front of him.

"Do you always eat fish soup?" Matthew asked, dipping a chunk of bread into the soup.

Dale shrugged. "Sometimes I eat fried fish or spread fish pate' on the bread. It varies."

Matthew laughed. "But it is always fish?"

Dale finally grinned, and Matthew discovered Dale's face was fairly good looking when he smiled. "Fish doesn't cost me anything but the effort to catch it."

Matthew looked around the room. "You are not married?" he asked.

Dale's smile faded. "It is hard for fishermen to find wives. Women prefer farmers or merchants. Even sailors have more appeal to a young lass."

Matthew took a risk. "Is there no young lady that you fancy?"

Dale's gaze became distant. "Aye, but her father is not happy with my profession."

"What does she think of you?" Matthew persisted.

Dale suddenly stood. "Enough talk. Tomorrow I go fishing again and you talk to your merchant uncle."

In the morning after a breakfast of fried fish and potatoes, Matthew walked back into town, and then along the main street down near the docks. He had to ask directions a couple of times, and then found the sign he was looking for, "Danforth Shipping". He pushed open the door and walked in.

The front of the business was an open room with two tables near the front window, a couple of chairs pushed up against them. Halfway back stood a waist-high counter running part way across the room. Matthew approached it, and saw on the other side two desks piled high with books and papers. Three bookcases hugged the walls, also loaded down with what looked like accounting books and ledgers. A thin older gentleman with spectacles sat at one of the desks, peering at a ledger, turning pages and making marks in it now and then.

Matthew watched the man for a few minutes, and then cleared his throat. The old gentleman peered up at him distractedly.

"May I help you?" he wheezed through a pipe stuck in his teeth.

"Yes, sir. My name is Matthew. I have a letter for Edward of Danforth." He passed his Uncle John's letter over to the man.

The old man opened the letter, read it, and then looked up at Matthew. "Master Edward isn't in right now. Come back after lunch." He tossed Matthew's letter onto a pile of papers and went back to his ledger.

Matthew hesitated. "Excuse me, sir. May I have my letter back for now?"

The old man stared at him a minute, then retrieved the letter and handed it back to Matthew before silently returning to his work.

Matthew tucked the letter carefully back into his shirt and then walked outside. He spent the morning down by the shipping docks, watching the ships come and go and studying the sailors at work. It amazed him how the men seemed to know how to set each sail and adjust the rigging just right to catch the wind and steer the ships through the harbor. They worked with a teamwork and rhythm that fascinated him. He heard captains and first mates shout commands to their crews, using terminology that Matthew had never heard before. He began to feel nervous about this whole sailing thing. What if he never figured out the sailor lingo?

Just as his stomach was getting hungry, Dale appeared at his side. He offered Matthew a chunk of homemade bread and some sardines to put on it. Matthew tasted one sardine, and then decided he would just eat the bread. The fish was a little too strong for his liking. The two men watched another ship tie up at the dock while they ate, Dale leaning up against a post.

"Impressive, aren't they?" Dale commented between bites.

Unsure if he meant the ships or the sailors, Mathew just nodded.

"I never tire of watching them sail in and out. Big ships, smaller schooners, they are all beautiful."

"Have you ever worked as a sailor?" Matthew asked with curiosity.

Dale shook his head. "I don't take well to a captain telling me what to do." He grinned. "I prefer to live or die by the decisions I make. Besides, I make a better fisherman than a sailor. I inherited my father's knack."

Matthew studied him. "When did you know what you wanted to do when you grew up?"

Dale shrugged. "I always knew. My pappy was a fisherman, and his pappy before him, and so on. One day I will teach my son…" Dale's voice trailed off, and he gazed out toward the sea. He turned back to Matthew. "My younger brother, Allen, chose to be a sailor. Thought it sounded more adventurous. He didn't get along so well with Pappy, so he left home at sixteen. Roberta left home at thirteen to train for the court life. Then it was just the two of us until he died. Pappy's heart gave out."

Dale kept glancing down the wharf as if he were looking for someone. Suddenly he averted his gaze and stared determinedly at his boots. Matthew glanced around and saw a woman walking in their direction down the wharf. She was carrying a basket of goods in her arms. She appeared to be in her early thirties, but Matthew couldn't be sure with the scarf wrapped around her head. She kept glancing in their direction as she drew near, and then made as if to pass them by.

Matthew stood up quickly and nodded his head to her. "Good day, Ma'am."

"Good afternoon," she responded, her gaze flitting back toward Dale. She set down her basket. "Greetings, Dale,"

Dale's gaze finally met hers. "Hello, Lisa."

Lisa smiled. "Has the fishing been good, Dale?"

He nodded dumbly. There was an awkward silence. Lisa looked questioningly toward Matthew.

Matthew extended his hand. "I'm Matthew. My sister Amber and Dale's sister Roberta are friends."

Lisa took Matthew's hand. "Glad to meet you, friend of Dale's." She looked back to Dale, who was inspecting the wharf again. She picked up her basket. "Well, I must be back to work. G'day, Dale."

Dale lifted his eyes briefly and nodded. Lisa turned and continued down the wharf away from them. Dale watched her until she turned around a building down a side street and disappeared.

Matthew studied Dale. "So Lisa is the girl?" he asked gently.

Dale's head turned to Matthew and his gaze slowly focused on him. "Well, must be back to fishing and selling," he sighed, and walked away from Matthew back to his boat tied to the dock.

Matthew walked thoughtfully back to his Uncle Edward's office. The old man with the pipe was still sitting at the desk behind the counter. This time Matthew could hear voices in the office room behind them. The old man took Matthew's letter and went into the office room with it. The voices stopped, and Matthew shifted his feet in the silence. Then a large man came through the office door and walked past the counter, Matthew's letter in hand. He peered at Matthew a moment, and then opened his arms wide.

"Matthew!" he greeted him in a big booming voice, giving him a hug. "Welcome to Portsmouth! You look like my brother Robert did at your age. Maybe a bit prettier though. How are your parents?"

"Fine!" Matthew hoped it was true. He stepped back and studied his uncle. Edward was not as grey as John, but he was three inches taller and much heavier than either of his brothers. There was definitely a family resemblance nonetheless. It had been twelve years since he had seen Uncle Edward.

Edward waved the letter in his hand. "John writes that you want to try your hand as a sailor on one of my ships. Let's see what we can do. Clarence? Bring me the Eastern shipping ledger."

Clarence adjusted his spectacles, went over to one of the shelves against the wall, and pulled off a brown ledger book. He carried it around the counter and laid it on one of the tables by the front window. Edward turned to the page of most recent entries and ran his finger down a list of ship names, mumbling to himself.

His finger paused at one, then he shook his head and moved his finger further down. This time he stopped with a big grin on his face. "Captain James of the Dauntless! There is no finer captain for teaching my nephew the ropes, so to speak. He arrives in port in two weeks. That gives you time to get familiar with sailing ships and the shipping trade." Edward turned. "Clarence, bring me maps of the Eastern trade routes."

Clarence brought over three rolled parchment maps. Edward unrolled all three and laid them out on the table, placing seashells and rocks from a basket onto the corners to keep them flat.

Edward pointed his index finger over one. "This is our island continent with the mainland across the channel. Captain James usually circles the Browning Isle exchanging goods, goes across to the mainland, and then continues down the coast to the far eastern countries for more exotic trade goods. You will be in for a real treat this journey." He traced a route on the other two maps. "Then he works his way back to us here. The journey takes about six months. It will be the experience of a lifetime!"

Matthew grinned at his uncle's enthusiasm. "Thanks, Uncle Edward!"

Edward pounded Matthew on the back, nearly throwing him off balance. "Clarence! Bring Matthew a book on the three-mast sailing schooners. We'll let him study the parts of a ship this afternoon."

Clarence took back the maps and hefted back a large old leather-bound volume with yellowed pages. Matthew opened it carefully. Each page showed drawings of ships, sail positions, masts and ropes, all carefully labeled. At the back was a glossary of terms many pages long; most were words that Matthew had never heard before. He looked up at his uncle, eyes wide.

"Uncle, am I supposed to learn all of this in one day?"

Edward leaned back his head and laughed, deep and rich. "One day? My boy, it takes most of us years to be good at sailing. I mainly want you to be familiar with the structure of a ship so you can appreciate the complexity of sailing, and how important it is to listen to your captain. That and be able to understand his orders. Every little rope and sail adjustment affects the function of the ship, and every sailor is vital to the ship running smoothly. Understand?"

Matthew gulped and nodded.

Edward peered at him. "You say, 'yes sir' or 'no sir' when your captain asks you a question. Understand?"

Matthew squared his shoulders. "Yes sir!"

Edward relaxed. "Good. Now I have some business to complete in my office, and Clarence here can help you if you need anything. Check in every couple of days to make sure you don't miss the Dauntless. Feel free to come in any time to study the books."

Clarence glanced up from his work briefly and scowled at Matthew.

Matthew looked back at his uncle. "Thank you, sir." Then he remembered Dale. "Um, Uncle Edward, may I ask you one more question?"

Edward turned back to him. "What is it?"

Matthew hesitated briefly. "There is a woman named Lisa, a friend of a friend of mine. I need to take something to her. Do you know where I can find her?"

Edward scratched his chin. "Do you know this woman, Clarence?"

Clarence didn't look up. "She works at Fisherman Joe's supply store, if that's the Lisa you want."

"Are there other Lisa's in town?" Matthew asked.

Clarence glanced up. "No," he answered shortly.

Matthew waited for more information but Clarence was back working on his ledger. 'Where is Fisherman Joe's supply store?"

Edward jerked his thumb up the wharf. "That way three blocks, and inland one street."

"Thank you, Uncle Edward," Matthew responded. He sat down and turned back to the first page of the ship's book. "Main mast, mizzen mast, fore mast," he murmured. Uncle Edward retreated back into his office.

After three hours Matthew's eyelids grew heavy and he felt his head nodding. Terms and images swam in his mind in a confused mixture. He had never really enjoyed book learning. He usually learned things better by doing them hands-on. He closed the book, stretched, and then carried the book back to Clarence.

"Thank you, Clarence," Matthew told him. The man placed the book carefully on the shelf. Matthew glanced at his uncle's closed office door. "See you tomorrow."

He exited and spent a few minutes watching sailors unload another ship. Then he walked up the wharf to find Fisherman Joe's. He went up three blocks, then inland to the next street. There were several shops catering to the clientele of a port town. Finally he spotted a wooden sign bearing fishing tackle and the words "Fisherman Joe's". Matthew pushed opened the door and walked in.

The shop was relatively small, but the owner had made the most of the space. Three walls were lined floor to ceiling with shelves displaying clothes, gear, tools, ropes and netting, and anything a fisherman might need. The fourth wall displayed more knick-knacks, including fishing themed mugs and plates, little toy boats, mini sized wooden fish of many varieties, and some shirts embroidered with the words "Fisherman Joe's, Portsmouth". Between other shelves in the middle of the shop lay a rowboat, containing various sizes and shapes of work boots. In the corner behind the door was a stand from which hung bright yellow rubber rain coats.

"May I help you?" a female voice called out

Matthew looked around. There were several customers milling through the shop, but the girl behind the counter was looking at him. It was Lisa. Matthew smiled and went over to the counter.

"Good evening, Lisa. We met this morning down by the wharf. I'm a friend of—"

"Dale's!" Her eyes brightened, and she extended her hand again to Matthew. "Yes, I remember." Her eyes clouded a moment, and she put on her business face. "How may I help you today?"

Matthew surveyed the shop. "I am hiring on as a sailor in two weeks with one of Edward of Danforth's merchant ships, the Dauntless. I am wondering what kind of gear or supplies I might need to take with me?"

"Oh! The Dauntless. That is a good ship." She looked him up and down. "Is this the only kind of clothes you have?"

Matthew nodded and Lisa shook her head. "Let me show you some things. You will need clothes that keep the wind from blowing through you, but dry quickly when you get wet." She sized him with her eyes, and then pulled four different shirts off the shelf. "You also need durable pants that won't tear with hard work, but yet are light weight in case you have to swim in them." She handed him two pairs of pants. "Wool socks, a good rubber rain coat, and a pair of rubber boots." She picked through several boots in the rowboat, and then handed him a pair. "These are my favorite, because they grip wooden decks even when they are wet."

She took him to a shelf where several funny looking shoe slippers were laid out. "These you will want for most of your ship work, because they allow you to easily climb the masts and ropes while gripping with your feet." She smiled at Matthew as he examined the funny shoes. "You better try them on to make sure they fit right," she advised.

She pulled a stool out from under the shelf. He laid aside his armful of clothes and sat down. The shoes felt a little odd, but they fit comfortably enough. He nodded.

She stood looking at him, her hands on her hips. "Most sailors choose their own type of head gear, whether head scarf or hat. You want to start with unobtrusive functional, and work your way up to flamboyant big as you go up in rank. Do you know what your position will be on the ship?"

Matthew shook his head.

"Well, no matter, you can figure the hat out later. Let's purchase your supplies. I assume you can pay now, or do you need credit?"

Matthew patted his money purse hanging from his waistband. "I can pay now."

While Lisa tabulated the items, Matthew took a deep breath. "So, Lisa, any sailors you have your heart set upon?"

She didn't even glance up. "No."

"Are you married or betrothed to anyone?" he pressed.

"No." She rocked back on her heels and stared at him. "Mr. Matthew, I don't know where you are going with these questions, but I don't intend to start a relationship with someone I don't know or have barely met."

Matthew leaned his elbows on the counter. "I am not asking on my own behalf. Is there not anyone in Portsmouth you are interested in?"

She pursed her lips together. "I am going to finish tabulating your purchases."

He studied her for a minute, his eyes never leaving her face. "Could you possibly fall in-like or in love with a fisherman?"

Her eyes met his, and a smile flickered on her lips. "It is possible."

Matthew straightened up and he tapped his fingers on the counter. "So what would be attractive about a fisherman? He smells like fish all the time, he has big calloused hands, and he never goes off anywhere exciting."

Her eyes took on a faraway look. "He doesn't go off and leave you for months at a time."

"He might know how to cook fish many different ways," Matthew suggested.

"He could have a strong back and arms, and know how to work hard," she replied, looking at him again.

"He would appreciate having someone keep him company who knows how to talk the fishing business," Matthew grinned.

"Do you think he would appreciate having someone who could sing to him sea ballads?" she asked wistfully.

"Undoubtedly," Matthew replied. "But the problem might be that he is very shy. I think he feels very awkward about talking to the girl he has a crush on. How do we solve this dilemma?"

Lisa smiled, revealing smile wrinkles at the corners of her eyes. "You tell him to cook up the finest fish feast for you and a friend that he can. I will come with my best biscuits to complement the meal. Then we'll see what the net can catch. Shall we put out the bait tomorrow night?"

Matthew nodded. "Yes. I will be prepared to carry the conversation if need be. Do you know where Dale's house is?"

She nodded. "I don't think you will have to worry about much talk. Do you play any musical instruments?"

"I have a flute," Matthew offered, feeling a pang as he thought of Sarah giving it to him.

"Perfect." She finished tabulating the goods and Matthew paid her. She smiled at him again. "Remember, don't tell him who is coming, just that it is a friend of yours. I don't want him getting cold feet."

Matthew nodded. "Good idea. See you tomorrow night, Lisa."

He picked up his bundle of purchases and whistled as he walked down the road towards Dale's house. It had been a good day. He just hoped tomorrow would work out well too.

Dale was cooking some fish soup when Matthew walked in. He looked up. "What have you got there?" he asked.

"Oh, I thought I better get some gear for when I go on board ship," Matthew responded. "I spent the afternoon trying to learn ship terms." He rubbed the back of his neck. "It's just like learning a foreign language."

Dale grunted. "You'll figure it out eventually. What's your plan tomorrow?"

Matthew's mind raced. "I need your help, Dale. I...I met a girl, and I want to treat her to a fisherman's feast dinner tomorrow night. You know, maybe fried fish, shrimp or crab, and clam chowder. I can cook a fish decently enough. The problem is I'm not very good at cooking most of this. Can you show me?"

Dale grinned. "Yes, I will show you. At dawn we'll dig clams at the beach. Then we'll fish for some mild white fish, girls like that. Perhaps cod." He frowned. "Shrimp takes a special trip to catch. We could trade for this in the afternoon. Then we cook."

Matthew pumped his fist in the air. "Perfect!" Then he looked crestfallen. "I would like to sing her a romantic sea ballad, but I don't know any. Can you teach me one?"

Dale scratched his head. "I know ballads that fishermen and sailors sing to the sea, of high adventure or lost ships. But a romantic ballad? Let me see." He thought for a few minutes, tried to hum a couple of different melodies, and then shook his head. "I can't come up with...Wait! My sister, Roberta, used to sing one, and I played a pan pipe for her. Let me get it."

Dale got his pan pipe and blew various different tunes while Matthew stirred the soup. Then Dale played the melody through, a catchy tune that made Matthew tap his foot. When Dale felt comfortable that he had the tune right, he tried to teach Matthew the words. Dale's voice was deep and a little hoarse, but he got the gist of the melody across adequately. Matthew sang it a few times, while Dale played his pan pipe. Then Matthew fetched his flute and played along with Dale, sometimes with the melody, sometimes harmonizing with it.

Dale put down his pan pipe. "You are good. Maybe we can play while your girl sings. Then you dance."

Matthew grinned. "I hope so. Thanks Dale! Let's eat."

The next morning before dawn Dale woke Matthew by pushing him on the shoulder. "Clamming," he grunted.

Matthew dressed in his new sailing clothes, with rubber jacket and fishing boots. Dale handed him a bucket and shovel and led the way down to the beach. Dale showed him how to watch for bubbles appearing in the sand after a wave went out. Dale would dig deep and quickly, and easily dug up two dozen clams before Matthew found and caught his first one. The buggers could dig down fast. They collected three-fourths of a bucketful by the time the sun was in the sky and the clams no longer were coming up to feed.

Dale then led Matthew to the dock where his fishing boat was tied up. They rowed near the mouth of a little river where Dale threw out his nets. He collected some fish there, and then rowed further upstream. After catching some fish there, he rowed back out along the shoreline near some rocks and caught more fish. Matthew sorted the different keeper fish into baskets: trout, bass, catfish and some cod.

Back at Dale's house he sorted which fish he would keep and which fish he would trade. They ate a quick lunch and then took the fish to the market. Within an hour they had traded for a basket of shrimp and headed back to the house.

Dale got a soup started on the stove, while Matthew cut potatoes and onions. Dale pried clams out of their shells and plopped them into the soup. They picked out five of the best fish, cleaned them, coated them in a special batter, and laid them in a frying pan to cook. Dale showed Matthew how to prepare the shrimp for cooking in a special garlic butter sauce. While Dale watched the fish, Matthew set the table with the best plates, cups and silverware he could find.

Matthew frowned at the table setting. It was too plain. He snapped his fingers and stepped outside. He walked toward the ocean and walked along the sand dunes, eyes focused on the ground. Then he spied what he was looking for, some early spring crocuses. He picked a handful of white and a handful of blue, and brought them back to Dale's little house. He stood them together in a mug with water on the center of the table, then stood back to analyze the effect. Not as good as Monica would have done it, but the table did look nicer.

There was a knock at the door. Matthew's hands suddenly felt sweaty. This wasn't even his girl! He glanced up at Dale who nodded encouragingly at him. Matthew went to the door and pulled it open.

Lisa stood at the door, dressed in a clean spring dress, her hair pulled back in a ribbon and hanging down her back. She smiled and thrust a basket of biscuits into Matthew's hands.

"Good evening, Matthew. May I come in?"

Matthew nodded and stepped back to let her in. As he turned around, he caught sight of Dale's face. It showed complete shock, a flash of joy, and then his eyebrows lowered into a glare aimed at Matthew. Matthew looked away and placed the biscuits on the table.

"Uh, Dale, this is Lisa. She helped me purchase my sailing gear. I think you know each other?"

Dale turned his glare at Matthew into an expression reminiscent of fear as he turned to Lisa. "Hello, Lisa," he mumbled.

"Hello, Dale," she curtseyed. "How may I help with dinner?"

Dale looked over at the fish forgotten on the wood stove. He grabbed a towel and pulled the frying pan off the heat. "Fetch the soup," he commanded.

Lisa reacted faster than Matthew, and expertly unhooked the pot off the fire hook. She carried the heavy pot over to the table and set it down on the towel Matthew set down for her. Dale poured the buttered shrimp into a bowl and brought it over as well. Then he stood gazing at Lisa.

"Which chair shall I sit in?" she asked him.

Dale unfroze and pulled out the chair closest to the fire. She sat in it and smiled up at him. Dale looked hopelessly at Matthew, who motioned with his hands that he should push her and the chair closer to the table. He did so somewhat clumsily. Lisa smiled at him again.

The men sat down across from her. Dale cleared his throat "It was my father's tradition to bless the food on special occasions. This feels like one of those. Is that all right?"

Lisa smiled. "That would be wonderful!"

Dale bowed his head. "Lord, we are grateful for this food and for this company. Bless it to our health. Amen."

"Amen," Lisa and Matthew echoed together.

While Matthew ladled soup into bowls, Dale served fish onto their plates. Then they passed around the shrimp and biscuits. As they ate, Lisa merrily told them stories about sailing and fishing misadventures of her family. Matthew occasionally asked questions to clarify terms he didn't understand, while Dale just watched her and listened.

Finally Lisa leaned back in her chair. "I am full. That was a wonderful meal, gentlemen."

Dale beamed.

Matthew stood up. "I have been learning a sea chanty on my flute. Do you sing, Lisa?"

"Oh, yes! What song is it?"

"The Seaman's Chanty," Dale informed her. "My sister, Roberta, and I used to sing it incessantly."

"I know the song!" Lisa clapped her hands.

Dale fetched his pan pipe while Matthew picked up his flute. When they were ready, Dale and Matthew began playing together while Lisa tapped her foot. After they played through the melody once, she joined in singing.

Lisa's voice was clear and beautiful. During the chorus Dale began tapping his foot to the rhythm. After the third verse he couldn't help himself. He dropped his pan pipe for the chorus, grabbed Lisa by the hand, and started dancing with her around the room. Matthew played through the melody again. After the final chorus she dropped into the chair breathlessly.

"My, that was fun! May we do another?"

The next song was one Matthew didn't know, so Dale played his pipes while Matthew and Lisa danced. Then Dale played another tune while Lisa sang. Matthew eventually picked up on the soulful melody to play along with them. He was nearly in tears by the time Lisa finished singing.

Matthew put down his flute. Dale and Lisa were gazing at each other intensely.

Dale put out his hand to her. "Come walk with me."

She nodded and placed her hand in his. He led her out the door and towards the beach. The setting sun cast an orange and pink glow on the waves and sand. Matthew grinned to himself and stayed inside the cottage. He cleaned the table and put away the leftover food. Then he sat in a chair and dozed by the fire.

It was near midnight when Dale and Lisa returned. They were still holding hands. And they were smiling giddily.

"I asked her to marry me," Dale announced gruffly to Matthew.

"And I told him yes," Lisa added.

"Congratulations!" Matthew jumped up and pumped their hands enthusiastically. "When is the big day?"

"In two weeks," Lisa responded. "I still have to tell my father and let the neighbors know."

"Waiting that long, huh?" Matthew grinned. "No sense in rushing things."

Lisa grasped Matthew's hand and held it. "Thank you for bringing us together."

Matthew looked at Dale. "I think you two were already together, you just hadn't admitted it yet."

CHAPTER 8

THE DAUNTLESS

The day arrived for Matthew to join the Dauntless' crew. He gathered his belongings, girded on his sword, slung his bow over his shoulder and said goodbye to Dale, who was up to see him off. Matthew arrived at the docks just as dawn started lighting the sky. Crews were already busy loading and unloading ships' cargo up and down the wharf. Matthew found the Dauntless, already busy loading cargo.

Matthew waited until there was a small break in the flow of workers, and then made his way quickly up the gangplank. One sailor, wearing a hat with a brim and a feather, seemed to be directing the others. Matthew approached him when he seemed to be between tasks.

"Good morning, Sir! I am Matthew of Sterling..." The name sounded presumptuous in his ears. "I am Matt. Master Edward signed me up to join Captain James and the Dauntless crew. Where should I report for duty?"

The man looked him up and down. "I heard you were coming. I'm Adam, first mate. Have you ever worked on a sailing ship before?"

Matthew shook his head. "I've been on rowboats and fishing boats. And I've been studying up on sailing ships."

Adam sighed. "Another landlubber to train." He used a language expletive that turned Matthew's ears red. "Oh, well. We'll find something for you to do. I'll have the cabin boy get you settled. Conrad!"

A fourteen year old boy climbed up quickly from below decks and ran up to Adam. "Yes, sir?"

"Take Matt here below decks and get him settled." Adam looked at a roster on the bottom of a stack of papers in his hand. "Give him berth 27. He can share that with Shorty." Adam looked up at Matthew. "I am putting you on the night shift under Don. It's the quietest time to learn the ropes." He grinned. "Plus, if you know what you are doing in the dark, you can do it in wind and storm. Now get on, both of you, so I can get these sailors back to work."

Conrad saluted. "Yes, sir!"

Matthew followed Conrad's example and saluted also. "Thank you, sir!" He followed Conrad below deck.

The space below was cramped but clean. They walked down a narrow passageway past doors leading into storage rooms, a galley and mess hall, and to the cabin berth area. The berths were wooden bed frames stacked three high, with straw mattresses. Under each of the bottom berths were six small wooden lockers. Conrad stopped at one of the far berths and pointed to the top bunk.

"This berth is yours, you sleep during the day, Shorty sleeps on it at night. Locker six at the bottom is where you store your belongings."

Matthew eyed the top narrow berth, just above his eye level, with the ceiling a mere two feet above that. "How do I get up there?" he asked.

Conrad grinned. "You climb. Just don't step on the men sleeping below you or you'll get trounced." He eyed Matthew's bow and broadsword. "Those are not going to fit inside your locker."

Matthew opened locker 6 and stuffed his clothes inside the narrow box. It was now full. He glanced at Conrad. "Any idea where I can put my weapons?"

Conrad shook his head. "Just throw them on your berth for now, I guess. We'll figure something out later. I need to show you around the ship."

Conrad took him one deck lower to the main cargo hold. It was divided into three main sections. Men were using winches to lower crates of goods through hatches into the fore and aft holds. Into the center hold a pulley system lowered a platform on which miscellaneous non-crated items were stacked. Conrad adeptly sidestepped sailors moving crates into stacked piles along the ship's bulwarks and strapping them into place. A couple of times Matthew almost ran into a sailor hefting a crate, but sidestepped just in time. It was rather like a dance, but not nearly as fun as dancing with Sarah…

The loading of cargo finished up and the hatches were closed. A shrill whistle blew, and sailors scrambled up the ladders.

"Come on," Conrad panted. "Captain is calling us up to the main deck."

Conrad mounted the ladder steps three at a time, hauling himself up by his hands on the handrails as much as leaping with his feet. Matthew followed as quickly as he could, two steps at a time. On the main deck the men were lining up, and Conrad slid into place at the end of the line. Matthew got in line next to him. The Captain, a gentleman in his fifties, wearing a hat with three long feathers, blew his whistle again and the men stood at attention. Adam walked down the line counting the men.

"Fifty-eight, Sir!" Adam barked. "All men accounted for."

"Fifty-eight?" Captain James looked over the men and his gaze stopped on Matthew. "Ah, yes, the new recruit. What was your name again, son?"

"Matt, Sir!"

"Welcome aboard, Matt," Captain James faced his crew. "All right, men, to your stations. Man the sails!" He turned back to Matthew. "Matt, come with me to my cabin."

Matthew followed Captain James to his cabin below the poop deck. There was a narrow bed on one side, a desk on the other side, and a table in the middle of the room with maps laid out on it. The captain sat in a chair behind his desk, and indicated Matthew to sit in a chair in front of it. Matthew sat down.

Captain James leaned back in his chair and touched his fingers together while studying Matthew. "You want to go by Matt, eh?" Matthew nodded. "Fine then. I read the letter from your uncle. I will take you on board as a member of my crew, but I expect you to work hard like everyone else, from swabbing the decks to cleaning the head."

"Yes, sir," Matthew assented.

"There will be no fighting, no stealing, and no getting drunk on board ship. Of course, the only alcohol I carry on board anyway is for use by the ship's medic to clean wounds. Unfortunately, what you do while off duty in port is beyond my jurisdiction. However, I expect you back in good condition to work when it is time to leave port."

"No problem, sir."

"You will obey my instructions promptly, even if they don't make sense. You will obey Adam, first mate, as though I am speaking. You will follow Don's instructions as if they come from Adam. Understood?"

"Yes, sir!" Matthew responded without hesitation.

"Any questions, Matt?"

Mathew squirmed a little. "I studied the ship's layout and sailing terms while in Portsmouth, but I am not certain what they all mean. I am worried I might make a costly mistake."

Captain James leaned forward and placed his hands on the table. "Good, then it means you'll be careful. Be observant of your crew mates, ask questions when you must. I trust you will pick it up quickly. You should go to Don or Adam with your questions before coming to me." He stood. "Time to go out there and work. Dismissed!"

Matthew left the captain's cabin and nearly got bowled over by a sailor rushing by. Matthew stepped back against the bulwark and just watched. Adam barked out commands from the poop deck above while sailors pulled lines, moved yard arms, and adjusted sails. The ship slowly turned and sailed smoothly past other ships in the harbor. Soon they headed out into the open sea, the waves rocking the sailing ship up and down. He swallowed his stomach and concentrated on what the sailors were doing.

Soon the crew dispersed; some went below to sleep, others went below decks to eat or perform other maintenance tasks. A third of them stayed above deck to man the sails. One young sailor approached Matthew.

"Welcome, I'm Mark," he introduced himself.

"I'm Matt," Matthew put out his hand to shake Mark's.

"You ever sailed on a ship before?" Mark asked.

"Yeah," Matthew hesitated. "Only as a passenger, not as a sailor. But I have been studying books on sailing."

Mark shook his head. "Not the same. I'll have to show you how it's really done."

"Thanks!" Matthew responded. "How long have you been sailing?"

"A year. I signed up so I could get away from my home in Mordred and see the world." Mark leaned in close to Matthew. "My Pa didn't want me to be a sailor so I had to wait until I turned eighteen. The minute I turned of age I signed up."

Matthew grinned. "Then we're about the same age! I turn nineteen this summer."

Mark leaned back. "Perfect! Well, we're on the night shift together, so that means we either sleep or fix things for the rest of this shift. Are you sleepy?"

Matthew shook his head.

"Neither am I. Let's go below and I'll show you the work tasks."

They climbed down the steep stairs and joined a group of sailors in the mess hall. Some were eating, and the others had various work projects laid out on the tables, from ropes and nets to sails and clothing gear.

"Cook doesn't like you to mix food and work," Mark explained. "Let's eat first; then we work."

Cook, a short overweight man, stood in the galley frowning with arms crossed, watching the men work on his tables. When Matthew and Mark arrived, he spooned something out of a big pot that looked like a mess of potatoes and vegetables in a meat sauce. Both of them grabbed a biscuit to go with the stew, and sat down at a table still being used for eating.

Matthew looked down at the stew, hesitating to dip his spoon in. Mark was already shoveling down spoonfuls.

"This food is why this is called the mess hall," Mark told him. "It may not look like much, but the taste is okay and it keeps some meat on your bones. Believe you me, hot food will really hit the spot after a cold night working." He took a bite of biscuit and then rolled it in his hands examining it. "It's the hard tack you have to watch out for. Cook makes these fresh when we are in port, but they get more stale the longer we are on the open seas. The best days are when we catch fresh fish and have a fish feast."

"Sounds awesome," Matthew responded, starting to eat.

Mark showed Matthew how to clean their bowls, spoons and mugs, and where to put them back on the shelf. Then they went over to the task list.

"Too bad," Mark commented. "The only thing left is rope splicing. That's brutal on the hands unless you have great finger calluses."

Mark grabbed some short and long ropes off a hook and took them over to a table, laying them out in front of them. "Do you have a knife?" Mark asked, pulling a small one from his pocket.

"In my locker," Matthew answered. He ran to get the dagger blade Harry had made for him years ago. He laid it out on the table when he returned.

Mark whistled. "That is some blade. It looks more like a short sword than a pocket knife. It would be useful against pirates though. Don't you have anything smaller than that?"

Matthew shook his head.

"Never mind. We'll get you a pocket knife at the next port. Right now we've got to splice rope."

Mark showed him how to weave together ends of rope, fuse them together under a little flame, and wrap the sealed portion for extra strength. Soon they had a long length of secondary back-up rope.

Matthew's mind wandered as they worked. "Mark, what you said about pirates, you were kidding, right?"

Mark gazed at him steadily. "Nope. There have been more pirate sightings the last three years than ever before. They've been attacking merchant ships, killing the crews and stealing their goods. That's why we charge more for the goods we bring to port. It's also why we get paid more working as crew on board ship. More risk, more pay." He grinned.

Matthew felt a little nervous. "Have you seen pirates?"

Mark shook his head. "Naw. I think pirates are mostly working the eastern trade routes anyway. We should be fine."

Matthew found his larger blade was more unwieldly than Mark's little one for working with the ropes. It was good for cutting off large frayed ends, but he watched jealously while Mark deftly cut into the rope ends with his small blade before weaving the rope ends together.

Finally they were finished. Mark showed him where to store the coiled finished ropes, then led him to the berth area. A gong rang to signal change of shift.

"We better get some sleep. Normally our sleep shift is right after deck work, but sometimes they let us change it up on port days."

Fortunately, Mark's bunk mate wasn't due to sleep until the night shift. Matthew wasn't so lucky. A tall sailor was standing in front of his bunk, holding Matthew's sword, bow, and quiver of arrows in his hand. He looked at Matthew accusingly.

"Can't sleep with this stuff on my bunk," he muttered.

"I am so sorry." Matthew took his weapons back.

"Shorty, this is Matt, our new crew mate," Mark introduced them. He turned to Matthew. "We call him Shorty because he's the shortest of his three brothers. Right Shorty?"

Shorty nodded. "Name is compliments of my father. I'm now taller than he is. My real name is Robin. I prefer Shorty."

"Glad to meet you, Shorty." Matthew held out his hand. "I guess I'm your bunk mate. I'm happy to sleep somewhere else this shift so you can have the bunk."

Shorty nodded and climbed up to the top bunk, deftly folding himself in. "Just keep the bunk clear in future."

"Can do." Matthew lay down on another bunk that Mark showed him. He tried to fit his weapons next to him.

Mark eyed him. "I know a place you can store your equipment, Matt. There is a broom barrel in the corner of the mess hall where they won't be in the way. Come, I'll show you."

When Matthew walked into the mess hall carrying his sword, bow and quiver of arrows, several of the sailors looked up from their meals to watch him. Some of them sniggered.

"Looks like our new boy is a hunter. Think he wants to catch whales?"

"Minnows, more like it. I don't think those darts are big enough to harm even a sea bass."

Face aflame, Matthew walked past them and stored his weapons behind the brooms in the barrel in the corner. As he turned to walk out again, one middle aged sailor grasped his arm.

"I'll be watching you, Landlubber," he told him. "If you don't pull your weight around here, I'll have you dropped off at the nearest port. You are on a sailing ship now, understand?"

"Yes sir," Matthew murmured.

As they left the mess hall, Mark turned to him. "That last sailor who talked to you is Don, our night shift boss. Keep your nose clean around him."

Matthew nodded. He was so wound up he wasn't sure he could sleep. But soon on the bunk he fell into fitful dreams.

He dreamed he heard a low whistling. Mark shook Matthew awake. It was getting dark through the portholes.

"Matt, wake up. We need to eat something before our shift starts."

Matthew's eyelids felt heavy. He had just gotten into a deep sleep. This night shift was going to be hard to adjust to. While they quickly ate, Matthew recognized Shorty, sewing a torn sail canvass in the lantern light. He did not look up from his work.

"If you have a jacket, you will want to wear it," Mark advised. "It gets cold on the night shift."

Matthew dug into his locker and pulled out a long sleeved shirt and put it on. Back on deck men were changing shift. Sailors were climbing down the rigging while others were climbing up. Others pulled at the lower ropes from the deck or adjusted booms while Don, the second mate, shouted orders from the poop deck. Another sailor stood at the helm, holding the course of the ship steady. Every now and then Don shouted out to turn the sails, and then the ship tacked for a while in a little different direction. Don would check the compass at the helm in the lantern light, and study the wind sock flying nearby. Don had Matthew stand next to him, and in between instructions to the sailors at the sails explained to Matthew what they were doing.

After half an hour Don turned to him. "Now it's your turn, Matt. I'm putting you on the foremast, lower topsail. Your job is to move lines or adjust sails as I instruct. Understand?"

"Yes sir!" Matthew stepped down from the poop deck and hurried over to the foremast. He found a rope ladder and climbed up partway. Then he gingerly ducked under stays, scooted across the yard for the lower topsail, and positioned himself halfway out, mimicking how the other sailors perched along the sails.

Matthew did his best to follow Don's instructions, but by the end of the night shift he was discouraged and exhausted. He had trimmed the sails incorrectly three times, nearly fallen off the rigging twice, and once got the sail so entangled in the lines that the ship listed badly until another sailor scooted over and untangled it.

"Thanks, sir," Matthew told him sheepishly.

"S'all right, mate," he responded with a grin. "We all have to learn some time."

Matthew hoped he didn't capsize the ship while trying to learn the ropes.

At dawn and the end of the night shift, they reached Greensbay port in the eastern country of Renling. The crew unloaded and loaded goods, and then Mark advised Matthew they better sleep.

"This is a short stop, and then we are off again," Mark told him. "During our repair shift I think I better show you how to work the sails."

"Thanks." Matthew hesitated. "I think you also better teach me how to tie knots. The sailors tied the ropes to the moorings a lot faster than I could even see it."

Mark nodded. "Sure, Mate. Can do."

Despite the sleep hours being shifted around, Matthew fell asleep quickly, this time in his assigned bunk. He awoke before the crew shift change whistle blew. They ate quickly in the mess hall, some sort of seafood soup and biscuits. Then Mark started showing him the knots he would need to use on board ship. Matthew did okay with most of them, but the bowline knot seemed beyond his ability to do.

"No matter," Mark told him. "You'll get it eventually. I need to show you how to adjust the sails."

Taking a piece of sail to be mended, Mark showed him some basic techniques for furling and unfurling the sails, plus how the lines should be moved to get the sails in correct positions. Then they went above deck to watch the afternoon shift in action. Mark explained to him how the sails needed to be turned or adjusted to tack the boat into the wind, to get it where it needed to go. By the time their shift was to start Matthew thought he could figure out most of the directions Don was likely to give him. Sure enough, the second night went better.

Early in the morning they had crossed the channel to the main continent and sailed into a little port for a small cargo exchange. Matthew jumped quickly onto the dock, eager to practice the knots he had learned to tie the rope to the moorings. He thought it looked pretty good until Don came over and yanked on it. The rope pulled loose and unraveled before Matthew's eyes.

"No! I was sure I wrapped it correctly!" Matthew moaned.

Don grinned. "You did until the very end. You have to flip a loop of rope over itself to secure it. Like this." He wrapped the figure eight loops around the mooring, and then showed Matthew how to create the securing loop. Then he untied the rope and handed it to Matthew. "Do it again," he instructed.

This time Matthew got the rope wrapped right. Don slapped him on the back. "I'll make a sailor of you yet," he commented. "Now go load some crates."

"Yes sir!" Relieved, Matthew jumped back onto the deck and hurried to move crates.

Adam supervised a quick exchange of crates while Captain James was on shore making agreements with future buyers. Then the Dauntless left port again to sail south along the coast.

While traveling along the coast, the work shift crews let down some fishing nets to restock the ship's food supplies. The next few meals offered some interesting new fish varieties, a shark and a squid. For breakfast there was turtle soup.

The next morning as they were falling asleep, Mark told Matthew about the big port they were coming to next.

"We'll probably have to unload during the time of our normal sleep shift, but Captain expects all hands to move crates. He'll just have a skeleton crew for most of our shift, run by the most junior members, which means us. Then we get paid for our work and are allowed twenty-four hours of shore leave. If you're tired we can nap a bit before we go on shore. I have some wonders to show you at Port Mer Eclat!"

"Sounds awesome!" Matthew fell asleep wondering what new experiences he would find at a big seaport.

Chapter 9

CLARISSE

Early in the morning, The Dauntless pulled into Port Mer Eclat, the large port across the channel from Matthew's homeland. Matthew was starting to get the hang of what was to be done on the ship. He actually managed to turn and drop his part of the sails without anyone having to show him what to do. As they pulled up against the dock, he jumped over the starboard bow and tied one of the mooring ropes. He wasn't as fast as the other sailors, but when Adam walked by to check his knot, he just nodded and didn't make Matthew retie it. Matthew grinned and followed the other sailors back up the gangplank. Captain James stood on deck, barking out unloading orders.

"Carry the crates off first, and pile them on the dock for now. Ye don't get your pay until the cargo is all unloaded. Hurry up now!"

Men rushed everywhere. A line formed on the stairs from the hold, men passing the smaller crates up the hatch to the deck. Other men used the pulleys and winches to haul up the larger and heavier crates through the big freight hatch, and then swing them aside from the ship onto the dock. Matthew helped others carry the smaller crates down the gangplank onto the dock. This was a large load, so it took several hours to transfer all the merchandise out. As soon as they were done, Captain James faced the men lined up before him.

"After you receive your pay, you have twenty-four hours shore leave. Be back by noon tomorrow to load up the next cargo. The ship leaves at high tide tomorrow."

Captain James walked down the row handing men their coins from the bag at his waist. Conrad walked behind him, marking down the pay each man received. Matthew was excited; Mark had told him this pay would be the biggest yet, timed so he could spend money in the big port. After getting paid, the boys napped a couple hours, then got up to start their shore leave.

"We should explore around town first," Mark told him. "Don't spend any money until you have seen everything, and then decide. Also, don't plan on spending all your money in one port. Most of the sailors do, then when they're flat broke they don't have anything to send home to their families, and they are stuck working the hardest, longest jobs."

As they got off the boat, they ran into Don, Adam and their friends hanging out on the docks.

"Where are you boys off to so fast?" Don asked.

"Looking around town," Matthew began.

"None of your beeswax," Mark retorted.

"Maybe they are going to find some toys to play with," Curly, one of the sailors, sniggered.

Mark shrugged. "So what if I am?"

Adam slapped Don's shoulder. "Let them go."

Don was eyeing Matthew. "I think you boys ought to join us for supper tonight at La Castille, for fine dining and entertainment. We could show you what grown men do in the city."

"Ah, lay off them, Don," Ricky, one of the other sailors cut in. "Let them be boys a little longer."

"Maybe you're scared to join us?" Don asked.

Mark stared him down. "No, we're not scared."

"All right then," grinned Don. "The fun starts around eight."

Mark was quieter than usual as he and Matthew walked into the city. He hardly seemed to notice as Matthew commented wondrously at the shops, the finely dressed people, and the multi-story homes. Even Portsmouth in Sterling was not this big or this busy. Soon they came to the marketplace, larger and more sprawling than any Matthew had ever seen. Mark finally became animated, looking at all the food, wares and weapons. Matthew found himself craving the fresh fruits. After buying and sampling almost one of every kind, Matthew finally felt satisfied.

"You know all that fruit is going to run right through you," Mark commented, eying Matthew sideways.

"I don't care," Matthew grinned, patting his stomach comfortably. "It's been a long time since I have tasted such good fresh fruit."

Mark stopped to look at a table of long daggers. "I think I ought to get one like yours, Matt. Which one do you recommend?" He picked up one that looked gold plated, glittering with jewels on the hilt.

Matthew ran his finger along the blade edge. "It's not very sharp. Also, gold is a very soft metal. This one looks more for show." He picked up and examined several, then handed a plain steel one to Mark. "Heft this one. Does it feel balanced in your hand, sturdy but not too heavy?"

Mark tested it in his hand, swooshing it through the air. "Aye, that feels good, Matey." He turned to the sword merchant. "How much?"

"Sixty," was the reply.

Mark gazed at the coins in his purse.

"Too much," whispered Matthew. "Barter with him."

"I can pay thirty," Mark offered.

The merchant shook his head. "Sixty."

Matthew pulled on Mark's arm. "Let's go."

Mark reluctantly followed. The merchant ran after them carrying the dagger. "Fifty!" he called.

Mark stopped. "Thirty-five."

The merchant looked uncomfortable. "Forty-five. Final offer."

Matthew nodded.

"Forty-five," agreed Mark. He paid the merchant, who gave him the plain steel blade in return.

"Nice job bartering," grinned Matthew. "That blade probably was worth at least fifty. Let's get you a scabbard for it. Any plain sturdy one will do. You don't want it to look too fancy."

After getting an inexpensive leather scabbard, Mark took Matthew by a shop with various hats. "You need your own sailor's hat, mate," he told him. "You should get one like mine." Mark touched the little feather on the back of his small brimmed hat.

Matthew laughed. "Fine, but I'm not ready yet for a feather." He looked around the shop until he spotted a plain brown brimmed hat that fit his head perfectly. He bought it and perched it on his head jauntily.

Mark laughed at him good naturedly. "Plain but useful. Now you are one of us."

Matthew bought bread and cheese for Mark and himself. They wandered back to the docks to watch ships coming and going out to sea, and feed the seagulls some of their bread crusts.

"Where did you learn how to barter?" Mark asked.

"A fellow named Dale in Portsmouth showed me. I didn't grow up doing much bartering. But I have had my share of talking other boys into doing things I wanted." Matthew grinned sheepishly.

Mark sighed. "In our small town we mostly traded goods, and anyone from out of town wouldn't sell except at their asking price. We couldn't afford much that wasn't manufactured or grown locally. It's hard to know what things are really worth."

They wandered back toward the city center as the afternoon grew later. They listened to some minstrels play in the court in front of the cathedral, and clapped as dancers spun to the music. One booth advertised tattoos.

"Hey, Matt!" Mark said excitedly. "We should get a tattoo. All the sailors have one."

Matthew shrugged, but looked over the designs with Mark.

"I think I'll get this shark one," Mark pointed it out. Matthew thought it looked more like a dolphin, but he didn't say so. Mark handed the man his coins, and the artist began applying it to Mark's right upper arm.

His assistant observed Matthew. "Here are some other fine tattoo designs. You should choose one that has special meaning to you."

Matthew wasn't sure any of the designs spoke to him. Finally Mark called over to him. "You better hurry up and choose one, slow poke. My tattoo's almost done."

Matthew's eye landed on an orchid design. "That one," he decided.

The assistant smiled. "Thinking of your lady?"

"Something like that." Matthew sat down and the man started applying it to his left upper arm. It stung more than he expected, as the man applied colored ink into his skin with a hot needle.

Finally they were done. Mark and Matthew looked at each other's tattoos.

"Now we are sailors," Mark commented proudly.

Matthew was already regretting having done it. He wasn't so sure his parents would approve. But beyond that, what if he decided a year from now that he didn't want the orchid design on his body anymore?

Soon eight o'clock drew near.

"I guess it's time to join Don's gang at La Castille," Mark stated.

"We don't have to go, you know," Matthew commented.

Mark looked both nervous and excited. "What do you think they'll do if we don't show up?"

Matthew grinned. "Probably call us Mama's Boys and Nappy Wearers. Doesn't bother me if it doesn't bother you."

Mark frowned. "I'd rather not be considered a toddler any more. I was the youngest brother for too long. It's time to be considered a man. That's one of the reasons I joined this outfit."

Matthew nodded somberly. "I'll go with you then."

They found La Castille on a side street in a seedier part of the city. The sign over the door portrayed a mug of spirits and a bed. Taking deep breaths the boys went inside.

The bar was noisy, full of men drinking and playing gambling games. Mark spotted Don in the center of a group of the Dauntless' sailors, loudly telling a bawdy story. He looked already partially inebriated. Adam was not among them. After Don finished the punch line, amid roars of laughter and groans from his mates, he looked up and spotted Mark and Matthew.

"Matt and Mark!" he yelled loudly. "I was beginning to think you weren't coming! Come on over and set yourselves down. First drink's on me!"

Mark and Matthew pulled up chairs to the table and looked around. The other sailors had drinks at various levels of fullness, and smelled of various levels of intoxication. Don waved a hand and a waitress came over.

"Get my two friends a drink. Mark and Matt, what can I get you?"

"Just an ale," replied Matthew.

Don laughed. "An ale? That's hardly anything. Get them the house drink, The Firebomb. That's a man's drink!"

Mark hesitated and then nodded. "Okay."

Matthew shook his head. "Just an ale," he repeated. "And a loaf of bread." It seemed to Matthew that Don's eyes narrowed momentarily, but then he turned to his companions to tell another story. Matthew determined to keep his wits about him tonight.

When the drinks came, all eyes focused on Mark as he took his first swallow. Mark tasted the edge of the mug, and then took a gulp. His eyes widened and watered, and then he choked, spraying some of his drink out onto the table.

Don laughed. "That drink is for sipping, not gulping!"

"Water!" Mark gasped.

"You might as well give him milk," Don commented harshly. "I knew he was a Mamma's Boy."

Mark took another sip, and managed to keep a straight face as he gazed at Don and swallowed. But his knuckles whitened where they gripped the mug's handle.

"The kid's got guts," Ricky commented. Don nodded, and they went back to their stories. Mark gasped as a tear ran down his nose.

Matthew tore off a chunk of his bread and handed it to Mark. "Here, eat." Mark nodded and as he ate the redness in his face abated.

Matthew had felt a tingling sensation in his hands as he watched Mark drink the Firebomb, which was why he had made Mark eat. It reminded him of the times when his sister Amber was about to do something stupid or dangerous. He didn't know why he seemed to know when she would need him to be there, but he had been able to rescue her several times, and stop her from making bad decisions. His connection to her had broken when she got married to Harry. He had experienced the tingling with his younger sister Stephanie to a lesser degree; she was not as likely to get into trouble as Amber had been. He wondered why he was feeling this now with Mark. Was it because he had felt a kinship with him, like the brother he never had?

Matthew glanced at Don entertaining the other men, and then turned back to Mark and spoke in a low voice. "Mark, we don't have to stay here. C'mon, let's get out of here."

Mark looked around at the other men. "I'm okay. I want to stay."

Matthew nudged him with his elbow. "I don't think I want to stay. Let's go."

Mark looked Matthew in the eyes, and then looked down at his mug. "You go ahead. "I'm staying. It's time to prove I'm a man."

Matthew felt the skin tingling more strongly. He was not going to abandon Mark now. "Fine. But we stay together. Just be careful."

Don turned back to them. "Mark and Matt, it's time to teach you how to play cards. First game is practice, and then we play for real." He explained the rules, dealt out the cards to everyone, and they played through. The rules were a little confusing, and the other sailors obviously had more practice with the strategy. Mark and Matthew finished last.

"Not bad for a first time," Don slapped their backs congenially. "This time we each put in a bit coin, and the winner keeps the whole pot. Ready?

Reluctantly Mark picked up a bit coin out of his money purse and put it on the table. Matthew scooted his chair back a bit and folded his arms.

"I'm just going to watch a bit," he stated.

"Whatever," Don commented, dealing the cards again. Matthew could tell he was disappointed, and he grinned a little inside. It felt good to throw Don off balance.

This game Mark played a little better, but he still came in last place. Don won and collected the money winnings.

"No fair, Don," Ricky grumbled. "Let someone else deal."

"Fine, you deal, Ricky." Don handed him the cards.

Ricky dealt around the cards, and everyone put in another coin. This time Ricky came in last place, and Curly won. Matthew thought he was picking up on some of the game strategy. He watched through the next game also just to make sure. Mark sweated nervously as he played, anxious not to lose any more money. He made some careless mistakes and came in last place again.

"I'm done playing," Mark exclaimed, throwing down his cards.

"Aw, don't quit now," Don goaded him. "We were just about to increase the worth of the pot." He threw in a larger coin, and the other sailors matched with theirs.

"I'll take his place," Matthew announced suddenly. "Isn't it Curly's turn to deal?" He scooted in between Don and Curly, and threw a coin into the center. Curly dealt the cards, and they began to play.

Matthew watched Don surreptitiously. He had observed him on the ship over the past month, and knew when Don was confident and when he was under pressure. Matthew made his plays thoughtfully, unafraid of making the other players wait. Based on Don's subtle reactions to the other player's moves, Matthew deduced some of what was going on in Don's hand, and made his own plays accordingly. When the game was done and everyone revealed their hands, Don had a pretty good hand. But Matthew's choice of cards actually beat Don's.

Don looked at Matthew incredulously. "I am impressed, Matt. Are you sure you haven't played this game before?"

Matthew shook his head, "Not this exact game." He declined to tell Don that he always had done well with patterns and mathematics.

Don, looking at Matthew, pulled out a gold piece and laid it on the table. "Play again?" The other sailors groaned.

"No thanks," Matthew scooted back, pocketing his winnings. "Once is enough for me."

"Well then, it's time for another round of drinks," Don announced. "What would you like this time, Matt and Mark?"

"I'll stay with my ale," Matthew replied firmly, stuffing another bite of bread into his mouth. "And I'll buy my own."

"Ale for me also," Mark answered, handing a coin to the waitress.

Don frowned transiently, and then turned to the other men to tell some more stories. Half way through his ale, Matthew felt the need to relieve himself. The waitress showed him where the water closet was at the back of the tavern. Mark followed him. When they came back to the table, Don greeted them jovially.

"Mark and Matt! I've just decided what I'm going to call you: M and M. Then it doesn't matter whose name I say first, I can address both of you together. M and M! It has a nice ring to it, don't you think?"

The other men laughed and nodded.

"I propose a toast," Don announced, raising his drink. "To M and M, the finest young men on the Dauntless!" He took a swig of his drink, but watched Mark and Matthew over the top of his mug.

Matthew started to drink from his ale, but the odor and taste was different. He pretended to take a deep swallow, and then put his mug down. Mark lowered his mug slowly.

Don nodded at them. "Another toast! To Captain James of the Dauntless!"

The men drank again. As he pretended to drink, Matthew kicked Mark's foot under the table. Mark coughed out his gulp of ale. Matthew reached over toward Mark to pat him on the back, and accidentally on purpose swept Mark's drink off the table.

"I am so sorry," he told Mark. "I'll get you a refill in a minute." He took his own mug and upended it toward his mouth, letting most of it dribble down his chin. "I'll also get myself some more." He grabbed Mark's arm to come with him.

As Matthew stood up, Don's brief look of fury was replaced by a determined smile. Mark followed Matthew over to the bar.

Mark coughed a couple more times. "What was that about?" he asked.

"I think Don is trying to get us really drunk," Matthew whispered. "That was more than ale in our drinks just now. I don't know what he plans, but I don't trust that snake. Best we stay clear headed." He gazed at the bottles of liquor displayed on the wall.

"What drink do you recommend for the adventurous of spirit?" Matthew asked the bartender loudly. He could imagine Don perking up his ears behind them. He slid onto a stool at the counter. Mark followed suit.

The bartender showed them several bottles. Matthew pretended to study each one." We'd like a drink that looks strong, but is really watered down," he told the bartender quietly. "What can you do for us? I can pay the full drink price."

"I've got just the drink for you in the back," the bartender responded loudly. "Just a moment."

Matthew sat looking toward the drinks. Mark looked around, and then nudged Matthew. "There are some ladies over there," Mark whispered.

Matthew glanced toward the corner of the room. Several women in colorful dresses with full-bodied skirts conversed and laughed with some men sitting at the table there. One woman sat down on the lap of one of the men and kissed him. One of the women turned, revealing a low cut dress. Matthew turned back toward the bar, his face burning.

"Whoa!" Mark gasped.

Matthew's mind was whirling. He knew now what Don's plan was. He grabbed Mark's elbow and pulled him back facing the bar.

"Listen to me, Mark. Whatever Don has in mind, you do not have to do it. You might choose to pretend to go along with it for now, but you do not have to prove anything to me or to Captain James. Remember that. I will leave with you any time you are ready."

Mark glanced at him. "I am not going to miss my chance to prove myself to the other sailors, Matt. Do what you want."

Matthew stared glumly at the bottles until the bartender returned. The two mugs nearly overflowed with golden foam. The bartender named his price and Matthew paid it reluctantly. He had charged them a full drink price. Matthew followed Mark back to the table of sailors and they sat down.

Don looked at the drinks approvingly. "Drink up men. You will need your courage for the next part of the show. It's almost time for the dancing."

Matthew looked up from his 'drink' with interest. He knew how to dance several dance forms. He wondered what dances sailors knew. Folk dances? Gypsy?

Suddenly a piano started playing. It was somewhat out of tune, but the melody was lively. A line of girls in the brightly colored dresses Mark and Matthew had seen earlier stepped out on stage, kicking their legs high in the air. The men in the room all clapped and stomped their feet in rhythm. Mark's eyes bulged. Matthew had never seen so much leg in his life. He closed his eyes tightly, feeling distinctly uncomfortable. He tried to focus on the colors of the skirts in his mind's eye.

"Now that's some dancing!" Curly commented as the other men whistled.

The girls danced four numbers, and then came down to mingle with the men. Three of them came over to the sailor's table.

"Bon jour, Don," one of the older women greeted him. "You have some new men with you tonight."

"Good evening, Connie," Don smiled at her dreamily. He introduced his crew. "And this is Mark and Matt, our newest mates."

Connie raised an eyebrow. "Are they joining you for the whole evening?"

Don grinned crookedly. "Aye. Who do you recommend for them?"

Connie studied Matthew and Mark thoughtfully. "Marie and Clarisse!" she called across the room. Two pretty girls about their age came over to join them. "I want to introduce you to Mark and Matt. Please keep them company this evening." They curtseyed and smiled at the boys. Connie touched a hand to Don's shoulder. "I will be supervising things a while tonight, Don. See you around."

"Save a dance for me, Connie," Don called. He looked after her hungrily as she walked away, swinging her hips gracefully. Then Don turned back to the table. Two sailors got up with the other two women, and joined them at more private tables. That left Don and Ricky, Mark and Matthew, Marie and Clarisse at their table.

Marie sat down and picked up a deck of cards. "We have a game to show you how to play."

Mark struck his hand to his forehead. "Not if it involves gambling money. I already know I am not good at those games."

Marie giggled. "Oh, we are not allowed to gamble with your money. This game is called 'Truth or Dare'. Depending on the card you draw, someone gets to ask you a question you have to answer truthfully, or they dare you to do something. Obviously it has to be something that can be done in this room."

Matthew groaned and Clarisse laid a hand on his arm. "Don't worry," she told him. "You don't have to do it if you don't want to."

Matthew thought of his sister, Amber, and the trouble she had gotten into eight years earlier by accepting a dare. But Clarisse's eyes looked so warm and innocent, he couldn't imagine getting into too much trouble.

"Fine," he answered a little more gruffly than he wanted to. "I'll play."

Ricky got up from the table. "I think I'll go have a drink at the bar. Coming, Don?"

Don nodded comfortably and left with Ricky. The girls made Mark and Matthew feel good, the way they listened and smiled at them. Marie dealt out the cards evenly among the four of them.

"The numbers Ace to six are Truth cards. Seven to King are Dare cards. Jokers are your choice. Clarisse and I will go first." Marie drew a card. "Nine. One of you boys dare me to do something." She looked at them expectantly.

Mark grinned. "Pat your head with one hand while you rub your stomach with the other."

Marie tried, but kept patting both or rubbing both.

Matthew laughed. "That is exactly what happens when my little sister tries to do that."

Clarisse drew a five. "Ask me a question."

Matthew nodded. "Tell me about your family."

Clarisse smiled sadly. "I was born in a little town near the shore in the south of the country. My parents died of the plague when I was nine. My younger brother and I were separated and sent to foster families. I ran away when I was thirteen and came to the city."

"I am sorry," Matthew mumbled. Clarisse shrugged.

Everyone was silent for a few minutes. Then Mark drew a card: Jack.

"Show me your muscles," Clarisse dared.

Mark flexed his arms, and then hefted a chair over his head. At the bar Don rolled his eyes and looked away.

Matthew drew a three.

"Why did you become a sailor?" Marie asked.

"I wanted to see the world."

"That is too cliché," Marie frowned. "Why else did you leave home?"

Matthew shifted uncomfortably. "I didn't want to become a knight. You are expected to defend the ladies which is fine, but you have to serve a Lord and risk your life on someone else's whim."

Marie drew a ten.

"Sing a ballad," Matthew asked her.

Marie nodded and stood up. She linked her fingers together in front of her and began to sing in a sweet soprano voice about "Beautiful Annabelle Lee". Mark closed his eyes as he listened about the lass, who loved and died in a kingdom by the sea.

Marie finished and Mark sighed. "That was beautiful," he breathed.

"Merci," she smiled and sat down. Customers in the tavern clapped and hooted and pounded their mugs. Marie blushed.

Clarisse pulled an ace card.

Mark tapped his chin. "What is your dream job or vocation?"

Clarisse stared off into the distance. "I really wanted to be a hair dresser. I wished to style lady's hair." She lowered her eyes. "But it is a fantasy."

Marie nudged Mark. "Your turn."

Mark pulled a queen. "Dare."

Clarisse's eyes gleamed. "Dance a jig."

"No! I am a terrible dancer!"

Marie signaled the pianist, who started plunking out a lively tune.

"Go on!" Clarisse pushed him up from the chair and started clapping a rhythm.

Mark started moving his feet in time to the music, performing a step that vaguely resembled a jig.

"Balance a mug on your head!" Marie suggested, handing him his nearly empty mug.

Mark balanced it for several steps, and then caught it as it toppled. He bowed while Matthew and the ladies clapped.

Matthew drew a two.

"Tell us about your first kiss," Clarisse asked him, leaning her chin on her hands, elbows on the table.

Matthew looked thoughtful. "This fine lady in the castle had just taught me how to make a berry tart. We were in the kitchen, and I threw myself into her arms. I totally melted her heart." He winked. "I was almost eleven years old and she was the matronly castle cook."

Clarisse laughed until the tears ran down. Mark just shook his head. "She means your first romantic kiss, mate."

Matthew ducked his head. "I really haven't kissed a girl that way. I've only kissed my sisters and my mother." He grinned. "There was this girl named Sarah I really wanted to kiss, but we were from different stations in life."

Mark looked at Matthew open-mouthed. "You haven't lived, laddie, until you have tasted a lady's kiss."

Marie drew a king. Mark grinned. "Kiss me, Marie. Let's show Matt how a woman kisses a man." Mark stood and held out his hand. Marie took it and faced him, her face unreadable. Mark cupped her chin with his hand and kissed her lingeringly on the mouth. When they parted, Mark raised his eyebrows at Matthew. "See? Easy." They sat down again.

Clarisse pulled a seven and laid the card on the table without looking up.

Matthew gazed at her. "Let down your hair, Clarisse."

She smiled a little, appearing slightly relieved. She pulled her hair pins out, unrolling a long braid that had been fastened at the back of her head. Her dark tresses fell past her waist. She loosened the braid and then sat with her hands in her lap.

Matthew put a finger under her chin and tilted her head up until her eyes met his. "You have beautiful hair, Clarisse. I can see why you want to be a hairstylist." He smiled and let his hand drop.

Mark shook his head at Matthew's missed opportunity and drew a six.

Clarisse pursed her lips thoughtfully. "Tell us what you like best about sailing."

Mark leaned back in his chair. "Ahh, my favorite subject. I love the sense of freedom and adventure, the wide expanse of ocean, and the cool wind in my hair." He tossed his head to shake the bangs out of his eyes.

Matthew pulled an eight.

Marie folded her arms. "Tell us a poem."

Matthew scratched his head. "The only one I can remember is one about a family going on a walk and Father falls into the pond."

Marie nodded. "Tell it."

By the time Matthew finished telling his dramatic recitation, the other three were gripping their sides laughing.

Mark sighed. "That is funny. Especially when I am tired and it is late at night."

Matthew's eyes were getting sleepy, and his head was feeling a little fuzzy from the watered down liquor drink. By now half of La Castille's patrons had left, and Matthew set down his empty mug.

"Ladies," he announced. "I am tired and we should go. I need to find a place to sleep." The moment he said it he knew he had worded it wrong.

"Oh, you don't have to go elsewhere to find a place to sleep!" Marie exclaimed. "There are rooms at La Castille. We will show you."

Marie grabbed Mark's hand, and beckoned the others to follow her. Clarisse latched onto Matthew's elbow and led him along. As they went through a door leaving the pub, Matthew caught sight of Don's grinning face at the bar.

"Sleep well…" his laughing voice echoed after them.

Matthew had not intended to fall into Don's plot for them. Instantly his mind became alert, searching for a solution to his dilemma.

Marie led them down a hall with closed doors. "This is the Inn portion of La Castille," she explained. "You can rent a group room from the Innkeeper, or you can get a single room through us." She stopped at a door and dangled a key in her hand. "The catch is, Mark, you have to share the room with me." She eyed him coyly.

Mark nodded and fumbled with his coin bag. "Okay, I'm ready." His voice cracked. Marie led him inside and shut the door.

Matthew looked at Clarisse. She smiled shyly and led him to another door. Inside, the room was sparse and smelled a little stale, but the bed at least looked comfortable. Clarisse locked the door and lit a candle, then turned to face Matthew. She started untying the bodice of her dress.

"Whoa, whoa, whoa!" Matthew quickly turned his back on her. "Don't...undress. I am not planning on doing...whatever you planned."

Clarisse froze uncertainly. "What? Why? Do you not find me pretty enough?"

Matthew cleared his throat. "You are very pretty, and I like you well enough that I cannot do this. And I want to save myself for my future wife someday. Didn't you tell me that you wanted your own hairdressing shop?" He turned to face her. "Why then are you here? Why don't you go start your shop?"

Clarisse bit her lip and looked up at the ceiling. "I cannot save enough money to leave here. They watch me all the time and I cannot run away." She suddenly looked terrified. "Where else would I go? They took me in here when I had no one else to turn to. Without money, no one else in the city will take me in. If I refuse to work...they will beat me." The last she said in a whisper.

Matthew sat down on the bed and just stared at her. She sank onto the bed beside him, twisting her thumbs with her fingers.

"What can I do?" Matthew asked her, his skin tingling like it had for Mark earlier that evening or for his sisters in years past.

She looked up at him pleadingly. "Don't make me leave you tonight. As soon as I go they make me find another...companion. Sometimes they are rough. I don't think I can face that tonight, not after remembering my dream... that I will never see come to pass."

Matthew had a sudden idea. He stood and dumped his purse full of money onto the bed. "I won a betting game tonight. I don't need this money. I'll earn more at the next port. Will this be enough to leave here and get your hair salon started?"

She gazed incredulously at it. "Yes," she breathed. "I think so."

"Good." He gathered it back into the purse and handed her the whole thing. "This is yours. Count it as my room payment tonight." He grinned. "And tie up your bodice again. I meant it when I said I wasn't going through with this tonight. You deserve to choose your own lover."

Clarisse complied, tears streaming down her smiling face. "You sleep on the bed," she told him, standing up. "You paid for it."

"Oh, no," he crossed his arms. "A gentleman and knight never puts his comfort above that of a lady. I will take a blanket and sleep on the floor."

She didn't move. "I am no lady."

Matthew grasped both her arms and pushed her gently back into a sitting position on the bed. "You are in my eyes. Every woman deserves to be treated as a lady. At least that is what my father says."

She wiped her tears with the back of her hand. "Your father must be a wonderful man."

Matthew nodded. "Stubborn at times and bit rough around the edges, but yes, he tries." He gathered a blanket around his shoulders and stretched out on the floor. "Good night, Clarisse. Sleep well."

She leaned over and gave Matthew a kiss on the cheek. "Merci, good Matt. Tonight for the first time in a long time I will sleep well." She lay down on the bed facing the little window, and pulled the covers over her shoulders. In a few minutes her breathing was even and steady.

Matthew sighed contentedly. He could still hear his mother saying, "Be true to the royalty within you."

When Matthew awoke with the early morning sun shining in the window, the bed was empty. A pink dancing dress lay in the corner, and the bedsheet was missing. The room's window to the alley was open. Clarisse was gone.

He sat up and looked around, his money purse lay on the bed, but it was empty. Next to it lay a hair comb with a silk orchid attached. He put the comb in his money purse and attached it inside his waistband. He washed his face in the basin on the little table and went out to the loo located off the main hall. On the way back he met Mark, whose hair was disheveled, his eyes squinting against the bright light.

"Morning, Mark," Matthew greeted him.

Mark winced. "Yeah. It is. Boy do I have a headache." He went into the loo.

Matthew waited for him. Mark came back out. "Hangover?" Matthew asked.

Mark nodded. "I am not drinking that Firebomb again. It burned going down and it burned coming out."

"Breakfast?" Matthew asked.

Mark shook his head. "Not unless you want to see me barf."

They walked back toward the beach. Matthew led them up a hill to the cliffs overlooking the ocean. They sat on the grass and watched the waves rolling in, a cooling breeze ruffling their hair. Mark lay back on the grass and closed his eyes.

"I am feeling a little better already," he sighed.

"Good. Just rest," Matthew commented. "Captain James and Adam will work us hard enough in a couple of hours."

"Matt?" Mark asked after a few minutes.

"Yes?" Matthew pulled up a stem of grass and stuck it between his teeth, sucking on it.

"Thank you for trying to get me out of La Castille last night. I kind of wish…I had left with you earlier." Mark opened his eyes and looked over at Matthew.

Matthew just grunted.

"It's not just the hangover. It's—" Mark took a deep breath. "The girls. I feel…kind of icky. It is not what I expected. You know, the way the other guys talk about it." He shook his head. "That's not quite it. It was initially exciting, but now I feel empty. Incomplete."

Matthew looked up at a cloud in the sky. "Hmm."

"Is that the way you feel?" Mark asked.

Matthew looked over at Mark and shook his head. "I didn't go through with it." He sighed. "I watched my sister marry the man of her dreams, and he saved himself for her. They are deliriously happy now, other than chasing after a very active little girl. My parents are also very devoted to each other. To them marriage is a very special relationship, a very exciting and satisfying one. I want that kind of experience too. I am not going to do anything to ruin that opportunity."

"Wow," Mark whistled. "I didn't know that kind of love happened in real life; I thought it was only in fairy tales." He was quiet a moment. "My parents fought a lot, and my father drank. I was glad to get out of the house when I turned eighteen."

Mark rolled over onto his stomach and watched Matthew chew on his stem of grass. "Matt, do you think it is too late for me to find the kind of love that your family has?"

Matthew looked him in the eye. "No. Not if you want it bad enough. But you have to be prepared to make sacrifices, to be the person who can offer that kind of love to a girl." He grinned. "Personally, I think you would make a fine husband one day. You work hard, and you are a nice guy."

Mark lay back on the grass. "It is a big responsibility, earning enough to support a family. I hope I am up to it."

"I hope I am too," Matthew commented.

"Being an adult is a lot harder than it looks, isn't it?" Mark asked.

Matthew sighed. "You got that right."

CHAPTER 10

STORM AT SEA

Captain James was standing on the Dauntless' deck checking his time piece as Matthew and Mark walked up the gangplank. Other sailors hurried on board, stowed belongings, and took their places loading crates. When the crates were loaded Captain James ordered the gangplank pulled. Four sailors pulled the gangplank in while dock workers untied ropes and pushed the ship away from the dock with thick sturdy poles. Adam shouted orders to set and unfurl the sails while Captain James stood at the helm, hand on the rudder.

Mark climbed up the mizzen mast while Matthew hauled on the mizzen stays below him. A peculiar tingling on Matthew's neck made him look around. On the dock stood a tall woman wrapped in a cloak watching their ship leave. In a flash of recognition, Matthew realized he was staring at Connie, the mistress at La Castille. Their eyes locked and Connie's face hardened.

Matthew imagined her voice in his head. "I know what you've done. You may have escaped me this time, but if I see you again you will pay dearly."

"Ho! Matthew!" Mark's voice filtered down to him. "Turn the sail!"

Matthew pulled the lines to move the boom which turned the sail. When he looked back toward the docks Connie was gone.

A heaviness settled in his stomach. Had he done the right thing helping Clarisse? What if they tracked her down? She had hinted she would be beaten; would they do worse? Would her friend Marie be punished? Yet she had known the risks and chosen to leave. Risk was the price of freedom and self-determination. Matthew sighed and turned back to his work.

The Dauntless followed the coastline, passing by villages, making quick stops every three or four days to do a small exchange of goods at larger towns. After a month the boat turned east and passed through a busy shipping channel. Many of the sailors lined the rails to watch as the Dauntless passed slowly by ships both small and large, of many styles of builds from many different lands.

Mark, standing by Matthew, was grinning widely. "From here on out our port stops get more exotic," he told him mysteriously.

Sure enough, at the next little port Matthew noticed many dock workers wearing turbans and beards. Many of the women they saw wore scarves to cover their heads. Matthew wasn't sure what goods were in the crates Captain James brought on board, but Cook started making a lot of rice dishes with spicy sauces. Mark pointed out that one particular golden sauce was a curry, which Matthew particularly liked. On shore in the ports, food stands sold new foods and pastry delicacies. Matthew fell in love with a nut and honey pastry that he bought every time he could find it in port.

One mid-day after eating lunch, Mark and Matthew went above decks to watch the sailors run the lines and sails again. It was a windy day, so it was a good day to observe how tacking and sail positioning was done. Adam was on the poop deck calling out orders to the helmsman and sailors.

Suddenly one of the sailors called down a warning, using a term Matthew had not heard before. Adam got out his spyglass and stared off to port for a minute. Then he shouted for Conrad, who came running.

"Get Captain James up here immediately!" Adam told him.

Conrad ran to the Captain's cabin. In a minute Captain James himself was on the poop deck, peering through the spyglass. The next moment Captain James was calling out orders to the sailors. The Dauntless turned from the coast toward more open seas. Mark ran to the rail to look behind them. He gestured to Matthew to come over.

"Look," he pointed to three black ships behind them on the horizon. "I think they might be pirate ships."

A chill ran up Matthew's spine. "What is Captain James going to do?"

"Outrun them, I think. It looks like we are trying to get away from the coastline a little bit also."

The boys watched for a while, but the ships seemed to be getting closer. Ahead of them the skies darkened. It looked like there was a storm brewing out on the sea ahead of them. The wind was getting stronger and the waves higher. Matthew had to hold on tight to the rail to keep standing. Lightning flashed in the clouds ahead. Mark looked worried.

"Matt, if you have any rain gear, you better put it on," Mark told him.

Matthew nodded. "I do."

The boys leaped down the hatch stairs and ran to get their rain gear on. Just then Adam's whistle blew three shrill blasts.

"All hands on deck! All hands on deck!" He shouted.

Sailors scrambled off bunks and out of the mess hall, leaving work tasks and dishes on the tables. As he ran past the mess hall door Matthew saw Cook hurriedly picking things up.

Up on deck sailors were climbing up the rigging or stationing themselves on the lines below. Captain James shouted commands, tacking the ship into the wind and toward the storm clouds. The black ships seemed to be losing some speed behind them, increasing the distance between them and the Dauntless. Matthew, hanging onto one of the aft sail lines, breathed a sigh of relief. Then he looked toward the storm ahead of them and caught his breath.

The storm clouds looked black, with lightning occasionally lighting up the sky. As the Dauntless reached the cloud bank, it seemed as if it entered under a waterfall, the sudden deluge of rain was so heavy. Many sailors without raingear were drenched, but even with his rubber coat the rain was cold and the wind whipped through Matthew. He hung onto the lines as the ship rose and fell with the ocean swells. Only half the time could he hear the Captain's shouted commands.

"Move the boom to port!" the sailor next to him shouted at him.

Matthew looked at him, then at Adam, who was waiving at him. Matthew swung the boom toward the port side and hung on to the lines there. Sailors above him were furling up the sails and tying them into place against the yardarms. Two sailors hung onto the helm, steering the ship bow first into the waves.

The rain lashed against Matthew's face, and the cold wind chilled his skin. He was soon shivering. The storm seemed to last forever into the night. His stomach lurched and was barely holding onto its contents with all the dips and falls of the boat, but he willed himself not to think about it.

One big wave hit the starboard side of the ship, tipping the ship so much Matthew thought they would capsize. He hung onto the lines with all his might, trying to keep his foot grip on the deck. He thought he saw the shadow of something falling from one of the mizzen sails. He cried out in alarm as it splashed into the ocean.

"Man overboard!" he thought he heard someone shout.

As the ship righted again, Shorty appeared out of the darkness toward the port side where the man had fallen. He tossed a small white painted barrel attached to a rope over the side of the ship. Shorty yelled over the wind for the man to grab it and hold on. In a few minutes Shorty and another sailor began hauling on the rope, pulling the barrel and sailor back in. Finally they had him on the deck, exhausted and shivering. Shorty helped him stand and took him below deck for Cook to dry and warm him up.

Finally the storm seemed to be diminishing, the wind less biting, and the pelting rain less cutting. Ahead of them there was a small bit of light, seeping between dark seas and heavy skies. As the light grew the storm calmed. Soon they were sailing out into a bright morning, sun glinting on the waves, green coast on the horizon ahead of them. Matthew felt relief and increasing warmth permeating his exhausted body.

He looked around at the ship and bedraggled sailors. Lines were broken, sails torn, deck coated with salt water and seaweed. Anything that hadn't been tied down had been washed off the deck or thrown around inside the ship. Worried about his bow, Matthew leaped down to the mess hall to check the broom barrel. It had slid around a bit in the storm, but the bow was safe nestled among the brooms. One of his arrows in the quiver had cracked a bit at the feather end, but he thought he could repair it with glue.

Captain James let most of the crew sleep for a few hours while limping to land. When Matthew awoke the ship was already docked in port. Captain James and Adam had gone ashore to bargain for repairs. Don stayed on board to guard the ship. When Captain James returned late afternoon, he gathered the crew together to speak to them.

"Men, thank you for your work getting through the storm." He wiped a hand across his tired eyes, and Matthew suspected he hadn't slept yet. Adam also looked exhausted. "The ship sustained enough damage that we will be in port for about a week making repairs." A cheer from the men started, but was cut short when Captain raised his hand.

"Unfortunately, I cannot pay you right now. We need all the coin we have and more to pay for new supplies, lines and sails. I also need some men to volunteer to work in town to pay for what we lack. Those who stay on board will work the repairs. Those who want to work in town go to my right, those who want to work on board go to my left. Those who don't care which location stay where you are and I'll assign you."

Mark nudged Matthew. "Want to work on land?" he asked.

"Absolutely," Matthew responded positively. "I want to see new places and people as much as possible."

"And eat new food," Mark grinned. They joined the group at the Captain's right.

While Don directed the on-board work crews, Adam brought a list of jobs that businesses on land had offered. Matthew scanned the list.

"I am familiar with horses, I can take the stable job," he offered.

"I know animals too, I'll go with him," Mark added quickly.

Adam nodded and wrote their names next to the job. "Fine. You start first thing in the morning." He gave them directions and moved on to the next sailor.

"This will be fun," Mark commented.

"It will be an adventure," Matthew agreed.

CHAPTER 11

MIRIAM

Before dawn the next morning Adam woke everyone with his shrill whistle. "Those working in town need to be there by sunup!" he announced.

Twenty-five men rolled grumpily out of their bunks, swallowed breakfast and left the ship. As Mark and Matthew walked down the main road of town, men in long white robes and draped headdresses suddenly spilled out of a large mosque and dispersed in all directions. Some women dressed in black robes and various colored head scarves headed toward the market carrying baskets of goods on their heads or in their arms. The townspeople glanced curiously at the foreigners, but did not bother the boys as they hurried to their own work for the day.

As the sun rose, Matthew and Mark left the center of town and headed up a hill toward what looked like a large palace set on top. Mark seemed unusually nervous as they approached.

"Matt, Adam didn't say anything about us going to the king's palace. Are you sure we are going to the right place?"

"Pretty sure. You remember the directions he gave. Did you see anything more likely, Mark?"

"No," Mark responded miserably. "I just thought we weren't going to THE largest house in town."

Matthew stopped. "Do you want to go back?"

Mark looked down the hill back toward the ship. "No, I'll stay with you."

Matthew studied him a minute. "What do you have against palaces?"

"Not palaces per se, but the rich and higher class snobs."

Matthew nudged him. "Out with it. There's more to this than you are saying."

Matt sighed. "There was this girl I liked," he began.

"Doesn't it always start there?" Matthew agreed.

"Well, she seemed to like me too, but her father was not happy with me. Seems he had a rich nobleman in mind for her. When he found out we were seeing each other he sent her away and married her off to the nobleman. He told me he would kill me if he ever saw me again. It was right after that I joined the Dauntless. So yes, I guess I am a little nervous around rich houses."

Matthew didn't say anything, but thought about Sarah's nervousness about his proposal to her. He hadn't really thought before about how people might view his family. Although his father had managed to bridge both worlds fairly well; perhaps it was his inner confidence of his self-worth, independent of birth or station. The people of Danforth tended to have that independent attitude.

They reached the courtyard of the palace. The wall was ornate but high enough to be protective and functional, and skirted the entire hill. They knocked on the gate and a robed man opened it.

"You are the sailor workers?" he asked. They nodded. "Come."

They entered and faced a grand palace set back on the estate, with mushroom shaped turrets and arched porches surrounding the various wings. Their guide walked past the palace and gardens toward a grand stable that looked large enough to house fifty horses or more. It was the finest stable Matthew had ever seen. Mark whistled in amazement.

"All this for horses?" Mark asked.

The robed man turned to look at him. "Horses are the king's prized possession," he answered.

The chief of the king's stables came over to meet them. "You are late," he announced. "Work starts at dawn."

"Our apologies, sir," Mark hurriedly replied. "We will be on time tomorrow."

The man nodded. "I am Assad. Come. I will show you your jobs."

Assad showed them how to feed and water the horses. Then he showed them mucking the stalls and the pasture. Matthew expressed surprise about cleaning up the pasture also; Assad explained that with valuable horses one does not want dirty or infected hooves.

The boys worked all morning. Mark was amazed at Matthew's speed and skill at tossing hay and shoveling horse manure. Matthew confessed that he had learned a little farming from his uncle John, but didn't tell him about mucking stalls as punishment as a boy. At noon a bell rang and the boys washed off the dirt at the stable faucet, and wandered toward the near side of the palace.

All of the palace workers filed from all over the grounds and buildings, lining up before a little mosque on the grounds. Curious, Mark and Matthew followed them. At the door, the men ceremonially washed hands and faces over one of two basins, and then filed inside. A man with a tall fancy turban met Mark and Matthew as they approached the door.

"Is this where we eat?" Mark asked.

The man shook his head. "You wish to pray?" the man asked instead.

"I suppose so," Mark answered.

"Yes!" Matthew asserted.

"You must cover your head," the man told them.

The boys looked at each other in dismay. "I left my hat on the ship," Mark stated.

"So did I," Matthew echoed.

The Imam turned to his helper and said something in another language. The assistant hurried inside the mosque and returned a minute later carrying two head cloths. The men helped the boys put them on and fasten them down with headbands.

"Next time come with clean robes," the Imam told them. "Now you may wash and enter."

The boys mimicked the actions of the other men, dipping their right hand and then their left into the water basins, and then applying water to their faces. Then they entered the mosque. The men were all standing in even rows facing the front. Soon the Imam entered, faced the worshippers, and spoke briefly. The worshippers all chanted together words the boys did not understand. In unison the men then bent halfway over in a bow position and chanted again.

Mark and Matthew bowed with them. "What are they doing?" Mark whispered.

"I think they are praying," Matthew whispered back.

Everyone stood up straight again, their hands over their chests, still chanting. Then they all knelt down in unison and placed their foreheads to the floor. The boys imitated them. The worshippers stayed down for a long time, still chanting together. Then they stood again. After a minute the men all knelt down onto their right knees, crossing their left legs over their right ankles. Finally the men all stood again, chanted one more time, and finished their prayers.

The Imam was at the door. When Matthew and Mark tried to return the head coverings, he waved them back. "You wear them while you work and worship here," he told them. "Return them when you are finished working here."

"Thank you," Matthew responded, bowing slightly.

The boys followed the men to a courtyard where everyone was given a bowl of rice covered with a yellow curry sauce and a chunk of bread, but no spoon. They sat down on the ground with the others, confused about how to eat their meal.

Mark nudged Matthew. "They are scooping up the rice with their fingers."

The boys began to eat, trying to scoop rice to their mouths without dropping food onto their shirts. Some of the workers stared at them disgustedly.

"Why are they staring?" Mark murmured. "We are eating the same way they are."

Matthew looked at Mark, and then studied the other workers. "Mark, I think they are all eating with their right hands, and you are eating with your left."

Mark raised his left hand to look at it. "So? I am left handed."

Matthew remembered something he had read during his book studies. "I think the left is the toilet hand," he told Mark. "Just humor me a minute and switch to eating with your right hand."

Mark awkwardly tried to feed himself with his right hand. A couple of the men nodded and smiled, and went back to their eating.

After lunch Assad met them back at the stables. "Now we groom the horses," he told them. "You have handled horses before?"

"No," Mark admitted.

"Yes," Matthew answered.

Assad's eyes gleamed. "I see." He pointed to a stall by itself where a smaller gray-white horse was kept. "Brush down that horse."

Matthew grabbed a grooming brush and approached the stall. The horse laid back its ears, showed its teeth, and rolled its eyes back. Matthew stopped. He pulled an apple out of his tunic that was meant to be his lunch and held it up.

"Assad, sir, may I feed this apple to that horse?"

Assad inspected the apple to make sure it had no worms. "Yes, you may try," he said. He couldn't keep from grinning.

Matthew cut the apple into four pieces and stood just outside the stall talking quietly to the horse. He rolled the first apple piece casually in his hands. The horse stopped rolling his eyes and looked at Matthew's apple. He stopped baring his teeth. He stretched his neck forward to sniff at the apple, which Matthew held just out of reach. The horse took a couple of steps forward and stuck its head just over the gate, his ears twitching toward Matthew's low droning voice. Matthew raised one hand to touch the horse's nose, and the horse drew back a little. Matthew kept the apple tantalizingly up near the horse's face until he stretched forth his nose again. Once again Matthew tried to touch his nose and the horse drew back. On the third try, the horse let Matthew hold his hand on his nose for a moment, and Matthew fed him the piece of apple.

Matthew took the second piece of apple and worked with the horse until he was able to touch the horse down its neck. Assad seemed surprised. With the third piece of apple Matthew got in the stall with him and laid his hand on the horse's back.

"What is the horse's name?" Matthew asked softly.

"Saitan," Assad replied, chewing on a strand of straw.

Mark and Matthew glanced at each other. "Why is he called that?" Mark asked.

"Try to ride him," Assad replied nonchalantly.

Matthew looked at Saitan, who eyed him suspiciously, ears twitching forward and back. "Not today," Matthew decided. He tossed the last quarter apple to Mark. "Here, you feed him the last piece."

Mark held the apple quarter out on his palm. Saitan nibbled it off his hand, lips tickling Mark's palm. "Wow! His nose is so soft!" he exclaimed, and patted the horse on the nose with his other hand. Saitan drew back slightly, and then sniffed Mark's hand as though looking for more apple.

"Come," Assad spoke. "You must groom the other horses."

He showed them the curry brushes and hoof hooks for cleaning the hooves. Mark brushed down the animals while Matthew cleaned hooves. At last they came back to Saitan's stall.

"Do you think he will let us groom him?" Mark asked.

"Maybe," Matthew replied, studying the horse. "Let me go in first and see how he reacts to the brush."

Matthew slipped into the stall and slowly approached the horse, talking in low tones. Saitan turned his head to stare at him. Matthew held out the brush for the horse to sniff. Then he touched one hand to the horse's neck and began brushing with the other. The horse stood still and let him.

"Come in and brush," Matthew told Mark.

Mark entered the stall the same way Matthew had, let the horse sniff him, and then joined in the brushing. Then while Mark stood caressing the horse's neck, Matthew lifted each hoof and cleaned it. Then they left the stall. Assad was there watching.

"We did it!" Mark grinned.

Assad clapped his hands softly. "You come back tomorrow and work again," Assad told them. "Tomorrow I have some robes for you so you can pray in the mosque with us."

Matthew inclined his head. "Thank you, Assad."

As they finished putting their tools away, the bell rang to call people to prayer. Assad excused himself and left for the mosque. As Matthew left the tool room, he noticed a pile of broken bridles and cinch straps.

"Hey, Mark, do you want to learn to repair leather tomorrow?" Matthew asked.

"Sure! Is it like repairing lines and sails?" Mark queried.

"Uh, a little bit. Come with your pocket knife tomorrow."

"And another apple. I want to approach Saitan again."

Matthew looked at him quizzically. "Are you sure? I have a feeling that horse mistrusts people."

"Maybe. But then I kind of mistrust people too."

Back at the Dauntless the other sailors talked about the jobs they were given to do. Mark and Matthew gathered their tools for the next day, and then went to bed. Matthew woke Mark up well before dawn.

"Are you sure you want to get up there so early?" Mark asked groggily.

"Yes. I have a feeling it means a lot to Assad."

"Fine," Mark mumbled, rolling out of his bunk and groping for his clothes in the dark.

As they hurried up the dark streets, Mark grumbled some more. "I don't know this Allah they are praying to. I don't know their language, and it hurts to kneel on my twisted left leg. Why are we doing this anyway?"

"It is respectful to follow the customs of the land you are visiting," Matthew told him. "When in Rome, do as the Romans do."

"We are not in Rome."

"No. So 'when in Arabia, do as the Arabians do'. Besides, I think our God is the same as theirs, just by a different name. I figure there is no harm in praying to my God while they pray to theirs."

"I don't pray," Mark mumbled.

Matthew wondered what he should say. Prayer was a natural part of his family's life; they prayed every Sunday in chapel and over every meal. A sudden thought hit him.

"Do you believe in God?" Matthew asked.

"Why should I?" Mark answered glumly. "What's he ever done for me? He took my mother in childbirth when my sister was born, he did nothing when my father beat me, and he let us nearly starve every winter. He allows sickness and inequality of wealth in the land. Why should I pray to a god who allows that?"

Matthew didn't know what to say. Mark had a point. Why should he pray to a God who allowed suffering? He himself had led a privileged and bountiful life, and experienced very little in terms of hunger, cold or scorn. But there were others around him who struggled, and his family had helped where they could. He remembered his mother saying that those who had plenty were responsible to help others in need. Did God help people by working through other people?

He thought about all of this as they entered the palace grounds, were handed robes by Assad, and prayed in the mosque. He pondered a response as he and Mark fed hay to the horses and mucked the stalls and adjacent meadow. He was thoughtful as he watched Mark feed slices of apple to Saitan, and then enter the stall to brush the horse down.

He heard a gasp behind him and turned. A young woman, dressed in riding skirt and bright pink headscarf, stood by the stall holding a bridle and staring at Mark.

"He's in the stall with Saitan," she remarked wonderingly.

"I think he likes the apples we brought him," Matthew replied and held out his hand. "I'm Matt."

She looked at his outstretched hand a moment, and then touched it briefly with her fingers. "I am Miriam. You are not from around here, I see." It was more a statement than a question.

"We are on the merchant ship, Dauntless. Our ship was damaged in a storm, and we are working to pay for replacement sails and supplies," Matthew told her. "That is my friend, Mark."

They watched Mark talk to Saitan as he brushed him down.

"He is very good with that animal. How long has he worked with horses?" she asked.

Matthew shrugged. "He tells me only a little bit. His family owned a donkey and a few goats."

Miriam laughed. "Saitan hates our most professional riders and horse trainers. Perhaps it is the novice who will succeed where others have not." She noticed Matthew's confusion and explained. "No one has been able to ride him yet, not even I. We inherited him from a peasant to pay off a debt."

Matthew grinned. "Maybe I can give it a try. I'm pretty good with animals."

He grabbed a bridle from a hook on the wall and stepped into the stall. He held up the bridle to make sure it was about the right size. Then he pulled a piece of apple from the pocket in his shirt. Saitan nibbled it happily. Then Matthew gently brought the bridle to the horse's mouth. Saitan tossed his head and backed up. Matthew wrapped the reins around the horse's neck and gave them to Mark to hold. Matthew approached Saitan's head again, talking gently. With one arm over the top of the horse's head to hold it steady, he brought the bridle up again.

"Come on, boy, you can do this. I have another piece of apple for you once the bridle is on."

The horse couldn't get away from Matthew this time, and gently he pushed the bit between the horse's teeth. Quickly he pulled the rest of the bridle over the horse's ears and fastened it around his neck. In a moment Saitan was munching on apple quarter number two.

"Nicely done," Miriam complimented him. "However, you are still not on the horse."

Matthew took the reins and opened the stall door. "Let's see, shall we?"

As he led the horse toward the corral behind the stables, several stable hands went running.

"The foreigner is going to try riding Saitan!" they shouted. Soon a crowd gathered outside the corral fence. Matthew hesitated.

"Go ahead!" Miriam urged him. "I want to see this."

"I am just going to ride on your back for a moment," Matthew whispered in the horse's ear. "Then you can have another piece of apple." He drew the reins around to the back of the horse's neck, and stood still a moment. The horse's eyes rolled back to look at him. The crowd around the corral fell silent.

Swiftly, Matthew hiked his stomach up onto the horse's back and swung his leg over. The horse stood still a moment, and Matthew heaved a sigh of relief. Suddenly Saitan laid his ears back and reared back on his hind legs. Matthew couldn't keep his knee grip around the horse's flanks and he slid off the back end of the horse into a mud patch. The crowd roared in laughter and went back to their work. Miriam ran over to help Matthew up. Saitan loped across the corral to the far end and began nibbling grass.

"I thought I had it," Matthew mumbled, rubbing a sore hip.

Miriam laughed gently. "Well, you did make it farther than most others have. I only made it halfway up myself."

Miriam and Matthew walked toward Saitan to guide him back into the barn, but he kept walking away from them along the corral fence.

Miriam threw up her hands and walked back inside the stable to work with her own horse. Matthew followed her.

"I noticed you praying with the men in the mosque this morning," she commented. "Not very many foreigners join us in prayers."

"Oh," Matthew didn't know what to say. "I like to experience different cultures."

"Do you have a big mosque where you come from?" she asked curiously.

"We have a little chapel where my family worships on Sunday. There is a lovely cathedral where most of the townspeople worship. They have a large choir that fills the cathedral with beautiful sound."

"Oh," she sounded wistful. "My mother sings beautifully, but I don't hear her sing very often. She sang more to me when I was little." She started brushing down her horse.

He grabbed a hoof hook from the wall. "May I check your horse's hooves for you?" he asked.

"Yes, thank you!" She smiled. He checked and scooped the hooves while she brushed. "How long have you been around horses, Matt?"

"I have been riding since I was little." He didn't mention anything about his squire training with horses. "And you?"

"I also have been riding since I was little. My father feels it is very important to be skilled in various arts. Horses are very important to the people of Sahaja, both for trade and war. Oh! Surprise!"

Matthew looked up. Miriam was looking out into the stable hall. Mark walked by with Saitan following close behind him, the bridle was off and there was no rope around him. As his stall door Mark let him in and closed the gate. Then he fed him an apple quarter. Saitan whickered softly and chomped the apple happily.

"You say Mark has only had a little time with horses?" Miriam asked softly.

"This is his first week, I think," Matthew answered, watching his friend.

"Interesting. Saitan seems to like your friend."

"Maybe it is the apples he brought."

"Maybe." She shook her head. "I have never seen the horse follow someone like that before, and we have tried a variety of treats."

The call for noon prayer sounded from outside.

"Oh, dear, I never got my ride in." Miriam put her brush away. "I must go to prayers. Are you going?"

Matthew looked down at his muddy trousers. "I will have to wash these off before going inside your mosque."

She glanced at the robes hanging on a hook by the stable door. "Just take them off. No one will see underneath the robes." Then with a mischievous smile she left.

Matthew looked down at his muddy clothes. Then in a moment of decision he went into an empty stall, took off his muddy trousers and shirt, and pulled the robe over his head. He left the dirty clothes in a corner, planning to wash them out right after lunch. Then he went to get Mark.

After prayer and lunch, Matthew washed out his clothes and laid them on the corral fence in the sun to dry. He kept the borrowed robe on. Then with Assad's permission they set to work repairing ropes, cinches and halter ropes. Assad inspected their work part way through and seemed pleased.

After Mark finished with rope repairs and while Matthew worked on one more saddle cinch, Mark wandered off to visit the horses. Matthew found him in the stall again with Saitan.

"You and that horse seem to get along," Matthew commented.

"You think so?" Mark asked. He studied the horse. "I feel like I almost know what Saitan is thinking. I don't think he likes being cooped up in this stall day after day. I bet he used to wander more freely before coming here."

"What do you think his previous master had him do?" Matthew wondered.

"Maybe he was used more to pull a wagon or a plow," Mark mused. "He doesn't seem used to being ridden, but he isn't wild."

"I wonder if there is a wagon harness somewhere we could try?" Matthew offered.

"And a wagon," Mark added.

They looked through a pile of harnesses, and Mark found something likely. He entered Saitan's stall and strapped the harness around the horse. Saitan continue to munch on his hay unperturbed. Mark and Matthew looked at each other hopefully.

"Now for a wagon," Mark stated.

Just then Miriam came into the stable. She looked at Saitan and the harness around him. "What are you doing with Saitan?" she asked.

"Investigating a theory, ma'am," Mark explained. "We were thinking that Saitan might have been trained to pull a wagon instead of being ridden. Do you have a cart or something we could test him with?"

"There is a little buggy I rode in as a little girl," she mused. "That might work."

"The only problem is how to guide the horse," Matthew commented. "Saitan doesn't exactly like bridles."

"Peasant horses often are guided by a rope around the neck," explained Miriam. "Perhaps we should use that."

They found a rope that Mark looped around Saitan's neck. While he led the horse out of the stable to the corral, Miriam showed Matthew where the little buggy was stored. Matthew pulled it out to the corral, and the three of them hooked up the buggy to the harness around the horse. Saitan stood looking at them expectantly.

"Who is going to ride in the buggy?" Matthew asked.

Miriam stepped back hesitantly. "Saitan and I did not get along well in the past," she told them.

"I will," Mark offered. "I've driven carts before." He went up to talk to Saitan, and then climbed into the buggy. He took the rope that was attached to Saitan's neck and slapped it up and down. "Go!" he commanded. Saitan didn't move.

"Maybe you need to speak the command in my language," Miriam suggested. "Adhhab!"

Mark repeated it. Saitan started walking, pulling the cart around the corral. Mark grinned and waved. Then he tried pulling back on the rope. "Stop!" he commanded. Saitan kept walking.

"Try, tawaquf!" Miriam called out. Mark repeated it and Saitan stopped.

"Well, now we know what language he speaks," Matthew commented.

"And we know now he is a work horse and not a riding horse," Miriam agreed. They unhooked Saitan from the harness and Mark led him back to his stall.

Just then Assad showed up. "Enough playing with the horse. You know how to fix fences?" Both Matthew and Mark nodded their heads. "Good. Then come."

Miriam shook her head. "You are both versatile sailors."

"With farming experience," Mark responded. He nodded his head to her and followed Assad out of the stable.

The boys worked quickly beside Assad and another man repairing some wood fences and some rock walls around the estate. They finished just before evening prayer time.

"You may go," Assad told them. "Perhaps tomorrow you help polish saddles."

Matthew nodded. "As you wish." He retrieved his now dry shirt and trousers and changed out of the robe before heading back to the ship with Mark.

The next morning the boys fed hay to the horses first, and then Assad led them into the saddle room. He showed them the saddle oil and cloths and how he wanted the saddles polished. They set to work and Assad left. When they were part way through, Miriam stomped into the saddle room, grumbling under her breath.

"Can't find anyone when you want them. I will have my ride this morning." She stopped when she saw Mark and Matthew.

"Good morning, Miriam," Matthew offered, inclining his head.

"Mm." She stared at the saddle Mark was oiling. "You are working on my saddle."

"I am so sorry, ma'am." Mark hurriedly started wiping off the oil.

She stomped her foot. "I am the king's daughter. You will address me by my title!"

"I am sorry, Your Highness. I will clean this up for you." Mark kept wiping.

Her face softened a little. "You may as well finish." She paused. "Thank you for working on the saddles."

Mark's face flushed. He stayed bent over the saddle, working silently.

Miriam spoke again. "I guess I am just a bit perturbed. I am used to riding alone, but now my father thinks I need an...escort." She lowered her voice on the last word.

Matthew smiled. "To protect you from the foreign strangers on his property?"

Miriam tucked in an end of her headscarf that had come loose. "Who knows? You don't look dangerous to me."

"No, Your Highness. We are more apt to protect you from danger, if anything," Matthew stood up and bowed to her over the saddle he was working on.

She laughed. "I thought so."

A short stout woman appeared in the doorway, covered in black robe and headscarf. She frowned. "What are you doing here, Your Highness?"

Miriam stopped smiling. "Fetching my saddle, Ana. They are still working on it."

Ana gazed at Mark and Matthew disapprovingly. "The princess has need of her saddle now," she ordered.

Mark hurriedly rubbed in the last spot of oil. "Done," he mumbled.

Matthew hefted up the saddle. "Let me carry it for you," he offered.

Miriam smiled. "Thank you."

When Matthew returned, Mark was finishing the last saddle. He stayed silent while they started mucking stalls.

Suddenly Mark turned to Matthew. "You didn't seem one bit afraid to talk to Miriam," he accused. "Don't you realize she is the king's daughter?"

Matthew continued shoveling out the stall. "Yes, I know she is. So?"

"So, that makes her a princess. Doesn't that make you a bit nervous around her?"

Matthew leaned on his shovel and gazed at Mark. "No. Should it?"

Mark stared at him suspiciously. "Okay, Matt. You have hinted about your family, but never given a lot of details. You come from an upper class family, don't you?"

Matthew nodded. "You could say that."

"You are familiar with weapons and horses, indicating some training in the defensive arts. Army?" Mark probed.

Matthew shook his head. "Knight's training. I'm a squire."

Mark whistled. "You gave up knight's training to be a sailor? Are you crazy? The ladies would be all over you as a knight."

Matthew sighed. "Sarah wasn't."

Mark grinned. "I thought there might be a girl behind all this, with your mysterious comments, sighing, and not connecting with other girls. Did she think she was too good for you?"

Matthew shook his head. "No. She thought she wasn't good enough."

"Not good enough for a knight or squire? What, is she crazy?"

"No. She's an orphan. She has no idea of her birth parents."

"Why should that matter? That should only matter when marrying royalty." Mark laughed. Matthew was silent. Mark stopped shoveling and just stared at him. "Matt, are you…are you royalty? Or should I be calling you Matthew?"

Matthew paused and then nodded. "My parents are the Queen and King of Sterling."

"That makes you a prince." Mark's face was pale.

Matthew looked miserable. "Please don't tell the other sailors."

"Dude, I'm not that dumb." Mark caught himself. "I mean, Your Highness."

Matthew shoved him gently on the shoulder. "Don't. I'm a regular guy like you."

"No, not like me. Your parents taught you Values."

"Yes, they taught me right from wrong. They taught me every person has worth. They taught me how to work, like you."

"Yeah, I do know how to work." Mark smiled, looking more like himself. "In fact, we better get back to work."

They finished their work early, and Assad let them go. On the way back to the ship Matthew suggested they walk through the local marketplace. Mark bought a curved machete' blade. Matthew stopped to look at a stall displaying many colorful scarves. His gaze landed on one that was black with pink orchids on it. He bought it.

"For your girl back home?" Mark asked.

Matthew nodded. "In case I ever get a chance to speak to her again."

The next day at lunch time Miriam showed up again at the stables. She carried a basket lunch for all of them. "Come, I have some place to show you," she told them.

She led them out of the stable and into the palace gardens. The boys were amazed at the variety of exotic flowers growing there, and told her so.

"My mother collects flowers," she told them. "Wherever my father goes on his journeys he brings her back a new variety of plant. He really adores her. I think that is why he only married one wife."

Mark looked at Matthew questioningly. Matthew shrugged.

They walked on to the far end of the gardens, then down a hill toward a pond. The land next to the pond was fenced off, surrounding a wild, more arid section of terrain. Miriam sat down on the grassy hill before the pond and opened the lunch basket. She passed out fruit, bread, and bowls of spiced meat and rice. The boys ate hungrily.

"No Ana today?" Matthew asked.

Miriam's face clouded momentarily. "She had to run an errand. She thinks I am studying in my room."

"Sounds like something my sister, Amber, would do," Matthew grinned.

"Won't you get in trouble?" Mark remarked.

Miriam squared her shoulders. "I don't care. I am not doing anything wrong." She smiled mysteriously. "Besides, I want to show you something."

She took a piece of meat from her bowl, stood up, and walked toward the fence surrounding the arid parcel of land. The boys followed her. She made a warbling sound in the back of her throat, held the piece of meat over the fence, and waited.

A warbling cry in the distance responded, and then repeated coming closer. A dark scaled dragon-like creature lumbered into view, approached the fence, and ate the piece of meat from Miriam's outstretched hand.

"What in the world is that?" Mark asked, stepping back startled.

"It's a Komodo dragon!" Matthew exclaimed.

Miriam turned to Matthew. "How do you know this?" she asked.

"A couple of Komodo dragons showed up on an island near my home about ten years ago. No one knows how they got there. I've had a chance to observe them some. May I try feeding him?"

Miriam hesitated. "You must be very careful; don't let him bite your fingers."

Matthew retrieved the last two pieces of meat from his lunch bowl, leaned over the fence, and dropped the meat pieces one at a time into the waiting dragon's mouth. Mark brought over his last piece and, hands shaking, also fed the dragon.

Miriam smiled. "See? Nothing to it. You just have to be calm and careful. My father thinks these creatures are amazing. Somewhat like him: wild and fearless."

They watched the dragon sniff around some for some ground creatures, then wander off into the brush again.

"Where are you from, Mark and Matt?" Miriam asked as they walked back toward the pond.

"The Kingdom of Mordred," Mark answered.

"The Land of Sterling," Matthew told her.

"Sterling..." Miriam looked thoughtful. "Something about that name seems familiar."

"It's the southern country on the island continent of Browning Isle," Matthew added.

She shook her head. "I know my geography. It's something more. Rock Rim,… Rim Stone…"

"Rimrock Island is where the Komodo Dragons showed up," Matthew suggested helpfully.

"There was a contest on Rimrock Island, wasn't there?" She asked.

"Yes. There is a tradition in my family to use this contest among suitors if a husband cannot be found for the unwed daughter at a certain age, like my mother," Matthew explained.

"I think my father participated in this contest," Miriam mused. "He doesn't speak of it much. I think it was a painful memory for a while, but he seems to have resolved it in his mind."

Matthew felt a growing suspicion rising in his mind. "Miriam…" he hesitated. Did he really want to know? He took a deep breath and plunged ahead. "What is your father's name?"

Miriam straighted her shoulders. "His Royal Highness King Abram Mohammed of Sahaja the First. May he live forever." She smiled proudly. "My mother is Fatima Rose Miriam of Aguala. What about yours?"

Matthew paused. "Robert of Danforth…and Elinore of Sterling."

Miriam's eyebrows furrowed a moment, and then her eyes opened wide. She stared at Matthew. "I have to go," she muttered. She hurriedly gathered up the lunch bowls, slammed them into the lunch basket and ran up the hill without looking behind her.

Mark watched her go and then turned to Matthew. "What just happened?"

"I think her father was a suitor to my mother," Matthew answered. "It didn't turn out too well between them. Let's go finish our work."

They finished the chores Assad gave them by mid-afternoon. Mark took some apple chunks to feed to Saitan, while Matthew leaned on the stall gate, deep in thought. Assad walked by, and then stopped in astonishment.

"He is on the horse!" he cried.

Matthew looked up at the horse. Mark was sitting quietly on the horse's back, occasionally leaning over to feed the horse a chunk of apple. Saitan was munching contentedly and calmly. There was no rope around his neck and no bridle on.

Mark was grinning widely. "I think he just hates bridles on his head."

Several men gathered around the stall, looking in amazement at Mark on the horse.

Assad whistled softly. "You are the first. I am impressed."

"I think it was the apples," Mark declared, sliding off the horse. He rubbed the horse's nose and Saitan whickered at him. The men stood back respectfully as Mark walked past them.

Assad put his palms together in a prayer formation and bowed to Mark. "There is no more work for you today. Tomorrow will be your last day."

"Thank you," Mark and Matthew echoed in unison.

The next day they mucked the stalls and corral, and then helped Assad fix a shed. They ate with the other men after noon prayers, and Mark visited Saitan one more time to feed him apples. There was no sign of Miriam. Late afternoon when the shed was repaired, Assad paid them their wages to take to Captain James. The boys returned their prayer robes and headdresses, and bowed their farewell to Assad. As they were walking toward the front of the palace grounds, a young woman's voice called to them from behind.

"Mark! Matt! Wait!" Miriam was running up to them. She stopped next to them, breathless. "You cannot go yet. There is something you must take with you. Come."

Curious, Mark and Matthew followed her. She led them toward the horse stables and stopped in front of Saitan's stall. She had a rope in her hands, which she handed to Mark.

"You take Saitan," she told him. "We cannot keep feeding and caring for him when no one else can ride him."

"But we go back onto a ship," Mark protested. "Where will we put him?"

"It is a merchant ship, is it not?" she asked. "There is usually a place for livestock. You just need to make sure he gets fresh water and hay until you get home."

"Is your father okay with this?" Matthew asked her. He suddenly noticed her eyes were red, as though she had been recently crying.

"We talked about...other things. This is my idea. I want you to have the horse."

"Won't you get in trouble?" Matthew probed.

Miriam shook her head. "Not much. I will just explain that you did extra work that needed more compensation. Please, take the horse! It's the least we...I can do."

Mark grinned, very pleased. "Wow! Thank you very much!" He put the rope around Saitan's neck and led him from the stall.

Matthew bowed his head to Miriam. "Thank you, Miriam. May you and your family be well."

She inclined her head to him. "May Allah be with you, Matt."

Saitan happily followed Mark off the grounds and through the town to the docks. Mark was almost giddy with excitement at the opportunity to have his own horse. He kept talking about how a horse could help him on a farm one day, and brightened his prospects for supporting a wife and family.

At the ship Matthew went on board to talk with Captain James and deliver their pay while Mark stayed with the horse. Resistant at first, Captain James finally consented when Matthew promised they would pay for the horse's passage and feed him from their own wages. With a little coaxing and another apple, Mark got the horse to follow him across the gangplank onto the ship's deck, and then onto the large pulley cargo platform to be lowered into the cargo hold. Mark stayed with the horse on the platform to keep him calm. Then they moved the horse into a little room with a porthole that let in the light.

Mark and Matthew hurried to the market place just in time before closing to get a bag of apples and two bales of hay, which they carried back on their shoulders.

The sailors spent the evening and into the night finalizing repairs on the lines, shrouds and sails. Early the next morning the Dauntless sailed out of harbor on the morning tide, and headed westward for the return journey home.

CHAPTER 12

MARIE

The Dauntless sailed back safely through the straits with all hands watching from the deck, away from where pirates lurked. Captain James appeared visibly relieved and went back to his cabin to rest. Adam returned to commanding from the poop deck, and the sailors divided back into their normal shift pattern. The Dauntless sailed northward along the coast again, stopping in various ports to exchange exotic goods for money and other supplies. Matthew found it was getting easier to understand Don's orders, and he felt more adept at climbing the rigging and adjusting the sails just the way Don wanted them.

At one larger town they were told their stop would be overnight, so Matthew and Mark went ashore for the afternoon. Matthew was feeling strangely restless, and told Mark he just felt like walking around the town.

Mark talked while Matthew remained mostly silent. He felt a low grade pressure in his stomach, like something was not quite right. When they came to a street that crossed the main street they were on he felt a little tingling in his hands. He turned down that cross street and followed it to the next street. This side street housed some smaller shops and businesses. The tingling in his hands grew stronger. He picked up his pace, looking at the shop signs as they went past.

Mark jogged to keep up. "Where are you going, Matt?" he puffed.

"I'm not sure yet," Matthew replied enigmatically.

Suddenly he stopped. The sign read, Clarisse's Hair Styles. The tingling in Matthew's hands was very strong now, moving up his arms to his shoulders. He patted the dagger at his side to make sure it was still there, and glanced at Mark. Mark's eyes were wide and astonished. They opened the door and went inside.

The shop inside was small but very clean, bright and welcoming. Two cushioned chairs were arranged by the window, with shelves of various tonics and hair décor along one wall. On the other wall hung a large mirror. In front of the mirror was stationed an upright chair on which an older woman sat, while a younger deftly braided up her hair with ribbons and combs. The younger woman's back was turned to the young men.

"I'll be with you in a moment!" she called. "Please have a seat."

Mark and Matthew sat down a little awkwardly in the chairs by the window. The tingling in Matthew's arms abated a little.

"There, Madame Bouffant. You are ready for your party tonight."

The older woman patted her hair while gazing in the mirror. "Thank you so much, my dear. It is perfect." She stood and paid the hair dresser, and swooshed toward the door. She glanced once at the boys sitting by the window, her expression turning sour as she smelled their fishy clothes.

There was a gasp from the back of the shop, and Matthew turned to look into the face of Clarisse, the girl he had met at La Castille. Her face was pale and she grasped for the salon chair to steady herself.

"You!" she whispered. "What are you doing here?"

"We are in port overnight." Matthew wasn't sure how to explain how he found her. "We were just wandering through town and found your shop." Mark glanced at him curiously.

"Oh," she breathed.

"I see you were able to set up the shop you dreamed of," Matthew commented. "I assume business is going well?"

She nodded. "Thanks to you." She looked around nervously. "Are you alone?"

"Yes." Matthew spread out his hands. "But something brought me here. Are you in any trouble?"

"No." She shook her head and paused. "But I am afraid Marie might be."

Mark jerked and took a step toward Clarisse. "Marie! What is wrong with her?"

Clarisse sank into the chair. "I have no way of knowing for sure, but I can only imagine. We worked together. I disappeared one night, and I am sure she was questioned about me. They would likely have beaten or starved her to make her talk. But she knew nothing, only that I had dreams about a different life." Clarisse gazed around her shop. "I prayed to God to help her, and then you came."

Mark stepped toward her again. "What can be done? Can I—we do something to help her?"

Warmth flooded over Matthew's body and the hand tingling disappeared. "That is why we have come, Clarisse. We are supposed to help Marie. What do you need us to do?"

She shook her head and thought. "If only someone could rescue her from that place, like you did me." She gazed up at Matthew.

He walked over to Clarisse and grasped her hand. "I believe our ship will dock in that port again in a few days. But I am not so sure we will be welcomed back into their establishment again."

"I am willing to try!" Mark pounded his chest with his fist.

"Shh!" Clarisse looked around nervously. "Perhaps we should plan over dinner tonight. I have two more clients this afternoon, and then I can close shop. Can you come back around five?"

"Yes!" Mark responded immediately.

Clarisse grasped his hand and squeezed it gratefully. "I think you are an answer to prayers."

Matthew and Mark left the shop and continued to stroll down the street.

Mark could barely contain himself. "Matt, maybe this is my chance to redeem myself for my, um, indiscretion with Marie. I hadn't been able to get her out of my mind."

Matthew nodded. "So once you rescue her, what will you do? I don't think Captain would let her stow away on our ship. That would jeopardize his ability to go to that port again."

Mark looked crestfallen. "I hadn't thought of that." He pondered for a few minutes. "I can give her all of my money. Maybe she can escape the same way Clarisse did."

"We don't have much money since spending it on your horse. And what if they chase her down and find her? How does she get to Clarisse?"

Mark's face furrowed. "Maybe I should go with her. An escort in disguise. But I only have sailing clothes."

Matthew shrugged. "We are about the same size. Maybe you wear the landlubber clothes I brought with me."

Mark's face lit up. "Could I? That would work, I think."

"You would not be able to catch up with the Dauntless again this season. We would leave port without you. Would Captain James take you back as a sailor next year if you left ship without advanced notice?" Matthew probed.

Mark frowned again. "Probably not. I would have to hire onto a different ship, or work on land for a while." He looked over at Matthew. "I might not see you again for some time, mate."

"Is this what you really want to do?" Matthew asked. "Once you start this rescue for Marie, there is no turning back until it's done and she's safely back here with Clarisse. Then what?"

Mark shrugged. "I don't know."

Matthew studied him. "Do you want to be a sailor all your life, Mark? You spoke once of farming."

Mark kicked the cobblestones with his shoe. "I don't think so. I would like to settle down sometime with a wife and have a family."

"With Marie?"

Mark blushed. "Maybe. If she would have me."

"You realize where she has been, Mark? Maybe she won't want to marry and have a family."

Mark turned on him angrily. "You don't know her, Matt. She has dreams too. Just because she is trapped where she is doesn't mean she can't have her dream come true someday too. Maybe I can be the one to make that happen for her."

Matthew held up his hands. "Okay! I just wanted to make sure you looked at the whole picture." He patted Mark on the shoulder. "I actually am glad you want to do this for Marie."

Mark looked at him slyly. "You could come with me and be here for Clarisse!"

Matthew shook his head. "My heart lies with Sarah back home."

"You mean that girl who jilted you? You need to move on, Matt!"

"I want one more chance to win her heart. If that doesn't work out I can come back and find you."

Mark suddenly paused in his walking. "Matt, how did you find Clarisse anyway? The whole thing was weird. I mean, it was almost like you were being led to her."

"Or driven," Matthew responded a little glumly. "I told God once as a boy that I wanted to help protect people, and I would follow Him if He would help me. Then I got this gift. I can sense when people close to me are in trouble."

Mark whistled. "I guess there might be a God up there after all."

At five o'clock Mark and Matthew returned to Clarisse's Hair Styles shop. She was waiting for them, welcomed them in and locked the door behind them.

"It isn't fancy, but the food will be hot," she confessed. She took them into the back of the shop and up a flight of stairs, to a one room loft that had a cook fire, table and bed.

She quickly heated up some soup over the fire, and laid out a loaf of bread and some fruit on the table. The boys sat in the two chairs at the table while Clarisse sat on the bed. The soup was tasty and the bread fresh.

After eating, Clarisse offered some ideas for getting Marie out of La Castille. Mark shared his ideas for getting Marie back to Clarisse, which included possibly using a horse. She drew a map on the table with charcoal, showing the towns and back roads that they could take. She handed Mark a black wig to disguise himself when he went to La Castille, and a little bag of money she had saved.

"Well, I suppose this is it," Mark sat back in his chair.

Clarisse grasped his hand. "You are so brave to attempt this," she told him. "I just know God will be with you in this endeavor."

Mark shrugged. "You have been kind to us. You both deserve some happiness in your lives."

Tears coursed down her cheeks. "This is no small thing. No one else ever seemed to care like this." Mark grasped her hand and squeezed it.

Matthew eyed the fading light out the window. "We must return soon if we are going to be able to spend the night back on our ship." He stood and shook Clarisse's hand. "I am glad you found your dream, Clarisse."

She kissed his cheek. "You will come back some day, Matt?"

He glanced at Mark. "How can I say no? I will have to come back to check on this shipmate of mine."

They made it back to the Dauntless just before Adam had the gangplank pulled for the night.

"Ah, just in time," he told them. "Can one of you help guard through the night shift?"

"I will," Mark answered. "I don't feel much like sleeping right now anyway."

"Send for me if you need a break," Matthew told him.

Matthew lay awake in his bunk for a while, a mix of emotions and thoughts in his head. He was glad Clarisse had found her way. He was worried for Mark and Marie. He wondered if there was something he could do to create a false trail away from their escape route, or a way to protect the Dauntless from blame. It would take three or four days to reach the main port where Marie was. That left them three to four days to work out the details of the rescue.

"The big question is whether we tell Captain James what we are planning," Matthew mused with Mark the next day. "If he gets some warning you might be able to sail with him again someday. But then the Dauntless becomes accomplice."

Mark shook his head vigorously. "The fewer people who know our plan, the better chance to leave unnoticed."

"Our men will notice the horse leaving," Matthew pointed out.

"Fewer will see if we take him out in the middle of shore leave," Mark responded. "Saitan will need to stretch his legs after all this time cooped up in the hold."

The ship arrived in Port Mer Eclat late morning. After unloading cargo and getting paid, most of the sailors left to spend their next twenty hours in town. The boys slept a couple of hours, and then prepared to take the horse off the ship. Mark tucked all of his savings plus the money Matthew gave him into his purse, tied to his belt and tucked inside his waistband. He wore Matthew's landlubber clothes underneath his sailor's clothes, the wig from Clarisse inside his shirt. He also tucked several apples and biscuits into his tunic to eat later. While Mark fed and watered the horse one more time, Matthew went on deck to prepare the winch and the cargo lift.

As the boys were hauling Saitan up the cargo lift, Adam came down from the poop deck to see what they were doing.

"Where are you going with the horse?" Adam queried.

"Giving him a chance to stretch his legs on land," Mark explained calmly. "We'll put the equipment back in order when we are finished."

"Fine," Adam nodded and went back to his observation deck.

"Smooth talking," Matthew whispered to Mark.

It took a quarter of apple to coax Saitan down the gangplank to the dock. After that the horse followed Mark happily down the cobblestone streets. The boys walked through the side streets toward the southeastern side of town. There were mostly farm fields to the south. They found a road heading east toward wooded hills, which Mark thought looked promising as an exit route.

Toward evening the young men led Saitan back into town and tied him up in a little alley about a block from La Castille.

"Sorry to do this to you, Saitan," Mark whispered in his ear. "But I can't have you following me this time. I need you to be here when I come for you." Saitan blew air threw his lips at Mark.

Mark grasped Matthew by the hand. "Thanks for everything, mate."

"Take care of yourself and the girls," Matthew admonished.

Matthew put on Mark's sailor's clothes over his own, and Mark pulled on the dark wig. Matthew studied him a moment, and then pulled an old beret cap out of his pocket. "Try this on," he told Mark.

Mark put it on his head awkwardly and Matthew fixed it for him. "That's better."

"Don't you think it is a little old fashioned?" Mark asked, adjusting the cap one more time.

Matthew shrugged. "Maybe it will become popular again."

Mark grinned a little nervously. "Show time."

"Good luck to you, mate," Matthew responded, then turned and left the alley.

Mark turned back to the horse and leaned into the horse's neck one more time for courage. "God," he prayed. "If you are really there, help me get Marie out safely."

Matthew walked back toward the docks, meandering along various streets, mingling with the night crowd. He followed a group of noisy young sailors into a pub a block away from the docks, and pretended to be part of their group as they sat down inside. The group didn't notice him at first. Then one sailor turned to him.

"You're not a sailor on the Reale. Who are you?"

Matthew hesitated, and then decided it would be best to use his real name, more or less. "Matt, I'm with the Dauntless." He stuck out his hand.

"I'm Davie," the sailor shook his hand. "You hanging out with us this evening?"

"Yeah, if that's all right with you."

"Sure. You want a drink?"

Matthew nodded. "I can pay. Ale please!" he told the serving girl and handed her his second to last coin.

The Reale's crew was a jolly lot, singing sea chanties and drinking freely. One group played some gambling card games, which Matthew was tempted only for a moment to play, deciding instead to get some dinner with his last coin. He joined in the laughter and singing and nursed his cup of ale along slowly, determined to stay clear headed. Around midnight when their group left the pub Matthew left with them. He wandered around the docks, singing loudly at times and pretending to be slightly inebriated. The Dauntless had already pulled in the gangplank, so at about two in the morning Matthew settled down beside some crates in view of the ship, and fell uncomfortably asleep.

Mark watched the entrance to La Castille Pub and Inn until a group of townspeople entered and then he followed them inside. He sat at a table alone, and ordered a soup and ale. He looked around but there was no sign of Marie. Soon another young woman approached him.

"Would you like some company?" she asked.

Mark hesitated and then nodded. She sat down.

"My name is Reine. How may I keep you company tonight?"

"Do you know any good card games?" he asked lamely.

She did and explained a game to him. He played halfheartedly, frequently glancing around the room, and lost to Reine every time.

"Perhaps we should try a different game?" she asked, bored.

"Yes." Mark suggested one he knew well, and explained it to her. As they started to play, he glanced up and spotted Marie entering with two older women. His eyes followed her as she stood glassy-eyed for a moment and then walked toward another table of guests.

Reine watched him. "Perhaps you prefer different company?" she asked, a little unhappily.

"Yes! Um, maybe," he fumbled.

Reine stood up and went over to Marie, glancing once at Mark and gesturing toward him as they talked. Marie nodded and approached him.

"My name is Marie," she stated. "I am happy to keep you company tonight. What is your name?"

"M-Meeker," Mark caught himself quickly. It was not yet the right time to reveal himself, and Marie obviously did not recognize him.

"You wish to play a game?" She asked, not really smiling.

"Um, yes!" He dealt the cards and explained the game. They played several rounds, Marie offered to refill his ale, and he bought her one too, which she partially drank. Finally he leaned back in his chair and stretched.

"I am tired. Do you have a room here where I could sleep?" he asked casually.

Marie nodded. "Would you like some company?" she asked automatically.

"Yes, if it is with you," Mark responded gently.

She glanced into his eyes momentarily, and then looked down again. "As you wish."

She stood and led him through a door to the back hall and toward some stairs.

Mark paused. "Do you have any rooms on the main floor?"

She shook her head. "Those rooms are not available to us."

She continued up the stairs and opened a door, let Mark in, and then shut and locked it behind them. Mark went over to the window and looked out. Below them was a dark alley that ran the length of the inn. He turned back toward the room where Marie had started unbuttoning her dress.

"Whoa, stop!" Mark held up his hands toward her. "Don't do that yet."

She looked puzzled. "You do not wish me to—"

Mark interrupted her. "You need to know who I really am." He pulled off his cap and wig. "I am Mark from the Dauntless. We came through here a couple of months ago."

She stared at him, unsure.

"My shipmate Matt was with your friend Clarisse the night she disappeared."

Recognition lit her face. Then she looked frightened. "You should not be here. They will arrest you. Perhaps they will beat you until you tell them where Clarisse is." She said this in a low voice.

He pulled her down to sit next to him on the bed. "I am here to rescue you from this place, if you wish it."

She soaked in this information, various emotions flickering across her face. "Yes, I wish it," she whispered.

She padded silently to the door and peeked through the keyhole, and then replaced the key. She next looked out the window. Then she sat down on the bed again by Mark.

"We must pretend to have a normal night of socializing. Things are most quiet around three in the morning. That is the best time." She sighed. "Alas, I have no money or extra clothes for travel."

Matthew jingled his purse. "I have the money. Perhaps we can borrow some clothes along the way."

She looked slightly hopeful. "That might work…"

He glanced toward the window. "Unfortunately we are on the second floor. It will be a challenge to climb out."

She shook her head. "It is fortunate actually. They now have bars on the first floor windows. We can use bedsheets to climb out here."

They heard footsteps in the hall, pausing outside their door. Marie turned to Mark. "Kiss me," she commanded.

Surprised, Mark obeyed, pecking her on the lips.

She slapped his face and jumped back. "Meeker!" she said loudly. "You forward b_____! Can't you even give a girl a moment to get ready?"

He cleared his throat. "Yes, but I can't wait all night!"

They held their breaths and listened. The footsteps continued down the hall. Mark and Marie fell onto the bed, giggling quietly.

She suddenly stopped laughing. "When Clarisse disappeared, I thought my world had ended," she whispered.

"She is in a town south of here several days' journey. She has her hair shop now. In fact she gave me this wig to wear. She asked us to come and get you out. I have a horse to help us get there."

She hesitated. "I don't know how to ride."

Mark grimaced. "Yeah, well Saitan probably won't let you ride him anyway. We'll have to get a wagon."

"They will jail us and maybe kill us if we get caught. Are you sure you want to do this?" she asked quietly.

Mark nodded and gazed at her solemnly. "I have never been so sure of anything in my life."

She returned his gaze and then lowered her eyes. "When I am free I think I would like to make dresses," she told him. "Nice ones for the proper ladies."

"A hair and dress shop would go well together. I think Clarisse would like that."

She looked him in the eye. "I wish no more intimate socializing. It will only be when and with whom I choose."

Mark felt something wither inside him. "I understand."

"What will you do after we get there?" she asked him.

"I have been thinking about working a little farm. My father was a farmer, and now I have a horse."

"What will we do for food on the journey?" She suddenly asked.

Mark drew the apples and biscuits from his tunic. "I am saving these for tomorrow, until we can buy food at the next town."

She smiled. "Good. I think we should rest a little now." She lay down on the bed.

Mark stood uncertainly at the foot of the bed. "I'm not sure where I should sleep."

Marie glanced toward the door and sighed. "On the bed with me, I suppose. But that does not give you any liberties to touch me."

Mark nodded and lay down on the edge of the bed far from her, turning his back to her. He supposed he felt glad that she was feeling some hope and independence now about her life. After about twenty minutes he heard soft even breathing behind him. He rolled over to look at her. She lay on her side facing him, her hand stretched toward him, a slight smile on her lips. He reached a hand toward hers, but did not touch it. Soon he closed his eyes and also slept.

Mark woke suddenly to Marie shaking his shoulder. "Wake up, Mark! It is almost four in the morning! We must go now!"

She had already removed her outer party dress, and was clothed in only her slip, shoes and stockings. She pulled the sheets off the bed and tied them end to end.

"Do you have everything with you?" she asked.

Mark patted the money purse and food in his tunic. "Oh! The wig and cap!" He snatched them from the table and put them on his head. "Let's go."

She opened the window and lowered one end of the sheet rope. Mark grasped the nearer end and held it firmly. "You go first," he whispered.

She lowered herself out the window and climbed down the sheets to the alley below. She stepped back and hugged her arms to herself in the night chill. Mark looked at her a moment, then at the sheets. He untied one and tossed it down to her. He threw the other back on the bed. Then he swung himself out the window and hung to the windowsill with his fingertips. He let go and fell to the ground below. He tried to land quietly but his shoes clapped on the cobblestone. Marie looked alarmed and turned to flee, sheet wrapped around her. Mark grasped her hand and pulled her the opposite way, toward where he had left his horse. They ran up the alley, turned down the next street, then into the covey where Saitan waited.

Saitan nickered softly as Mark untied him. Hurriedly they led the horse away to the eastern edge of town. As they reached the last house, Mark paused in the shadows. Dawn touched an edge of the sky.

Mark turned to Saitan and pulled out a piece of cut apple, holding it in front of the horse's nose. "Saitan, I have a favor to ask. This is really important. We need to ride you for about two miles to the woods. Then you will be free of riders again. I want you to meet Marie."

Mark took Marie's hand, put the apple slice in it, and held her palm up under the horse's nose. The horse nibbled the apple from her hand. Marie laid her hand on Saitan's nose. The horse held still and let her rub his face. He blew on her hand and then lowered his head, ears forward. Mark carefully led her to Saitan's side. He climbed up first and sat for a moment on Saitan's back, holding onto the rope around his neck. The horse's ears moved forward and back, but he stayed still. Then Mark pulled Marie up behind him. She grasped Mark tightly around the waist. The horse stayed calm.

"Grip the horse's side with your knees," Mark instructed. "Saitan, you may go now. Adhhab!"

Saitan started walking forward. Soon the horse was trotting, and Mark had to grip Saitan's mane to keep from falling off. Marie perched precariously behind him, but managed to stay on. Saitan partially followed Mark's lead as he pulled the rope on one side to keep him heading towards the woods. Finally they neared the trees, Mark spoke "Tawaquf!", and gratefully the two slid off Saitan's back. They looked back toward the edge of town, seeing people begin to wake and move in the growing light. Then Mark led them deeper into the trees.

"The road shouldn't be too far from here," he told her. "Can you make that sheet look more like a dress?"

She nodded and wrapped it differently, tying it around her shoulders and waist. "Do you think you should remove the wig now? They might be looking for a sneak called Meeker."

He took off the wig and threw it deep into the woods. The cap he put back on his head. "I think my name will be Morris now."

Marie laughed. "I'll be Maude. Don't you think you should have kept that wig, just in case?"

Mark looked chagrined. "You're right. Clarisse might want it back. I'll have to reimburse her for it."

After an hour of walking they found the road. Marie looked nervous, even though there weren't many people traveling yet. Whenever someone came by she hid in the trees until they passed.

"I need a real dress and common shoes as soon as we reach the first town," she told Mark. "A girl wearing a bed sheet is unusual enough that people will notice."

"Who will they tell?" Mark commented.

"My boss will send out the Recruiters to search for me," she responded grimly.

In another hour they reached the outskirts of a town. Marie hid in the woods with Saitan while Mark went exploring. In half an hour he returned, a bundle of clothes in his arms. He showed her a work dress, smock and cap.

"Perfect!" Marie exclaimed and quickly changed out of the sheet. The dress was loose but adequate. She glanced down at her dressy shoes. "I think I need some clogs or something."

Mark cut some pieces off the sheet with his pocketknife and wrapped them around her shoes. "Will this work for now?"

Marie nodded. "Now cut my hair,"

Mark gazed at her waist-long locks. "Your beautiful hair—" he began.

"Will grow again. I need it shoulder length. Now!" she commanded.

He took his machete' blade in one hand and her hair in another, and hesitated. Then in one swift movement he cut her hair off. It was slightly crooked at the edges, but Marie was satisfied. She carried the cut strands into the woods for the birds and animals to use.

"All right, let's go," she told him and started walking down the road.

Not willing to throw the sheet away yet, Mark tied it around his waist like a sash. This time they blended in more with the travelers on the road. They each ate a biscuit as they walked.

Several miles past the first town a horseman trotted down the road behind them. Mark glanced back. The man seemed to be studying each traveler he passed. Instinctively Mark pulled the cap lower over his eyes. The horseman came up even with them and matched their pace for a while.

"Good morning," the man spoke.

Mark nodded. "Hm." Marie did not look up, but Mark noticed her posture and gait had subtly changed, mildly stooped and stiff.

"Where are you off to this fine morning?" the man asked.

Marie did not respond. It was up to him. "To my sister's," Mark replied gruffly.

"Why are you not riding this fine horse?" the horseman asked.

"He doesn't seem to be a riding horse. More of a cart-pulling horse," Mark answered truthfully.

The man laughed. "Not much of a horse then, is he? Selling him or giving him away?"

Mark shrugged.

"Where did you say you were from?" the man asked casually.

Mark mumbled the name of the town they had just passed through.

The horseman seemed satisfied. "Well, good day." He said cheerfully and rode on ahead. Then he turned and looked back at them. "By the way, Marie, Connie has been looking for you."

Marie flinched. In a second the man leaped off his horse and ran toward Marie. Mark met him, machete' in hand, while Marie cowered against Saitan's side.

"Move aside, thief," the man growled, sporting a sword in his own hand. "This girl doesn't belong to you."

"No, she doesn't belong to anybody," Mark didn't back down. "She is a free person like the rest of us, free to choose her own life. Free to claim her basic human rights."

"No one is really free," the man stated and lunged at Mark.

Mark dodged, and swung his machete' but it missed. The man came at him again, sword jabbing toward him. Something burned in Mark's left side as he parried. Enraged, he charged the man and stuck his blade up into the man's chest.

"That is for all the terrible things you have done to her and others like her," he grimaced.

The man fell at Mark's feet, eyes open and staring. Marie shuddered and looked away. Mark dragged the body off the road into the trees, gagged a bit over a bush, and then returned to Marie, who was holding the recruiter's sword. He placed a hand on her shoulder.

"Are you all right?" he asked her.

She nodded. "Get his horse," she whispered.

Mark looked at the mare, standing in the road and waiting. He cut a piece of apple and approached her, hand outstretched. The horse gobbled the apple and let Mark take the reins. As he led the horse back, he felt something wet and sticky at his side. He looked down and saw blood oozing from his left side. He started feeling a burning pain again.

"Oh, you are hurt!" Marie cried. She took the sheet and wrapped it around Mark's trunk over the wound. "You must ride," she told him.

"Then you should ride the other horse," he breathed.

She looked uncertainly at the horse. "How do I get up?"

Mark led her to the horse's side and bent a knee. "Step on my thigh, then put your left foot in the stirrup, and swing your leg over the horse's back."

On the second try she was on. He handed her the reins and briefly told her what he knew about guiding a horse. Then he went over to Saitan's side, put a hand on the horse's neck, and jumped up to mount.

When his stomach landed on Saitan's back, pain seared in his side again. He lay there for a minute while he caught his breath, and then swung his leg over.

"Are you all right?" Marie asked.

"Yes," he breathed through gritted teeth. "Let's go. Adhhab!" Marie's horse followed Saitan.

"I think I'll call this horse Sadie," Marie commented. Mark just nodded.

When they reached the next town, Mark stopped his horse in front of an inn. "I need to rest," he told Marie.

They slid off their horses, tied them up at the side of the inn and made their way inside.

"We'd like a room, please," Marie told the innkeeper.

He looked at them suspiciously. "What do you need a room for?" he asked.

"My name is Maude, and this is …my brother, Morris. We have been traveling through the night and just need a few hours' rest."

"And a hot meal," Mark added, handing the innkeeper some change.

The innkeeper nodded, and had one of his staff lead them to a room on the main floor. Mark collapsed onto the bed gratefully. Marie unwrapped the bedsheet bandage to look at the wound. It was still oozing. Marie washed her hands at the basin in the room, and then returned to Mark's side.

"I need to explore the wound and see how deep it is," she told him.

He nodded and turned his head. She probed a finger inside. It only went up to the first knuckle, but the bleeding increased again.

"I need to stitch this up," she told him, pushing the sheet dressing back over the wound.

There was a knock at the door and a girl brought them a tray of hot food.

"Miss," Marie asked her. "I tore my dress. Do you happen to have a needle and thread I could borrow to mend it?"

The girl nodded. "I will bring it right to you." She left and returned in a moment with the items.

After she left again Marie turned to Mark. "This will hurt a little bit." She washed the wound with fresh water, poured a little ale over the wound, and then proceeded to stitch it up. Mark grunted each time the needle pierced his skin, but let her finish the job. The bleeding appeared to stop.

She leaned back and wiped the back of her hand across her brow. "There, that should do it. No more bumping your side. I don't want the stitches to tear."

"Yes, ma'am," he smiled wanly. "I'm thirsty."

She gave him a mug of ale. He drank deeply and leaned back. "That's better." He closed his eyes.

She sat on the edge of the bed and laid a hand on his. "Mark, thank you for what you did for me back there."

"You're welcome." He was silent a moment. "I shouldn't have…killed that man. I was just so angry." Mark grimaced.

"That was self-defense!" Marie protested. "If you hadn't, he would have killed you and taken me back to…" She couldn't finish, but covered her face with her other hand.

Mark opened his eyes. "I've never killed anyone before. It still feels awful."

Marie kissed him lightly on the cheek. "You are different from any other man I've met before."

"Is that a good thing?" Mark asked gently.

"Yes, that is a good thing."

Mark sat up in the bed. "Where is that hot food? I'm hungry!"

They ate, and then Marie washed the blood out of the bedsheet, throwing the dirty water into the plants outside the window and hanging the sheet up to dry. While Mark slept she crept out to run an errand.

Mid-afternoon she woke Mark up. "I don't think we should stay here. We need to at least get to the next town," she told him. She slipped the recruiter's sword inside the waistband of her skirt where she could retrieve it easily.

His side was stiff, but he was otherwise feeling better. She checked his wound one more time; it was still dry. Still, she wrapped the sheet around his trunk underneath his shirt for support. They left the inn and went to get their horses. This time there was a mounting block to use.

"You have different shoes!" Mark exclaimed.

"Yes. While you were napping I traded my other ones for a set of clogs," she confessed. "The woman I traded with will get a little surprise when she next comes outside to fetch her shoes." They both laughed.

Outside of town they found a stream and long grass to refresh the horses. Then they rode on. Late that evening they reached the next town. Mark counted his coins.

"I think we can stay one more night at an inn, and then we better save the rest of the money for travel food," he told her.

"Put that money away," she told him. "I have an idea how we can earn our keep tonight."

Marie led him into the inn and talked to the innkeeper's wife while Mark waited by the door. Soon she was back with a smile on her face.

"I'll serve some guests while you wash dishes and clean floors. I told her you hurt your back and can't chop wood today. Madam said there is a little room off the kitchen where we can sleep tonight," Marie told him.

Mark nodded. "That will do."

They went to work. Around eleven pm Marie slipped back into the kitchen and began helping Mark wash dishes. Fifteen minutes later Madam huffed into the kitchen, leaned against a table and wiped her brow.

"I can't believe that man! He didn't want to pay for his food, and he kept yapping on about a runaway girl who stole his horse. He was creating quite a disturbance in the main room. I had to take a broom to his backside to get him out of here." She frowned. "He even tried to take your horses!" Then she grinned. "The white horse bit him on the arm. Serves him right!"

Mark and Marie smiled at each other.

Madam looked at them. "You have worked hard, you cute couple, and I thank you. Eat some supper and get some rest. I suggest you leave early in the morning before that man tries to bother you again, dears."

"Thank you, Madam." Marie kissed her on the cheek. "You have been most kind."

The woman patted her on the cheek. "Anything for someone who reminds me of my own daughter."

The bed in the little room was narrow, and Mark hesitated to join Marie on it. But there was no other place to sleep.

Marie scooted her back up against the wall and patted the bed beside her. "Lie down, Mark, I won't attack you. You need your sleep as much as I do."

"Yes, ma'am," Mark smiled gratefully. He lay down carefully and was soon fast asleep.

Mark woke before Marie this time. He slipped out into the kitchen and peered out the window. It was still dark out, but with a hint of light on the horizon. He carefully brought in some small loads of firewood and laid them by the stove. Then he went back to wake up Marie. She looked tired like she hadn't slept very well.

"I'm all right," she told him. "I'm used to functioning on very little sleep."

"I think we ought to turn south now," Mark told her. "I'd like to shake off the trail of any who are following us. The question is whether we travel through the country or follow the roads?"

Marie considered this while she checked his side. The dressing was dry and the wound had no redness. "Stick to the road," she answered finally. "It will be harder to follow tracks, and we can blend in better as normal travelers. Plus it will be faster traveling for us. I want to get as much distance behind us as possible."

Mark nodded. "Agreed. Let's go."

They grabbed some fruit and bread from the kitchen, and went outside. Their horses were still there, and Mark gave each horse half an apple.

"You are going to spoil them, you know," Marie told him.

"I'm just buying their loyalty," Mark responded. "It helped us last night, you may have noticed."

They took the road south as the sun came up. As Marie's confidence in riding Sadie grew, they took their horses into a trot, then a gentle lope. Mark was still guiding Saitan by a rope around his neck, but the horse responded to the gentle rope tugs and verbal commands. They passed through two towns, eating the bread as they journeyed. Night fell before they reached the next town. Even though stars filled the sky to light the way, Marie slowed her horse to a walk.

"When do you think we'll reach Clarisse's town?" she asked.

"At this rate the day after tomorrow, barring any mishaps," he replied.

"May we stay in an inn again tonight?" she asked. "I need a real bed. I am sore from riding."

"Me too. I am willing to pay for it tonight."

They finally reached the next town, rented a room, and fell exhausted onto the bed. Mark was almost asleep when Marie spoke.

"Mark?"

"Yes, Marie?"

She hesitated. "I never told you how I ended up at La Castille."

"No. I assumed you would tell me what I needed to know when you were ready. I'm okay with that," he answered.

"I want you to know." She took a deep breath. "I did not intend to end up in any place like that. I was sixteen when I came to the city to work. My family was too poor to feed me any longer and it was time for me to make my own way. I started off looking for cleaning and mending jobs, but they were hard to come by. So I took a job serving at an inn for a while. Then one day my boss told me I was being transferred to another "inn" where I could earn a higher wage, wear pretty dresses, and get free room and board. It sounded really nice. I was tricked."

Mark listened silently, but reached out and grasped Marie's hand. She gripped it tightly.

"When I found out what my new job really entailed, I tried to leave, but it was too late. They have ways to blackmail you, or come after you to bring you back," she whispered. "Many of the girls are kidnapped off the streets and brought in. I think that is how Clarisse ended up there."

Mark's throat felt tight. He could hardly say a word if he had wanted to.

"I used to dream I might find a man of my own to marry and have children, but my career at La Castille has probably lost me that chance." She was crying. "Mark, is there any chance you would want me after... you know...where I've been?"

Mark's voice cracked with emotion. "Yes," he told her simply. "I think that is why I came back for you."

"Oh, Mark! I don't know what I want anymore. There are times I don't want to see another man in my bed ever again." She leaned her head into his shoulder, letting loose a few sobs. Then she calmed. "You have treated me very well. I think I do like you enough to let you..." She reached for the lacing on the front of her dress.

Mark grabbed her hand and sat up. "No, Marie!" He stood up and paced. Marie stared at him, shocked. He stopped and faced her. "Don't get me wrong. I do want you. I want you very much. But a princely friend once showed me that there is a better way, a happier way. You deserve a proper wedding—"

Marie interrupted him. "I don't deserve—"

"Everyone deserves a chance for happiness and change, even us. Let's put that other part of your life in the past and do things now the way they should have been." He sat back on the bed and took her hand in his. He wanted to ask her the big question, but realized now was not the time. She needed time to heal first. "Marie, you are a lovely girl, and I would like a chance to get to know you better. Would you consider letting me court you?"

"I don't know if I am ready for a boyfriend," she finally responded. "What long term prospects do you offer?"

"Hm, funny you ask. I have a horse, and I grew up on a farm. Once I find a town that I like, I plan to work until I can purchase a small plot of ground, and then start my own little farm, which I predict will grow bigger. I will save enough to build a comfortable cottage, big enough for a family. When I find the right woman, I will ask her to marry me, and we will live happily-ever-after." Mark smiled hopefully at her.

"Perhaps you are right, we should get to know each other better first," she responded.

He nodded. "You do not have to accept any commitment until you are ready. I can be your friend Mark, or your brother 'Morris'."

She peered at him. "You don't look like a Morris."

"Maybe I should have kept that wig."

She laughed. "I like you better as Mark. Thank you for giving me the space I need." She leaned forward and kissed Mark meaningfully on the mouth. He responded tenderly. She drew back smiling. "I rather think I liked that kiss better than any I ever experienced before."

"I did too," he told her, and kissed her again. "Now it's time to go to sleep. No more distractions."

"Yes, 'Morris,'" she smiled, lay down and closed her eyes, a smile on her lips.

Mark covered her with the blanket, and then curled up on the edge of the bed to sleep.

The sun was well up when they awoke. They hurriedly packed up their things and went to fetch their horses.

"I can't face riding on the horse again today," Marie groaned. "What if we walk?"

Mark assented, also sore from the previous day. About an hour later, Marie saw something off to the side of the road and went to investigate.

"It's a broken wagon," she told Mark. "Do you think you could fix it? Then we could ride more comfortably."

They brought their horses over and Mark examined the wagon. One wheel was off and was missing some spokes. The axles were straight, but the bed of the wagon was cracked and one side rail had fallen off. The wagon leaned precariously, one wheel in a ditch.

"I think I can fix this," Mark mused. "And with the horses we should be able to pull it out of the ditch."

He and Marie tore the old sheet into strips and he fashioned a harness to attach Saitan to the wagon shafts. With some coaxing he got the horse to heave forward. Marie pushed the wagon from behind. The wagon finally rolled out of the ditch and onto flat ground. Mark fed Saitan a portion of the last apple he had been saving, then untied him and went to examine the wagon again.

"It looks like a metal pin is missing that goes through the end of the axle to hold the wheel on. I think I can fashion one from wood if we can't find the metal one," he told her.

They searched the ditch and along the side of the road, but found no metal pin. While Mark cut a strong thin branch and started whittling it to the right size, Marie explored the woods. She came back with some branches and laid them in the wagon bed. Mark looked at her questioningly.

"I thought it should look more like we are taking a load to the next town. Some more camouflage for our identities," she explained.

"Good idea!" Mark told her. He finished up the stick whittling. He wrestled the wheel back onto the axle, and while Marie leaned on the wheel, he worked the stick into the hole, finally pounding it into place with a rock. While Mark hefted up the corner of the wagon to lift the wheel off the ground, Marie spun the wheel. It spun mostly straight and the wooden pin held.

Mark smiled. "That should hold for a couple of days anyway. Let's hook up the horses and go."

He fastened Saitan again to the wagon shafts to pull it, and tied Sadie's reins to the back of the wagon to follow them. Mark and Marie seated themselves on the wagon seat and Mark gave Saitan the command to go. Saitan seemed to know what to do. Mark held onto the rope fastened around his neck to guide him when needed. Marie settled back in the wagon seat, grateful to be off the horse for a while.

Just outside of the next town a horseman rode by them, rough cut, and studying the faces of all the travelers going by foot. Marie hunched her shoulders and kept her head down. The horseman did not pay them much attention. After he was long gone she finally heaved a sigh of relief and relaxed.

"That was another recruiter," she told Mark. "I would have thought we were far enough away that they would have stopped looking for me."

"They are persistent," Mark mused. "Or desperate. You must have been very good."

"I don't think that's it," she replied. "I think they don't want any other girls to think it is possible to escape."

Mark thought about that for a few minutes. "Someday someone should change all that. There should be laws against it." He sighed. "For now, it is about time to turn back west toward the coast. What do you think, do we dare?"

Marie nodded. "I am afraid to stop any more places until we arrive at our destination."

At the next crossroads with a westbound road Mark turned onto it. He coaxed Saitan into a trot, and Sadie obediently followed at the same pace. Periodically he slowed the horses to check his makeshift axle pin. So far it held.

They paused a couple of times between towns to let the horses eat and drink. Marie found some berries and roots in the woods for her and Mark to eat. It grew dark and they still traveled on. Finally they saw the lights of a larger town ahead, and then caught sight of moonlight glinting on a harbor as the road descended toward it. Mark tried to remember the direction of the street where they had found Clarisse three weeks before. Finally he drove along the docks until he found a street that looked familiar. He turned inland, found the right street, and in five minutes stopped in front of Clarisse's Hair Styles shop. Marie jumped out of the wagon and pounded on the shop door.

"Hello! Clarisse!" she shouted.

Mark finished tying up the horses out front just as Clarisse opened the shop door, dressed in a robe over her dressing gown.

"Marie! Oh mon Dieu, you are really here! Come in, come in!" She pulled Marie inside and embraced her friend. Both girls were crying.

"Mark! You are also here! Thank you so much!" Clarisse drew Mark into the group hug with one arm. Then she stepped back. "But where is Matt?"

Mark hesitated briefly. "He is sailing on to return to his homeland."

Clarisse looked sad. "But of course. I think his heart lies in that direction. I understand. But you are here! For how long do you stay?"

Mark glanced at Marie. "I think I am here to stay for good."

Marie grasped his arm with her hand. "I think he is going to become a farmer. He already has a horse and wagon."

Clarisse turned to Marie. "And you? What are your plans?"

Marie glowed. "I would like to try my hand at dressmaking."

"Then you must share my shop with me!" Clarisse hugged them both again. "But tonight you sleep here at my place. Tomorrow we start our new lives together."

Matthew was awakened by someone kicking at his foot. Dawn was lighting the sky, and the air was crisp and chill. He raised his stiff neck and looked up into the face of a middle aged dock hand, carrying a box on his shoulder.

"Time you be getting out of here, mate. The docks will be getting quite busy soon. Your night snooze needs to come to an end."

"Thank you, sir." Matthew pushed himself stiffly to his feet, picked up his sailor hat and put it on his head, and looked around to locate his ship.

The man was staring at him curiously. "You look familiar to me somehow. Where are you from?"

"Oh, not from around here. I grew up in Sterling. I'm just sailing for the summer on my uncle's ship."

The man lifted the cap from his head, scratched his scalp, and replaced the cap. Matthew thought it looked a lot like the beret he had found in the cave back in Sterling.

"Nice cap," Matthew commented. "I used to have one like it."

The man's eyes narrowed. "These caps are traditional to my little village in the mountains near here. I know of no other people in the world who wear them."

"That's the funny thing," Matthew told him. "I had never seen that kind of cap before. I found it in a cave near Sterling Castle."

The man's face paled and he stepped back to lean against a pile of crates. He put down the box he was carrying.

"Are you all right, sir?" Matthew grew concerned. "May I get you something to drink?"

The man shook his head. "No, no. I'll be fine." He pulled a flask from his tunic and took a swig. He sat down on his box, but continued to stare at Matthew.

"Are you sure?" Matthew asked. "I can go fetch someone. What is your name?"

"Andre'," the man whispered.

"I'm Matt. Did you have anything to eat yet today? You really don't look well. I can get you something."

Andre' shook his head but stayed sitting.

"Wait right there." Matthew ran down the wharf and across the gangplank to the Dauntless. Sailors from the Dauntless' crew were already starting to gather and move winches and boxes for loading. Matthew jumped down into the hold, grabbed some biscuits and sausage from the galley, and then ran back onto the deck, dodging other sailors. Andre' was still sitting on the box on the wharf when he returned. Matthew handed him the food.

Andre' chewed on the biscuit and sausage obediently, still staring at Matthew. "I was in Sterling once," he stated flatly.

"Oh?" Matthew sat and watched him eat. "What were you doing there?"

"This and that," Andre' replied vaguely. Suddenly he seemed to decide something in his head, and leaned forward toward Matthew. "What are your parents' names?"

Matthew hesitated. "Elinore and Robert."

Andre' mumbled to himself. "Hm. Figures."

"What did you say?" Matthew asked him.

Andre' didn't reply, but finished eating. Then he sat up straight and rearranged the cap on his head. "Matt, have you ever done something you regret, and wish you could have done it differently?"

Matthew nodded. "I guess so."

Andre' sighed. "Yeah well, I did. I've always wondered if I would ever get the chance to make amends. But maybe I will." He stood up and looked down at Matthew. Matthew stood also. "Well, Matt, nice meeting you." He patted Matthew on the shoulder. "Don't do anything you will seriously regret, boy. Take it from someone who knows. Thanks for the breakfast, kid." Andre' hefted the box and walked off down the wharf, whistling. He turned back once to look at Matthew and nodded his head toward him.

Matthew walked slowly back toward the Dauntless, confused. That was the strangest encounter he had ever had with a total stranger. It was almost like that man knew his parents...Matthew stopped and looked down the wharf where Andre' had gone, but couldn't see him. There had been one of his mother's suitors whose name was something like Andre', but that name could belong to any number of people. It would be an incredible coincidence if he were the same man. Matthew turned and hurried back to the Dauntless.

Don was on the wharf directing the loading of crates onto the ship. "Where have you been, Matt? Hurry and get loading. Where is Mark anyway?"

Matthew shrugged and grabbed a crate.

"Never mind," Don commented and turned to direct other sailors.

Matthew heaved a sigh of relief and crossed the gangplank. In an hour the cargo was all loaded and Adam lined the crew up to make the count.

"We are missing a sailor," Adam remarked suddenly. "Who is missing?"

They were interrupted by a sudden commotion on the dock. Connie was there with two rough looking men, trying to get past Don to cross the gangplank onto the Dauntless. Captain James leaned over the rail toward them.

"What seems to be the problem, ma'am?" he called to them.

"The last time you were in port, mister, one of my girls disappeared from La Castille. Today another one is gone. I demand to get on board and search your ship!" she shrilled.

Captain James looked over at Adam. "Did you see any ladies come on board, Adam?" Adam shook his head. Captain turned back toward Connie. "Sorry, ma'am, but I don't think your girls came this way."

Connie pointed her finger at Matthew. "That one knows where they are!" she screamed. "Ask him!"

Captain James looked at Matthew. "Were you at her establishment last night?" he asked.

Matthew shook his head truthfully. "No sir. I was actually at that one over there last evening." He pointed down the wharf.

Andre' and two of his friends sauntered up, shirt sleeves rolled up to show off their strong biceps. "What is going on here, madam?"

Connie was nearly frothing at the mouth. "That boy is responsible for my girls disappearing! I demand he be hauled off that ship and questioned!"

"Shall I call for the constable, madam?" Andre' asked calmly, towering over her.

Connie paused. "No, that won't be necessary. My men can handle this."

Andre' stepped closer to her. "What is your evidence that that young man was involved?" he asked.

"He was intimately involved two months ago when the first girl disappeared. I saw him with my own eyes. He is back in port now when the second one is gone. That is evidence enough for me."

"And he is the only person at La Castille that you have seen both these times?" Andre' asked, folding his arms across his chest.

"No," Connie faltered and she glanced toward Don. Don looked uncomfortable. "But he is the new variable in the situation." She pointed her finger at Matthew.

"I happen to know that he was not anywhere near your establishment last night, madam." Andre' glowered over her threateningly. "Now, do you want to press the matter with me and my men, or will you quietly leave my wharf?"

Connie looked at Andre's men and her face set hard. "You will not see the end of this," she stated. She turned on her heel and stomped down the street, her men following her.

Andre' looked up at Captain James. "I suggest you set sail right away, Captain," he called up. "If she returns with more men I may not be able to protect you from her boarding. I really don't want to get the constable involved. That investigation could trap you in port for months."

Captain James nodded. "Understood. Thank you, sir." He turned to Adam and his crew. "Man the stations. Get ready to sail." Adam gave the signal and the men ran to their positions. Matthew glanced back at Andre', who nodded and touched a hand to his eyebrow toward him, and then took up a position guarding the dock, arms folded. The sailors untied the ropes and Don's men pulled up the gangplank. The Dauntless sailed slowly out of port.

As land passed behind them, Matthew finally felt able to relax. As he climbed down from the yards of the upper sails, Conrad met him on the deck.

"Captain wants to speak with you in his cabin, Matt."

"Thanks, Conrad." Matthew headed toward the Captain's cabin, his stomach tightening. He entered the cabin and shut the door behind him.

The Captain was writing in a ledger book on his desk. After a minute he closed the ledger, put it away on a bookshelf and closed the glass door over it. Then he turned toward Matthew. "Have a seat, son," he directed, sitting back down in his own padded chair. Captain James leaned back, touched the tips of his fingers together in front of him, and studied Matthew. Matthew returned his gaze a little nervously.

"I am not going to ask about your activities at La Castille," Captain James told him. "That is beyond the scope of my authority, nor do I wish to know any details." Matthew relaxed a little inwardly. "However, I believe I do have a right to ask if you happen to know where your shipmate, Mark, is? Or a certain temperamental horse named Saitan?"

"He took his horse off to explore the countryside. He might consider settling down here," Matthew told him.

The Captain studied Matthew. "I assume he realizes that leaving without notifying me with enough advanced notice to find his replacement means I can no longer hire him on my crew again?"

Matthew nodded. "I believe he was aware of that, sir."

Captain James gazed out his window. "Pity. He had the makings of a good sailor." He looked back at Matthew. "Will you stay on with me another season, Matt?"

Matthew was silent a moment. "I am not sure, sir. I think I need this winter to reconnect with a certain young lady to clarify our intentions with each other. "If it does not work out, I would very much like to sail with you again."

Captain James laughed to himself. "You are very welcome to sail with me again, young man. But I get the sense I should not take you back to Port Mer Eclat again."

Matthew ducked his head a moment, and then looked the Captain in the eye. "Probably not, sir."

Captain James nodded. "You are dismissed, Matt."

As Matthew left the Captain's cabin and went below deck, Don accosted him near the galley.

"You just cost me my chance to return to La Castille, boy."

Matthew met his gaze. "Somehow, Don, I think you'll survive."

Matthew tried to push past him, but Don grabbed his shirt front. "Where is Mark? I think you know more than you are telling."

"Mark is taking his horse to settle down in the country," Matthew told him. "Now let me go."

Don pushed him away. "Fine, but I don't want you on my night crew anymore."

"That's fine by me," Matthew retorted. He bit back a remark about certain people's moral depravity. Instead he turned around to head back up the stairs. "I'll see if Adam can use me on his shift."

Adam was willing, and reassigned another sailor to night shift. Matthew scaled up the foremast to skinny out by the topsail. He always felt free up here, and today he needed that more than ever. Without Mark on the ship he was again feeling lonely and without purpose. He was determined to talk to Sarah again and…apologize, grovel, beg her to reconsider him? But at least he was heading back toward home.

CHAPTER 13

PIRATES!

It was wonderful to be on the open seas again, sailing carefree with the wind in the sails. Matthew enjoyed the morning shift a lot. He could see more in the daytime, including seagulls and an occasional albatross patrolling the skies. Matthew was getting better at working the sails, and seemed to have a knack for unravelling knots when the lines tried to tangle. He could now climb and balance himself almost anywhere along the yards and masts.

Their first stop was to be at Greensbay, Renling, on the east coast of Browning Isle. Then they would hit the main port of Mordred northward, Borden on the west coast, and finish up in Portsmouth, Sterling, where the ship would dock for the winter after unloading all its cargo. Matthew wondered if Mark had gotten Marie out safely and reunited with Clarisse. He found himself thinking more and more about Sarah, wondering if she would reconsider his proposal of marriage. If she didn't, well…he wasn't sure what he would do.

At dawn on the third day on open sea the crew was awakened by shouting. "Pirates!"

A moment later a whistle blew three shrill blasts. "All hands on deck! All hands on deck!"

Matthew leaped down from Mark's old upper bunk, narrowly missing Shorty who rolled out across from him. Shorty fumbled in his locker and pulled out a long knife.

"Take your weapons," he growled, and ran off down the corridor.

Matthew retrieved his dagger and followed. He paused at the galley and a sailor bumped into him from behind.

"Move!" the fellow grunted.

"Sorry!" Matthew ducked into the galley room. He glanced into the corner where his sword, bow and arrows were stored, and felt a mild tingling in his fingers. He quickly belted on his sword, fastened on his quiver, strung his bow and threw it across his back. He then followed the other sailors up on deck.

The Captain was shouting instructions to move the sails and change direction. A handful of sailors were hauling two small cannons up the cargo lift onto the deck. Matthew quickly climbed the aft mizzen mast to help with the sails and get a better view.

Matthew could see three dark ships. Two appeared to be heading westward toward land; they could just be seen on the horizon. A third ship was much closer and was heading toward them. He could see a black flag waving from its main mast.

Captain James was directing the turning of the ship in a more southwest direction. Matthew could understand the strategy. If two ships were moving to the eastern port of Renling, they stood a better chance heading south with only one ship following them.

The wind caught in the Dauntless' sails and she surged forward, gaining speed. Matthew looked back toward the pirate ship. It was maintaining course and speed with them. A thrill of fear and excitement gripped his stomach. He had heard stories of battles with pirates, and of how determined and ruthless they could be. He wasn't sure he wanted to confirm this for himself, but felt some confidence that the knights he had trained under had prepared him well for combat.

He glanced at the pirate ship again. It seemed to be gradually gaining on them. He heard a boom, and a moment later a cannonball tore through one of the main sails.

"Fire the cannons!" Captain James shouted.

Two smaller booms sounded from the Dauntless. Two cannonballs splashed into the water short of the pirate ship. Another boom sounded from the pirate ship, and a cannonball ricocheted off the main mast, shooting splinters across the deck.

"Damn it!" Don shouted from where he stood in the fore of the ship. "Their cannons have greater range than ours. We must outrun them, Captain!"

"Agreed," Captain James responded. "Run full with the wind!"

Adam and Don shouted commands to the sailors, who scrambled to fully unfurl the sails and turn the ship to make the best speed with the wind. The next chance he had to look, Matthew glanced back at the pursuing ship. It seemed to be dropping behind.

They held this course, practically skimming across the water. But soon the pirate ship grew closer again. Matthew had the sinking feeling that the Dauntless would not outrun them, due to its smaller size and fully loaded cargo hold. As it neared, Matthew could see that the pirate ship's shape was built for speed.

Again the sailors on the Dauntless heard a boom and a cannonball roared through the sails. Captain James ordered his men to make their cannons ready to return fire when he gave the word. The pirate ship skimmed closer and let loose another ball. This time it hit the mizzen mast, which splintered but held. Sailors clung to their positions above.

"Aim for the body of the ship!" Captain James instructed. "Fire!"

One cannonball fell short into the water, but the other hit the side of the pirate ship just below the rail. There was a clang of metal ball hitting the metal-wrapped side of the ship, and the cannonball dropped harmlessly into the water. This pirate ship was also built for battle.

Two more cannonballs from the pirate ship struck the Dauntless' main mast, while other balls tore through main sails. Several sailors jumped or fell to the deck from above. One sailor did not jump up again, but dragged himself over to the bulkhead, dragging his right leg behind him, and then lay there groaning. It looked like a ball had shattered his leg.

Captain James shouted commands to aim cannonballs at the pirate ship's masts and sails. Dauntless was able to shoot two balls for every 6 coming from the pirate ship. The pirate ship's sails blossomed some new holes, but the Dauntless was looking ragged, lines cut and sails beginning to flap in unwanted directions. Despite brave sailors trying to keep the ship sailing forward, the Dauntless was losing speed.

"Land ahoy!" someone yelled.

The Dauntless continued toward shore. Various small islands and rocks stood out along the shoreline. Captain James made sure they stayed clear of them, but the ship's maneuverability was diminishing.

Another cannonball hit the upper part of the main mast, and the top started toppling. Several sailors scrambled down from the top yards, while others hurriedly shifted sails to protect them from tearing. Matthew concentrated on adjusting his sails to the Captain's orders, and stopped watching the approaching pirate ship. He did notice, however, that Captain James was steering them into the inlet of a larger island.

Suddenly there was shouting from the decks below, and Matthew peered down. Sailors were gathering at the starboard bow, pulling out long knives and cutlasses. He looked across the water and his heart nearly stopped.

The pirate ship was almost upon them.

Instinctively, Matthew stabilized his position sitting on the upper crosstree of the mizzen mast, swung the bow off his shoulder and knocked an arrow to it. Several voices from memory ran through his mind. First was old Sir Bentley's advice to never strike the first blow, to only use force in defense of family, lord and kingdom. This was followed by Sir Lamborgini's accented statement that sometimes the best defense was to strike the first offense. Matthew quickly realized that Sir Lamborgini's advice was more useful in this situation. He raised his bow, took aim on a man on the pirate ship's main sails, and let loose an arrow. It flew silently, hit the man in the stomach, and with a cry he fell into the water.

The other pirates looked around briefly, and then faced the Dauntless' crew again. Matthew let fly three more arrows and two more men fell from the sails to the decks. Several of the pirates started shouting and pointing into the sails where Matthew sat. Two pirates turned a cannon in his direction. Matthew sent two arrows in their direction and the pirates collapsed to the deck. Two more cannons pointed at him. He downed the pirates at one cannon, but the other managed to fire. The cannonball came very close to Matthew's leg and hit the crosstree. He scooted out onto the sail yard and reached for more arrows. There were three left.

Matthew gazed across the pirate ship's deck to see if he could see the captain. There was a fellow with a large hat sporting many large feathers. He took aim and felled the man. Then he saw a pirate with an even more impressive hat. As he pulled back the bow, another cannonball swooshed by his shoulder. He instinctively ducked back. His arrow flew across the bow of the pirate ship into the water. He had one arrow left.

A cannonball hit the yard he was on, which broke and fell downward. Matthew grasped a stay and swung to the nearby shroud along the mast. He repositioned his bow and surveyed the pirate ship one more time. It was almost alongside the Dauntless. He had to find the pirate captain!

He realized he could not keep his position on the shroud without gripping it with at least one hand. He thought of Karl's acrobatic archery tricks. He repositioned his bow by placing his right foot against the bow grip, grasped his last arrow and the bow string in his right hand, and extended his leg outward to aim. The pirate with the big fancy hat was shouting directions to his men as they prepared to jump across to the Dauntless.

Matthew let his arrow fly. The bow dropped to the deck, but Matthew clung to the shroud one last second to see where his arrow would land. It hit the pirate captain in the left shoulder and he paused, startled. Then grimacing, he broke the arrow off mid shaft, raised the cutlass in his right hand, and shouted his men forward. Matthew slid quickly down the shroud to the deck and drew out his sword.

"Nice work, mate." Curly slapped him on the back and then turned to face the pirates coming aboard.

Matthew's mind and body went into gear with his melee fighting techniques. The Dauntless sailors fought bravely, but the pirates were ferocious. As he danced around the deck felling pirates, Matthew noticed that the sailor with the crushed leg lying against the bulkhead was slashing the legs of any pirates that passed him. With this assistance Dauntless' sailors managed to overpower more pirates, and a pile of bodies was growing around him. Still, the sailors were outnumbered as more pirates poured from the larger pirate ship.

Matthew felt some tingling in his hands and looked up to see the pirate captain approaching the poop deck. He quickly worked his way through the battling sailors and arrived at the foot of the stairs as the pirate captain reached the top of the deck. The pirate captain cut Adam down easily as he stood in front of Captain James to protect him.

"I am Captain Spike of the pirate ship Dread Knot!" the pirate growled. "Surrender!"

"Never," Captain James gritted his teeth and raised his sword.

"Then face my wrath!" Captain Spike raised his cutlass overhead and struck downward. His cutlass met steel, but it was not Captain James' sword that met his.

"You will not hurt my Captain," Matthew grunted and pushed the pirate back.

Captain Spike laughed. "You dare to try and stop me, young whipper snapper?"

He struck and thrust at Matthew, who countered each strike with precision. Circling around the helm, neither could get the advantage of the other. Then with an evil smile, Captain Spike attempted a move to disarm the sword from Matthew's hand. Barely even thinking, Matthew employed the defense he had used against Lamborgini's disarming technique. The cutlass flew from the pirate's hand and flew over the side of the ship into the water.

"Call your men off," Matthew demanded, pointing his sword at the pirate's chest.

Captain Spike's face hardened. "Never." In one swift move, he leaped over the helm toward Captain James while pulling a dagger from his tunic, grabbed Captain James and thrust the dagger against his throat.

Matthew started forward and the pirate captain pressed the dagger deeper against Captain James' throat. Captain James gasped slightly. Matthew stopped.

"You care for your captain, don't you? That is as it should be. Drop your sword, young man. Refuse my demands or step any closer and I kill him."

Matthew slowly laid his sword on the deck. "What do you want with us?" he asked.

"Oh, I don't want the people, I want the cargo," Captain Spike responded. "Although, if you want to join us in our campaign we could make a spot for a fighter like you."

Matthew's mind was racing to figure a way out of this situation. He glanced around at the sailors fighting desperately below. He also noticed with surprise that the ships were in a small lagoon of all places, Rimrock Island!

"Call off your men and we can talk," Matthew offered.

Captain Spike pushed Captain James toward the railing of the poop deck. "You call off your men first," he demanded.

Captain James glanced at Matthew, who nodded. Captain James brought a whistle to his lips and blew five times. "Men of the Dauntless! Stop your fighting!" he yelled hoarsely.

"Stop the fracas!" Captain Spike shouted.

The fighting gradually calmed down. The men stood looking up at the poop deck uncertainly. One pirate thrust his cutlass into the chest of the poor sailor with the crushed leg. He gurgled once and lay still. Matthew closed his eyes and fought the urge to vomit.

"I said, stop!" The pirate captain fumed. His face almost turned purple. He took a deep breath and calmed himself. Then he addressed the sailors below. "We are taking possession of this ship and its cargo. I have offered this young man a position on my crew. Any fighter who wishes to join us on our campaign is welcome. Either a blood oath or a bloody death. What say you?"

There was silence across the decks. It was broken by a single question. "What is your campaign?" Matthew asked loudly.

Captain Spike looked pleased. "Ah. Good question. You see, most people think we only want to get rich and retire in obscurity. This time we are going for full power of an island continent. We have been working for the last five years destroying the economy by hijacking every shipment we can, then demanding exorbitant prices for goods and food. We have infiltrated the various trades, and are at this moment entering all the seaports to control them. From there we will force the ruling class and royalty to relinquish control of their countries to us. So you see, yours is a lost cause."

"Who is 'us'?" Matthew asked. "Who is the one man in charge? Is it you?"

Captain Spike looked taken aback for a moment. "It is a gentleman's agreement. We are all equal."

"Yes, but what if one of you decides to take ultimate power, and conquer the others? And who is 'we' anyway? A dozen pirate ship captains? A thousand sailors? Will every man and sailor have an equal share in the bounty and the rule? What say you, captain? Your men are listening." Matthew waited.

Captain Spike was speechless for a minute. His men shifted uncomfortably on the decks. "It is a gentleman's agreement," he repeated, a little uncertainly.

Matthew lifted his arm to indicate the shoreline. "And what of this land, captain? How do you propose to take the Land of Sterling? I hear it is a fiercely independent land. The people are likely to die fighting rather than submit to your rule."

The pirate captain squared his shoulders. "We get to Portsmouth and make our way to the castle, where we surprise and capture the royal family. We will force the people to obey us or see their monarchs killed. It is simple."

"Uh huh," Matthew mused out loud. "The moment you try and take over the port, word will get to the King and Queen and they will not be surprised when you come. Besides, they would rather die than submit to a pirate."

Captain Spike grinned wickedly. "Then I torture and threaten the children."

Matthew nodded thoughtfully. "That might work. Although the children weren't there the last time I knew." He hoped this partial truth would dishearten the pirate.

Captain Spike merely shrugged. "Then I torture the queen until the king relents."

Matthew let out a forced laugh. "You really don't know much about Sterling, do you? It is the Queen you have to convince, not the King. And she would rather die than give her country over to you. But I expect she will fight you to the end to save her country."

The pirate's eyes narrowed. "What makes you the authority on Sterling, young whippersnapper?"

Matthew's knees trembled for a moment, but he knew what he must do to have a chance to save his shipmates and country. He must bait the pirate captain. He squared his shoulders and announced to everyone aboard the ship in a loud clear voice: "I am Prince Matthew Robert of Sterling, son of Queen Elinore and King Robert. And I say to you, Captain Spike, I will never join you or your campaign. In fact, I will oppose it to the end. I plan to jump ship, swim across to the mainland right here where the castle lies, and warn them here and now. I suspect my crewmates feel the same. I dare you try and stop us."

Captain Spike gave a guttural cry and lunged toward Matthew. Unable to reach his sword in time, Matthew ran across the poop deck and looked down into the water to check its depth. Glancing over his shoulder to make sure the pirate captain was still following him, he dove off the ship into the water. Then with strong swift strokes he swam to the island shore. Captain Spike dove off the Dauntless to follow him.

Reaching the beach, Matthew stumbled slightly to get his feet underneath him. Sounds of steel against steel rang again from the ship's decks. Matthew ran up the beach to his left toward the rocky waterfall portion of the island. He needed to find a place where he could have an advantage over the pirate. As he ran he drew out his dagger, the one his cousin Harry had made for him years ago. Glancing again over his shoulder, he was grateful to note that the pirate captain still only had a dagger himself. The shoulder arrow wound did not seem to be slowing him down very much. Would he be better leading the pirate through the forest trees, the nettle patch, or the quicksand bog? No, he didn't want to trip himself up in the process.

The sandy beach ended and Matthew's feet found better traction on the hard packed earth leading inland. His pace slowed again as he neared the Komodo dragon nesting ground. Picking his way carefully around several nests of eggs, he veered away from two mothers who eyed him suspiciously. He crooned to them reassuringly until he reached the other side. Then he began scrambling up the layers of rock toward the island's waterfall. Partway up he looked back to see where the pirate captain was.

Captain Spike was just entering the nesting ground. Intent on his pursuit he tromped through two nests of eggs. Matthew cringed as several eggs crunched and broke. The pirate did not notice that the two Komodo mothers had arisen from their nests and were following him. As Captain Spike neared another nest of eggs Matthew couldn't take it anymore.

"Stop, Captain! Don't smash the eggs!" he shouted out to him.

The pirate did not see the Komodo dragons behind him. "What, these?" he laughed, and stomped a couple more." This is what I'll do to you when I catch you!" He started again toward Matthew.

Matthew scrambled up the rocks until he found a flat ledge to stand on. There he turned to face Captain Spike, who had started climbing. Matthew readied his dagger. He wished he still had his longer sword. The pirate grinned up at him wickedly, a long dagger in his hand. As he reached the flat rock where Matthew waited, he suddenly lunged toward Matthew's feet with his dagger. Matthew jumped back, jabbing toward the pirate's face.

Captain Spike shrieked out a frightening war whoop and was upon him, lunging with his blade. Matthew parried deftly, but the strength of the onslaught forced him back against the rocky wall behind him. The pirate was beginning to protect his wounded left shoulder. At the first opportunity Matthew jabbed at the pirate's face and then ducked under his free left arm to get behind him. This time the pirate pushed him toward the open edge of the rocky ledge. Matthew swiped and thrust, but was unable to touch the pirate at all. Captain Spike was good.

Suddenly a swipe from the pirate's blade whisked across Matthew's cheek. He instinctively shied backward, and found himself teetering on the edge. He grabbed the pirate's left arm and pulled himself back upright. As Matthew used the same left arm to thrust the pirate away from him, he saw the two Komodo mothers climbing laboriously up the rocks toward them. Captain Spike grunted and grabbed his left shoulder. Matthew ducked toward the back rocky wall again.

"The dragons are coming," Matthew told Captain Spike.

The pirate laughed. "What, those lizards? I am not afraid of you or your distractions."

He swiped again at Matthew with his dagger. At the same moment one of the Komodos had reached the rock ledge and gained firm footing. The second one was right behind her. The first one struck and latched onto Captain Spike's right leg with her teeth and started dragging him back down the rock toward the nesting ground dirt. The pirate struck at her with his blade, and the other Komodo bit down on his knife arm. Captain Spike screamed, kicked and flailed, but the dragons did not let go. Matthew averted his eyes as he heard the crunching of bones. Soon the pirate lay still among the shards of eggs he had broken.

When Matthew opened his eyes again, he was horrified to see the mother Komodos once again climbing the rocks toward the ledge where he stood. Hoping against hope, he began to whistle and croon to the dragons, trying to soothe and calm them. They kept coming. He looked around and decided the best escape was to continue climbing upward.

He thought about climbing to the cave partway up this end of the island, but decided against it. If the Komodos could climb to the ledge, they could climb to the cave, and he had no desire to get trapped inside with two angry Komodo mothers.

He looked to his right, where the more gradual rocky slope became steep and cliff-like. A waterfall cascaded down into a pool, which left by a stream to feed the island. Perhaps he could escape the Komodos by that route. He would have to move quickly. Once the Komodos reached flat land they could move surprisingly fast.

As Matthew scaled across the cliff face toward the waterfall, he was careful with his foot and hand holds. He did not want to fall as he had eight years ago when climbing this wall searching for one of the treasures of Rimrock Island with his sister, Amber. He could not afford a broken bone at this point.

Once he was close to the waterfall and the pond below, he risked a quick look at the Komodos. One was still on the flat ledge where he had dueled the pirate captain. The other was waddling down the rocks toward the stream. He was out of time.

Holding his breath, Matthew pushed off from the cliff wall and jumped toward the pond below. The cold water washed over him, refreshing him. Pushing to the surface he swam quickly downstream until he was among the trees. He climbed out and ran through the trees to the beach. At the beach he started pushing back up toward the Dauntless resting in the lagoon.

He didn't get far before a Komodo crawled onto the beach from the nesting ground. Matthew slowed his pace and veered closer to the shore. The Komodo changed direction to meet him. Matthew stopped and watched her continue to come toward him, her baleful eyes fixed upon him. He was tempted to pull out his dagger, but instead stretched out his empty hands, palms up, and began to croon at her.

He kept holding up his empty hands. "I am not going to hurt you, sweetheart," he coaxed. "I am so sorry your babies got smashed. I promise it won't happen again." He whistled, trying every way he could to stop her angry approach. He backed into the water to keep his distance from her.

Suddenly a larger male Komodo careened into her side, flipping her over. She got to her feet and faced him. He let out a warning cry and rammed her again, pushing her back up the beach.

Matthew stumbled out of the water. "Creedo, good boy," he crooned to his friend. "You saved my life. Thank you." Matthew took off running toward the ships in the cove.

Fighting was still going on upon the decks of the Dauntless. He swam toward his ship and looked up, hoping to see a rope he could climb. He spotted Shorty above him.

"Shorty! Throw me a rope!" he shouted. "It's Matt!"

A moment later a rope dropped over the hull and Matthew climbed up quickly. Dagger out, he ran his way to the poop deck, jabbing any pirate that blocked his path. He leaped up the steps and by happy chance nearly stumbled over his own sword. He picked it up and held it aloft over his head. He took a deep breath and let out a long piercing whistle.

"In the name of King Robert of Sterling, I command this fighting to stop!" It was the loudest, most commanding voice Matthew had ever used, but it worked. All eyes turned toward him.

"Men of the pirate ship, Dread Knot," he continued. "Your Captain Spike is dead. I saw it with my own eyes, as the dragons which inhabit this island ripped him apart." He shuddered slightly but maintained a fierce stare at the pirates. "Any who doubt me may go see for themselves, at risk of their own lives." He nodded toward the beach, where Creedo still stood guard, watching the ships in the lagoon.

"Now in the name of the King and Queen of Sterling, in whose waters you lie and whose emissary I am, and on behalf of the fearless Captain James on whose ship you stand and dare try to desecrate, I give you these terms. Continue fighting and die, or surrender now to the brave crew of the Dauntless, and you will receive a fair trial and a just hearing from the King and Queen of Sterling." He let his words sink in.

"Never!" one of the pirates shouted. "Live free or die!"

Don knocked him over the head with the butt of his cutlass and the pirate crumpled to the deck. "Anyone else?" Don yelled, teeth gleaming. Matthew was glad he was on the same side as Don this day.

Captain James strode to the center of the ship's deck and cleared an area at the base of the main mast. "Throw your weapons here, ye pirates. Men of the Dauntless, take the pirates to the brig in the hold."

As the pirates dropped off their weapons, they were taken down into the hold. The only room he knew of that was empty and could be locked was where Saitan had been stalled. He didn't think all of the horse manure had been completely removed, and grinned to himself at the thought.

Shorty and Don tied up the unconscious pirate and carried him down to the "brig". Captain James climbed the stairs and joined Matthew on the poop deck.

"I thank you this day for your timely and valuable assistance, young Matthew," Captain James said, laying a hand on his shoulder.

Matthew inclined his head. "Always a pleasure to serve a fine Captain." His face clouded over. "How is Adam?"

"Not good, I fear." They both hurried over to Adam's still form on the deck and bent over him. "Still breathing, but barely," Captain James declared. "Help me carry him down to my cabin."

Matthew lifted Adam by the shoulders while Captain James took his legs. Matthew backed down the stairs first. They laid him on the Captain's own bed. Captain James opened Adam's shirt, revealing a deep cut across his chest.

"Fetch the ship's medic," Captain James commanded, grabbing a towel to hold across Adam's wound.

Matthew found the medic on the main deck, wrapping up various wounds. "Captain James needs you right away," Matthew told him. "First Mate is hurt pretty badly."

The medic nodded and handed the bandaging cloths to another sailor. He followed Matthew to the Captain's cabin, and after washing his hands, bent over Adam and explored the wound with his fingers. Adam groaned incoherently. He leaned his ear against Adam's chest and listened for a minute.

The medic straightened up. "There are several lacerated muscles and cut ribs. The right lung sounds are decreased but his heart is beating okay. It will be a long recuperation, but he might live. He will need more care than we have on board ship."

Captain James sat down heavily in his chair, face discouraged. "The Dauntless is not going to make it very far in its current condition."

Matthew cleared his throat. "Captain James, I may have a solution. About half a mile away from here at the shore lies a boathouse where we can dock. From there it is about a two mile walk to Sterling Castle. I am sure the castle doctor could care for Adam there for as long as he needs. Bring any others of your wounded. We could put the pirates in our prison and handle their trials there. Do you think we can limp the Dauntless over to the shore?"

Captain James smiled wearily but gratefully. "Aye. That I think we can do."

Captain James gave Don his instructions, and then returned to his cabin to care for Adam. Don gathered the sailors that were able, and they unfurled the sails. Most of them were still in good enough condition to function, and the Dauntless sailed slowly away from Rimrock Island. Matthew guided Don toward the boathouse and dock on the shore. The water was just barely deep enough to handle the size of the ship.

"We'll take the most wounded men with us this first trip," Captain James decided. "I wish to go and watch over Adam's care."

"Aye, aye, Captain," Don saluted. "I'll stay here with the rest of the men to guard the prisoners."

Matthew nodded to Don. "I'll send guards as soon as possible to take them to our castle prison."

It was a bedraggled group that left the ship, those with wounded arms helping those with wounded legs. Three men had to be carried on bedrolls, including Adam. Matthew helped Captain James carry him. The walk to the castle was slow and tedious, with frequent pauses. At the base of the castle hill Matthew told everyone to stop and rest. He ran up the hill road to get help. He arrived breathless at the front doors and burst through, startling Malcolm who was walking through the entry hall.

"Prince Matthew! What a pleasant surprise!" Malcolm started toward Matthew to greet him.

"Malcolm! Where's Doc Howser? I've got wounded men at the base of the hill. I also need help bringing them up."

"Why? What happened?"

"Our merchant ship was set upon by pirates. We actually have them in the ship's hold at the dock. I'll explain more later. Can we get help now?" Matthew looked around for more castle workers.

Malcolm nodded. He put his fingers to his mouth and blew three sharp long whistles. Castle workers began pouring forth from various castle rooms.

Matthew stood surprised. "I didn't know you could do that!"

Malcolm smiled primly. "One of my many secret talents." He turned to the castle workers. "We have wounded men at the base of the hill. I need help bringing them up, and beds set up in the ballroom. I'll need bandaging supplies for Doctor Howser. And hot food too. Now go!"

Workers scattered in all directions. Matthew led a group of men down the hill to fetch the wounded sailors. By the time they arrived in the ballroom, makeshift beds were set up and Doc was ready with his supplies. He examined Adam first, and then turned to Captain James.

"It is as your ship doctor said. The pirate's blade cut through muscle and ribs, but missed any vital organs. He will need strict rest and medical attention to prevent infection, and at least three months of rest to recuperate. Are you able to leave him here with us?"

Captain James nodded. "I would be most grateful for your care."

Just then King Robert and Queen Elinore entered the room. All talking fell silent.

"Brave men of the Dauntless, welcome to Sterling Castle," Queen Elinore greeted them. "In a short while we will have a hot meal for all of you. Please carry on."

There was a quiet cheer from the sailors, and the castle workers resumed their dressing of wounds. Matthew ran over to his parents and they greeted each other with warm embraces.

"Amber told us you were probably going sailing on one of Edward's ships," Robert commented. "You have had some adventures, I see. Tell us about them."

"I will later," Matthew said quickly. "The danger from pirates is not passed. Right now pirate ships are arriving at Portsmouth and at other ports in all the four coastal kingdoms. They have joined forces to take over our island continent. They are behind the increasing trade and import prices over the last five years."

Elinore looked shocked, but Robert nodded. "That would explain some things."

Elinore turned to Malcolm. "Please call Sir Lamborgini. I need him to take his troops to Portsmouth and secure it from the pirate coup."

Malcolm bowed.

"Oh, Malcolm?" Matthew interjected, touching a hand to his cheek where it was starting to sting. "Will you thank Sir Lamborgini for teaching me some unconventional fighting techniques? They came in handy against a very persistent pirate captain today."

Malcolm smiled and inclined his head. "I will be happy to, Prince Matthew."

Elinore examined Matthew's cheek. "Celia!" she called. "Fetch me a cloth and some water!"

"Yes, Your Highness." Celia disappeared to fetch the supplies.

King Robert was grinning. "Fighting pirate captains, eh? Our son is growing up!" He caught Elinore's eye and she looked thoughtful.

"Mother," Matthew suddenly remembered. "The Dauntless is holding about thirty pirates in her brig. Can we send some guards over to bring them back? I promised them Sterling would give them a fair trial when they surrendered."

Robert was chuckling now. "A fair trial? For piracy and conspiracy? That could still be a steep sentence."

Matthew rubbed his chin. "Could we make it not a death sentence? Maybe we give them a few years to work back what they stole from our people. And offer to rehabilitate them to become contributing citizens instead of thieves."

Elinore nodded. "I like the sound of that." She took the wet cloth Celia offered her and washed the blood off Matthew's cheek.

Matthew looked around the room. "Where are Amber and Stephanie?"

"The traveled back to Adonia about a week ago. They wanted to get back before the pass closes," Elinore told him.

Matthew felt a sudden tingling in his hands and feet. It was strong. "Mother, they are in trouble. I am afraid the pirates may have reached Adonia. I must go now. Is there a horse that I may take?"

Robert nodded. "Take my horse Flint. He is getting older but still has some strength to get you there."

Matthew hugged his parents, grabbed a loaf of bread and sausage from the kitchen, and then ran to the stables. He saddled Flint and galloped down the hill toward the dock. He passed the castle guard marching down the road toward the Dauntless. Once on board the ship he gathered his bundle of clothes, bow, empty quiver and sword. He met Don on deck as he was leaving. They looked at each other uncertainly.

"You are leaving?" Don asked.

"Yes, sir." Matthew responded. "I must travel to Adonia to protect them from the pirate coup." He paused. "Don, thank you for teaching me the ropes on a sailing ship. I learned a lot from you."

Don nodded. "You were a hard worker." He looked uncomfortable. "I guess you were all right. A bit different, but all right."

Matthew grinned. "Thanks, mate." He saluted Don, then turned and left the ship. He jumped on Flint and galloped off toward the Black Forest and Adonia.

CHAPTER 14

SIEGE IN ADONIA

M atthew galloped on Flint through farm fields empty and bare before winter. He passed his family's cottage with barely a glance. He entered a trail into the Black Forest that led past a certain cave. Here he slowed his horse to rest and get a drink from the stream. As he looked up, he noticed a wolf lying in the entrance of the cave watching him. Matthew stood up and approached the wolf cautiously, hands outstretched.

"Wolf, is that you? You have been here the last six months?"

Wolf whined and crawled forward to meet Matthew. Matthew broke off a piece of sausage and fed it to him. Wolf licked Matthew's fingers. Matthew scratched his ears. When Matthew stood up to go, Wolf stood up with him.

"I have to travel to Adonia," Matthew told him and moved toward his horse. Wolf followed him. "So you wish to follow me, eh? Come on then."

Matthew mounted Flint and galloped off down the trail. Looking back, he saw Wolf following him, tongue lolling out happily. Matthew was glad for the company. When he reached the road coming from Borden on the west, the sky began darkening to dusk. Matthew hoped he would be able to find the trail leading off to South Wolf Pass. He kept his horse to a trot, trying to find the trail head.

He heard a whine behind him. He turned and saw Wolf sitting on his haunches by the side of the road. He turned Flint and went back.

"What is it, Wolf?"

The moon came out from behind the clouds, and Matthew saw a trail going off among the trees. "You found it!" Matthew told Wolf. "Thank you."

He turned his horse down the trail and Wolf followed him. The trail began rising into the foothills of the mountains and Matthew pressed on. Flint was sure footed even in the dark, for which Matthew was grateful. At the foot of the pass Matthew reached the clearing where he had spent the night with Thomas six months earlier. Unable to keep his eyes open any longer, he rolled up in his rain coat against the grotto wall, and with Wolf curled up against him, fell fast asleep.

Matthew woke to the sound of distant wolf howls. He opened his eyes. Wolf still lay next to him, but had lifted his head to look toward the trees, ears forward and listening. Flint paced a little nervously where he was tied to a tree. Matthew arose, saddled Flint in the light of dawn, and started up the trail again. Wolf occasionally looked back down the trail, but silently kept pace behind Matthew.

There was some day-old snow in the pass, but it was only a couple of inches deep. Flint pressed on with a good pace, and Matthew tucked his hands under his arms to keep them warm. Finally they reached the top of the pass. As they came down out of the mountains Matthew could see down into the valley. A light layer of snow glinted off the roofs of Adonia City below. Everything looked peaceful, and Matthew's heart took courage.

He rode Flint down the trail as quickly as he could, Wolf still following at his heels. As they entered into town mid-afternoon it seemed unusually quiet. No one was on the streets and homes were shuttered. On a whim, Matthew turned down a side street and rode to Lance and Lark's house. He tied up his horse, and Wolf lay down against the wall of the house. Matthew knocked on the door and waited.

After a couple of long minutes a little shutter up high in the door slid aside and a pair of eyes looked out. Then it closed and the door opened halfway.

"Matthew! Inside quickly!" Lance let him in, and then bolted the door again behind them. They stood staring at each other.

"What's going on?" Matthew asked in a low voice. "The city looks like a ghost town."

Lance sat down wearily on a chair. "We are invaded. Two days ago a legion of pirates and robbers who had joined them rode into town declaring a new national government. Join them and prosper; fight against them and be imprisoned or killed. Some tried to fight. Many of us are in hiding."

"Where are Lark and the children?" Matthew whispered. Lance glanced upward toward the attic. "Where are the pirates now?" Matthew asked.

"They have taken over Adonia Palace. The Royal Family was taken hostage. Sir Royce and the palace guard fought the best they could, but they were caught by surprise and overwhelmed. We think they are being held in the palace dungeon with half of the army. We tried to send a message out to the rest of the army up north to come help. The palace gate is too heavily guarded to attack right now. We feel trapped in our own city. I don't know what to do, Matthew." Lance looked at his hands discouragedly.

Matthew suddenly sat up straight. "Lance, I know a secret way into the palace from outside. It is near the squire training ground on the back side of Palace Hill. There is a tunnel that goes inside the hill and comes out in one of the storage rooms. Perhaps we can free the prisoners to help. How many men could we gather to sneak inside?"

Lance grinned. "Quite a few, I think. Give me an hour and we could gather a nice group. Others could wait outside the gates for us to let them in."

Matthew calculated in his head. "Our best chance of getting into the tunnel unseen would be after dark. Let's give it two hours and meet at the base of the hill right after dark. Have them bring whatever weapons they have. Do you have a place where I can keep my horse?"

Lance nodded. "Put him in the shed behind my house. There is enough room next to our donkey." He came out to help Matthew move his horse. He looked uncertainly at the wolf that followed Matthew. "I don't think my donkey will allow the wolf in the shed with him."

"I don't think Wolf will stay in there," Matthew replied thoughtfully. "He seems intent on staying with me."

Lance shrugged. "Fine. Just as long as he doesn't attack my people." Wolf sat back on his haunches looking at Lance, tongue hanging out. He seemed to be laughing.

Lance and Matthew divided up to quietly spread the word of their revolt. They had to be careful; periodically they would pass a little patrol of robber-pirates. Matthew went to the smithy, livery stable, and carpentry shop where he had trained before, then to the homes of the squires he knew lived in town. Then he returned to Lance's home to wait for him in the shadows by the shed. Soon Lance returned with a few other men and they went inside his home.

Lark descended from the attic with the children to hug Lance goodbye. She kissed him long and hard. "Don't die," she whispered hoarsely.

"That is definitely my intention. I plan to live a long and happy life with you," Lance responded.

One of the men watching out the window curtains ducked his head back in. "It is time," he told them.

Matthew checked his sword and made sure his scabbard was strapped on tight, then slung his bow and empty quiver across his back.

"No arrows?" Lance inquired, eyebrows raised.

Matthew shook his head. "Used them up on pirates. I'm hoping to find more at the palace."

Lance went into a back room and came back with five arrows. "Take these."

Matthew accepted them gratefully and stuck them in his quiver. Then they were off, slipping down side streets to avoid the patrols, other men joining them in the dark. They skirted around the hill among the trees to an area below the training field. While the others waiting in hiding, Matthew, Lance and Wolf ran across the field toward the hill. They crept along until Matthew found the shrouded entry. He gripped the edge of the door with his fingernails, and with Lance's help, swung the door open. Lance stepped out to signal the others to start joining them.

As the first group arrived, Matthew directed them further into the tunnel. A couple of them lit torches and waited. The second group arrived. As this group passed him, one smaller figure slipped passed him, head bowed. He took a second look, then followed, and suddenly pulled off the hat. Long hair fell down around the shoulders.

Matthew sighed. "Ma'am, this is a dangerous rescue we are undertaking. It is not a garden party. You should not be here."

She stared back defiantly. "Why not? This is my kingdom as much as anyone else's. I know how to fight." She partially drew a sword out of its scabbard. "Besides, I want to do something. My father was injured in the takeover, and there is no one else in my family able to fight," she added miserably.

"What is your name?" he asked.

"Donna," she answered.

Matthew laid a hand on her shoulder and smiled. "You remind me of my mother. Perhaps there is a special task you can do in rescuing the children, Donna. Stay near me and we will see what is needed." He turned to the others as the last group joined them. "This tunnel ends in a storage room. From there we will need to spread out and take down any robbers or pirates we meet until we can open the gates and free our people. Are you ready?"

Everyone nodded. Matthew took a torch and began leading the rescue party up the winding tunnels, Wolf at his side and Donna right behind him. As they climbed up the hill, Matthew walked through the palace in his mind. Where would the royal family most likely be held? He would need to be very careful in their rescue. He suspected the pirates would threaten or injure them at the slightest provocation. It would be best to free the other people and dispatch as many pirates as possible first.

When they reached the trapdoor at the end of the tunnel, Matthew had everyone extinguish their torches and quiet down. He pushed on the trapdoor and lifted it up. He climbed through, and his head found that the table still hovered over the trapdoor behind the storage barrels. He crept to the door of the room, pulled it open carefully, and peeked down the palace corridor. All was quiet and empty. He went back and got everyone out of the tunnel. Thirty-five people crowded into the storage room in the dim light from the hall.

"I need a group to go down into the dungeon to free our people," Matthew whispered. "Does anyone know where that is?"

John the master smith raised his hand. "I do. I have had to repair locks there a few times." He raised a metal pick. "I can unlock the cells with or without a key."

Matthew grinned. "Perfect. Take five or six men with you."

Lance spoke up. "I can get to the armory and procure weapons for the people we release. "I'll need about six men with me."

Matthew nodded. "I need about five people with me to go to the upper floors. That leaves the rest of you to clear the main floor of the palace and then the surrounding grounds. Hopefully more of our people will be able to help you with obtaining possession of outside." He paused a moment. "I am not asking anyone to kill unless absolutely necessary. However, pirates are known to kill ruthlessly. If you have any survivors, knock them out, tie them up, and put them in the dungeons. But don't get hurt and don't die. Understand?"

Everyone nodded. They checked to make sure each group had a balance of weapons. Someone found some rope in the storage room and passed it out.

"Let's go," Matthew told them. "And may God be with us."

One group silently followed John to the back stairs and down to the dungeons. Another group followed Lance toward the Armory. Matthew took Donna and five men to the back stairs and up toward the bedrooms. The rest of the rescuers divided into three groups. One crept into the inner palace courtyard to clear it, one group to the east wing and one to the west wing on the main floors. Candles lit the halls; the rescuers kept to the shadows as much as possible.

At the top of the stairs, Matthew sent four men down one hall, and took Donna, Wolf, and another fellow named Mike with him toward the royal chambers on the east wing. He listened carefully for any noises coming from downstairs. Occasionally he could almost feel more than hear a thump. He wished he could see down into the courtyard or assess the progress of the others.

Matthew decided to clear all the rooms of the east wing as they went. While his companions guarded the hall, he suddenly opened the door of the first room facing the back stairs and looked in. It was dark. He walked through, checking under beds and behind furniture. It was empty. He closed the door and they prepared to turn the hall corner. He peeked carefully around the corner, and then quickly drew back. Three pirates guarded doors down the hall. He quietly unstrapped his bow and grabbed an arrow.

While he tried to decide what to do, he heard a muffled yell from the west wing. He heard footsteps running down the hall toward him. Mike stepped in front of Matthew, grinning eagerly and waited for the fellow to run around the corner, and then thumped him on the head with the hilt of his sword. Mike and Donna tied his arms and legs and dragged him into the room they had just cleared. Matthew listened but all was quiet again. He nocked the arrow to his bow and began to step around the corner again.

He came face to face with a pirate, who looked just as startled as Matthew felt. Before Matthew could stop it his fingers released the arrow and feathers sprouted in the pirate's throat. He collapsed to the ground, eyes still surprised and hand still gripping his cutlass. When Matthew looked up, the third guard had disappeared from the far end of the hall.

Feeling a tingling begin subtly in his fingers, he crept to the door the first pirate had been guarding. He thrust the door open and came face to face with Karl, who was holding a chair leg in his hand like a club. A bruise and small gash graced his forehead, but Karl's eyes looked fierce before widening in surprise.

"Matthew!" he gasped.

Matthew put his fingers to his lips, and soon Mike and Donna joined them, followed by Wolf. Huddled on the couch were Karl's father and a couple of the older palace courtiers. They looked frightened but unharmed. Donna closed the door behind them.

"Where is the royal family?" Matthew whispered.

"In King Gilbert's suite, I believe," Karl whispered back. "I think the pirate captain is personally watching them. Be very careful."

Matthew nodded. "We are freeing those in the dungeon. Then we'll tackle the gate guards."

Karl's father looked confused. "If there are still gate guards, how did you get in?"

Matthew smiled. "Through the secret tunnel Karl found."

Karl smiled briefly and nodded. "Figures you would find a way."

"How did the pirates get control of Adonia Palace?" Matthew asked quietly.

Karl didn't respond immediately. "I think we weren't expecting anything to happen, so we were caught completely by surprise. The gate guards don't usually close and lock the gates at night, so it didn't take too many pirates to overpower them. A portion of our soldiers were out on country patrol, and the others were captured while sleeping in their quarters. The rest of us upstairs were similarly surprised in our sleep. I got knocked out and my father hid me under the bed in the commotion, so I wasn't taken to the dungeon with the other younger palace inhabitants. Since then I have been waiting for the right moment to do something."

Matthew laid a hand on his friend's shoulder. "Now is the time. We brought about thirty-five people in through the tunnel with us."

Karl's face looked grim and he nodded toward the window. "Be careful. There are a lot of pirates or robbers on the top of the outer palace walls. They have been watching for an attack from outside, but they can just as easily shoot at opponents within the walls."

Matthew looked at him worriedly. "We need to warn our people about them, and figure out how to bring them down before they know we are here. Lance was getting swords and things from the armory, but I think they'll need bows. Take mine and lead the offensive."

Karl nodded, took Matthew's bow and quiver of arrows, and beckoned to his father and the other courtiers. They shook Matthew's hand and left the room. Matthew led his team to the next room that had been guarded.

As he reached for the doorknob, an electric shock seemed to go through him. This was the door to Sarah's suite. When he hesitated, Donna pushed past him and threw the door open. A muffled scream came from within, and a little plate broke against the door near Matthew's head. Pieces of shattered glass spattered them, and one stuck in Matthew's left jaw. Mike jumped through the door brandishing his sword, and Wolf growled and bared his teeth.

"Don't hurt us!" a female voice begged from the shadows.

"Then stop throwing things," Mike growled. "We are here trying to rescue you."

"Oh!" A female figure stepped from the shadows into the candlelight, holding another dish up ready to throw it. "You don't look like pirates or robbers."

"No!" Donna retorted. "We are from Adonia City. We're trying to help break the siege."

Matthew couldn't help but stare at her as he recognized Sarah. Her hair was disheveled and her right cheek was smudged with soot, but she was the same Sarah he remembered.

She finally noticed him and furrowed her brow. "You look familiar... Matthew!" she gasped. "I almost didn't recognize you!" She suddenly marched over to him and slapped him on the right cheek. "That is for leaving me without even saying goodbye!"

Matthew stared at her, astonished. "I was under the impression that you left me!"

"Well you thought wrong." She suddenly burst into tears. "No, you are right, Matthew, and I have regretted it all summer." She looked at his face more closely. Something in his left cheek glinted in the candlelight. "Oh! I hurt you. Let me take a look."

She touched Matthew's cheek and the piece of glass cut deeper. He winced and pulled back. Another woman brought the candle closer. "I see it," Sarah told him. "Hold still and I'll get the glass out." She grasped the piece with her fingernail and finally managed to pull it out. The hole started bleeding a little, and Sarah brought him a piece of cloth to hold over it.

Matthew went to the window overlooking the inner courtyard. Figures moved quietly and swiftly in the darkness. "Sarah, where are my sisters being held?" he finally asked.

"In the king's chambers," she answered. "The entire royal family is guarded by the pirate Captain Jambalaya himself." She paused. "Amber has a little boy named Samuel."

"Marvelous!" Matthew smiled. "Sarah, I need to see outside the palace to the outer courtyard. Are the rooms across the hall safe?"

Sarah nodded. "I believe so."

Matthew motioned Donna to stay with the women, while he and Mike slipped across the hall and into the empty chamber on the other side. They peered out the window into the darkness. All seemed quiet, but then they saw shadows moving across the outer courtyard. Several thunks and groans could be heard, and then they saw a body fall from the parapets.

Matthew felt a presence behind him and turned to see that Sarah had entered the room. "How are you going to rescue the royal family?" she whispered.

"Barge in, I suppose," Matthew answered quietly. "Unfortunately, their guard saw us and has probably already gone in to warn their captors. I fear they will have an ambush waiting for us."

Sarah was silent a moment. Two more figures fell from the parapet walls. "There are secret connecting doors between the royal suite's bedchambers," she finally confessed. "I think those will not be so heavily guarded."

Matthew smiled. "Perfect!"

"However, you and anyone else who uses them tonight must promise to keep their existence a secret."

Matthew and Mark nodded their agreement.

They returned to Sarah's chambers to prepare. Sarah went into her bedroom and returned with a dagger. "I am going with you to get the children."

Matthew began to protest, and then saw the look of determination in her eyes. He nodded. "Then let us go."

Sarah led Matthew and Donna to Harry and Amber's suite, while Mike positioned himself by the door to King Gilbert's. They slipped into Harry's bedroom, where Sarah pulled back a wall tapestry to reveal a door. She tapped on several stones next to it, and then pushed on one until it slid inward. The door latch released, Sarah pushed the door inward a few inches and slid it to the side. There was about two feet of space between the stone walls of the rooms. Ahead of them was another door. Again Sarah felt around for the right spot, and then pushed another stone. This door released also. Matthew felt a mild tingling in his fingertips, so he paused to listen. Hearing nothing, he let Sarah pull this door to the side also. He slipped behind the tapestry covering the doorway.

He heard some commotion from the sitting room beyond, and thought Mike must be at the door of the suite. He slipped out from behind the tapestry and saw some figures huddled on the bed: a woman holding a baby and two little girls. The bedroom door was partially closed. One of the little girls yelped at seeing him, and huddled closer to the woman.

"Amber, Stephanie?" he whispered.

The older one of the girls launched herself at him. "Mattie!"

"Stephanie!" He hugged her tightly. "Hurry, Sarah is behind the tapestry and will take you out of here. Now go!" He pushed her toward the tapestry covering.

Meanwhile Donna had entered and was hurrying Amber and Sabrina off the bed and toward the tapestry. Matthew turned toward the door of the sitting room.

There was mayhem inside. Mike was bravely fighting two pirates by the door. King Gilbert and Harry were dodging four others around the sitting room. Harry had only a short dagger; Gilbert had no weapon at all. However, they were making great use of furniture as shields, vases and pillows as weapons and projectiles. Mike and Harry managed to take down one pirate each. Matthew slipped into the room behind another and hit him over the head with the hilt of his sword. He crumpled to the floor.

Suddenly Captain Jambalaya's voice rang out over the room. "No one move! I have the king! Stop fighting this instant!"

Everyone froze and the room fell silent. Captain Jambalaya stood behind King Gilbert and was holding a knife to his throat. The pirate captain grinned. "That is better. Now, King, abdicate the throne to me or I will kill you."

Gilbert gazed at his son. "No. I cannot and I will not," he stated hoarsely. The pirate's grip around his throat tightened, and King Gilbert's breath rasped raggedly. A drop of blood appeared on his neck where the pirate's dagger pressed.

Captain Jambalaya leered at Harry. "You, Prince. You have the power to save your father. Give me the throne and I can let you both go."

Harry hesitated a mere moment. "Never!" he shouted and lunged at Captain Jambalaya.

One pirate robber near Matthew tried to intercept Harry, but Matthew tripped him, tackled him to the floor and disarmed him. Wolf grabbed him by the throat and held him there.

When Matthew looked up, he saw Harry standing behind Captain Jambalaya, his knife stuck between the pirate's ribs. As the pirate captain toppled to the ground, he released King Gilbert, who sank slowly to the floor, bleeding from where the pirate's blade had stabbed into his throat.

"No, no, no, no," Harry mumbled as he cradled his father's head in his arms. King Gilbert reached up a hand to grasp Harry's arm, and gazed lovingly into his son's eyes. Then his eyes glazed over and his arm dropped to the floor. "Nooo!" Harry leaned back his head and began to weep.

The pirate underneath Matthew suddenly began to struggle. Matthew hit him over the head and knocked him out cold. He looked up at Mike, who had just taken down the last pirate robber.

Mike nodded at Matthew. "I'll go find some rope."

Matthew stood guard over the unconscious pirates and waited. Donna slipped into the sitting room from the bedroom.

Harry suddenly looked up at Matthew. "Amber!" he cried. He jumped up and rand into the bedroom, and almost immediately returned. "Amber and the children are gone!"

Donna curtseyed. "Your majesty, we took them out through a secret passage to the next room. Come." She led Harry into the bedroom and through the passage behind the tapestries.

Mike returned with rope, and he and Matthew trussed up the pirates. They gazed down at King Gilbert's body.

"Perhaps we should lay him on his bed?" Mike suggested sorrowfully.

Matthew nodded. "Let me clean him up a little." He got a wet towel and washed the king's neck and shoulder, and then wrapped a clean cloth around his neck to hide the neck wound. Then together they lifted the King's body and arranged him on top of the bed. Mike bowed his head in respect before they left the room.

They found Harry reunited with his wife and the children in Amber's chamber. Harry was hugging Sabrina tightly while Amber leaned against him, holding her baby Samuel. Stephanie sat in Sarah's lap where they were comforting each other.

Matthew cleared his throat. "Um, excuse me, Harry, but I think we are needed outside. Your townspeople are still trying to clear the parapets and gates from the pirates and robbers. We need to go help them."

Harry looked up at him. "Right." He gave Amber a kiss and stood up.

Amber clung to his arm. "Harry, be careful."

He looked at her with concern. "I hate to leave you unprotected…"

Donna moved swiftly in and knelt before him, her sword across her knees. "I will stay and protect your family, Your Highness."

Harry smiled and laid a hand on her shoulder. "Thank you. For that I am most grateful."

Mike turned from looking out the window. "I think it would be easier to track down the pirate robbers if we could shine some light out onto the parapets."

Sarah spoke up. "Leave that to those of us still in the palace. We can put lamps in all the windows and light the roof torches."

Matthew smiled gratefully at her. "Be careful. Protect yourself."

She brandished her dagger at him. "Aye. Be ye pirate or be ye friend? Your answer could have dire consequences."

Matthew laughed and then grew serious. "Friend. Always friend." He stepped closer, wanting to kiss her, but thought better of it. Instead he squeezed her hand and then went to the door. "Coming, Harry?"

"Yes, let's go." Harry took one long look at Amber and the children, and then followed Mike and Matthew out the door into the hall.

"I need to get another bow," Matthew told Harry. "Can we stop by the armory on the way out?"

"Absolutely," muttered Harry, holding up his dagger. "I need a longer blade myself."

Matthew found a bow and quiver of arrows, while Harry picked out a good sword. Then they all slipped out a side door to the outer courtyard.

The women inside the palace had started by putting lights in the rooms on the top floor. Someone had ascended onto the roof parapets and lit torches on each of the four corners of the palace. This had the advantage of keeping the courtyard grounds in shadows while lighting up the outer wall parapets. Matthew joined other Adonians in shooting down pirate robbers. Some tried to escape by descending down the stair wells, but Harry and his soldiers met them at the exits. Soon all was quiet.

"Adonians, to me!" Harry's voice rang out over the palace courtyard. "Ascend the walls and clear out every hiding place there is!"

Harry led the charge. Men entered stairways and ascended the outer walls. A few more pirate robbers were found and dispatched. The parapets were clear. Harry peered over the wall near the closed front gates at the group of pirates guarding the road.

"Ho there!" he shouted down. Some of them looked up, confused. "Pirates and robbers, the siege of Adonia palace is ended. I, Prince Harry of Adonia, give you a chance to surrender and live. Fight on and you will be slain. In a moment I will open the gates and come out, and you must decide."

One pirate looked up at him. "You and what army?"

Harry blew on his horn a long loud blast. His men on the parapets leaned over, pointing drawn arrows at the pirates in front of the gates. Townspeople emerged from the shadows and started up the road toward the palace. They brandished a variety of tools and weapons as they came. A patrol of Adonian soldiers could be seen galloping down the road from the north toward them.

Harry gazed down at the pirates calmly. "Your Captain Jambalaya was slain by my own hand. I repeat, surrender and live, or fight and die. Open the gates!"

As Harry's soldiers poured out of the gates, the leader of the pirate gate guard raised his sword to fight, and other robbers followed suit. Several arrows from Prince Harry's men on the wall parapets felled them. The rest of the pirates and robbers dropped their weapons and raised their arms in surrender. Harry's men took them down to the palace dungeon.

Harry hurried down the stairs to the gates to meet the villagers and the incoming Adonia soldiers. "We need to sweep through Adonia City and ferret out any remaining pirates. Bring all surviving robbers to the palace for lock-up. On the morrow we can clear out the rest of Adonia."

Through the night the city of Adonia was searched, and several dozen more pirate robbers were brought to the dungeons. Prince Harry finally let everyone settle down to get a couple of hours of sleep.

Matthew felt like he had barely closed his eyes when there was a loud knock on the door of his suite. When he opened it Harry stood there, his eyes red and his face tired.

"Harry, didn't you sleep?" Matthew queried.

Harry shook his head. "I tried. Too much on my mind. Meet me in the throne room." He turned on his heel and went downstairs.

Matthew washed his face, put on his shoes and hurried down to the throne room. There Harry was meeting with the general of his army, the mayor of Adonia, the chief of police, and Sir Royce.

Harry looked up as Matthew came in. "Prince Matthew, do you know if your parents were planning on sending any assistance to our neighboring countries of Renling or Borden? I assume we will be the closest to Mordred."

Matthew shook his head. "I left just as they were sending troops to stop the pirates in Portsmouth, Sterling. I do know pirate ships were landing in Renling about three days ago. I can only assume the same for the other countries."

Harry covered his eyes with one hand. "Then we will need to send troops to all three countries." He lowered his hand. "I will take a group of men and soldiers north to Mordred. I will need horses for all of my men to get through the snows I am sure we will encounter now that winter is near."

He turned to his knight. "Sir Royce, I need you to take a group of men through the East Adonia Pass to Renling and offer your assistance there."

Harry looked around the group of men, glanced at his general, and then rested his gaze on Matthew. "Prince Matthew of Sterling, your assistance in Adonia has been most appreciated. I wonder if we could request your further help in aiding our brothers in Borden? General Tobasco would accompany you with his troops. You will have to go through South Wolf Pass."

Matthew inclined his head. "I would be honored to serve any country of Browning Isle."

Harry looked at the group before him. "Then it is settled. Upon our return we will bury King Gilbert in state ceremony."

While palace workers gathered and packed food supplies, soldiers and as many men from Adonia City as could be spared prepared their horses, weapons and travel gear. By noon they were ready.

Harry led one hundred soldiers and civilians, all on horseback, out of the city by the north route. Their plan was to free any towns from pirate robbers that infested them, and leave some civilian fighters to protect them. The rest would forge through the North Pass into Mordred and help free them if needed.

Sir Royce led a hundred fighters and squires towards the East Adonia Pass and Renling, figuring the pirates would have targeted the capital port city of Greensbay. The palace guard and a handful of squires including Karl stayed behind to protect Adonia Palace and the royal family.

Matthew, General Tobasco and their one hundred men on horseback prepared to head toward South Wolf Pass and from there on toward the capital city of Borden. As Matthew saddled his horse, Wolf trotted around some of the other horses who shifted nervously. Matthew hoped Wolf would leave Borden's sheep alone. He did not know how to tell the animal to stay behind. On the other hand, he almost felt safer having Wolf by his side.

Just before the troops left, Sarah came running out of the door of the palace. She met Matthew in the front courtyard preparing to mount his horse. She stopped in front of him and shifted her feet in uncertainty.

"Will I see you again, Matthew?" she finally blurted out. She blushed.

"I certainly hope so. But it may not be until next spring. I will need to return to Sterling after freeing Borden." He saw her forlorn look and took her hand. "I want you to know I still think you are the most lovely woman in the world, and the most desirable to me. It doesn't matter to me who your parents were." He smiled at her. "To me you are an exotic orchid of great beauty. I don't care how many other flowers I have seen. Remember that, Sarah."

He mounted his horse and turned to follow the rest of General Tobasco's troops. He looked back to see her still standing in the courtyard, an uncertain expression on her face. He waved once to her and she raised a hand slowly toward him in farewell.

CHAPTER 15

BORDEN

Matthew, General Tobasco and their men traveled rapidly over South Wolf Pass, reaching the east-west road on the other side of the pass by sundown. Knowing time was of the essence, they continued traveling west toward Borden, horses trotting down the dark road under the trees. Some men dozed in their saddles, including Matthew, who hadn't slept much the previous three nights. By dawn they reached the edge of the woods and General Tobasco called a halt so the horses could rest and let the men grab a bite to eat from their food rations.

Matthew slid down from Flint and was met by Wolf, tongue out lolling, looking up at him happily. Matthew scratched the animal's ears and then went into the trees to relieve himself. Wolf followed him. When they returned to the group, Matthew crouched down in front of Wolf, held onto his ears and looked him in the eyes.

"We will be entering sheep country," Matthew told him. "You are not allowed to eat any of Borden's sheep. If you do, I will have to put a tether on you. You are allowed to eat rabbits, snakes and other vermin. And you may have some of my rations."

Wolf grinned at him. Matthew had no idea if the animal understood him, but he fed him some of his strips of dried meat to make sure.

Just as the men were getting ready to climb back onto their horses, five mountain men emerged from the depths of the trees and approached General Tobasco. As Matthew neared them he thought one of them looked familiar. Sure enough, the man was his previous traveling partner, Thomas.

"General," one of the men was saying. "There are pirates in Borden."

"Yes, we know," the general responded. "We have come to help."

"General Tobasco," Matthew chimed in. "Perhaps these men can help us scout out the enemy, and lead us to where our fight would be most effective?"

The five men nodded. "The pirates are holed up in the king's chateau. We will come with you," the one named Baer offered.

General Tobasco smiled. "Your help is most welcome. But we do not have extra horses for you."

Thomas shrugged. "We walk fast."

Matthew offered to carry Thomas' pack on the back of his horse, and several soldiers did the same for the other mountain men. Thomas walked beside Matthew in comfortable silence. Wolf, who seemed to recognize Thomas, walked beside him happily.

They did pass many herds of sheep and cattle in the rolling hills of Borden. Wolf's ears picked up and forward as they neared each sheep herd, and Matthew talked to Wolf each time to keep him near him.

He fed Wolf a little scrap of food each time they finished passing a herd successfully. By late afternoon they reached the main town of Borden, a community along a river with dense trees running alongside it.

"The town of Borden is smaller than I thought," Matthew commented to Thomas.

"People more spread out to farm," replied Thomas briefly.

General Tobasco called a stop and had the troops set up camp among the trees by the river. Then he called a meeting among his lieutenants, with Matthew and the five mountain men. "We need to scout out where the enemy is if they are here at all, and then regroup to carry out the rescue," he told them.

"We will meander through town and gather information," offered Baer. The other mountain men nodded their agreement.

"Perfect," General Tobasco responded. "We also need someone to approach the King's chateau and see what is going on there. I am afraid my presence would alert any enemies to our intent."

"I will go," Matthew volunteered. "I can look like an innocent visitor from out of town. If the pirates are there and let me in, I can send a signal to let you know when you can come to the rescue."

Thomas accompanied Matthew to the grounds of the King's chateau. The house sat on a little hill beside a small lake, but was most easily approached by a wide road from the direction of town. A stone wall the height of a man ran around the grounds, with a wood and iron gate guarding the entrance. Some rough looking guards stood outside the gate.

Thomas stayed back among the trees along the river, while Matthew walked up the road toward the chateau with Wolf. He had left his sword and bow back with Thomas, but carried his long dagger in its sheath hidden underneath his trousers. The guards watched him warily as he approached.

"Good day!" Matthew greeted them cheerily. "Is the good master of the house at home?"

"He is not accepting visitors today," one of them replied gruffly. "Begone."

"Oh, that is too bad." Matthew looked crestfallen. "I bring interesting news from beyond the realm. Perhaps tonight or in the morning? I was really hoping for a meal and a place to sleep tonight. I have come from afar."

"Where did you say you traveled from?" the guard asked curiously.

"Oh, from hither and yon." The guard didn't look satisfied. "I hail from Danforth City," Matthew finally told him. "Have you heard of it?"

The guard shook his head. "We will inform the master of the house." He turned to his associate. "Go and tell Long John we have a persistent visitor with news."

Matthew sat down at the side of the road to wait. Wolf lay down beside him and Matthew rubbed his ears. He resisted the urge to look back into the trees where Thomas waited. He wasn't sure if he wanted to get inside the chateau right now or not. He and Thomas had talked briefly about different strategies and possibilities; it would be better for General Tobasco's troops if there was a man inside to let them in.

After about twenty minutes the guard returned. "Long John will see the visitor."

Matthew stood up and nodded at the guards. "Thank you. I have long heard of the hospitality of the Lord of Borden."

The guards exchanged looks. "Uh, sure. Well come on in."

Matthew did not look back and followed them in. No signal to Thomas meant that pirates were in the chateau, and that General Tobasco needed to prepare his troops for battle.

The guard looked at the wolf following Matthew. "Is he tame?"

Matthew grinned. "I don't think so. But he has been my traveling companion for some time now. He seems to prefer to stay by my side."

At the front door of the chateau another guard met them. "Search him for weapons."

When Matthew's escort attempted to approach Matthew to search him, Wolf bared his teeth and growled menacingly. The fellow drew back in alarm. Matthew took off his traveling cloak and turned around to show he wore no scabbard or obvious weapons. The guards seemed satisfied.

"Go on in," the one at the door told them.

Matthew and Wolf followed their escort into the chateau, through the messy main hall into a large room that looked like a small throne room. At the far end a throne stood on a dais, and upon the throne sprawled a large bearded fellow tearing bites of meat off a large ham bone he held in his hand. Scraps of food and bones lay on the floor around the throne where two dogs lay, chewing on bones of their own. Wolf wisely stayed quiet and close to Matthew's heels as they approached. The guard escort stayed by the door and waited.

"You must be Long John," Matthew stated.

The bearded man put down his ham bone and grinned. "I am the master of the house, the Lord of Borden, as you called me. You may bow to me."

Matthew ignored the last request. "Nice little place you have here. Not quite the size of the throne room in Sterling, nor the grandeur of the palace of Adonia, but twill do for the little shepherd kingdom of Borden."

Long John's grin disappeared and he put his feet onto the floor. "How does this compare to Renling and Mordred?"

Matthew looked around the throne room. "Well, Renling's palace sits atop a cliff overlooking the sea. It has lovely open halls to let in the sea breezes, and is carved in the shapes of the local forest trees. Mordred Castle overlooks a deep green fjord amongst rugged mountains, and the great halls are made of the white and gray marble stone found there. It is truly impressive."

Long John scowled. "You said you hailed from Danforth City. I have not heard of it. What country does it belong to?"

Matthew smiled. "Oh, the city state of Danforth belongs to no other country. Its people are fiercely independent."

Long John looked troubled. "Who is Danforth's king?"

Matthew shook his head. "Danforth has no king. It is ruled by the people, who vote in their leaders for six year terms. It is a very equitable way of running things, and no single person is in charge."

Long John shifted uncomfortably on the throne. "You said you brought interesting news."

Matthew looked at him slyly. "I will give you news for a dinner meal."

Long John studied him a moment. "Very well." He clapped his hands and shouted loudly, "Bring this man a meal!"

A middle aged woman brought in a plate of meat and potatoes for him, but with no fork or knife. Matthew sat down on the floor and began to eat with his fingers, occasionally tearing off a piece of meat and feeding it to Wolf. Long John watched him impatiently. Matthew ate slowly, savoring each bite. Finally Long John could wait no longer.

"I have fed you. Now tell me the news!"

Matthew chewed his last piece of meat. "There seems to be new management in the kingdoms of Browning Isle."

"What do you mean, 'new management'?" Long John asked, eyes gleaming.

"New governors, new lords, new masters. What shall I call them?" Matthew eyed Long John.

"New kings?" Long John suggested hopefully.

"Perhaps you could call them kings, though I doubt any of them come from royal lineage. They seem a little rougher than that. And they all came on the scene about the same time, and through some violence. Rather like a coup. And rarely do the majority of the people like a coup."

Long John furrowed his brows. "Does every country have a new king?"

"Except Danforth, of course," Matthew mused. "I wonder which new leader will be the High King?"

"The High King?" Long John looked eager and worried at the same time. "What is this High King?"

"Oh, the High King rules over the other kings. Rather like the father of the first four kings and one queen who founded the kingdoms of Browning Isle. The High King basically tells the other kings what to do."

"How does one become the High King?" Long John asked, the corner of his mouth drooling.

"I suppose you would have to prove yourself wiser in council, stronger in battle, or wealthier in trade. Then you get the other kings to vote for you to be their leader." Matthew yawned and stretched. "I am tired. Is there a warm corner near a fire where I may sleep?"

Long John waved a hand distractedly. "Find a room with a warm fire where this fellow may sleep."

Matthew nodded his head. "Thank you, Master Long John." He returned to the door of the throne room. The guard seemed uncertain where to take him. "Just point me the way to the fires in the kitchen," Matthew suggested. "Those fires should stay warm most of the night."

The guard took him to the kitchen and then returned to his post. Matthew glanced at three women huddling in the corner of the kitchen, nodded to them, and proceeded to stretch out in front of the fire. "Good night, ladies," he said, wrapping himself in his cloak and closing his eyes. Wolf curled up against his back.

After several minutes the three women came out of the corner and crept over to peer down at Matthew.

"Is he one of them?" one whispered.

"I don't think so," another one answered.

"How can you tell?" the third one asked.

"He is cleaner than the others, and more polite," the second one stated. Matthew laughed to himself. It had been at least two days since he had even sponge bathed.

"He looks nicer," the first one said. "More wholesome. Something in his countenance, something almost royal inside."

"You dream, Cindy. You are always looking for a prince in sheep's clothing," stated the second.

"At least he's not a wolf in sheep's clothing," retorted Cindy.

Wolf let out a low growl. The women stepped back.

"Do you think the wolf is dangerous?" asked number two.

"Not as dangerous as those pirates, Veronica," responded the third woman. "At least they are keeping us working in the kitchen and not in their bedrooms."

"Poor Stacy and Sally," moaned Cindy. "Whatever shall we do?" Cindy began to weep.

"There, there, girls," comforted number three. "It's not the end of the world. Something or someone will tip the balance of things and we'll find a way out."

"You can talk, Madeleine, but those pirates didn't kill your brother," hissed Veronica.

The women were silent for a moment.

"Come on, girls," Madeleine suggested. "Let's stop talking and get some sleep."

"Good idea," spoke Matthew in a low voice from under his cloak. "It's hard to sleep with all this chatter in the room." He rolled over to look at them and gave a friendly smile.

Cindy covered her mouth. "We are so sorry, sir. Did you hear all we said?"

Matthew nodded and sat up. Veronica grabbed a long kitchen knife from the counter and pointed it at him. "Don't move, traveler, until you tell us where you are from and what you are doing here. If you are another pirate, I swear I will kill you right here and now."

Matthew gazed at her steadily. "I have just come from six months of sailing, but it was on a merchant ship, not a pirate ship." He held out his empty hands. "I have come to see if the same fate befell Borden as other kingdoms of the Isle."

Veronica lowered her knife. "Then it is true, pirates have captured the other kingdoms as well?"

Matthew nodded. "They did in Adonia, and possibly Renling and Mordred. I hope Sterling was warned in time."

"Then you are truly from Danforth as you said?" Cindy asked.

"My father is from Danforth, and my mother from Sterling," Matthew told her.

"So what is your plan?" Veronica asked sarcastically. "Are you and the wolf going to free us from the inside?"

"Something like that," Matthew grinned. "I have a little Adonian army waiting by the river. I just have to find a way to signal them and let them in."

Cindy bounced on her heels. "This is so exciting!"

Madeleine smiled slightly at her enthusiasm. "There are guards outside the kitchen doors. How do you plan to get past them?"

Veronica raised her kitchen knife. "He can have this knife."

Matthew smiled. "Thank you. I do have one of my own. You may need to keep that one as back up. I may need your help in creating a distraction for the guards when it is time to slip out of here."

Cindy looked at him shyly. "May I ask your name, kind sir? I would like to be able to address you properly."

"My name is Matthew." He glanced out the window. "I think we should get some sleep or at least pretend to, until the pirates are mostly asleep." He lay down again by the fire.

He heard Cindy gasp. "Matthew! Father from Danforth, mother from Sterling, bringing an army from Adonia! Madeleine, he is a prince in sheep's clothing!"

Matthew smiled to himself but lay still. Cindy was pretty smart, figuring that out.

He felt someone tapping his shoulder. "Sir, are you Prince Matthew of Sterling?"

He rolled over and looked up into Cindy's earnest face. "I am," he told her.

"Ooh! I knew it!" She first hugged Madeleine and then Veronica. "We are saved!"

"Not yet," Matthew told her seriously. "We first have to let Adonia's little army in, then defeat the pirates and release Borden's king. By the way, where is your king being held?"

"King William is in the dungeon," Madeleine told him. "The pirate chieftains have taken up residence in the royal suites upstairs."

"And his family?" Matthew asked. "Where are they being kept?"

"King William is a bachelor," Cindy giggled.

Matthew smiled at her. "Noted. When Adonia's army gets inside the gates, will you ladies take some soldiers with you to let him out of the dungeons?"

"It would be my pleasure," Cindy giggled again.

Veronica stared at Cindy disdainfully. "We will also free the other prisoners down there."

"Good," Matthew responded. "Then I will plan to remove the menace from upstairs. Meanwhile let's pretend to get some sleep, shall we?"

"I'll stay up and let you know when the pirates are asleep," Madeleine told him.

Around midnight one of the pirate guards opened the door to the kitchen. All he saw was Madeleine knitting by candlelight, and a traveler sleeping by the fire next to two kitchen wenches. He closed the door again, and the chateau grew quiet. Madeleine put down her knitting and roused the others.

Matthew sat up and rubbed his eyes. He had dozed off after all. "Is there any way to flash a signal light from an upper window toward the river?" he asked Madeleine.

She nodded. "I can take some medicine up to one of the servant's rooms upstairs that looks outward, pretending one of the girls is sick. I can flash a candle light out the window."

"Perfect. Flash it in sets of three. I will give you about ten minutes before I slip out into the courtyard to free up the gate."

While the others hid in the shadows, Madeleine took her candle and a bottle of medicine, talked her way past the guard at the inner kitchen door and headed upstairs.

Veronica tapped Matthew on the shoulder. "I have an idea to get you past the guard on the outside door."

Matthew listened and liked the plan. He stood behind the outside kitchen door in the shadows, dagger in hand. Veronica stood on the other side of the doorway, heavy frying pan in her hand. Cindy pulled open the door and poked her head out. The pirate guard looked around at her.

"You have to stay inside, wench," he told her gruffly.

"I know, mister. But we heard strange noises coming from inside the chateau and we were afraid. We wondered if a strong brave man like you could come check it out for us," she pleaded.

The pirate guard, flattered by her words, walked through the door into the kitchen. Matthew hit him hard on the head with the handle of his dagger and he toppled to the floor. Cindy and Matthew began tying him up with linens and a pulled a burlap sack over his head.

The inner kitchen door opened and the other pirate guard looked in. "What was that thump?" He asked. He saw them bending over the prostrate form on the floor. "Hey, what's going on here?" he asked, striding toward them.

He didn't see Veronica standing in the shadows, frying pan still in hand. Tiptoeing from behind she hit him over the head and he too crumpled to the ground. Another burlap sack and two kitchen towels later, two pirates were trussed up and rolled under the table.

"Well, that takes care of both doors," Veronica smiled with satisfaction. "While Prince Matthew has his fun in the courtyard, I think Cindy and I will free some of our friends upstairs."

Cindy picked out a frying pan and kitchen knife of her own. "I'm ready," she said bravely.

Matthew was concerned. "These are ruthless pirates you have here. I advise waiting until the extra soldiers arrive before trying to free anyone."

"As you wish," Veronica smiled sweetly.

Pacified, Matthew borrowed a cutlass from one of the trussed up pirates. He peeked out of the kitchen door and then slipped outside, Wolf padding silently beside him. Staying in the shadows from the moonlight he approached the front gate, listening for any unusual sounds. All was quiet. Six men stood on the inside of the gate; shadows of at least two dozen more stood outside the gate. Matthew leaned against the wall of the chateau and waited.

Matthew sensed more than heard a low whooshing, a thud thud thud, and then six of the men outside the gate collapsed to the ground. There were cries of alarm from the others, and those inside the gate turned to look. Matthew and Wolf leaped from their hiding place into the midst of the guards on the inside. Before they knew what was happening, Matthew took down two of them, while Wolf nipped at legs and created chaos.

Matthew reached the lock at the gate and attempted to open it. Alas, it required a key. As he turned around to look for it, he saw one of the pirate guards raising a cutlass over his head to strike down on him. As Matthew raised his borrowed cutlass in defense, a furry body launched itself onto the attacker. The pirate fell, wolf jaws clenched around his throat.

Matthew downed two more attackers while Wolf faced off against the last guard, teeth bared and growling. The last attacker fled. Matthew finally found a set of keys on the guard that wolf had first downed. He grabbed them and hurriedly unlocked the chateau gates. Captain Tobasco's grinning face met him as the gates swung open.

"About time you let us in. Where do you want us now?" He asked.

Matthew suddenly felt tired of fighting pirates. "I think Captain Long John will be in the king's suite upstairs. I suspect his other main henchmen are up there also. Take your men up there and have some fun. The only thing I ask is a few men to go with me to free any people of Borden who are in the dungeon."

General Tobasco saluted. "Yes sir. Take a dozen men with you."

By the time they reached the door of the chateau, the pirates were alerted to their presence and were pouring out the front door. Fighting erupted on the front steps and swept into the main halls. Matthew and his dozen men pushed their way through, only fighting pirates directly in their way, looking for any stairs leading downward. Finally they located a narrow stair spiraling down below ground level. They quickly took it, Wolf following Matthew.

At the bottom of the stairs they found two unconscious pirates sprawled on the ground. One sported a nice red welt on his forehead. The men with Matthew looked at him questioningly. He shrugged. They followed the corridor around a corner and nearly stumbled over two more pirates on the ground. One of these men was bleeding from a shoulder knife wound.

More cautious now, Matthew and his men crept down the corridor. Torches in the wall flickered. Matthew heard a sound around the next bend and prepared himself. Brandishing his borrowed cutlass, he leaped around the bend and came face to face with…Madeleine.

"Eep!" she exclaimed and then covered her mouth with a hand.

Matthew lowered the cutlass. "What are you doing here?" he whispered.

She took his arm and led him past some empty cells and around another bend where the floor started sloping downward. Veronica, Cindy and three other women had just finished knocking out two more guards.

"Yes!" Veronica pumped her hand in the air, waving a frying pan. "I love this weapon!"

"Have we found the keys to the cells yet?" Cindy asked.

Madeleine searched the pockets of the most recently downed pirates. She straightened up, dangling a ring of keys from her hand. "Found!" she exclaimed triumphantly.

Some of the men with Matthew continued further down the corridors to make sure there were no more pirates lurking beyond them. Madeleine started opening cell doors and letting out Borden citizens, chateau workers and guards.

Cindy ran further on, looking through barred windows. Near the end of the hall she started jumping up and down. "I found him! Madeleine, get over here with the keys quickly! I found King William."

Madeleine unlocked the cell door and Cindy entered the cell. King William was lying on a wooden bed, eyes closed. Cindy ventured over to him and touched his arm.

"King William! Your Highness, we are here to get you out. Wake up!"

He opened his eyes groggily and slowly sat up. He looked around, a little disoriented. "What is going on?" he asked, and rubbed his eyes.

"We've come to get you out of the dungeon," Cindy told him again. "Come!"

King William swung his feet over the sides of the bed and then spotted Matthew. "Thank you, sir, for rescuing me," he told him.

Matthew held up his hands. "It wasn't I, Your Majesty. These women actually did all the work in your rescue. I only arrived minutes ago after they dispatched six pirate guards."

King William looked at Cindy, as though seeing her for the first time. "Thank you, Cynthia," he said respectfully and gratefully.

She beamed and held up her frying pan. "It's all in the wrist." Then she took his arm. "Come, Your Highness. We need to get you out of here."

He stood up and wobbled a moment. "Just a little dizzy," he mumbled and started tipping over toward Cindy.

She tucked her shoulder under his and wrapped her arm around his waist. "It's okay, you may lean on me, Sire."

He nodded gratefully and she helped him out of the cell. Other prisoners were leaving their cells and running up the corridors toward the stairs. The soldiers who came with Matthew went with them.

King William touched the side of his head gingerly. "I think I got hit on the head. How long have I been down here?" he asked.

"Four days, Your Highness," Cindy responded.

"I think they fed me a couple of times," King William murmured. "Whew, I feel weak."

Matthew walked with them, watching for any dangers and prepared to help support the king if needed. Cindy was doing a fine job herself. By the time they reached the main floor of the chateau, the fighting was finishing up. King William commanded that all the surviving pirates be put into the dungeon cells. Long John bared his teeth at King William as General Tobasco's men took him down to the dungeon.

"This isn't the end," Long John sneered.

"Oh yes it is," King William told him. "You know the punishment for treason." He watched the pirate captain dragged down the dungeon stairs. "I am in the mood for a proper hanging."

King William sagged, and Cindy helped him over to a chair against the wall of the entry hall. "You need nourishment," she told him. She ran to get him a pitcher of water, fruit, bread, cheese and sausage.

He ate and drank hungrily. "I feel better," he finally said and sighed. He spotted General Tobasco. "General, thank you for your service this day. I would like to meet with you and your officers in the throne room so you can tell me how you accomplished our rescue." He turned to Cindy. "Cynthia, I'd like you to come to the throne room also. Bring anyone else in the household who can enlighten me on the events of the past few days."

She curtseyed and ran to fetch Madeleine, the butler and the captain of the guard. General Tobasco indicated that Matthew and Thomas should also join them. In minutes they joined King William in the throne room.

"Tell me how all this got started," King William commanded, relaxing into his throne.

The butler came forward. "It is my fault, Your Highness. One of the pirates came dressed as a traveler, requesting a place to stay for the night.

I let him in, fed him and put him in a guest room. He let in his fellow pirates in the night."

Matthew thought that sounded familiar. He wondered that Long John had let him in the same way. He glanced down at Wolf, lying quietly at his feet, and bent down to scratch his ears. Perhaps Wolf made it look like Matthew was more of an innocent mountain man then he realized.

The captain of the guard stepped forward. "I also share some of the blame, Sire. I was off shift and a new recruit was an assistant on duty. He did not raise the alarm speedily enough. But he fought bravely and dispatched several pirates before he succumbed. Alas, they overran us and locked us in the dungeon before we could stop them. Any citizen of Borden who approached the chateau was also imprisoned."

King William rubbed his head. "That must have been when they entered my room and hit me over the head. All I remember is waking up in the dungeon cell and sleeping a lot."

Madeleine curtseyed. "Your Highness, you should know of more atrocities that these pirates have committed. Several of the ladies of your household and girls from Borden were brought to the pirate's rooms and forced against their will. Some of us were luckier and served in other capacities."

King William's somber expression turned angry and he gripped the armrests of his throne tightly. "They shall pay double for this!"

Cindy, standing next to his throne, ventured to reach her hand out and laid it on his arm. He looked up at her pale face for a moment, then turned his arm over and grasped her hand. He took a deep breath and calmed himself.

"General, tell me where you are from and what brought you to Borden?"

"Your Highness, my name is General Tobasco. I and my troops serve King Gilbert—" He caught himself, and a shadow of sorrow crossed his face. "Er, Prince Harry of Adonia. We also were besieged by pirates, and have just been rescued ourselves. Apparently this was a massive plot to take over every kingdom on Browning Isle." He glanced at Matthew. "We were sent to offer our assistance, and were guided here by your neighboring mountain men, who had observed where the pirates had taken up residence in Borden." Thomas nodded.

"And who are you?" King William turned his attention to Matthew. "How do you fit into this saga?"

Cindy spoke up before Matthew could. "Your Majesty, this is Prince Matthew of Sterling. He pretended to be a traveler with interesting news, and Long John let him sleep in the kitchen with us. He helped us escape from the kitchen and let in General Tobasco's troops."

Matthew nodded his head. "It is as she said, Sire."

King William chuckled. "So the pirate captain got fooled by his own trick! That feels like justice."

Matthew smiled. "Meanwhile, Cindy and her friends got busy freeing your people. You should be proud of her."

King William glanced at her again. "I am quite pleased." Cindy blushed and tried to pull her hand away, but William kept it in his grip.

Matthew inclined his head. "Your Highness, now that your kingdom is restored to you, I request leave to return to my home. I left my parents on the verge of a battle themselves."

King William smiled. "Yes, I give you leave. Thank you for your service to Borden. I will not forget it."

General Tobasco shook Matthew's hand. "Thank you for your assistance, Prince Matthew. We are most grateful for all you have done for Adonia and Borden."

Madeleine kissed him on the cheek. "You truly are a prince in sheep's clothing, as Cindy said."

Matthew glanced down at Wolf, who stood up to follow him. "Or in wolf's clothing," he smiled to himself.

As he headed to the front door of the chateau, Veronica met him. "You are leaving so soon?" she asked. "We are preparing a feast for celebration."

"I can't stay," he told her regretfully.

"Then let me send you with food," she told him. She returned a few minutes later with a bulging bundle. "Good journey's to you, Prince Matthew."

Outside the chateau, Matthew realized he had no idea where his father's horse was. King Robert would be very disappointed if he returned without Flint. Matthew saw some horses milling around inside the walls by the side of the chateau, and went closer to look. One of General Tobasco's soldiers came running up to him.

"Prince Matthew! Are you looking for your horse?" Matthew nodded. "Then follow me. I believe Thomas rode your horse in and put him in the stable."

Sure enough, the horse was in a stall, still saddled. Flint whinnied when he saw him. Matthew leaned his head against the horse's neck, and breathed in his horse scent. Then he straightened up.

"Are you ready for another journey?" Matthew asked him. "We are finally going home."

CHAPTER 16

KNIGHTHOOD

As the sun rose in the sky, Matthew galloped Flint along Borden's highway toward the Black Forest, Wolf running happily alongside him. He thought his parents would have defended themselves just fine against the pirate's attempted coup, but he wanted to make sure. Fortunately he had a full day of daylight for travel. If Flint held up, he should arrive home before sundown.

Several times Matthew slowed Flint to a walk to pace him, and twice they stopped at streams so Matthew and his companions could drink and rest a short while. By late afternoon Matthew arrived at the main wagon road that turned off toward the town of Sterling. Half an hour later the road reached the edge of the Black Forest.

"We are almost there," Matthew told Flint. He glanced down and noticed that Wolf was hesitating at the edge of the forest. "Wolf! It's okay, you can come with me this time."

Wolf grinned and leaped after them again. They turned off the main road at the edge of town and followed a smaller road leading to Sterling Castle. Matthew slowed Flint to a walk and looked around. The sounds of a normal town activity wafted over to him, and he passed one wagon traveler coming toward him from Castle Hill. The man tipped his hat to Matthew and he nodded back in return. Everything appeared to be in order. Still, he was cautious as he rode up Castle Hill to the gates. The sun was sinking to the horizon, and the sky was colored with pink and orange hues.

The gates were open and a full guard contingent stood within and without. The lieutenant saluted Matthew and let him pass.

"Welcome home, Prince Matthew. Your parents are inside. All is well."

"Thanks," Matthew nodded and rode Flint to the stables. He removed Flint's saddle and brushed him down well. Then he brought the horse a fresh bucket of water and fed him some oats. Wolf drank from Flint's water bucket and then followed Matthew to the main castle door.

Matthew hesitated a moment, then pushed the doors open and went inside. There were voices coming from the dining room and Matthew wandered that way. Queen Elinore and King Robert were sitting at one end of the dining table, deep in conversation. They appeared to have already finished their meal. They looked up when Matthew walked in. Wolf lay down just outside the dining room door to wait.

"Matthew, son!" Robert jumped up and met him with a bear hug.

Matthew hugged him back. Suddenly he felt tired and hungry and ready to curl up in the comfort of his parents' presence. "I'm home," he murmured and slid into a chair at the table.

Elinore reached across the table and grasped his hand. "Can you stay longer this time?" she asked. He nodded. "Monica!" she called, smiling. "Bring another plate of food! Matthew's home!"

The food arrived within minutes and Matthew ate hungrily, not caring that it was lukewarm. His parents waited until he finished, just enjoying watching him. Finally he pushed his plate aside and gazed back at them.

"I missed you," he remarked. "I didn't realize how much until now."

"It has been a year," Elinore said quietly. "I imagine you have had a variety of experiences and adventures."

"Yes, I have." He thought about all the people he had met, the dangers he had faced, the choices he had made, and the things he had learned. How do you explain all that in one sitting? Instead he looked at his parents and smiled. "Thank you for all you have taught me over the years. I can report that I have done nothing that would shame either one of you." He paused. "Except maybe getting a tattoo."

Elinore raised her eyebrows.

"May I see it?" Robert asked with curiosity.

Matthew pulled up his left sleeve and showed them.

"An orchid?" Elinore smiled.

"Yeah well, I was thinking of someone at the time," Matthew confessed.

"Sarah?" Elinore probed.

Matthew stared at his mother. He hadn't really told anyone except Lance his feelings about her, and could not conceive how his parents knew about her.

"Who told you?" Matthew asked. "Amber? Stephanie? Because I didn't give them permission to talk behind my back. And besides, it wasn't working out between us, so…"

"So you went sailing on the Dauntless," Robert finished the thought. "I must thank you for warning us about the pirates arriving in Portsmouth. We were able to apprehend them soon after they landed. Then I went with some troops to Renling. After some negotiations between them, us and the troops Sir Royce brought from Adonia, they decided it was better to relinquish their designs than die fighting. I just got back myself today."

Matthew felt relieved. "Good. General Tobasco is currently helping King William clean up the mess left by the pirates' invasion of Borden. Now we only need to hear about Mordred's ordeal."

"Harry's troops weren't needed there," Elinore told Matthew. "The king of Mordred discovered the pirates the moment they landed, and ambushed the pirates instead of the other way around."

"How did you find all this out so quickly?" Matthew asked, calculating in his head the days and travel miles involved.

"Mordred sent emissaries to Adonia, who arrived right after you left there. Adonia's messengers arrived this afternoon." Elinore explained. She and Robert exchanged meaningful glances.

"It is impressive to me how all the countries on Browning Isle have been able to work together through this crisis," Robert observed. "If nothing else, those pirates have unified us even more tightly. I don't think they intended that."

"That should make it easier to negotiate better trade prices this next year," Elinore responded.

Matthew yawned. "I am tired. I didn't sleep much the last five nights. Mother, Father, I love you both. Good night."

They both stood and gathered around him in a group hug. Then Matthew went upstairs to his bedroom suite, Wolf padding along beside him. He looked around his old room once, put down his bundle of belongings and fell into bed, Wolf stretching out on the floor beside him.

It was late morning when Matthew finally awoke. He finally felt refreshed and rejuvenated. His muscles felt mildly sore from the exertions of the past week, but the cut on his cheek was almost healed.

After grabbing some bread and an apple from the kitchen, he wandered out into the Queen's Garden, Wolf at his heels. The air had the slight cool of autumn, but the sun was warm. He walked past the family garden of sunflowers, daisies and tulips, and walked down other rows of various bushes and flowers imported from other countries. He stopped in front of a group of flowers that he hadn't really noticed before, but now were eerily familiar to him.

"Orchids," he murmured. "When did Mother plant these?"

"Matthew!" a voice shouted behind him.

Matthew turned to see his friend Karl from Adonia. "Karl, what are you doing here?" He greeted his friend with a hand clasp.

"We brought news from Adonia and Mordred," Karl answered. "Didn't your parents tell you I was here?"

Matthew shook his head. "They said messengers came from Adonia, but didn't tell me any names. Boy, it is good to see you!"

"Oh," Karl paused. "How did Borden fare?"

"Adonia's troops were needed to free King William." Matthew glanced down at Wolf. "The pirate captain thought I was a mountain man or something, so he let me in to tell him news from the other countries. I think he was hoping to hear about his colleagues' successes. Instead I let our troops in right under his nose."

"I bet he was surprised." Karl looked down at Wolf. "I never asked you how you got your wolf companion, my friend."

Matthew scratched Wolf's ears. "He found me when I was crossing South Wolf Pass this spring. I pulled a thorn from his paw and he followed me to the Black Forest. He waited for me for six months and was still there on my return. We've been inseparable ever since."

"Amazing. I have never seen a wolf take to a human like this before."

"Nor have I." Matthew laid his hand on Karl's shoulder. "Karl, I have to thank you for your creative archery lessons. I got to test out some of your tricks shooting at pirates from the sail yards on the Dauntless."

Karl grinned. "Brilliant. That makes me happy." He paused and studied his friend. "So, now that all the countries are saved from piracy, what is your plan?"

Matthew rolled his eyes skyward. "Everyone asks me that question! I have no idea."

"You could become a knight," Karl suggested. "I think you would make a very fine knight. All the ladies would swoon for your affections."

"Naw, I don't think I would like to be tied down to serving one lord. And I don't need all the ladies' attentions." Matthew looked thoughtful. "I think I should like to go back to Adonia one more time before the winter passes close."

Karl looked sly. "So there is a certain girl you still have your eye on?"

Matthew sighed. "Yes. I suppose I need to swallow my fears and face her one time, to see if there is any chance she will consider me again." He looked at Karl earnestly. "Do you think she would?"

Karl began walking away from Matthew. Matthew just stood, watching him leave. Karl looked over his shoulder.

"Come!" he commanded.

Matthew followed him, puzzled. They walked down one path, and then turned onto another. One more turn and they approached a bench where a woman sat, back turned to them. Karl stopped in front of her, didn't say a word, but looked up at Matthew approaching. She turned to glance behind her and froze.

"Sarah!" Matthew gasped. He suddenly felt like his breath was taken away. "Wh-what are you doing here in Sterling?"

She stood and faced him. "I volunteered to be the messenger to bring Sterling word of Mordred's victory. Karl accompanied me. And I had other reasons."

"What about Amber's children? Who is caring for them?" Matthew asked.

"I got my friend Erica from the orphanage to take my place. They are in good hands."

They gazed at each other in silence.

"How long will you be staying?" Matthew asked dumbly.

Sarah glanced up at the sky. "Hard to say. It depends on whether the passes are closed by the time my business here is done."

"What other business do you have here?" Matthew asked.

Sarah didn't answer right away, but began walking. Matthew followed her. "Do you remember last spring when you told me my birth status didn't matter to you or your family?" She paused. "Well, I came here to find out if that was true. I came to talk to your parents."

Matthew stopped walking. His heart leapt in his chest. Dare he hope against hope? "And what did you find out?" He kept his voice steady.

She smiled. "Your parents are lovely people."

Matthew found it curious that his parents hadn't mentioned to him last night that Sarah was here. He didn't get the sense that they were opposed to her, or they might have said so. Perhaps they were leaving this relationship entirely up to Sarah and him.

He suddenly realized they had stopped by the patch of garden where the orchids grew. It seemed like a sign. He reached out, grasped her hand, and turned her to face him.

"I saw and learned many things the last six months while sailing around the world. I must confess, Sarah, everything I came across reminded me of you." He reached into his money purse and drew out the bundle he had been saving for her. He unwrapped the hair comb with an orchid on it, and the black and pink orchid designed scarf. He handed them to her.

"Orchids!" she exclaimed.

"Yeah, I even got an orchid tattoo," he confessed, pointing to his left upper arm.

She giggled.

"That was the most wild I got," he reassured her. "But orchids remind me of you, unique and elegant."

"Me? Elegant? No, I'm just plain me, an orphan—"

Matthew laid a finger on her lips. "I don't care where you came from. That doesn't determine who a person is. It is who you choose to be that matters. Sarah, I love the person you have chosen to be, daring and thoughtful, full of life and caring for others. I would like…" He paused. "Would you consider…" He took her hand again and dropped to one knee.

"Sarah, I love you. I want you by my side for the rest of my life. I promise to be true to you, and to do my best to make you happy. I may be young, but I have seen enough of the world to know that you are the woman I love and adore. Will you marry me?"

Sarah stood, weeping. "I thought my world had ended when you left last spring. How foolish I was to push away the man I had grown to love. I promised myself that if another chance came, I would not close that door again. Yes, Matthew, I will gladly marry you." She knelt and wrapped her arms around his neck.

He embraced her back. When he kissed her, she responded passionately.

They heard clapping from the other side of the hedge. Karl stuck his head through the bushes. "Congratulations, you two! It was about time!"

They stood up quickly and looked at each other sheepishly, but still holding hands.

Karl caught up to them as they walked back toward the castle door. "What a gorgeous day," he chatted. "I am so glad I came to Sterling. This is an adventure I didn't want to miss."

Matthew and Sarah just smiled at each other. Wolf padded along beside Matthew. Sarah did not seem bothered by the presence of the animal. Matthew laid his free hand on Wolf's head as they walked.

Queen Elinore was in the middle of holding court, but the young people found King Robert in the stable looking over Flint.

Robert stepped back from the horse when they came up to the stall. "Well, Matthew, Flint looks good. Thanks for not damaging him or wearing him out. I did miss him on my recent campaign, though." He noticed Sarah and Matthew holding hands. "Do you have something to tell me, son?"

Matthew drew a deep breath. "Father, I have asked Sarah to marry me," he announced.

Robert peered at them. "Looks like she is agreeable. She's a fine young lady, if you ask me."

"Then you approve?" Matthew breathed.

Robert nodded, grinning. "Come here, son." He hugged Matthew, and then drew Sarah into the embrace. Karl put his arms around all of them. Then Robert stepped back and looked at them. "Have you decided where you are going to live yet?"

Matthew and Sarah looked at each other in a little uncertainty.

"I suppose we will live in Adonia in the winter and Sterling in the summer, so I can continue watching Amber's children," Sarah suggested. "Or am I still allowed to do that?"

"Fine with me," Matthew nodded.

"So what will you be doing, Matthew?" Robert asked. "Do you intend to continue sailing?"

"Not anymore," Matthew smiled at Sarah. "I suppose I can keep polishing my skills at defense and negotiation. Do you have any position for that?"

Robert nodded. "Maybe. Have you considered completing your knight's training?"

Matthew shrugged. "It was a possibility under Sir Royce, but Sir Lamborgini seemed to be convinced that I was not very good at it."

"On the contrary," Robert observed. "He saw great potential in you. That is why he held you to a higher standard than the others."

"Was that it?" Matthew thought back with new perspective. "Perhaps. But I have an issue with promising fealty to one Lord. I feel more loyal to my country." He caught Sarah's eye. "Well, now to two countries."

"Hm." Robert looked thoughtful. "Anyway, your mother and I would like a detailed report of your journeys over dinner tonight. Let's make it a welcome home feast."

That evening Matthew, Karl and Sarah dressed up for dinner, and then went down to the dining room together. This time Wolf padded in quietly and lay down behind Matthew's chair. Queen Elinore raised her eyebrows at Matthew when the animal followed him in. He shrugged and raised his hands in a helpless gesture.

Tonight Elinore sat at one end of the table, Robert at the other end in their formal positions, Matthew to his father's right, Sarah between Matthew and Elinore, and Karl across from them. Everyone practiced their best manners.

After the soup was served, Elinore turned to Matthew. "Matthew, I want to hear everything about your journeys."

"Everything, Elinore?" Robert asked, straight faced. "You want details about the chamber pots in Adonia and the head on the ship?"

Karl laughed into his napkin, Sarah lowered her eyes, and Matthew grew red faced. His father could be a country boy at times.

"No, dear," Elinore smiled prettily. "I want to know about the things he has learned and the people he has met."

Matthew told his parents about wintertime in Adonia Palace, and learning how to ski. "I wasn't very good though. You should see Sabrina ski."

"He did very well for the first time," Sarah chimed in. "And you must know, Adonia Palace was warmer this past winter and cooler this summer with the hay in the attic."

"He also bagged a boar on the Christmas hunt," Karl informed the King and Queen.

"Yeah, after you slowed it down for me," Matthew smiled. "Harry actually got the biggest boar. And there is this lovely secluded waterfall Sarah showed me last spring. Mother, you should see it."

Karl grinned wickedly. "I hear it's called Bridal Veil Falls. Great name for a wedding place."

Sarah and Elinore smiled at each other. "I think that could be arranged," Elinore commented.

"Yes, well, then I took off and went to Portsmouth. I learned some fishing techniques from Roberta's brother Dale while waiting for the Dauntless," Matthew reported. "Uncle Edward has gained some weight."

Robert patted his own stomach. "It's the Danforth genes, the milk and honey diet."

"On the Dauntless I met Mark, another sailor my age from Mordred. He turned out to be my best shipmate, taught me a lot about repairing ropes and sails. We had a lot of adventures together." Matthew thought he better not mention Clarisse or Marie.

"Then there was this really tall sailor named Shorty sharing my top bunk, who was pretty cool," Matthew went on. "My night shift boss was Don. He was okay on the job, but he tried to get Mark and me drunk at one of the ports. He made Mark drink something called The Firebomb. Whooee! We thinned our drinks after that. Don called us the M and M's."

King Robert grinned. Elinore just shook her head.

"When we headed to the eastern ports, we got to try a lot of wonderful exotic foods. Then pirates chased us into a big storm, and we had to stop for a week in port getting the ship repaired. Mark and I worked at the King's stable. His daughter showed us the Komodo dragons he kept there."

"Komodos?" Elinore turned to Robert. "Do you suppose the East is where those dragons on Rimrock Island came from?"

Matthew kept his suspicions to himself. "Anyway, as we left, Miriam gave Mark this horse named Saitan that no one could ride but him. It seems Saitan would rather pull a cart or wagon."

Sarah giggled. "Saitan?"

"Yes. We had to find a room on the ship to stable the horse, until we reached a port across the channel where Mark could take him off again." Matthew paused wistfully. "Mark decided to settle down there and take the horse to do some farming."

"Bet you miss your ship mate," Karl observed.

"That isn't the half of it. Don got upset with me, so I moved to the morning shift under the first mate, Adam. That was when the pirate ship Dread Knot chased us to Rimrock Island. There was quite a battle, I tell you. That's where I got to use those archery moves of yours, Karl, from the sail yards. Cannonballs whooshing by us, tearing holes in the sails, splintering the masts, pirates yelling at us and brandishing their cutlasses."

Sarah shivered, staring wide-eyed at Matthew. Karl was listening with rapt attention, inspiring Matthew to share more of the details.

"So pirate Captain Spike jumps up on the poop deck to destroy Captain James of the Dauntless, and Adam throws himself in front of his Captain armed only with a dagger to protect them. Spike cuts Adam in the chest, and is about to swing his sword down on our Captain's head, when my sword blocks his blow. We dance around the helm, and I'm employing every move Royce and Lamborgini ever taught me. When I disarm Captain Spike, he is so mad he follows me off the ship to Rimrock Island and through the Komodo nesting ground, stomping eggs along the way. The Komodos are so angry they tear Captain Spike to pieces. I barely escaped myself from their wrath."

Elinore and Sarah stared at Matthew horrified. "I knew there was a reason I didn't want you on that island," Elinore whispered.

"No really, Mother, I was all right. My friend Creedo protected me from the other Komodos."

Karl clapped his hands. "Then what did you do?"

"Back on the ship I informed the pirates that their Captain Spike was dead. I had already defeated their first mate with my arrows, and Don knocked out a stubborn pirate who wanted to keep fighting. So they surrendered and we locked them up in Saitan's old stable room."

Robert chuckled. "Had it been cleaned out after the horse?" Matthew shook his head and grinned.

"That's when I brought everyone up to Sterling Castle," Matthew finished. "The end."

"Oh, that is not the end!" Sarah broke in. "That is when Matthew came to Adonia and rescued us!"

"How did you get past the pirates guarding Adonia Palace?" Robert asked. "We had to cajole our way in at Renling to speak with the pirate captain. I think it was only the threat of total annihilation from three country's armies that prevented a battle there."

Matthew glanced at Karl. "There was a secret entrance Karl and I discovered over the winter. I got some armed friends from Adonia City to slip in with me, and we cleared the pirates from inside-out."

Sarah smiled proudly. "I got to help get Amber and the children out through a secret passage, right out from under the pirate Captain Jambalaya's watch."

"She was very brave," Matthew agreed, smiling at her.

"I took a team to shoot down the guards on the walls," Karl added. "It was a marvelous routing!"

"Tell me how my cousin Gilbert died," Elinore requested softly.

Matthew grew serious. "Several pirates were in the room during the rescue and the pirate captain got King Gilbert with a knife against his throat. He demanded Gilbert and Harry abdicate the throne to him. Neither would relinquish, so Harry jumped Captain Jambalaya at the same time the pirate got King Gilbert. I don't think that they could have talked that pirate out of his intent."

Elinore nodded, a tear running down her cheek.

"I am afraid Harry feels it is his fault that his father was killed," Matthew added sadly. "I don't think he expected to take on the responsibilities of the kingdom of Adonia quite so soon."

"What does this do to Amber and the children coming to visit in the summer?" Robert asked Elinore.

"Or to the joining of Adonia and Sterling?" Elinore pondered. "I don't think it has to speed that up just yet."

"I can escort the children back and forth, Mother," Matthew offered. He glanced at Sarah. "I mean, we!"

"Elinore nodded. "That would be wonderful."

"Tell us about Borden's rescue," Robert interjected.

"General Tobasco and I took a hundred men from Adonia. Five mountain men joined us at the border. I took Wolf with me up to the chateau, where Captain Long John thought I was a traveling mountain man with news of his fellow pirates' victories. He let me in and gave me a place to sleep in the kitchen. From there I let in General Tobasco's men and they defeated the pirates. The ladies of the chateau freed King William. It wouldn't surprise me if there is a royal wedding soon in Borden." He winked at Sarah.

"That would be wonderful!" Elinore exclaimed.

"So tell me about Wolf?" Robert asked, eyeing the animal. Wolf raised his head and blinked at the king.

"Wolf first found me on this side of South Wolf Pass when I was leaving Adonia this spring. I pulled a thorn out of his paw and he followed me to the cave we found in the Black Forest. Apparently he stayed there all summer awaiting my return. He has followed me ever since." Matthew reached down and scratched Wolf's ears. Wolf let out a long sigh of contentment.

"Fascinating," Elinore murmured.

"I have heard of wolves occasionally befriending a human," Robert mused. "But normally they are more loyal to their wolf pack."

"Maybe his pack abandoned him or kicked him out," Karl suggested.

Matthew nodded. "That's what I think too. He was pretty scrawny and scratched up when I first found him."

"I think he needs a bath," Sarah commented, wrinkling her nose.

Matthew looked thoughtful. "He did follow me into the baths room this afternoon, but he seemed a little nervous. I might need some help actually getting him into the water." He glanced over at Karl.

Karl put up his hands. "Whoa, I have bathed dogs before, but not wolves."

Robert looked interestedly at the young men and grinned. "I will have to watch this."

"Maybe we will need your help, Father," Matthew told him slyly.

After they finished eating the main course, King Robert looked over at Matthew. "Sir Lamborgini wants to promote you, Matthew," he commented casually.

Matthew looked at his father, puzzled. "Promote me? What do you mean?"

"He thinks you are ready to be knighted," Robert announced.

Silence fell around the table. They all stared at Matthew.

"B-but I quit his squire training," Matthew stuttered.

"Maybe not," Robert said thoughtfully. "You could call it a temporary leave of absence. Besides, I understand you continued training under Sir Royce."

"Yes, he did!" Karl chimed in. "He got really good at archery in Adonia, and he taught us some superb sword fighting skills."

"Helping train other squires fulfills one qualification," Robert told him.

"But doesn't a knight candidate have to fulfill a quest and prove himself in battle?" Matthew asked.

"You figured out and solved what was behind our continent's economic decline," Elinore pointed out. "That's quest enough for me."

"You fought pirates in battle," Karl told him.

"And rescued Adonia and Borden," added Sarah.

"I think that proves your battle skills," Robert told him. "Any other excuses?"

"I used to want very much to be a knight. But what if that's not what I want to do all my life?" Matthew asked falteringly, gazing at Sarah.

"I don't think it has to bind him to only one course and purpose, do you Robert?" Elinore asked. "It could be a useful title to pull up now and then when the situation requires it."

"Oh, please say yes!" Sarah's face glowed and she clasped her hands together in petition. "It will be easier for me to tell my friends I'm married to a knight rather than a prince," she added. "The prince part sounds too presumptuous."

"But I really am a prince," he told her, dejectedly.

"Yes, I know. But I don't have to tell them that." She batted her eyelashes at him.

Matthew laughed. "Fine. I accept. But I'm keeping Wolf. And I'm still bathing him in the morning."

Queen Eliniore and King Robert stood, went over to Matthew who also stood, and they folded him in their combined embrace. "I'm proud of you, son," Robert said a little gruffly.

Elinore wiped a tear from her eye. "My boy is all grown up."

The next morning Matthew, Karl and Sarah took Wolf to the baths. Robert was detained by Sir Lamborgini and couldn't make it. Wolf followed Matthew to the door of the baths but would not go in.

"Maybe he is afraid of the water," Sarah suggested.

"Or the smell of steam and soap," added Karl.

"Maybe I shouldn't get wolf hair in the baths anyway," sighed Matthew. "Mother would have me flogged." Karl's eyes widened in alarm. "Well, figuratively anyway, not literally. Let's see if we can get Wolf to go into the washing room."

The washing room was quiet and empty. Wolf followed them into the room without hesitation. Matthew pulled down a big washtub off the wall while Sarah closed the door to the room. They each grabbed a bucket and started filling the washtub with water from the rainwater cistern. Wolf backed up against the wall and watched them warily. Then Matthew turned to Wolf.

"Come on, Wolf. We're going to get you clean. It's just like swimming in a stream."

"Do wolves swim in streams?" Karl asked.

Matthew shrugged. "I have no idea. Probably not. Maybe I'll have to show him." He pulled off his shoes and stockings, tunic and shirt. Then he stepped into the tub of water. It was a little cold. "Come, Wolf. The water won't hurt you." He sat down in the water for effect. Wolf just blinked at him.

"That worked really well," Sarah laughed at him.

"Maybe I need to bribe him with food," Matthew commented thoughtfully. "That's what he initially started following me for. It was strips of dried meat."

"I will be glad to get some meat scraps for you," Sarah offered. "Just wait right there."

"I'm not going anywhere with wet breeches," Matthew responded.

Karl stayed with Matthew, watching Wolf warily out of the corner of his eye. Wolf lay down and just observed Matthew. Matthew made a show of washing his torso with a bar of soap for Wolf's benefit.

"See? The water and soap won't hurt you," he coaxed. "After washing hair or fur it is so much softer."

Sarah came back with a bowl of raw meat scraps. Wolf's ears twitched and he lifted his head to watch her. She took the bowl over to Matthew.

"It's nice to see you know how to bathe once in a while," she teased him.

"Just give me a couple of meat scraps, woman!" he gruffed with a grin. He dangled a meat scrap from each hand. "Come here, Wolf. Get in the water with me and you can have a piece of meat."

Wolf crawled closer, but stayed on his stomach. Matthew dangled a piece over his own mouth. "Yum! Mighty good meat here! I know you want some." Wolf scooted up next to the washtub. Matthew stood up and held the meat up higher. "You have to come and get it!" he told Wolf.

Wolf cocked his head to one side, considering. Then he got up on all fours and stretched his neck up toward the scrap of meat.

"Just a little higher," Matthew told him. "Up!" Wolf stood up on his back legs and Matthew fed him the piece.

"Up again!" Matthew held up the second piece, but stepped back a step in the washtub. Wolf stretched forward, placing his front paws against Matthew's chest. The sudden weight threw Matthew off balance. Attempting to catch his balance he sat down in the washtub with a splash and Wolf fell in on top of him.

Sarah stifled a small scream as Wolf appeared to be trying to bite Matthew.

"I'm okay!" Matthew's muffled voice arose from just above the water. "He's just trying to find the meat scrap I lost. Pour water on him quickly!"

Karl grabbed a bucket and poured water on Wolf just as the animal found the piece of meat. He chewed happily seemingly oblivious to the water being dumped on his back. While Sarah passed meat scraps to Matthew to feed to Wolf, Karl soaped down the animal's back and rinsed him off. He finished at about the same time Sarah ran out of meat scraps.

Matthew showed Wolf his empty hands. "That's all I have for you, buddy. Bath's done."

Wolf sniffed around Matthew another minute, then jumped off of him and out of the washtub. He shook the water out of his fur coat, spraying Karl and Sarah with great drops of water.

"Eeek!" Sarah protected her face with her arms.

"Whoa!" Karl stuttered. "Stop, dude!"

Matthew sat up and climbed out of the washtub, shivering slightly. "Mission accomplished," he commented satisfied, and reached for his shirt.

"Matthew! Your chest is all scratched up!" Sarah covered her mouth with her hand.

He looked down at his chest. Sure enough, Wolf's claws had dug into his skin in several places. The skin began to sting. He looked over at Wolf, who was shivering and attempting to shake off more water. He hurriedly pulled on his shirt.

"I'm all right," Matthew told her. "I've got to get Wolf outside in the sun to dry off."

He pulled open the outer door to the courtyard and Wolf raced outside. The cool September morning air struck his damp skin and wet pants and chilled him. Wolf ran up and down the courtyard, reaching one end and rebounding off a wall, then racing around the clothesline pole at the other end. Suddenly inspired, Matthew took off after Wolf, whooping and hollering with the sheer joy of running in the sun. Karl and Sarah watched them from the doorway until Matthew and Wolf stopped in front of them and collapsed laughing on the ground. Wolf licked Matthew's face, and then looked up at Sarah and Karl, panting and grinning.

"Warmer now, Mattie?" Sarah asked him.

"Better, but the pants are still damp," Matthew told her. "I'm going up to change."

"I'll bring some salve for those scratches," Sarah told him.

"And I'm coming along to chaperone," Karl winked at them.

Matthew changed into dry pants, and then let Sarah and Karl into his suite. He obediently lay on the bed while Sarah applied the healing salve to the scratches. He closed his eyes blissfully to feel her soothing touch on his skin.

"All finished!" she announced, standing up and going over to the dressing table to wash her hands in the basin there.

Matthew opened his eyes. "Shouldn't you put on another layer, just in case?"

Sarah cocked an eye at him and shook her head. "What I put on will do for today."

Karl handed Matthew his shirt. "Tut, tut. Time to let the lady go. You have to get ready for your interview with Sir Lamborgini this afternoon."

Matthew groaned. "I am not looking forward to that."

"What, is the brave young knight afraid of something?" Karl grinned at him.

"Not afraid, exactly," Matthew confessed. "More embarrassed at my behavior a year ago. I don't think I gave Sir Lamborgini enough credit or respect. And I am not a knight yet, just a squire."

"An amazing, accomplished squire, I might add," Karl told him. "One I would be proud to associate with all my life."

Sarah merely smiled and dried her hands. "I will leave you two to your conundrums."

"Not without a kiss, my Lady," Matthew teased her. "I need a token of your affections." He pursed his lips.

She swatted his arm with her towel. "Not when you make funny faces at me."

He clasped her around the waist and drew her to him. "But I love your face." He kissed her lips. She kissed him back and he responded hungrily.

"Okay, you two," Karl intervened. "That is quite enough. We have to make it to what, a spring wedding?"

"You're right," Matthew sighed and let Sarah go.

She straightened her dress. "See you tonight, Mattie, Karl." She nodded at them and slipped out of the room.

Matthew waited nervously outside the throne room while Queen Elinore and King Robert conversed with Sir Lamborgini. Then the door opened and Matthew was allowed to enter.

"Are you sure he is old enough?" Matthew thought he heard Queen Elinore ask. "Isn't the usual age twenty-one?"

"He has completed years of squire training and mastered the various skills," Robert commented.

"He has proved himself in battle and shown leadership skills," Lamborgini asserted.

They all stopped talking and watched him. The walk to the far end where the three waited for him seemed farther than usual. When he reached the thrones where the King and Queen sat, Matthew bowed formally and waited.

Elinore looked down at him. "Matthew Robert of Sterling, it has come to my attention that you have desires to become a knight in the Land of Sterling. There were three who nominated you for the status of knight: King Robert of Sterling (once of Danforth), Sir Lamborgini of Sterling, and Sir Royce now of Adonia."

Matthew was surprised but glad to hear that Sir Royce had also put in a good word for him.

"There was also a commendation sent from King William of Borden for your recent services." Queen Elinore smiled briefly. "Thus we are gathered to review your training and actions to make sure that you fulfill the qualifications of knighthood."

Queen Elinore's formal tone made Matthew realize that the proceedings were serious and not just a formality. His stomach tightened slightly.

"Sir Lamborgini, you trained him during his squire years. Please comment on his qualities," Queen Elinore requested.

Sir Lamborgini cleared his throat. "Squire Matthew was talented, he learned the skills of horsemanship, sword and lance quickly. But he was also quick tempered at times, and tended to give up easily if he didn't perform the skill to his immediate satisfaction."

Matthew squirmed slightly. Sir Lamborgini's words were true.

"Nevertheless," Sir Lamborgini went on. "He was creative in problem solving. He found a way to outsmart my Disarming Technique. "He smiled proudly at Matthew.

Elinore turned to King Robert. "Robert, you spoke with Sir Royce. What were his comments?"

"Sir Royce noticed a marked improvement in Matthew's archery skills while in Adonia. He also became more adept at smithing and carpentry, and taught much of his swordsmanship skills to the other squires." Robert smiled proudly at his son. "But he was not so keen on the book learning and etiquette classes. He skipped out on some of those days to accompany the princesses on their excursions."

"Hm, a mixed review, but still mostly positive," Elinore mused. "I have observed a willingness to assist others, such as accompanying and protecting the royal family on their journey to Adonia. He has always shown an ability to do hard work. He has had a tendency to be a bit frivolous at times, but I will attribute that to his youth."

Queen Elinore straightened in her seat. "Now we come to the main required qualities of a knight: Chivalry, Charity and Chastity. Matthew, what examples can you share with us that demonstrate these traits?"

Matthew thought long and hard. There were some little things he had done here and there, but none of them seemed sufficient to the question. Then he remembered Clarisse and Marie. He paled. He had not intended to share this experience with anyone. But it was the only one that fit the question.

He took a deep breath and began. "On the Dauntless a sailor named Mark befriended me. He had been sailing for a year already, and was willing to show me the ropes of how to do things. There was an older sailor who seemed determined to show us all the experiences a sailor might have while in port." Matthew paused.

"Well, Mark seemed really interested in going along with it, and I didn't feel comfortable leaving him to face the experience or possible danger alone, so I went with him to this inn which turned out to be more than just a typical inn." Matthew sighed. "Several times through the evening I tried to get Mark to leave, but he would not. Soon I found myself alone in a bedroom with this girl, Clarisse."

Queen Elinore paled, Sir Lamborgini frowned, and King Robert looked stern. "Did you partake in this activity?" Robert asked flatly.

"No, Father, I did not indulge. It did not seem right. I kept thinking of your happy marriage, and Amber and Harry's. Of how Mother always says, 'Remember and be true to the Royal within you.' And I thought of Sarah and how she is the only girl I really want."

Elinore breathed softly in relief, and Robert's face relaxed. "Then what happened?" he asked.

"Clarisse had always wanted a different career, so I gave her what money I had and she escaped that night."

"Interesting story," commented Sir Lamborgini.

"That didn't turn out to be the end of it. Mark and I ran across Clarisse again in a different port town, and she asked us to get her friend Marie out. Mark decided to help her. While I established my presence in a different pub, he went back with his horse to help Marie escape.

I believe he was successful; the Dauntless was forced to leave port in a hurry because of it." Matthew glanced at his mother, debating whether he should tell her that a man named Andre' helped them.

"Helping two women in need and giving them money, standing by a friend, and maintaining his virtue; I think this meets the qualifications, don't you, gentlemen?" Queen Elinore asked.

Robert nodded and Sir Lamborgini agreed. "Yes, Your Highness. I would still support the decision to make Matthew a knight."

Queen Elinore smiled. "So be it then." She turned to Matthew. "Matthew, do you have any questions before we adjourn?"

Matthew hesitated. "Yes, Your Highness. Something has been troubling me. We talk of chivalry and charity, yet a knight must be ready to kill in battle. I have killed several times in the last few days, sometimes when I had no choice and sometimes unintentionally." He thought of the man with an arrow in his throat. "How do I know when it is the right thing to do?"

Elinore nodded. "A mature question. Was it in self-defense?"

"Sometimes," Matthew answered.

"Were you defending the weak and innocent?" Sir Lamborgini asked. Matthew nodded.

"Were you protecting home and family and country?" King Robert inquired.

"Yes to all of those," Matthew responded.

"Did you ever kill out of anger or a desire for revenge?" Sir Lamborgini asked.

Matthew thought of Captain Spike. Did he lead him through the Komodo nesting grounds out of an angry desire for revenge? Or was it more out of creative desperation? "I don't think so," he responded.

"When you have no other choice, and it is in defense and for just causes, then you are relieved of guilt if you have to kill," Queen Elinore told him. "A knight is justified in these cases."

Matthew sighed in relief. "Thank you for clarifying."

"Then if there are no other questions or issues, we will adjourn," Queen Elinore announced. "We will start the ceremonies on the morrow eve. Sir Lamborgini, will you assist this young man in choosing a suit of armor?"

Sir Lamborgini bowed. "Yes, Your Majesty. Come, Matthew."

Matthew followed Sir Lamborgini out of the throne room. Karl and Sarah were waiting outside the door.

"Well?" Karl asked eagerly. "Did you pass?"

Matthew pretended to look crestfallen. "Yes," he mumbled. "Now I have to go pick out a suit of armor."

Karl punched him playfully on the arm. "You joker. I'll come with you."

They all trooped into the armory. Several types of protective gear, shields, chain mail shirts and suits of armor were on display. Matthew examined them closely in a way he never had before. This was real to him now.

"Look at this red and gold suit of armor," Sarah pointed to one.

Matthew shook his head. "Too flamboyant. That actually belonged to Sir Royce in his younger years."

Karl studied a black armor piece. "What about this one?" he asked.

Matthew looked at it for a minute. "That feels too much like a pirate color or a somber old man. It doesn't feel like me."

They drifted around the room. Matthew felt drawn to one suit that appeared silver colored though it was somewhat tarnished. Karl and Sarah joined him looking at it.

"Not bad," Karl commented. "I could polish that up for you, and it could look quite dashing, in a less flamboyant way."

"Any color of plumage would go well with silver," Sarah commented. "Be it feather or shield design."

"Try it on," Karl urged. "It looks about your size."

His friends helped Matthew put on the armor. Some places could use some oiling, but it allowed him for the most part to move as he needed to.

"It looks good on you," Sarah commented, smiling. "The Silver Knight from Sterling."

"All right," Matthew told Sir Lamborgini. "I'll take this one."

Just then Queen Elinore entered the room. "Oh!" she exclaimed when she saw Matthew. She walked around studying him. "That was my grandfather's suit of armor. It fits you well." She smiled. "I rather like seeing that on you. I always thought Grandfather looked very regal in that suit of armor. As a little girl I always begged him to put it on for tournaments and holidays. He always humored me until he got too old to walk under the weight of the thing."

"Time to take it off," Karl instructed him. "I have a lot of oiling and polishing to do."

"I'll help you," Matthew began.

"Oh no," Karl stopped him. "Polishing the armor is your squire's job to do. A knight is much too important to do the polishing himself. In fact, I should be sharpening your sword for you too."

"Thanks anyway," Matthew told him. "I like to polish my own sword."

He allowed his friends to help him take off his armor. Sarah staggered a bit under the weight of the pieces.

"How are you able to walk under all this weight, let alone fight in it?" she huffed.

"Weight training," Matthew explained straight faced. "That's why men throw rocks and logs at each other."

Sarah looked shocked. "I thought that was just for Mordred's Highland Games!"

"Oh, not just for the games," Karl replied. "It's included in the weekly squire training. We have to do it in secret so the ladies don't see the savage side of us."

Sarah looked from one to the other, unsure whether they were serious or not, until the young men doubled over laughing. "Oh you!" She sputtered, swatting Matthew's arm with her hand. "First you tease your sisters and now me. Is this the kind of life I am doomed to live?"

"Absolutely," Matthew told her, leaning over to kiss her.

"Matthew, you also need a chain mail outfit for the ceremony," Sir Lamborgini reminded him. "The ones in the best shape are wrapped up in linens over there."

Matthew tried a couple of them on before he found one the right size. Then they looked through the various tabards hanging on the walls.

"I suppose I ought to wear one with the Sterling insignia," Matthew mused. He found a dark red tabard with a ship's anchor on the back, but it had a crown on the front. He put it on over the chain mail. "Is this too presumptuous?" he asked.

Sarah shook her head. "I think it is perfect. After all, you are of royal lineage."

"Now you need to pick out a shield," Sir Lamborgini told him. "It doesn't matter if the crest is not quite right, we can fix that later. Pick one that feels good on your arm."

Matthew looked at several and tried on a few. Sir Lamborgini picked up a sword and swung it at Matthew so he could practice blocking with the shields. They mostly felt okay, but he wasn't satisfied yet. He looked around some more, at shields leaning against the walls and on display. In a back corner of the room he came upon an old red shield hanging unobtrusively on the wall with a curious design on it. He took it down to inspect it more closely under the torch light. Karl and Sarah peered at it over his shoulder.

In the center of the shield was a green tree with five main branches. Surrounding the tree were five smaller symbols: a weaver's loom, a boat anchor, a woodman's axe, an iron anvil, and a boar's head.

"Ah," Sir Lamborgini remarked reverently. "It is the crest of Browning Isle, the shield made for the father king. It shows the crest symbols of all five countries. This is a find."

"Do you think we could polish it up?" Matthew asked. "It is very striking." He hefted it on his arm, and Karl tapped it with a nearby sword. "It still feels sturdy for being what, three hundred years old?"

"The crest is more like two hundred and fifty years old," Lamborgini corrected. "Yes, I think there is something around here to polish it with."

After the polishing, the metal looked bright. The crest design still appeared a little faded however. Sir Lamborgini suggested trying the strength of the shield. While Matthew held it, Sir Lamborgini swung a sword at it full strength. The tone rang true of metal on metal, and the shield held.

"Strong shield, well made," Sir Lamborgini commented.

"It feels natural on the arm," Matthew replied. "I like the crest design too. I'll take this shield."

"It looks good with the tabard you are wearing," Sarah noted.

"I'll have the castle artist brighten the crest design," Sir Lamborgini told him. "Now you all run along and get ready for dinner."

Over dinner the young people described to King Robert the bathing of Wolf. He laughed until he had to wipe his eyes. "Nearly drowning… feeding meat scraps to get him in the water…getting everyone wet…That is hilarious."

Queen Elinore put down her dessert fork. "I need to meet with Karl and Sarah tonight," she announced. "Robert, you need to get the tournament grounds ready for the celebration tournament games. Matthew, Sir Lamborgini needs to go over with you tonight your part of the proceedings. You are excused from the table."

"Yes, Mother," Matthew swallowed his last bite of pie and left the room.

He found Sir Lamborgini waiting for him outside the dining room door. "Come with me, Matthew."

Matthew followed him to the stables. "We need to pick out a war horse strong enough to carry you in your armor," Sir Lamborgini told him. "There are three that would do. You may not have my horse."

Matthew walked around the horses that had been used in squire's training. He stopped in front of Thunder. This horse had carried him in various training and tournament events. He raised his hand to rub the horse's nose. Thunder lowered his head toward Matthew and blew out his lips at him. Matthew laughed. "Thunder is the one I want, Sir Lamborgini."

"Very well. I'll have someone get him ready for you." Sir Lamborgini sat down on a bench in the stable, and had Matthew sit by him. "Tomorrow night you will be asked to do an all-night vigil. This is customary for the knight to prepare himself for his commitment to God, lord and country. You will dedicate your sword and soul to serving others. After morning mass the knighting ceremony will be held. Queen Elinore will do the honors, but I will give you your sword. Do you have one in mind?"

"Yes. I like the one I made in Adonia the best. It has a sharp blade and excellent balance."

"Very good. I assume Karl is your first squire?" Sir Lamborgini asked. Matthew nodded.

"Then Karl will escort you through the ceremony. In the afternoon we will have the demonstration part of the tournament. Which three events do you prefer?"

Matthew grinned. "Archery, sword fighting, and jousting."

"Perfect. And I assume Sarah is your lady." It was more of a statement than a question. Matthew nodded. "Sarah will prepare a favor for you to wear during the tournament," Sir Lamborgini went on. "It is also customary for the new knight to embark on another quest after his knighting. But I believe Queen Elinore already has something planned."

"Just as long as it doesn't interfere with a spring wedding," Matthew told him.

"I think the Queen is aware," Sir Lamborgini said with a slight smile. "Any questions?"

Matthew paused. "Sir Lamborgini, why are you recommending me now for knighthood, rather than two years from now?"

Sir Lamborgini studied him. "Do you want to continue being in squire training?"

Matthew shook his head. "Not really. Is there more I should learn?"

"Not much. There is more you could teach others now. And I perceive you feel restless, and ready to move on with your life. I think you would be happier with broader creative problem solving. You have always been good at that." Sir Lamborgini smiled at him.

Matthew slowly nodded his head. "Yes. I think you are right." He gazed at his mentor. "I haven't really thanked you for all you have taught me. I do appreciate it, Sir Lamborgini."

Sir Lamborgini grasped Matthew in a forearm and hand clasp, which Matthew returned. "You make me proud, Sir Matthew. I am honored to have been part of your training."

The next morning Karl got busy early with Sir Lamborgini in the armory preparing Matthew's armor and shield. Sarah disappeared with Queen Elinore and her lady Celia preparing their dresses and hair for the ceremonies. King Robert went out to the tournament grounds to guide the preparations there.

After polishing and sharpening his sword, Matthew was left to wander the castle and grounds trying to find entertainment. He couldn't concentrate on any books in the library, he got bored playing his flute after half an hour, and Wolf got restless inside the castle. When Matthew took him out into the courtyard Wolf ran up and down, sometimes stopping in front of Matthew begging him to play with a "woof!", head down by his front paws and tail waving up in the air.

Matthew pulled a string from his pocket to wave at Wolf, who tried to snap at it. Suddenly inspired, Matthew went to the gardening shed and found some thin rope. Thinking of the rope splicing on the Dauntless, he wove the rope into a thicker bundle. He tied big knots in the middle and at both ends. Then he sat down in the courtyard again to watch Wolf run. The next time the animal stopped in front of him. Matthew waved the knotted rope in front of Wolf's face. Wolf grabbed the knot at one end and held on. After playing tug-of-war a few minutes, Wolf ran again. When he came back Matthew threw the rope across the courtyard. Wolf leapt after it, grabbed it in his teeth and brought it back to Matthew. After tugging together on it, Wolf let go and allowed Matthew to throw it again. This time he tussled and growled at the rope on the ground for a few minutes before bringing it back.

The morning went by, and finally Monica called him to eat some lunch. Then Matthew spent some time brushing down Thunder. Finally, unable to stay away any longer, Matthew went down to the armory. Sir Lamborgini welcomed him in. He and Karl looked tired and sweaty. But the suit of armor shone its polished silver beautifully. Matthew examined it in wonder.

"Wow, that cleaned up nicely!" he commented happily.

"Yes," Karl sighed. "But you should have seen the gunk in between the joints. Next time I am not agreeing to clean an ancient piece of armor, even for you. You better stay on top of the cleaning and care of this suit, is all I can say. I'm heading off to the baths now so I am presentable for dinner."

Sir Lamborgini wiped his brow. "Karl talks a story, but he really did enjoy fixing up the suit of armor for you. And he did a fine job. He could teach Sterling's squires a thing or two about armor care."

Matthew noticed a cloth-covered shield leaning against the wall. "Is that my shield?" he asked, going over to it.

"Don't uncover it!" Sir Lamborgini stopped him. "It will be revealed tomorrow at the knighting ceremony. Now go eat dinner and take your ritual bath."

Supper that evening was eaten quickly and quietly. Afterward old Malcolm fetched Matthew to take him to the baths. Wolf watched from the corner of the room as far away from the pool as possible. Malcolm supervised Matthew's washing in order from head to toe, making sure every inch was scrubbed clean. Then Malcolm draped him in a clean robe and escorted him to his suite. There Malcolm shaved Matthew's face smooth and trimmed his hair. Then he helped Matthew dress in black dress pants, white shirt, red tunic, clean stockings and shoes. Malcolm stepped back a bit to examine him.

"I suppose that will have to do. I can't make you any more presentable," Malcolm told him with a contented sigh.

"I always was a difficult case," Matthew replied with a wicked gleam in his eye. "I always felt like I should loosen up the dress clothes a little after putting them on, by crawling under the table or up into a tree. Shall I do that today?"

"No!" Malcolm responded adamantly, holding a hand to his heart. "No dirt or tears in your clothes are allowed today!"

Matthew laughed and threw his arm around Malcolm's shoulder. "Thank you, Malcolm, for putting up with me all these years. I'm afraid I was a bit of a rascal growing up."

"More than a bit, young man," Malcolm smiled. "Now hie you over to the chapel for the vigil." He swatted Matthew on the behind as the prince scooted out of the room, followed by Wolf.

Matthew met Sir Lamborgini at the door of the chapel. Sir Lamborgini brought Matthew's sword in its sheath and handed it to him. Together they walked inside and up to the front.

"Lay your unsheathed sword on the altar," Sir Lamborgini instructed him. Matthew laid his sword carefully on the altar cloth, and put the sheath on the ground next to it. "Now kneel."

Matthew knelt before the altar, facing Sir Lamborgini who was standing on the other side where the priest usually stood.

"Squire Matthew, on the eve of being knighted, it is customary for the applicant to hold a night vigil here before the altar of God. On the morrow you will pledge your services, your sword, yea possibly your very life in the service of God, in defending truth and right and the weak ones of the world. This night is the time for you to prepare your heart, mind and body for the oath. Do you understand?"

Matthew nodded solemnly.

"Very well. I leave you now. You will be released from this vigil at dawn when we will join you for the morning Mass. Good night." Sir Lamborgini inclined his head to Matthew, then he exited the chapel and closed the doors behind him. Wolf lay down next to Matthew, resting his head on his paws.

Matthew stayed kneeling at the altar as instructed. His attention was drawn to his sword. He could see the imperfections in the blade and hilt. True, he had made it to be sharp and strong, serviceable but not necessarily beautiful. A little bit like himself. He looked up at the stained glass window above him, depicting Jesus on the cross. This man was the Son of God, and He descended to the imperfections of mortality to save mankind. But Jesus was perfect. Matthew desired to be perfect, but fell short of that often. And he liked to joke around. Jesus did not seem to be the frivolous type. Matthew sighed. He would have to be more serious as a knight. Like Sir Lamborgini. That man was serious. Matthew laughed to himself. Maybe he didn't have to be that serious. Sir Royce still had a sense of humor.

He directed his attention back to his vigil. As a knight he would have to focus on protecting his people. That meant continuing to train in the art of warfare, probably training squires and pages. He didn't know if he would have the patience for pages. Well maybe he would; he liked to joke around with his sister and niece, but he wasn't sure if that was the right approach with training boys. On the other hand, that would be more interesting for him than the serious training of squires. He could imagine some fun games with the pages while also teaching them skills in the bow, sword and lance.

He probably would have to travel some. What would that mean for his new wife? He was sure she would be fine, but would worry about him while he was gone, especially if there was fighting involved. Tournaments could also be dangerous. He would have to be careful not to get seriously injured or killed. He wanted to make sure he took good care of her and always let her know how much she meant to him. And when children eventually came he would need to take care of them too. His heart quavered a bit at the thought of having children. He was ready for a woman in his life, but wasn't sure if he was ready for children. He would have to teach them proper values, and put up with their crankiness and stubbornness. He knew the teen years would be challenging. But he would have Sarah to help, and she was a good patient teacher. He still felt too young to be a parent. His father was almost thirty when he married, but his mother was nineteen, Matthew's age. And she did just fine.

He shifted his weight on the kneeling cushion. He had never knelt all night long. And he usually did a lot better staying awake when he could move around. It was going to be a long night.

Matthew began thinking about his country, the Land of Sterling. The country was stable, with good laws. The people were for the most part content. But there was still poverty, and many people still struggled for a living, to keep enough food on the table and have adequate shelter. He wondered if there was a way to raise their standard of living. He thought of Roberta, Amber's lady-in-waiting, who risked everything to try to leave the life of a fisherman's family. She was able to rise above that life by training in the royal court. She learned to read and write, improved her skills in sewing and cooking, and was trained in etiquette. She would be able to find work anywhere now. Perhaps others could benefit from more education like her. What if schools were built in the towns and villages, where the children could learn reading and writing? The schools would have to be free, so anyone could attend. The problem would be to not take away too much time from their ability to work and earn for their families, or from their apprenticeships for trades. The schools could meet in the evenings, perhaps even parents could attend. He chuckled to himself. He had always hated sitting in a classroom, and here he was thinking of offering or even mandating it for everybody! Despite the work that had been involved he was now glad for the education after all.

He thought of the other countries of Browning Isle and their recent economic downturn due to piracy. Things should get better now, but Matthew wondered if there was more that could be done to protect national and international trade. Were the laws adequate to prevent price gouging and to protect the individual tradesmen? Could he, as a Prince of Sterling, do something to make sure free trade was protected and stabilized? Possibly. He would have to look into that and discuss his ideas with Queen Elinore and Prince-soon-to-be-King Harry.

Matthew's thoughts drifted to the people he had met on his journeys along the mainland. He worried particularly about those who were forced against their will to work in jobs they did not want. He felt a rising anger against those who took young victims and enslaved them in dangerous, demeaning and devilish labors. There had to be a way of stopping such trades and freeing the victims! He was under no illusion that he could change man's tendency toward such behaviors as greed, power-seeking and lasciviousness, unless it was through changing one person at a time. But perhaps he could do something to encourage other countries to make laws of protection for the innocent and to uphold those laws. He sighed. Who was he that he thought he could even begin to make a difference over there?

He looked up again at the lone figure of Jesus, held up against a dark background in the night. The candles around him flickered, the only light in the chapel now that the castle torches had mostly been put out. He suddenly realized that being a knight was a lonely big job. There was a lot of evil in the world out there. But there were also many good people, who could become a force of strength when gathered together and led the right way. One candle may not seem very strong, but it was amazing the amount of light it could give in a dark room. Perhaps Matthew could make a difference in the world after all.

"God," he prayed. "I have promised to follow you in my life. Now I dedicate myself more fully to your service. But I need you to strengthen me and keep me from temptation. Forgive me my sins and the mistakes of my youth, and any future mistakes I may make. Make me a tool in your hand to accomplish your work. Guide me to where you need me to be to serve you. Amen."

Matthew's eyes grew heavy. He would just close them for a moment, and then continue his vigil. Minutes later his head dropped to the cloth of the altar and he slept.

Matthew was awakened at dawn by someone shaking his shoulder. "Wake up!" Karl's voice spoke in his ear. "Matthew, your vigil is finished."

Matthew raised his head and gazed bleary eyed at his friend and squire. "It is dawn?"

"Yes," Sarah's voice spoke on the other side of him. "Come sit down for Mass."

Matthew tried to stand but his legs had fallen asleep. Karl and Sarah each took one of his arms and helped him stagger to a nearby pew. He moved his legs to get the circulation going and then grimaced as the nerves came painfully alive. In a few minutes the pain had abated. When he looked up, the rest of his family had arrived, and Sir Lamborgini, the castle squires, and most of the castle staff were seated. He noticed his two uncles seated next to his parents on the front row. He turned back to face the front and realized the priest was ready to begin.

"I left my sword on the altar," Matthew whispered to Karl. "Should I go get it?"

Karl shook his head. "Too late. I suppose they will tell us if we need to move it."

The priest did not seem to mind, and proceeded with the service. He invited Matthew up to the front at one point to bless Matthew and his sword at the altar. At the end the royal family exited the chapel while the choir sang, "Hallelujah, praise the Lord in holy songs of joy." The piece was magnificent and fit the celebration occasion perfectly.

After retrieving Matthew's sword, Sir Lamborgini and Karl escorted Matthew to the armory where they helped him dress in his chain mail and Sterling tabard. Sir Lamborgini then led the way to the throne room, carrying Matthew's sword sheathed in its scabbard and the shield still wrapped in its cloth. Matthew, Wolf and Karl followed him.

By now many other people from the town of Sterling and the land beyond filled the throne room, leaving an aisle through which Matthew's entourage could enter. They proceeded up to the thrones and bowed to the King and Queen. The room fell silent. Queen Elinore stood.

"We welcome all of you today to the solemn occasion of making a squire into a knight," she stated. "Sir Lamborgini, bring forth the squire's sword."

Sir Lamborgini presented Matthew's sword to the queen. She grasped the scabbard above his hand but did not yet take it from him. "Sir Lamborgini, has Squire Matthew met all of the requirements to become a knight?" she asked him.

"Yes, Your Highness, he has."

"Then present him to me so he may take the oath of knighthood." She took possession of the sword.

Sir Lamborgini indicated that Matthew should come forward and kneel before the Queen. Matthew did so.

"Squire Matthew Robert of Sterling," she declared. "You have trained as a page and a squire and have shown forth your skills of warfare on the field of battle. You have demonstrated your honor in standing for the right and in defending others. You will now repeat after me the oath of knighthood." Matthew nodded his assent.

"I, Matthew Robert of Sterling," she began.

"I, Matthew Robert of Sterling," he repeated each phrase after her.

"Do vow with all my heart...to follow the code of chivalry...which is to protect the weak...to always defend a lady...to uphold the virtues of truthfulness, loyalty and compassion...to fight against wrong-doers... and to always serve God and the church.... I swear before God...to fight with my strength and sword if need be...to protect all the countries of Browning Isle to the end of my days. Amen."

Matthew's heart soared within him. He had not imagined such a solution to his dilemma of fealty. "To protect all the countries of Browning Isle to the end of my days. Amen." Matthew finished.

Queen Elinore pulled the sword from its sheath and dubbed Matthew on each shoulder with it. "I name you Sir Matthew of Browning Isle, Wolf Friend."

The crowd erupted in applause.

"Now Sir Lamborgini, you may gird on his sword and give him his shield," Queen Elinore instructed, handing the sword in its sheath back to him.

Matthew stood and raised his arms while Sir Lamborgini girded the sword around his waist. Then Sir Lamborgini unwrapped the shield he had brought and handed it to Matthew. The crest of Browning Isle had been skillfully repainted. But there was a new figure, a wolf lying at the base of the tree. The crest was now Matthew's own. Sir Lamborgini bowed to Matthew and stepped back.

"Sir Matthew, I give you your next quest," Queen Elinore spoke. "As a knight for all of Browning Isle, it is your task to teach them to defend themselves from any future invasion. For too long we have been at peace and I fear we have become complacent. Our countries must become more closely joined in unity, trade and cooperation. To find a way to accomplish this is your assignment. Do you take this quest, Sir Matthew?"

Matthew nodded. It was as though Queen Elinore had heard his prayer last night. Or perhaps God had put it into both their minds and hearts? "Yes, Your Highness. I do."

"Very good then." Queen Elinore nodded. "You may present your squire and your lady."

Karl came forward and bowed to Sir Matthew. Sarah stepped from the sidelines, curtseyed to the King and Queen, and then took Matthew's arm. They faced the audience and received their applause.

"And now," Queen Elinore announced. "You are all invited to a feast in the dining hall in Sir Matthew's honor!" She took King Robert's arm and led the procession out of the throne room to the dining hall. Sir Matthew and Sarah followed them with Wolf at Matthew's side. Karl and Sir Lamborgini followed them.

At the door of the dining hall Matthew stopped and knelt down by Wolf. "I think you should stay outside the door," he told the animal. Wolf continued to follow him into the dining room. Matthew looked at Sarah helplessly.

"Let's get some food and take it out to the veranda," she suggested. "It shouldn't be as crowded there."

Matthew nodded. "Good idea." Sure enough, Wolf seemed a little less nervous outside away from the crowds. Matthew fed him some meat tidbits from his plate.

"You are going to make him fat," Sarah told him.

"Maybe not. I think there will be a lot of walking ahead of us," Matthew responded thoughtfully.

"It will be difficult getting to Adonia and Mordred in the middle of winter," she commented. "Are you planning on taking Karl with you?"

"Good question," Matthew answered. "My first assignment to my squire is to get my lady home safely. Perhaps I will have him join me after the winter snows are gone."

Sarah ventured to scratch Wolf's ears. He blinked at her but let her touch him. "We will have to leave first thing in the morning to get through the pass. We came by horseback so we could travel more quickly."

"I am glad you did." Matthew was already starting to miss her, but this time with an element of belonging and anticipation. "I suppose the next time I see you will be in Adonia for our wedding."

"Yes," she smiled and her dimples showed. "It will be a fun winter planning that. The little girls will love helping. And so will Princess Amber, of course."

"Soon to be Queen Amber. I can hardly believe it." Matthew shook his head.

Sarah's face looked sorrowful. "You will miss King Gilbert's funeral, if they haven't held it already. I suspect Harry's coronation will follow soon thereafter."

Matthew took Sarah's hand. "That's all right. You will be there."

Some visitors of the feast found Matthew on the veranda and extended their congratulations to him. A steady stream of well-wishers came by. Soon Karl found them.

"The demonstration part of the tournament starts in an hour," Karl told him. "We need to get you suited up."

"Oh!" Sarah gasped. "I need to get ready too."

"Very well, squire. Lead on!" Matthew and Wolf followed Karl out through the crowds of the dining room and back to the armory. Matthew felt like he was beginning to live there.

Sir Lamborgini met them there. He and Karl helped Matthew pull on the pieces of armor and fasten the parts together. The suit moved smoothly and with minimal clanking after Karl's oiling and polishing. Sir Lamborgini lastly put the helmet over Matthew's head and made sure that the visor worked. He stepped back to evaluate the effect.

"Very good," Sir Lamborgini commented. "Silver plated steel will endure well and blind your opponents. Everyone you meet will have to take you seriously."

"As long as I don't spill soup down my front while eating," Matthew's muffled voice spoke from within.

Sir Lamborgini lifted the visor. "You will not be eating in this suit. It is only for fighting."

"And ceremonies," Matthew clarified, taking off the helmet. "I am hoping I don't have to do much fighting in this armor. I rather prefer the flexibility of fighting without it; chain mail is ok."

Sir Lamborgini shrugged. "Depends on what troubles you get yourself into. Karl, will you help me get my armor on?"

While the two of them worked on dressing Sir Lamborgini, Matthew realized he needed to relieve himself one more time before everything started. He walked down the hall toward the toilet room, suit clanging a bit as he walked. Once in the room, he struggled a bit trying to remove the crotch-cover piece of armor without removing his gauntlets. Just then his father walked in.

King Robert stared at him a moment. "Having troubles, Sir Matthew?" He began to chuckle.

"I think I need some help," Mathew confessed.

Robert helped him unhook the right cover piece so Matthew could go. Then he leaned against the wall, held his ribs and guffawed. "Now I know why I never wanted to be a knight," he finally gasped while wiping his eyes.

Matthew didn't think it was very funny. "How do they do this in the middle of battle?" he asked, trying now to fasten the piece up again.

"I don't know." His father helped him, still chuckling. "Maybe they just pee their pants as they go."

"Gross. There has got to be a better way," Matthew replied, but he was smiling now. "I'll have to invent something that works better than this."

"A trap door," Robert chuckled as he took his turn at the toilet.

"Yeah, with a safety latch. Just don't lose the key," Matthew added. The two of them were laughing harder again now.

"Well," Robert finally breathed. "I've got to get my robes on. See you at the tournament grounds, son."

"Thanks, Father," Matthew told him. "I'm glad I'm related to you."

Robert winked at his son. "Most of the time anyway."

Matthew clanked back to the armory. He sat in a chair and tried to pet Wolf. The animal sniffed at him but didn't seem to like the feel of the metal gauntlets on his head. Matthew just waited. Finally Sir Lamborgini was dressed in his grey and gold suit of armor. Karl pulled a colorful tunic from his home country over his suit of chain mail. Then they all clanked over to the stables to get their horses.

Karl led Thunder, already clad in his protective armor, over beside a mounting block so Matthew could get on him. Once he was situated, Karl helped Sir Lamborgini mount his warhorse, and then he got on his own. Together they rode out of the castle gate and down the hill to the tournament grounds.

As they rode into the tournament arena, the crowd stood and applauded and stomped their feet. The squire and knights rode around the arena, waving at the crowd, and then stopped before the royal reviewing stand. King Robert stood.

"We welcome all of you to the demonstration portion of this tournament, honoring the knighting of Sir Matthew." The king paused while the crowd roared their approval. "We welcome Sir Lamborgini!" The crowd shouted loudly while Sir Lamborgini raised his hand. "Sir Matthew!" Matthew waved and the crowd shouted louder. "And Squire Karl!" There were a few shouts and mild applause. Karl turned slightly red faced.

"Before we begin, Lady Sarah has her favor to give." Robert turned to smile at her.

Sarah stood, and Matthew noticed she was dressed in pink, with a familiar black and pink orchid scarf draped across her shoulders. He brought his horse up alongside the reviewing stand so she could reach him. She opened up her hand and revealed a piece of the black orchid scarf in her hand. She tied it around his left wrist. Their eyes met.

"I love you," she whispered.

"I love you too," he mouthed through his open visor. He raised his left arm to show the audience her favor. The crowd roared its approval again.

King Robert raised his hand and the crowd quieted down. "Let the joust begin!"

Sarah hurriedly ushered Wolf onto the reviewing stand where he would be out of the way.

Karl and Sir Matthew went to one end of the field where Karl set Sir Matthew up with his lance and shield. Another quire readied Sir Lamborgini with his. Then Sir Matthew and Sir Lamborgini lowered their visors and faced each other for their joust.

On the first run Sir Lamborgini and Sir Matthew parried their lances harmlessly away from each other. As they turned their horses and prepared for the second run, Matthew thought of Sir Lamborgini's advice that a good defense was often a good offense. He rebalanced the lance in his right hand and gritted his teeth. Kicking his horse into a gallop, he concentrated on aiming the point of his lance toward his opponent's chest. As they passed each other, Sir Matthew's lance tip struck Sir Lamborgini square on the upper chest. Sir Lamborgini's lance struck into Matthew's right shoulder, which he met with a lunge forward. As Sir Matthew slowed his horse and turned around, he heard the crowd groan and cheer. Sir Lamborgini was leaning back and to the left in his saddle, desperately trying to regain his balance. After an agonizing moment he managed to pull himself back upright with the horse's reins, and the two faced each other again.

As Sir Matthew hefted his lance, he felt a quick pain shoot into his right shoulder. It must have been bruised by the blow. Concentrating on the task ahead, he spurred his horse forward again. This time Sir Lamborgini's lance struck him full on the chest, and before he knew it, he landed with a hard thump onto the ground.

The crowd stomped in shouts and cheers. With the heavy armor, Sir Matthew had some trouble getting up. He felt Karl's arm pulling him upright and to his feet. He noted some soreness on his back left hip, but limped it off.

"That's all right!" Karl's voice sounded through the buzzing in his ears. "You gave Sir Lamborgini quite a scare that second round!"

Sir Lamborgini rode around the arena, his arm raised and drinking in the applause of the audience. Then he dismounted from his horse and took the sword his squire brought him.

"Sir Matthew, your sword," Karl advised him, handing him his sword.

Sir Matthew raised his visor for better visibility, and grasped the sword. "Thanks."

The two knights approached each other and took up their ready stances. Sir Lamborgini's sword flashed out unexpectedly and whacked Sir Matthew on the head before he could even respond. The crowd cheered and booed. Sir Matthew struck out and Sir Lamborgini easily parried his blow with his shield. A few more strike attempts and Sir Matthew started getting into a rhythm of how to move in the suit of armor. Soon they were pushing each other up and down the arena using every strike and parry technique they knew.

Suddenly Sir Lamborgini started the arm twist around Sir Matthew's sword that foretold the beginning of the Lamborgini Disarming Technique. Without much thought, Sir Matthew employed his defense maneuver. Sir Lamborgini's sword flew out of his hand and up into the air. It landed point down in the dirt and quivered there.

The crowd was silent a moment and then jumped to their feet in ecstatic applause. They had never seen anyone beat the Lamborgini Disarming Technique before. Sir Matthew pulled off his helmet and waved to the crowd. In the reviewing stand Sarah was standing and clapping also. Sir Matthew went over to Sir Lamborgini and shook his hand.

"Nice job, Sir Matthew," Sir Lamborgini congratulated him.

"Next is archery!" King Robert announced.

While squires and pages set up three hay bale targets at one end of the field, Karl helped Sir Matthew remove his armor.

"It feels so good to have this armor off," Sir Matthew commented.

"I bet it gets hot in the summer," Karl puffed.

"I don't even want to know." Sir Matthew got the last piece off. "Now you get to show off your skills, Karl."

Karl grinned. "I can't wait."

They collected their bows and met Sir Lamborgini out on the range. They lined up two hundred yards from the targets. In the first round they were to hit a small circle placed in the center of their hay bale.

"You may begin!" King Robert shouted.

They each shot their six arrows. Sir Lamborgini got five arrows on the circle. Sir Matthew's first four arrows hit the circle, but his shoulder muscle zinged in pain on the fifth one and the arrow barely hit the edge of the target. He waited a moment and then drew his bow for the last arrow. Gritting his teeth he managed a better shot, but it was just outside the circle. He turned to look at Karl and saw his friend grinning happily.

"Six in the center of the circle," he crowed.

Matthew slapped his friend on the back in congratulations.

The pages removed the arrows from the targets and returned them to the three archers. The designs were changed to look like rabbits.

"Round two!" King Robert called.

Sir Matthew pulled back his bow. Again the sudden twinging pain in his right shoulder caused him to release his arrow early. It sank into the ground at the foot of the target. He stared at the target in chagrin and rubbed his right shoulder. Maybe he could shoot left handed? He moved the bow to his right hand and fit an arrow to the string. It took him a minute to figure out which eye to sight with, but at least the shoulder didn't hurt with the pushing as it had with the pulling motion. He let the arrow fly. It stuck in the target near the rabbit's tail. Not bad. He shot his next four arrows and three of them hit the rabbit.

Sir Matthew looked up. Karl and Sir Lamborgini had long ago finished their shots and were watching him.

"Shooting left handed, eh?" Sir Lamborgini remarked. "Trying to show off?"

Sir Matthew shook his head. "I seem to have injured my right shoulder," He explained.

Karl grinned at him. "Have you ever shot left-handed before?"

Sir Matthew shook his head. "No. Have you?"

While the pages retrieved arrows and changed the target shapes to birds, Karl moved his bow to his right hand and practiced sighting toward the target. "We'll see," was all he said.

Sir Lamborgini cracked a smile. "It seems we will all be trying something new." He also switched his bow hand.

Sir Matthew was quicker this time. He got four arrows into the bird shape. Karl's first arrow hit the target but missed the bird. The other five hit the center of the bird. They turned to watch Sir Lamborgini struggle with his bow. The first two arrows missed the hay bale, the second two hit the hay bale but missed the bird, and the last two hit the bird. When he finished, Matthew and Karl went over to him, each grasped one of Lamborgini's hands, and they all raised their hands together toward the audience. The audience in turn stood and stomped and cheered. Then the three men walked over to the reviewing stand and bowed to the King and Queen.

King Robert stood to address the crowd. "We have witnessed fine demonstrations of skill this day!" he announced. "Including some unconventional archery shooting." He smiled down at the men. "And now to announce the winners of today's matches. Sir Lamborgini is still the best at jousting!" Sir Lamborgini raised his arms to the audience and bowed. "Sir Matthew won the sword fighting!" Sir Matthew waved with his left arm and bowed with a flourish. "And Squire Karl of Adonia clearly won in archery!" Karl waved both arms and blew kisses to the ladies in the audience.

"And now we will adjourn until tomorrow, when the rest of the knights and squires will compete. You are dismissed!" King Robert sat down and reached for Queen Elinore's hand.

Matthew had barely turned back to the reviewing stand when Wolf leaped off the banister onto Matthew, knocking him to the ground, and began licking his face.

"All right, all right, that's enough!" Matthew turned his head to the side laughing and trying to push the animal away with his left hand.

Sir Lamborgini reached a hand toward Matthew to help him up Wolf raised his head and growled briefly deep in his throat. Sir Lamborgini quickly drew back his hand

Sarah reached Matthew's side "It seems Wolf thinks you were trying to attack his pack leader and friend," she explained "It was about all King Robert and I could do to keep him from leaping onto the field during the jousting and sword fighting."

Matthew took Wolf's head in his hands and looked him in the eyes. "Sir Lamborgini is our friend," he told him. "You will not attack him." Matthew got up and stood beside his mentor. "Friend. Come say hello to our friend." Matthew took Sir Lamborgini's hand and held it out toward Wolf.

Wolf stepped closer to them and sniffed Sir Lamborgini's hand. He did not growl, but sat back on his haunches and studied the two men.

"That's right," Matthew told him. "We were playing. He would not hurt me."

"Certainly not on purpose," Sir Lamborgini agreed.

Wolf cocked his head, and then licked Sir Lamborgini's hand once. He nuzzled his head under Matthew's hand. "Good Wolf." Matthew scratched his ears. Then he looked over at Karl. "Do you mind if I walk back with Sarah?"

Karl shrugged. "Go ahead. I'll use Thunder to carry your armor back to the castle."

Matthew carried his bow in one hand and clasped Sarah's hand with the other. They walked silently for a while, just basking in each other's presence.

"Karl and I need to leave tomorrow to return to Adonia," Sarah finally commented. "It will be a long winter without you near."

Matthew nodded. "I suppose we'll just have to keep busy until spring then. I may try to visit Mordred by boat in between working with Renling and Borden."

"Be safe," Sarah advised. "I don't want to lose you right after finding you."

Matthew raised his left wrist. "That's why you gave me your token. I am bound now to return to bring it back to you."

"That's right, Sir Matthew, and you better do it." She stood up on tiptoe to kiss him.

Back at the castle Matthew put his bow away in his room, and then went to soak in the baths. When he returned to his suite, Karl was there to return his sword.

"Feeling better?" Karl asked.

"Much more human," Matthew replied. "I think I have a couple of new bruises though."

"I thought you might. I asked Lady Sarah to stop by before dinner to apply more liniment to your wounds." Karl winked.

Just then a knock sounded on the door and Matthew opened it to find Sarah there with her salve. "I understand the knight needs a treatment," she offered.

"Absolutely," Matthew acquiesced and pulled off his shirt for her.

She examined his shoulder. "Has your doctor looked at this?" she asked.

"I think I'll be fine," Matthew told her, rotating his arm. "It just doesn't like strength-pulling right now."

She applied the salve to his shoulder and the wolf claw scratches, then put the container of salve on Matthew's dressing table. "You'll have to apply it yourself tomorrow," she told him. "It is time to meet your parents for dinner."

Matthew pulled on his shirt again and a clean tunic over it, and they went downstairs. Queen Elinore and King Robert were already there beginning the soup course. Robert stood as Sarah walked in and held her chair for her.

"Mighty fine day of celebration," King Robert told them. "Enough to earn a rest tomorrow."

"You have two more days of tournament to direct, Robert dear," Elinore reminded him.

"I know," he sighed, sitting down. "But I sure could use a rest already."

"Maybe I could spell you off, Father," Matthew offered. "I don't feel the need to participate any more in the events."

"I would love to have your help," Robert nodded.

The rest of dinner passed with small talk mostly between Karl, Elinore and Robert. Matthew suddenly felt exhausted. Right after dessert Sarah excused herself to go pack, and Karl left with her. Matthew stood to leave also.

"Son, I'm proud of you and who you are becoming," Robert told him.

"You behaved magnificently and magnanimously today," Elinore added. "It will be exciting to see what you do with this new vocation."

"Yes it will," Matthew mused. "Thank you, Mother, for giving me this opportunity. It will be interesting to see where it leads. Good night."

Matthew let Wolf outside briefly to do his business. Then they returned to Matthew's suite and fell quickly and soundly asleep.

Matthew woke at dawn to a tapping on his door. Karl poked his head in. "We're heading out, Matthew," he said. "We wanted to say goodbye."

Matthew jumped out of bed and pulled his shoes on. "I'm coming down."

Sarah was already in the courtyard tying her pack of belongings behind her saddle. She was dressed in pants and boots and warm cloak. She turned from her horse to face Matthew, and then threw herself into his arms.

"Take care of yourself," he told her. She nodded.

"I'll take care of your lady, too," Karl added. "After all, I'm first squire to the best knight of Browning Isle."

"I'm the only knight of Browning Isle," Matthew clarified. "The others belong to Sterling and Adonia and…"

"You know what I mean." Karl grasped Matthew in an arm-and-hand clasp. "It means the world to me to be your friend and ally."

"I feel the same, Karl. Thanks for everything."

Karl mounted his horse while Matthew helped Sarah up on hers. Then they headed out of the castle gates and down the hill. Matthew watched them from the gate, hand resting on Wolf's head. Sarah turned once in the saddle to look back and wave. Matthew waved back.

Matthew stood at the gate until their figures disappeared into the distance. Somehow, even with them gone, he didn't feel lonely and lost anymore. He had a task to do and a purpose in life. He had a best friend and a woman who wanted to be his wife. He looked down at Wolf and scratched his ears. And as an extra bonus he had an animal to be a companion on his journeys.

Life was good.

Printed in the United States
By Bookmasters